NORTH ON DRUMMOND

KC BURN

ISBN: 978-0-9981807-5-5

This work was first published by Loose Id in 2015.

Copyright © 2015 by KC Burn

Cover Art: L.C. Chase

❀ Created with Vellum

ACKNOWLEDGMENTS

As always, I have to thank my super support group: Alex, Dottie, and Chudney. Thanks also to my fantastic book club, who listened to me moan week after week about the book that never seemed to end! And lastly, thanks to some new beta readers who helped me out: Tammy, Jennifer, Shelly, and Su.

CHAPTER 1

Sunlight flashed off the ocean on Cliff Garcia's right as he drove along the two-lane road toward Sandy Bottom Bay. Salty air rushed into the car as he opened the window, and he drew in a deep breath, the scent making his homecoming seem more real than it had until now. He'd lived in Los Angeles for the past eight years, and despite frequent trips to the beach with friends, for some reason the Pacific just wasn't the same as the Gulf Coast of Florida, where he'd grown up. Maybe it was because he couldn't shake the stink of smog out of his nostrils, even at the beach. Maybe it was the aridity of California. Most people didn't enjoy the thick, muggy humidity of a soggy Florida summer afternoon. Cliff didn't much either, not when he was enduring it, but strangely, he found he'd missed even that while he'd been in California.

Not that he'd been perpetually homesick. The big city had taken some getting used to, for sure, but he'd made great friends and enjoyed the nightlife LA had to offer, when he wasn't working. He'd left Sandy Bottom Bay as soon as he could after high school graduation and hadn't ever expected to return, despite the fact that being a cop in LA hadn't been what he'd expected.

Florida had a different vibe, a different scent, a different way of life. One that wasn't always congruent with being gay, at least not in his tiny hometown. But then, he hadn't been out on the LAPD either. The cynicism and nonstop threat of violence had worn him down in four short years on the job and turned him into a jaded, world-weary man at the tender age of twenty-six. It hadn't taken long before he'd begun to wonder if he'd made a mistake living in LA. Cliff wasn't entirely sure small-town life suited him, but here he was, back again, for the foreseeable future. Maybe there was nowhere he truly belonged. Nowhere he could be himself. Nowhere he could be happy.

Statistically, there had to have been other gay people in Sandy Bottom Bay, but Cliff had never known any of them. Instead, as one of his high school's best athletes, he'd pretended to be straight, counting the days until he left for university.

California had seemed ideal, for a while. He'd been close enough to visit his dad in Pasadena; he'd had boyfriends, one-night stands, a job he both loved and hated, and his best friend, Pete. When the boyfriend cheated, the job became less satisfying, and Pete died in an accident, the allure of California vanished. A shiver ran through Cliff. Maybe he was only running away. Again. Maybe he didn't have the strength of character to suck it up and stick it out when things got tough. His stomach churned. Was he a coward? Weak?

He wasn't going to hide, though. Not this time. He was tired of hiding. If Sandy Bottom Bay didn't like him as he was, he'd soon be on his way again. Hell, he'd flown in three days ago and found a long-term rental motel about ten minutes out of town, then spent the intervening time stocking up on supplies and relaxing in front of the television. He hadn't set foot in Sandy Bottom Bay yet, nor had he told his mother he was returning. There would be plenty of time for that, for finding an apartment, getting his stuff shipped from California, and changing his driver's license. Despite taking a job with the SBBPD, he still had one foot ready to run from this place.

A rueful chuckle escaped, the sound rusty since Cliff hadn't spoken to anyone outside of requesting the room at the motel and ordering food for delivery. He couldn't quite escape the knowledge that, as much as he hadn't ever intended to return to Sandy Bottom Bay, events in LA had sent him running just as surely as when he'd run to LA in the first place. Where would he run to next? Would he even recognize a place he could make his home?

A billboard framed by palm trees caught his eye. White sandy beach, glistening blue water, and the words VISIT SANDY BOTTOM BAY! VOTED BEST BEACH IN FLORIDA.*

Cliff slowed his car, since there was no one on the road with him, to read the asterisked disclaimer, written in small enough font that most people wouldn't be able to read it as they tore down the road at sixty-five miles an hour—or more, depending on whether they were defying the posted speed limit.

The disclaimer made him cringe. It represented everything he despised about his hometown, which wasn't their probable lack of acceptance of his sexuality. This was the reason his parents had broken up. This was what his mother loved more than his father, more than him, more than anything in the world, as far as Cliff could tell. His mother's delusions were not only accepted in Sandy Bottom Bay, they were actively encouraged. If it weren't for the crackpots, con men, and charlatans who lived in and flocked to Sandy Bottom Bay, maybe his mother would be able to accept that she needed professional help. That she was only driving away people who cared about her and welcoming people who only wanted to exploit her wealth, status, and position.

VISIT SANDY BOTTOM BAY! VOTED BEST BEACH IN FLORIDA.*

*BY READERS OF *PARANORMAL BROADCAST WEEKLY*

A lengthy honk pulled Cliff's attention from the billboard, and he realized he'd come to a full stop right there in the middle of the road. He quickly got back up to speed, but he couldn't deny that the billboard, which looked brand-new, had soured his mood even more than having to venture into the town where he'd accepted a job. Where he'd have to find an apartment if he was going to stay for any length of time.

The next billboard, right at the city limits, made him let loose a growl.

SANDY BOTTOM BAY—COME FOR THE HAUNTS, STAY FOR THE BEACHES!

This was going to be harder than he'd thought. He might resent his mother for what she'd done to his family with her belief in the supernatural, but he still loved the woman. This town and its delusions of ghosts only bilked the unsuspecting or gullible into parting with their hard-earned cash, in ways that seemed innocuous. His mother was the matriarch of the town, her family having lived in and supported it since the area had been settled. However much she bought into the occult crap, he wasn't going to let her get taken advantage of by the townspeople. He didn't give a shit about the money, except that he didn't want his mother to give it away to people who pretended to buy into her delusions, in the hopes of financial gain.

Quaint buildings in faded corals and yellows came into view as the thick foliage on either side of the road thinned out. His hometown made him want to run away again. Leave his new job, leave his boss in the lurch, and drive as far away as he could. Cliff had never felt more divided in his life, not even when he pretended to be straight, dating one of the hottest girls at SBB High. A heavy sensation weighed down his stomach. He had an uncomfortable hunch that he was going to be a resident for a long while.

A glance at the clock confirmed he was going to be very early for his first shift. He wasn't ready to start working yet, so he pulled into the parking lot of the Publix. Might as well grab something for lunch at the grocery store's sandwich counter while he had the time. There were far more cars in the parking lot than he would have expected for that time of day.

Before he got out of the car, a flash of bright red hair, gleaming in the early morning sunlight, had him staring.

A simply gorgeous man, a few years younger than his own twenty-six, walked out of the store, clutching a loaf of bread and jar of peanut butter. Tall and lanky, he moved swiftly through the parking lot. Cliff didn't know who the hell the red-haired man was, but he was going to find out...and also find out if by chance Sandy Bottom Bay had another gay resident. Because not even the frown that pulled fair eyebrows together could change the fact that Cliff had spied one of the best-looking men he'd seen in a long time. Cliff had never been with a ginger before, but he loved how they looked, this one more than any.

From the number of people waving at him, and the fucking gorgeous smile he returned to them, the guy was undoubtedly a Sandy Bottom Bay resident, although he must have moved to town sometime after Cliff left. The smile made him hotter and sexier, with a hint of innocence Cliff hadn't seen on any of the men in California.

With another big smile, the ginger stopped by an old Chevy, where an elderly woman was attempting to put her groceries in the trunk. After placing his peanut butter and bread on the roof of the car, he made short work of loading the groceries for her, then stood for a moment chatting. Cliff wasn't parked close enough to get a hint of what the guy's voice sounded like, but the sweetness of watching him do a good deed was a turn-on even while it warmed something inside that had become dark and cold in LA.

After a few minutes, the guy nodded and strode away to return the cart. When he continued to walk in the opposite direction of the elderly woman, Cliff unsnapped his seat belt, intending to call out, let him know he'd forgotten his own groceries, but was too late. The woman called to him, but not loud enough for Cliff to catch the guy's name, and he rushed back, cheeks reddened in embarrassment. A few more words were exchanged before he grabbed his stuff and headed for the sidewalk.

The almost shoulder-length hair was practically aflame, and as the guy walked through the parking lot toward the sidewalk, heading for the main strip in town, Cliff continued to stare. Between the hair, the adorable blush, and the round, peachy ass enclosed in thin, faded jeans, Cliff might actually weep if the man wasn't gay.

Unlike many of his friends, Cliff had never been interested in straight men. There was no magic to "gay for you," no cachet to turning a straight man. In his opinion, a straight man who got seriously involved with a gay man had only been lying to himself until then and either wanted to keep his orientation a secret or had a mess of baggage Cliff didn't have the time or patience to deal with. Not that Cliff hadn't had more than a few guys call him a hypocrite for not being openly out at work, but he just hadn't been comfortable putting his life on the line and trusting his fellow officers would do what was right when the chips came down.

If this man were bi-curious or straight, though, he might change Cliff's mind about GFY, although the more Cliff watched, the more the guy pinged Cliff's gaydar. Or maybe that was just Cliff's wishful thinking.

The slow, steady throb of his cock, filling to full hardness in his uniform pants, surprised him. He was beyond—or so he'd thought—the unruly, unwanted erections that had plagued his younger years. The gorgeous ginger had gotten him all hot and bothered with nothing more than peanut butter and a good deed. For a few minutes, Cliff let himself picture stripping the red-haired hottie down to nothing, kissing skin that was amazingly pale for anyone who'd spent time in Florida.

But Cliff's mental vignettes were only making his cock more eager for relief, and he wasn't about to spend his first few minutes as an SBB police officer jacking off in the station bathroom, fantasizing about some guy who could be straight or taken.

"Cliff, it's good to have you aboard." Gary Walker, the chief of police for Sandy Bottom Bay, shook Cliff's hand. Although his personnel file had *Northcliff* plastered all over it, he was relieved the chief didn't mind using only part of his name, as he'd insisted for as long as he could remember.

Cliff shuddered. Northcliff Somerset Garcia. His mother, in her infinite wisdom, had saddled him with a name a *Gone with the Wind*-era hero would be proud to own, but all it had done was embarrass him. Early on, he refused to answer to anything but Cliff, much to his mother's dismay. At least he had his father's last name. Cliff Garcia was a solid, respectable name. Northcliff Somerset sounded like a flighty asshole who needed servants to wipe his ass.

"Thank you, Chief. I'm eager to get started."

The chief had bulk that came from years of bad eating and sitting behind a desk, but then, it had probably been years since the chief had found it necessary to engage in intense physical activity to perform his job. The pace of life in Sandy Bottom Bay was slower, more relaxed. It was one of the reasons Cliff had chosen to move back and, more than likely, was the reason Chief Walker had chosen to retire from the Pittsburgh police force to move here.

"Good, good. Now, if I recall from our interview, you said you grew up here, didn't you?"

Cliff nodded. Eighteen years he'd spent in the backwater of Sandy Bottom Bay, with its weird haunting festivals and reputation for ghosts. Now he was back, eight years after having shaken the swamp water from his heels. He wasn't exactly unhappy to be back, but neither was he happy about the reasons that had persuaded him his return was a good idea.

"Yes. My mother still lives in the area." Cliff could have bitten off his own tongue for admitting that. If the chief didn't already know who his mother was, Cliff didn't want to tell him. But Chief Walker just made a noise of acknowledgment in his throat and continued with his onboarding speech.

"Then you're aware that tourism is a huge revenue generator for us. I've doubled the number of full-time officers over the past five years. Normally a town of this size wouldn't require almost twenty officers, but with the influx of tourists and the associated theft and brawling that often accompanies them, well, it's prudent to have a strong police presence to deter criminal acts as much as possible."

Cliff wasn't sure the statements required a response. He could see the chief's reasoning, and maybe the situation had deteriorated since he'd left. Honestly, he hadn't paid much attention to the crime rate in Sandy Bottom Bay when he'd been an eighteen-year-old. Aside from some bullying in school, which he'd done his best to prevent when he could, and some underage drinking, which he'd participated in,

Cliff hadn't been aware of any significant crime. Certainly not like the crime he'd seen as a police officer in Los Angeles. There were neighborhoods in LA where young kids couldn't help but be aware of the potential for violence and be concerned for their safety. Life in Sandy Bottom Bay wasn't like that, and crime or no crime, Cliff had grown up feeling safe, as long as he kept his secret. He'd been upfront with the chief in his interview, though. He wasn't about to wear a rainbow flag, but neither was he prepared to continue life in the closet, and he hadn't wanted his new boss to be blindsided.

Fortunately, Chief Walker hadn't given a damn.

"Yes, sir."

"That doesn't seem to do anything about the Drummonds, however." The chief made a face, and Cliff wanted to make one of his own.

"The Drummonds?" If a school kid could be said to have a nemesis or two, Cliff's were Rob and Wyatt Drummond. The twins hadn't passed grade four the first time and were left back. From grade four on, they'd been his...well, *mortal enemies* seemed an absurdly strong and melodramatic term, but he'd had run-ins with them all the time. Bullying, stealing, generally being assholes. Cliff had done his best to shield other students who'd become their targets, partly because he was as strong as they were, even at a year younger, and partly because his mother had enough money to wipe the Drummonds from Sandy Bottom Bay if Wyatt and Rob had seriously thought to fuck with him.

Why hadn't it occurred to him earlier that he'd be returning to a Sandy Bottom Bay with full-grown Drummond twins to make his life hell?

The chief's jaw hardened. "In the grand scheme of things, they could be worse. Both of us coming from big cities, we've definitely seen worse. But they're an annoying infestation, like damned cockroaches, the lot of them."

An unwelcome sensation of vindication filled Cliff, as shameful as it was to feel it. Good to know it wasn't just he who had no time or patience for the Drummonds. Of course, the chief was undoubtedly talking about the whole clan, not just the twins. Not that Cliff had ever had any real interaction with any of the Drummonds aside from Rob and Wyatt, but he'd heard plenty of rumors in school about the rest of their family. Somehow, it didn't surprise him a bit that the police force found them aggravating.

"Well, I'm going to have Scott show you around. However familiar you may be with the town, living in it isn't the same as policing it. He'll also be sharing babysitting duty with you until after Haunt Fest; he'll go over the basics."

"Babysitting?" As the new guy, Cliff had expected to get some shit jobs, but babysitting didn't sound good.

Walker rolled his eyes. "Some woo-woo celebrity is in town, got here early this morning to film yet another illogical television segment. But since his visit overlaps the Haunt Fest, he needs some extra protection from his fans. The mayor insisted on having police presence for good publicity."

Good to know his new boss didn't believe in the occult any more than Cliff did, however much he respected the power of its tourist dollars.

"Ah." Cliff had interacted with too many minor celebrities in LA, his ex-boyfriend one of them. For the most part, they were arrogant and needy, a combination that set Cliff's teeth on edge, but at least this was only for a few days.

The chief turned away from Cliff and bellowed. "Hunter!"

Hunter? Scott Hunter?

The solid thump of boots on linoleum had Cliff turning around. The broad, muscled man heading for him at a swift pace had the same coloring as the Scott Hunter he'd known in school, but it couldn't be the same guy. He was so damn big.

The other officer skidded to a stop, and an instantly recognizable goofy grin split Scott's face.

"'Bout time you headed back this way, Cliff."

"Scott, I can't believe you... Look at you." Cliff would readily admit he sounded like an idiot, but Scott was one of the few people he'd regretted not keeping in touch with when he left.

"Ha. Bet you never thought the runt you had to help pass gym class would ever look like this." Scott posed like he was in a muscle mag, and Cliff laughed.

"I guess I don't need to worry about introductions. Hunter, stop fucking around, and show Garcia the ropes." Walker's words didn't have a lot of heat in them, and while Scott stopped posing, it didn't erase the goofy grin. Walker's bark must be worse than his bite. The man walked away without any more orders, and Cliff just stood there, taking in the differences between high-school Scott and grown-up-cop Scott.

"You're an asshole, you know." There was no change in Scott's expression or real heat in his words, but Cliff's cheeks warmed nonetheless.

"I know." If Cliff could have chosen one guy out of the circle of four he used to hang around with, he would have said Scott was his best friend. Once he'd realized he was gay, he'd found it hard to spend too much time with any one of his friends, for fear they'd discover his secret. But he'd missed Scott.

Scott's smile slipped away. "You just... You never... I didn't know graduation was going to be the last time I'd see or hear from you for eight years, you know?"

Regret and guilt crashed over Cliff. He'd better get used to the emotional overload because it would probably be a hundred times worse once he finally got the balls to go see his mother. Tell her he'd gotten a job in Sandy Bottom Bay and was moving back.

"I know. I'm sorry. There were...circumstances."

"Yeah. Sucks that your parents split, but I missed you."

Cliff suppressed a grimace. His parents' divorce wasn't the only reason he'd distanced himself from his hometown, and he knew he'd have to come clean to Scott sooner or later. Later was better. "Yeah, missed you too. I'm sorry, I should have... Maybe we can catch up with a beer after our shift is over?"

"Sounds good. Except it'll have to wait until Mr. Big Shot has gone."

Great. Cliff had already forgotten about their babysitting gig, but at least Scott hadn't lost his sweet, forgiving nature. "Is he going to need round-the-clock protection?" It would suck sweaty donkey balls if Cliff had to spend the next week guarding a hotel room while the TV princess got his beauty sleep.

"No, the security at the hotel ought to be able to cover overnight tonight. In fact, we'll probably be partnered for most of the day with the TV crew, but our shifts will be longer than normal because most days they expect to start midafternoon, then shoot well into the night."

Right. Paranormal claptrap never happened until dark, and those ghost-hunter shows never failed to make use of all that green night-vision shit. Only made it easier for them to scam an unsuspecting and uncritical public.

"Okay, then, show me around. Let's get started."

"Follow me. Everyone's a little squirrelly today, though."

Just today? Cliff didn't say that aloud. "Oh? Any particular reason?"

"Had an unexpected death out on the..." Scott swallowed his words, looking a little green. "Uh, don't you know this already?"

A chill swept through Cliff's veins, along with a heaping dose of guilt. Surely his mother was okay. Surely Scott wouldn't have been so cheery if something had happened to her. And surely someone in this podunk town would have called Cliff. An unexpected urge to speed directly for home gripped him.

"Don't know what?" Somehow Cliff managed to grit out the words.

"Oh. Well, the town's handyman died out at your mom's place yesterday. Name of Andy Wilson, midforties, came down here to escape the frozen north a few years after you left. Possibly escaping other stuff too, because he seemed a bit too comfortable with the Drummond twins."

"Who killed him? Did you run a background check on this Andy?"

Scott's eyes widened, and he shook his head. "You, my friend, have been out in La-La Land too long. Andy didn't have a record, and the medical examiner confirmed he died falling off a ladder. Nothing suspicious. Blood alcohol wasn't quite high enough to get him a DUI if he'd been driving, but high enough it wasn't hard to imagine him losing his balance."

Nothing suspicious except for hanging around the evil Drummond twins. The tension in Cliff's body faded away. His mother was fine. But the incident did highlight that no matter how conflicted his feelings were for his mother and for Sandy Bottom Bay, he needed to get back and visit her sooner rather than later. Even if she hadn't been hurt herself, having someone die on the estate would upset her and might exacerbate her delusions of the estate being haunted.

DREW DRUMMOND WAS SO hungry he could eat a whale. Not that he could afford such an extravagance. Instead he slathered peanut butter on one slice of bread, grape jelly on another, and slapped the two together. With his hastily made sandwich and a cold glass of milk, he slumped down in a kitchen chair and took a bite. If he hadn't woken up at an ungodly hour this morning and dashed out to the local Publix, he'd be licking grape jelly off a spoon for lunch. Not going grocery shopping earlier in the week had been a mistake, one he might regret at every meal involving peanut butter for the next few days.

He knew better. Sandy Bottom Bay, renowned for being the second-most haunted town in Florida, was busy gearing up for the haunting season. With the ghost festival coming up the first week of October, then Halloween, the fall saw a huge influx of tourists. As the only psychic tarot reader in town—thanks somewhat dubiously to his family—the fall tourist season brought Drew enough income to see him through the rest of the year if he was frugal. But that meant he had enough appointments and walk-ins that he should know skipping breakfast was a bad idea. And that was without the previous day's death of the town's resident handyman, Andy Wilson. Not that Drew knew him well, nor was it a shock to anyone that ladders and alcohol weren't the best combination. But the fatal accident at the Somerset estate had brought in a number of walk-ins from his regulars wanting to share the gossip. Especially since his brother Wyatt had found Andy. Put a Drummond next to a dead body, and the tone of everyone's words took on an uncomfortable bite.

Midchew, Drew heard the tinkle of a bell at the front door announcing the entry of yet another client, and he groaned. Glancing at the clock, he realized it was almost three. Not surprising he was faint with hunger. Still, whoever was out there could wait a few minutes until he was done eating. He wasn't in the habit of turning away business, because the psychic tarot reader gig wasn't going to make him rich, even in Sandy Bottom Bay. But damn, he was starving.

He swallowed and brought the sandwich to his lips again before he shot to his feet.

Shit.

His client had to be none other than Helen Somerset; she'd called wanting an extra appointment this week. Her patronage had sometimes been the difference between the luxury of peanut butter and the desperation of ramen noodles cooked with swamp water, so he didn't want to piss her off. That wasn't the only reason he wanted to stay on Mrs. Somerset's good side, but it was the only one he'd admit to aloud.

With a resigned sigh, he dropped his barely touched sandwich and stood, plucking at his damp T-shirt. September was so damn humid that it had only taken minutes of wear in the hotter, private part of his home before he'd sweated through his clothes. Drew had window air-conditioning units for the front of the house to keep it just cool enough for clients coming in out of the Florida heat and humidity to feel comfortable, but he didn't want to spend extra money to air-condition the rest of the house. He was a Florida native; he ought to be able to get by with ceiling fans and open windows most days.

Sitting at the kitchen table was the most comfortable, especially when he opened all the windows and the screen door that led from the kitchen to his tiny backyard. Air cooled by the greenery over-hanging and shadowing his back yard would flow in through the screen door. Today, though, not even a breath of a breeze stirred.

He shucked off the sweaty T-shirt and pulled on his mystic's robes, navy trimmed with gold. Once fastened, the robes still exposed a rather large vee of naked chest that made Drew extremely self-conscious, but he didn't know what he could wear that wouldn't make him drown in his own sweat or ruin the illusion that he was the all-seeing, tarot-reading psychic Malachi.

If he weren't such a skinny-ass beanpole, the bare skin might get him bigger tips. Still, he could only work with what he had.

The robes themselves were damp, but at least he'd had them made of material that was easy to wash and quick to dry. A faint scent of laundry detergent still clung to them. If the heat broke a little, he might be able to go another day before he had to wash them again.

After shrugging into the robes, he placed the turban on his head and went into the bathroom to inspect his appearance. The thick black eyeliner he'd applied before opening his doors had only smudged a little. Using a piece of toilet paper, he quickly corrected the smudging. Unruly red hair spilled out in untidy waves below his blue-and-gold turban, and he stuffed as much as he could into the turban. He wasn't fond of the outfit, but his granny had sworn up and down that people were more likely to buy into the readings if he looked the part. Since she'd been the only one in the family, besides himself, who'd managed to escape any brushes with the law, he didn't think he had a choice. At the beginning, he'd left off the turban, and he'd soon found that even the tourists were distracted by his hair and weren't fully invested in the whole tarot experience.

Hiding his red hair, adding eyeliner and the robes, he could main-tain the fiction with clients, especially those who'd been clients of his grandma before she died, that he truly was a mystic and not just that weird, skinny Drummond kid. Not that anyone would have ever called him that. There were more Drummonds in and around Sandy Bottom Bay than any other family, and despite the fact they were, as a group, on just about everyone's shit list, no one with any sense messed with a Drummond. It wasn't healthy or smart.

Turning away from his reflection, Drew took a moment to picture his grandma before she'd do a reading, turning himself into the poised, mystical Malachi.

CHAPTER 2

Ready for business, Drew stepped through the door that separated the tiny living space of his home—kitchen, bathroom, and bedroom—from the reading room. He rearranged the draperies so they hid the door—no sense in advertising exactly how to enter his home—and walked across the room to yet another set of draperies. Embroidered with mystic symbols in gold thread, they were the same ones his grandma had used. They might be a little threadbare now, but no sense in fixing what wasn't broken. Psychic readings weren't exactly a booming business, although he did okay for himself.

The tourists were hard to deal with sometimes, but if he turned away drunk or obnoxious tourists, he'd be out some much-needed bucks. Even the random drop-ins with his regulars, like he'd had yesterday and today, were a little annoying. Appointments, especially with a nice lady like Helen Somerset, were Drew's preference every time.

Drew peered through the black curtains that separated the reading room from the tiny reception area at the front of the house, making sure it was, in fact, Helen waiting for him.

Helen Somerset was an older woman, her perfect makeup unable to hide the creases at the corners of her eyes and alongside her mouth. Her perfectly dyed blonde hair was twisted into a fancy updo Drew wanted to call a chignon. He'd read the term in one of his grandma's romance novels, and it sounded sleek and sophisticated, just like this woman. Of course, he had no idea what a chignon actually looked like for real.

She sat with a regal air, ankles crossed and pale yellow skirt suit displaying not one hint that she'd just come in from 90 percent humidity and ninety-two degrees. She was Sandy Bottom Bay's resident lady of the manor—or at least the wealthiest woman in the area and owner of the Somerset Estate. If she took the bay's haunted reputation a little more seriously than most folks, even those who made a living on the supernatural, Drew was willing to forgive. He was never sure if she patronized his business because she truly believed in the hokum Drew and his granny before him had concocted, or if it was simply a way to support the town. A number of residents, especially those who hated the tourism influx, had made a lot of derogatory statements about her, but never in her hearing.

Drew had a soft spot for Helen, though, beyond the regular and reliable appointments she made with him.

Helen Somerset was the mother of one Northcliff Garcia, the guy who'd been indirectly responsible for turning Drew's world upside down—in a good way—eight years ago. Drew still carried a torch for the boy who'd confirmed Drew was unequivocally gay as well as convincing him to turn his life around. Weighty baggage for a guy Drew had never actually spoken to, but his unrequited and unquenched crush on Northcliff made him treat Helen Somerset with the same reverence and respect he'd used with his grandma.

The guy had never gone by Northcliff, to Drew's knowledge. It had taken a few sessions before it had truly sunk in that when Helen Somerset spoke about her son, Northcliff, she was referring to the Cliff Garcia who'd consumed Drew's thoughts since he'd hit puberty. In fact, he'd quickly surmised that even she rarely used Cliff's full name. Drew loved the name, even occasionally tested out the shorted *North* like a special nickname that was his alone to use. Stupid, really, but then, so was he for still crushing on a guy he hadn't seen in eight years. It was a secret he'd shared only with his best friend, Kyle. As far as the rest of the town knew, Cliff was the only name Helen's son had, assuming anyone else remembered him.

"Good afternoon." She'd asked him to call her Helen the first time she'd come to him in a professional capacity after his grandma died and he'd inherited her house and business, but he'd never quite managed to do it. She was Sandy Bottom Bay royalty, and he was... one of the dirty Drummonds.

Never once, in all the times she'd graced his front room, had a hint of a sneer appeared on her face. Most times, Drew looked forward to her visits. Although Cliff hadn't returned to Sandy Bottom Bay since he left for college, Drew often picked up tidbits about his life in California from things Helen said or questions she had for the cards.

"Good afternoon, Malachi. How are you today?"

While Drew appreciated that she never broke character, by always calling him Malachi, this wasn't the first time he'd wondered if she had any idea he was a Drummond. After all, there was no reason for her to know or care, especially since his grandma had taken back her maiden name long before Drew's birth, after Grandpa Drummond had been killed in prison.

"Just fine," Drew answered. "Did you want to come right in?"

"That would be lovely, thank you."

With a flourish of his long, bony fingers, Drew ushered her past the mystically embroidered curtain. Quasi-occult-looking implements, relics, and charms filled the reading room. Candles, incense, and herbs rounded out the ambiance. When he'd decided last year he needed an additional revenue stream, he'd hit on the idea of selling those same things, both out of the shop and online. He provided a greater variety for sale than he used in his own readings, and he hoped this year would see a boost in his income. He was doing okay, but if a big expense cropped up, like major house maintenance, he could be in trouble.

Helen seated herself at the table and smoothed her hands over the black crushed-velvet tablecloth while Drew readied the incense that his grandma swore facilitated card reading. Probably patchouli and sandalwood had been incredibly exotic when she had started using them. After lighting a few candles, Drew turned back to Helen, who had a wistful smile on her face.

"Smells exactly the same as when Marina read for me. I can hardly believe she's been gone two years now. You must miss her."

Drew blinked. He hadn't expected a personal and maudlin turn to the conversation. And of course it smelled the same. He wasn't about to futz with a recipe that had worked for his grandma for decades.

"I do, yes, but she's in a better place, and even drops in for a visit now and again."

Helen blinked, her surprise quickly masked. There was little reason for surprise, considering Drew's profession and Sandy Bottom Bay's hauntings. Assuming one believed in psychics, ghosts, and the supernatural.

Drew sure as hell didn't, not even when his grandma had sworn up and down that she had the second sight. But he wasn't about to bad-mouth the source of his livelihood. Perhaps this moral ambiguity was the last bit of shady Drummond he'd been unable to scrub clean, but the readings he gave provided comfort to his clients.

Time to move things along. He wanted a chance to finish his sandwich before a wandering tourist or gossiping resident happened by his place. Although he felt bad about Andy Wilson's tragic accident and the fact that his brother Wyatt had discovered the body, Drew hadn't known the man, and twenty-four hours later he felt the town had already discussed the shit out of it.

"Ready?" In one smooth movement, Drew seated himself opposite Helen and placed the deck of tarot cards in the center of the table.

"Shuffle the cards while thinking on what you want to know. When you're done shuffling, cut the deck into thirds." No matter how many times a regular came to see him, he always started with the same instructions. Put his clients in the right mindset. He might only be twenty-two, but after being raised by an extended family of criminals and con men, as well as having training from a "psychic" grandma, Drew was a natural at reading people's expressions and words to tell fortunes.

Helen picked up the cards and followed Drew's directive while he sat back and waited. As Drew did each time he read for her, he stared intently at her while she prepared the deck. No matter how hard he searched her features, he could see very little of Cliff in her. Still, she was a covert connection to Cliff, one he wasn't ready to give up.

Today tension deepened the creases by her eyes, and the slightly thicker makeup application spoke of something to hide. Helen had exceptional skill at suppressing or hiding her emotions, and she'd proved to be one of his most challenging clients. Even armed with his grandma's excellent teaching, it had taken him a while to figure out Helen's tells. He usually only saw the faint hints of stress when she was worried about Cliff, and each time, Drew had had difficulty keeping his heart rate even and his voice properly modulated. Lately, though, something else had been bothering her. Maybe it made him a bad person, but he kind of hoped her stress today was due to the death of Andy Wilson on her property and not anything to do with Cliff.

They'd get to this week's question soon enough. Even with Helen's familiarity with the process, she didn't like spitting out her question first thing any more than his other clients did. As usual, Drew would start out with some simple probing before getting into the real reason a client showed up for a reading.

Drew took the stack of cards back from Helen and laid out three lines of seven cards each. Touching a few cards as he spoke, he continued his standard patter about what the cards meant in terms of placement in the three lines. The layout had the most cards, and he used it frequently, sometimes interchanged with a Celtic Cross layout, but Helen always got three lines. He'd get into more specifics about each card's meaning eventually, interspersed with seemingly innocuous questions. Although her face was still difficult to read after all this time, once he'd realized the majority of her concerns were about her son, his job had gotten so much easier. The past few readings, however, she'd had something else on her mind, specifically a growing obsession with ghosts and haunting.

"I sense a conflict. Here." Drew pointed at the cards. "Related to family."

"My great-grandmother was reputed to be a witch, and there were rumors she killed her husband after she caught him with a servant girl."

Drew blinked. The past few readings, she'd brought up a number of deceased family members, and if Drew hadn't known for certain that she already patronized Eddie Price, the medium, he might have suggested she go visit Eddie. Then again, maybe he wouldn't. Not only was Eddie one of his most significant competitors, he was an ass, and neither of them had supernatural powers. Drew's fortunes and readings were designed to give hope, make people feel better about their lives. If circumstances called for it, he encouraged his clients to seek medical or legal assistance. But in his opinion, Eddie outright lied to people. Dead was dead. Spirits didn't exist any more than psychics, no matter what the neon lights in his window proclaimed.

The problem was, he wasn't sure where to go with this reading.

Helen took the decision out of his hands. She tapped the death card, which came up far too frequently for Drew's liking. Always required some fancy talk to avoid spooking his clients. Probably should just take the damn thing out of the deck altogether.

"Do you believe in ghosts?"

Shit. He didn't want to out-and-out lie. "The more important question is whether you believe. But the cards aren't dealt for me."

"A conflict." Helen tapped the card again. "I know the house is haunted. I've heard the spirits before, felt their presence. My mother watching over me. My father protecting me. I've sensed my grand-mother at times too."

Despite the muggy heat that remained in the room, a shiver slid down Drew's spine, like a ghost of his own. This wasn't the first time she'd referred to ghosts, more so recently. Ghosts weren't his gig, and he did his best to deflect Helen, but the whole tone of the appoint-ment had changed. Helen wasn't paying attention to the cards. She wasn't letting him guide the reading. But she was worried about something, and Drew wanted to help, like he wanted to help all his clients.

He opened his mouth, hoping something appropriate would fall out, but Helen beat him to it.

"The spirits have been more restless. More intrusive in their communications."

Drew might have grown up in the second-most haunted town in Florida, but he'd never seen hide nor hair of one single ghost. Didn't change the fact that Helen's conviction was creeping him right the hell out.

"How so?" Drew bit his lip. That question wasn't going to get things back on track.

Helen quirked her lips up in a tiny half smile. "Louder. Definitely louder. Things moving around. Doors slamming. Usually my family is fairly sedate in their haunting. I don't know..."

She broke eye contact and stared down at the cards again, but Drew was certain she wasn't really looking at them.

"You don't know what?"

"I don't know what I've done to upset them, but I'm very worried they had something to do with that poor man's death."

Drew's eyes widened. This delusion was getting worse, clearly exacerbated by Andy's death. Conflicting emotions prevented him from speaking. Should he try to contact Cliff? Maybe Cliff knew already. Then again, maybe she was just distraught and exhausted from everything that had been happening. He'd keep a careful eye on her during the next few weeks. If she got worse, he'd see if he could figure out Cliff's contact information, but for now...for now he needed to ease her mind. That was what he got paid to do.

"No. Not your fault. You can't blame yourself for his death."

Drew gathered the cards together, heedless of the unfinished reading. He wasn't going to cloak the message in his normal oblique patter.

"Listen to me. Even if ghosts were responsible for Andy's death..." Drew just about choked on the words, but he wasn't about to try and convince a believer she was wrong. Not now and not while she was laboring under the conviction the ghosts might be killers. "You weren't the one acting. Please do not blame yourself. Besides, have you ever heard of malevolent spirits in Sandy Bottom Bay?"

Helen took a deep breath and shook her head, tears glittering in her eyes, but not one fell to her cheek.

"Exactly. Sure, the town's reputation is founded in a pretty horrific massacre, but even that wasn't enough to bring back malicious spirits. I can't believe there's anything you could have done to make them mad at you."

Helen was a nice woman and, despite her money and station, didn't treat him like he was dirt.

"Thank you. I appreciate that. There was... I'm the only one in my family who has gotten a divorce."

The slightly bashful look that battled with her distress was a little odd.

"Forgive me, but...the divorce isn't recent, is it?" Drew had never been so direct with any client, but then, he'd never had a client worried her *ghosts* had killed a man. Maybe considering contacting Cliff wasn't quite so self-serving after all.

"No, no. Eight years. But I'm...seeing someone now."

Drew smiled. "Good for you." The stress of moving on might be the reason for her distress. He hoped that was all it was.

With a little shrug, Helen gave him another tiny smile.

At the end of her reading, Drew hadn't given Helen a full measure of relief. But the set of her shoulders was a tiny bit more relaxed and her smile as she pulled out her gold credit card just a little brighter. A success in the world, according to Drew.

Smiling, he walked her to the door and was about to bid her good-bye when his stomach grumbled loudly, reminding him of the sandwich he had yet to eat.

Helen smiled at him, a motherly smile, the likes of which he'd not seen since his grandma passed. "You didn't skip lunch to see me, did you? You need to eat more. You're too skinny." She patted his cheek while he blushed.

"It's been a busy day."

She tsked. "Put up the closed sign, and go eat something, Drew. Don't make yourself sick over work."

Drew gaped at her. He'd never heard her call him by his name, hadn't even been aware she knew what it was.

"Um, yeah, I'll do that," he mumbled.

"Good. I don't want to see you getting sick." Her attention strayed to his shoulder, and her hand reached out to tuck an escaping lock of hair back under his turban. "It's a shame you have to wear the turban. Your hair is such a lovely color. I'll see you in a few days."

Helen smiled, patted him again, and was gone in a cloud of Chanel No. 5. If it had been anyone else, Drew might have thought she was hitting on him, but she'd sounded so much like a mother. He couldn't imagine why the matriarch of Sandy Bottom Bay would bother trying to mother him, of all people, and why now. His grandma had done her best, but Drew had survived without a mother for a long time. As he made his way back to his kitchen, he wondered exactly why it was Cliff never came back to visit Helen. She was so sweet and caring, and Drew was determined to keep an eye on her.

Walking into his living quarters was like walking into soaking-wet cotton, warmed to boiling. Even for him, it was fucking hot, and sweat immediately dripped down his spine.

The peanut butter sandwich on his table, one bite taken out of it, looked like a feast, and Drew began salivating. He almost didn't want to take the time to remove his robes and turban, but he also didn't want to have to wash his costume any sooner than he had to. He grabbed a dry T-shirt from his clean laundry, swapped out robes and turban for stretchy cotton, and poured himself another glass of milk. Room-temperature milk wasn't worth the effort of drinking. With a tired grunt, Drew dropped down into the hard vinyl chair and picked up his sandwich.

He wolfed down half of it before he was able to relax and actually taste what he was chewing. Pounding at his back door had him swallowing before he expected, and he couldn't determine the identity of his visitor, eyes watering as he coughed.

After he cleared his throat and his eyes stopped tearing up, he blinked at his best friend, Kyle, who stood close enough to the door that if he'd been a cat, he'd have been hanging from the screen by his claws.

"You done with your death rattle yet? Let me in already."

Defiantly, Drew stood and shoved the last two bites of sandwich into his mouth, chewing while he took the few steps to reach the screen door. He rubbed the back of hand across his eyes to remove the tears that had accumulated, groaning when his hand ended up smeared with black.

"Hold on, sweetie. Let me fix it." Kyle dashed to the bathroom and returned with Drew's eyeliner. Kyle licked his thumb and stroked it under Drew's eyes before he stroked on more sooty black makeup. "You really ought to get some waterproof stuff."

This was an old argument. "I don't like the waterproof stuff."

"With the humidity in this place, you must look like Alice Cooper on a crying jag half the time. I'm so broke I could use a fourth job, but even my apartment has air-conditioning. How can you stand this?"

A snort escaped Drew's lips. Like he could afford to buy another window unit, never mind power it up. He wasn't religious, but he prayed every day that the units his grandma had put in the client areas didn't crap out. They were getting more aged every day, and he dreaded having to replace them. The part of his business that involved selling incense, candles, and herbs had required more outlay than he'd anticipated and was only just beginning to get some traction.

"You get rid of your fat butt, and you'll be perfectly comfortable in the heat." Drew playfully slapped his friend's ass.

Kyle sniffed. "Quit feeling me up. My ass is perfect, as we both know. We can't all be broomsticks like you."

True. He was skinny enough that he rarely had issues with the heat, but today was exceptionally hellish.

"Don't tell me you came over to bitch about the temperature and give me makeup tips. Aren't you supposed to be..." Actually, Drew wasn't sure where Kyle was supposed to be. The guy held down three different part-time jobs. This was a busy time of year for him because not only were his evening ghost-walk tours in great demand, but he was also in the beginning stages of preparing choreography for the high school cheerleading squad's trip to Orlando for the national championship competition. Somewhere in there, he also squeezed in time to teach little girls ballet at the dance studio, but he usually cut back on his dance fitness classes in the fall.

"Whatever. They won't even miss me, I bet. Those girls will never be ready for February. This year, they're all graceless, more concerned with texting than anything else. Of course, they'll be even more hopeless when I go to New York."

Drew laughed because Kyle was twenty-two, just like him, and yet he always sounded like a world-weary technophobe whenever he discussed his charges.

Kyle's life wasn't what he'd dreamed, but when he'd blown out his knee partway through his dance degree at Florida State University—while Drew was eking out his two-year business degree at the local college—Kyle's dreams of dancing in New York had changed. Despite the fact that he still spoke about going to New York as though he was poised to leave at any minute, Drew thought Kyle was mostly happy being back in Sandy Bottom Bay. No one besides Drew and his family knew why Kyle had suddenly switched majors to return to the bay and take up his odd assortment of jobs while he finished his degree online; he refused to admit to the physical impossibility of being a professional dancer. Drew was happy Kyle had enough mobility to teach dance. If Kyle had had to give it up altogether, his friend would have been even more devastated.

"Did you want a sandwich?" Drew was going to make himself another one. It was possible Kyle wasn't here for any other reason than to vent or chat.

"All those carbs? No, thank you." Kyle opened the fridge and rummaged around for an apple while Drew prepped another sandwich. They both sat at the same time, and Kyle used Drew's plate and knife to cut his apple and smear tiny bits of peanut butter on each of the segments.

After a few moments of silence while they ate, Kyle threw his hands up in the air. "I can't believe you didn't tell me Helen Somerset was one of your clients. Is that new? Did it have something to do with Andy's death?"

"What if today was her first visit?"

"Was it? So, then, it was about Andy."

Drew caught himself before answering. He made a point of not discussing his clients. Most of them came to him for help with things that were upsetting them. They didn't deserve to have him gossiping about them to all and sundry, although that particular pastime ran rampant through Sandy Bottom Bay's residents. No one needed to know Helen's visit was about Andy.

"It wasn't, was it?" Kyle's tone was accusing. "What did she want to know?"

"You know I don't talk about that, not even with you."

Kyle rolled his eyes. "What, the clairvoyants' ethics committee will suspend your tarot-reading privileges? C'mon. Spill."

Drew couldn't be mad at Kyle, not when the guy made him laugh. But he did shake his head, causing more dramatic arm flourishes.

"Okay, okay. Don't tell me. But I came over because I heard some of the girls talking."

Yeah, Kyle could bitch about working with the cheerleaders all he wanted, but this wouldn't be the first time he had imparted some tiny bit of gossip that had helped Drew provide a more accurate reading for someone.

"And?" It couldn't be about Andy's death, because they'd already discussed it the previous day.

"Guess who's at the hotel right now?"

Drew shrugged. "Dunno. Probably another well-off ghost hunter. Or maybe an author looking for authentic atmosphere. But I've never heard of any of these 'big-name' authors who've come to visit."

The bed-and-breakfast was the most popular lodging in Sandy Bottom Bay, partly because it was rumored to be haunted and partly because it had the best location, right on the main strip just blocks from Drew's place. There were a couple of motels near the highway, and a small hotel on the edge of town, but the bed-and-breakfast was far and away the best experience a visitor could get. Serious ghost people stayed at the B&B, the motels drew the budget-conscious, and the rich dilettantes booked rooms at the swanky but too-new-to-be-haunted hotel.

Kyle shook his head in exasperation. "You are no fun at all. Brett Cavanagh. He's supposedly filming a segment about Haunt Fest."

It took a moment for Drew to assimilate the name. "Brett Cavanagh? *The* Brett Cavanagh? From *Phantoms*?"

Holy shitballs. That was big news. *Phantoms* was one of the best-rated supernatural programs on television, due in no small part to the charisma and sheer good looks of its star, Brett Cavanagh. Drew didn't usually keep up with all the paranormal, ghost-hunting shows out there because he had to deal with it all on a daily basis. *Phantoms*, on the other hand, had captured his attention.

"Yes." Kyle almost, but not quite, squealed.

"You think it's true he's gay? The media can't seem to make up its mind."

"And he's never confirmed anything in any interview. So I suggest we find out for ourselves. We'll go to the Angry Parakeet at, like, seven, and from there we can hit all the places he might show up. We can try to *accidentally* run into him."

Drew wanted to say no, that everyone else in town would be trying to do the same thing. In fact, he wouldn't be surprised if the hotel was mobbed by people "just passing by." But he was as tempted as Kyle to see the man in person. Would he be an asshole? Would he be shorter or fatter or just plain less attractive when he wasn't on camera?

"Okay, okay, it's a date."

"Date. Puhleaze. Not only to do I have better taste than that, I want there to be no doubts about me being single."

Drew stuck his tongue out at Kyle. "Fine, but—"

His words were interrupted by the bell at the front door announcing yet another client.

"Kyle, I'm so sorry. I gotta get this." He'd have much rather sat in his sweltering kitchen discussing Brett Cavanagh, especially since they hadn't had much time to hang out recently.

"Hey, I get it. Business first."

Business first. An odd concept, considering most of his family did the bare minimum to keep afloat, often rounding out their income with a variety of semilegal or completely illegal activities. If Drew wanted to stay on the straight and narrow, he couldn't afford to ignore paying customers.

"Help me get back into this crap."

Drew pulled off his T-shirt and got his robes straightened while Kyle arranged the turban and hid his hair.

Somehow, at the tender age of ten, Drew had become friends with the only other guy in Sandy Bottom Bay who would eventually come out. There was Eddie Price, ten years older than they were and bisexual. Drew wasn't entirely sure it counted, since Eddie seemed to lean more toward women, although that might have been more a function of opportunity than anything else. Sandy Bottom Bay wasn't exactly a bastion of gay pride. In fact, Drew might not have come out either if it weren't for the fact his brothers figured it out and were surprisingly accepting. The Drummonds might not have the most sterling or upright reputations, but no one messed with them without good reason. And gay-bashing or bullying the youngest of Frank Drummond's boys wasn't a good reason, not by a long shot. Kyle's association with Drew afforded him the same protection, and although his family all assumed he and Kyle were boyfriends, they were too much like brothers to have that sexual spark. He loved Kyle like, or maybe better than, his brothers.

Ready to face the next client, Drew smiled at Kyle. "You can stick around if you want."

"In this sweatbox? Not even if Brett Cavanagh himself were stripping in your kitchen."

Drew gave him a disbelieving look.

"Well, maybe for that," Kyle conceded. "Besides, I should get back to those cheerleaders. But I'll be by at quarter to seven tonight. You better have closed up shop by then. There are some things more important than money, and celebrity-stalking Brett Cavanagh is one of them."

With that pronouncement, Kyle whirled around and dashed through the door, leaving Drew chuckling behind him. He couldn't disagree either. Drew had never had the opportunity to catch a glimpse of a celebrity up close, and he was looking forward to the evening.

CHAPTER 3

I t was nearing dinnertime when Cliff finally had to ask. "Scott, man, I appreciate the tour. And I've learned a lot of things I never knew about town, but weren't we supposed to be on babysitting duty?"

"Eager to meet our celebrity, are you?"

Not fucking likely. He'd seen more than his fair share of B-, C-, and D-list celebs in LA, enough to know that half of them were more trouble than they were worth.

"Just don't want to shirk duties on the first day."

Scott laughed. "That's the last thing I would have thought of you. No, the television crew were having some sort of discussion or planning session or some shit in the hotel today. Our first official duty is hitting the Angry Parakeet tonight for dinner."

Cliff hadn't even met the guy yet but wondered if the Angry Parakeet would measure up to the foodie snobbery of a television celebrity. Sandy Bottom Bay wasn't exactly the center of haute cuisine, but the Angry Parakeet was just as good as some of the places his ex had taken him in Los Angeles. His ex would have hated it, but Cliff had missed the weathered charm of Sandy Bottom Bay's relaxed lifestyle.

Scott pulled into the hotel driveway and parked the cruiser beside an enormous shiny red pickup truck. The giant, gas-guzzling vehicles that dominated the road were something he hadn't missed about Florida.

Cliff had the door open, ready to get out, but thoughts of his ex made him freeze in place. An unpleasant sensation, like milk curdling in his soul, filled him. He'd been preoccupied today, what with spying a gorgeous guy he'd like to get to know better, starting a new job, and worrying about how to tell his mother he'd moved back to Sandy Bottom Bay, however temporarily. Perhaps he could have been excused for not asking one very important question and for not drawing some significant and probably correct conclusions.

"Scott, just who is this celebrity?"

Scott's eyes widened. "Chief Walker didn't tell you? It's Brett Cavanagh from *Phantoms*. I can't wait to meet him. That show is so cool. I can't believe they're going to feature our little town."

Of course it was Brett. Damn it.

Like a kid's before Christmas morning, Scott's eyes were bright, and he was practically bouncing in excitement. Cliff, on the other hand, was about as ecstatic as those kids opening up skeletons and severed doll heads during *The Nightmare Before Christmas*. Well, this wouldn't be the first time he'd had to pretend he and Brett didn't know each other. This time Brett could be on the receiving end, because Cliff had no intention of airing any dirty laundry in front of his new colleague, and knowing Brett, there would be *plenty* of filth to deal with.

Scott beckoned Cliff to the door of the hotel.

"Uh-huh. You don't believe all that ghost shit, do you?" Cliff had to ask, although he tried hard not to sound too disparaging. He didn't want to alienate Scott, but they were cops, for God's sake. A lot could change in eight years, but he didn't remember Scott being into all that woo-woo nonsense when they'd been friends in high school. Sandy Bottom Bay's eccentricity was strangely compelling to some people.

"Ha, no! Remember when we pulled that trick on old Eddie Price? That guy really buys into his own bullshit."

Cliff laughed. When he'd lived here before, Eddie Price had been a self-important prick who claimed to be a medium, and the guy had zero sense of humor. None. It hadn't been hard for Cliff's buddies to get him to go along with the joke, pretending to haunt Eddie's garden shed. After all, Sandy Bottom Bay's reputation just begged for pranks of that sort. Old Eddie Price—a bit of a misnomer, since he was only five or six years older than Cliff—had not been happy. The prank had been fucking awesome, but it had also been the first time Cliff's eyes had been opened about his mother. His mother had been pissed because Cliff was mocking something she believed in. Boggled his mind, it did, that anyone in this day and age believed in ghosts and spirits, but apparently it took all kinds, and most of the weirder ones ended up in Sandy Bottom Bay.

"Is he still around?" Cliff didn't really care, but the closer they got to Brett's hotel room, the more he'd like to focus on something other than seeing his ex again, which he'd hoped would never happen once he'd decided to move to the opposite side of the continent. Didn't hurt to find out more about the locals he was going to have to deal with.

"Oh yeah, he's one of the top dogs in the field, or so he says. He does a pretty brisk business. His biggest competition is the psychic tarot reader."

Psychic tarot reader? Was that what they were calling con men who played on gullible old ladies?

Scott wasn't done, though. "But as much as old Eddie would like to run him off, the psychic is a Drummond, and well, we all know that would end badly for Eddie." The man shrugged, and Cliff had a momentary desire to smack him.

The Drummonds weren't even a violent gang like those he'd seen in LA. How did they manage to garner so much power? Surely the threat of a broken nose or a busted lip wasn't that scary. Things would have to change around here. The "psychic" might be a good start. Keeping an eye on a business—Cliff almost choked just thinking the word, as it gave the psychic a legitimacy he shouldn't have—run by a con man was only reasonable. Last thing they needed was their resident charlatan bilking money out of unsuspecting victims.

"And you'd never guess it, but that guy is like catnip for women."

Cliff didn't have time to respond to that shocking revelation or ask if Scott was talking about Eddie or the psychic tarot reader, because Scott stopped in front of a door and knocked. Cliff would worry about them another time. For now, he had an ex to confront, and that would be stressful enough.

Moments later, the door was opened by a beautiful woman with shoulder-length black hair, pale skin, and lips so red she looked like she'd been drinking blood. Then again, Kristi Ellis was the closest thing to a vampire Cliff ever expected to meet; at least she looked the part.

"Good evening, officers. I'm Kristi Ellis, the producer for *Phantoms*." Cliff wasn't sure if she truly didn't remember him, until she lifted an impeccably manicured eyebrow when she looked at him. Kristi had never liked him, so he still wasn't sure if Brett was intending to keep their connection on the down-low or if Kristi just didn't care enough to acknowledge Cliff in a friendly way now that she no longer had to put on a good show for Brett.

"Good evening, ma'am." Scott was as pleasant and eager to please as a new puppy, and not for the first time, Cliff realized how much recent events had aged him mentally. He and Scott were both twenty-six, but Scott seemed so much younger. Witnessing the aftermath of some of LA's crimes had been soul-destroying, snuffing out boyishness like nothing else. Cliff would never wish that pain on anyone, least of all Scott.

Kristi turned her back to them to call into the room, "Brett, your bodyguards are here."

Scott practically wagged his tail. Cliff elbowed him and tried to convey the message "be professional" with a few hand gestures and eyebrow wiggles. He must have gotten his point across, because when Kristi moved out of the doorway to allow Brett to approach, Cliff was certain they both appeared professional and emotionless.

Brett glanced at Scott but then left his gaze on Cliff while he spoke. "Hello, gentlemen. I appreciate your company. Shall we?"

The rather lengthy stare at Cliff's groin would have, at one time, had him erect and panting in a matter of seconds, but there was nothing. Cliff would have to come clean with Scott sooner rather than later, but for the moment he was grateful his partner didn't notice anything untoward and that neither Cliff nor his cock reacted to Brett's frank and lustful perusal. Nice to know good sense and betrayal overrode lust.

Then again, Brett looked worn and plastic compared to the freshness of the gorgeous red-haired man Cliff had seen earlier that morning. He'd spent half the day suppressing the urge to ask Scott if he knew any red-haired guys who lived within walking distance of the Publix. It had been a long time since Cliff had been so eager to meet a guy that the fluttery anticipation in his belly was both heady and scary as fuck. But his new interest only strengthened his armor against Brett's arrogant charm.

Was that plastic look something Brett had always had and Cliff was only noticing now, or was it something that developed over time in response to Brett's desperation to increase his celebrity status? Whatever the reason, Cliff wasn't going to be snared by Brett again. Which only made him more suspicious about Brett's presence in his hometown.

Brett pulled a ball cap on over his perfectly highlighted hair and strode out into the hallway without a glance backward. Kristi gave Cliff an exasperated look before she turned a big, fake smile on Scott and made an exaggerated show of looking at his name tag.

"Office Hunter? If you don't mind staying back with me for a few minutes to go over the plans for tomorrow, I'd appreciate it. Brett and your partner can go on ahead, and we'll meet them there shortly."

"Of course, ma'am." Scott's response was absolutely perfect, but the reddened tips of his ears told Cliff he'd flashed on one of those lame porn premises where the helpful cop gets lucky.

Unless this was all some elaborate setup by his ex, Kristi was merely giving them the chance to clear the air, since this was the first time Cliff had laid eyes on Brett since finding out he'd cheated on Cliff. With a woman. Not that Cliff would have tolerated cheating with anyone, man or woman, but he knew damn well Brett had only done it for the publicity, since she was a rising star in the business, and as far as his adoring fans were concerned, any of them had a chance of scoring with him. Especially since Brett was more than adept at flirting with either gender.

Probably Cliff should be thankful. If the media had found out he and Brett were in a relationship, they'd have hounded him, making it difficult for him to stay closeted at work. Cliff hadn't been aware that Brett wanted the benefit of being single and having a boyfriend at the same time and had been manipulating Cliff every bit as much as he manipulated the media.

Out in the parking lot, Brett stood beside the fucking enormous pickup. "This is me. Shall we go in my car?"

Of course Brett had rented that monstrous red penis stand-in. In California he drove a top-of-the-line hybrid, but in Florida it had to be the biggest and baddest of the pickups. Cliff assumed there hadn't been a Hummer available; otherwise Brett would be driving that.

Cliff opened his mouth to politely but in no uncertain terms tell Brett *no fucking way*. He was tempted to throw Brett in the backseat of the police-issue vehicle and drive him to the Angry Parakeet like he was a prisoner, but then Cliff remembered Scott had the keys to the cruiser.

"By all means, let's take your truck."

"What's with the ball cap?" Not the question Cliff wanted to ask, but he hadn't ever seen Brett risk hat head to wear a ball cap.

"Obviously I'm here incognito."

Incognito. Right. "It's not working. Especially since you commissioned bodyguards from the local police force."

Brett shrugged and turned the key in the ignition. "Fame is something you'll never understand."

Presumably, Cliff was meant to feel sorry for Brett, but it was hard when he despised the man so much. At least they'd never been in love. Cliff had hoped they'd been heading that way, but he should have known that if it hadn't happened after a year, it wasn't going to happen. He'd been happy—or at least content—and he'd thought Brett was too. He'd been hurt by Brett, and he wasn't going to give the man the chance to do it again.

Cliff waited until the truck was in gear and heading out of the hotel parking lot before he broke. "Brett, what the fuck are you doing here?"

"Well, Cliffy..." Brett paused to let the hated endearment erode Cliff's patience. Although he'd never divulged his full name to Brett, he'd rather be called Northcliff than *Cliffy*, for fuck's sake. But he wanted answers, and letting Brett get to him over something so minor would only lead them off onto a useless tangent. This wasn't his first time at Brett's narcissistic rodeo.

"I'm waiting."

"Cliffy, I'm just doing my job. I'm the host of a nationally syndi-cated paranormal show. Sandy Bottom Bay is reputed to be the second-most haunted town in Florida and has a well-respected ghost festival. It's the perfect subject for a midseason hiatus special. I think the only surprise here is that I haven't visited sooner."

Cliff curled his lip into a sneer. "And it's only coincidence you show up within days of me taking a job here and moving across the country?"

After all, Brett had tried to get him back a couple of times, but Cliff hadn't bought into his lies. Nor was he willing to trust his sexual health with a man who couldn't keep it in his pants and had been alarmingly vague about whether he'd used protection.

Cliff had been at loose ends after his friend Pete had been killed in a car accident, grief making his life grate on his nerves. His work had become unfulfilling, and his social life had seemed fake and pointless without Pete. The job opening in Sandy Bottom Bay a few months after Cliff discovered Brett cheating had been one of the most serendipitous things to ever happen to him. He also couldn't deny he was a little worried about what seemed to be his mother's tenuous grasp on reality, and the deeper she got into the supernatural shit, the more likely someone like the Drummond tarot reader would take advantage of her.

"Oh, come on, Cliffy. I mean, you were an okay lay, but it wasn't earth-shattering enough to chase you across the country."

Cliff coughed, caught off guard by the unexpectedly low blow. This was a new tactic. Apparently Brett was forgetting the tearful message he'd left on Cliff's cell phone. Nevertheless, the comment had been designed to hurt, to prick deeply at a man's psyche, and Cliff couldn't deny it had been effective. He might have been the one to break it off, but the fact that Brett had gone looking for something Cliff couldn't provide had eroded his self-confidence. Irritating but true, and yet another reason to wonder why Brett bothered chasing after him.

"So you're really here for work?" His skepticism was clearly audible, but maybe Brett was telling the truth. Maybe. It would be a long time, if ever, before Cliff trusted another word out of Brett's mouth. Come to think of it, the tactful retreat of Kristi was the biggest concession he'd ever gotten out of her in the entire time he'd dated Brett. And that was suspicious too.

"Of course I am. The network wouldn't send me out here if there wasn't a good reason, and trying to get into your pants isn't a good reason."

They stopped at a red light, and Brett took the opportunity to twist in his seat and give Cliff a much more lascivious perusal. "At least, it's not a good reason for them. You're looking good, but then you always did in uniform. Maybe we can entertain ourselves when I'm not working."

Cliff rolled his eyes as his suspicions returned tenfold. "You just finished telling me I was a shitty lay. And you didn't seem surprised to see me at your hotel. You didn't request I be included in your protection detail, did you?" If that wasn't a horrifying thought, he didn't know what was. The arrogant and self-absorbed Brett Cavanagh with enough power to influence Cliff's new job. He was going to have to change his name and move to Australia.

"Well, no, I wasn't surprised, exactly." Brett laughed, a burbling, happy sound Cliff had once adored, until he'd realized how fake it was.

The light turned green, and Brett guided the truck into the Angry Parakeet parking lot.

Cliff waited, wondering if Brett would admit to using his celebrity status to pull strings.

"After all, you'd told me you were coming back here to work. It wasn't a stretch to think that, in a town this small, you might end up as one of my bodyguards."

Rubbing a hand across his head, Cliff wondered if he could believably call in sick until *Phantoms* had finished filming their show. Since they were scheduled to be here until the end of Haunt Fest, he sort of doubted it. Not unless he were coughing up a lung or losing a limb.

"So, are you out here?" Brett didn't wait for his answer but pressed a hand to his crotch. With a grimace, Cliff grabbed Brett's wrist, squeezing a trifle too hard, and pulled it away.

"What the fuck is wrong with you?"

"I guess that's a no. You're in the closet."

He wasn't, not really, but he should at least tell Scott before Brett did something stupid. Because Brett was bound to do something stupid, and he had a lot of fucking nerve bitching at Cliff for being in the closet. Back in Los Angeles, Cliff had only been in the closet at work, and most of his close friends weren't police officers. Brett, on the other hand, wasn't exactly the model of discretion, but it was his relationship that had been the dirty little secret, not that Brett was happy to dip his wick in people of either gender. The ultimate in fan service.

"Whether I am or not, that's highly inappropriate while I'm on duty."

"Oooh. On duty. Like that's stopped you before."

Cliff's face flamed. Brett had seduced him a couple of times while he'd been on duty. In fact, Cliff suspected it might have been the uniform more than anything else that had attracted Brett in the first place and kept him around.

"That's the past. Here, in Sandy Bottom Bay, you're an assignment. We're not friends; we're not lovers. At best, we're acquaintances. Got it?"

Brett smiled, conciliatory and sweet, making Cliff instantly suspicious. Again.

"Of course, Cliffy. And as old acquaintances, could you maybe do me a teensy-tiny favor?"

The muscles in Cliff's jaw turned to stone.

"Could you arrange an interview with your mother? Her house is the focal point of a lot of the spectral activity around here, and we've got permission to film a couple of places on the property as well as in the house, but she's refusing to appear on camera and tell us about the activity."

"If she's made up her mind, I won't be able to change it." Because Cliff had tried. Many, many times. But he was a little surprised she'd agreed to filming on the property at all.

The predatory look in Brett's eyes intensified. "Or you could tell us about it. The camera would love you and your cheekbones. It would add extra authenticity if you were to appear in uniform. I could clear it with your boss, I'm sure."

Cliff's pulse sped up, and he clenched his hands in fists. "No fucking way. Get out of the fucking truck."

Like always, Brett was using him. And this time Cliff couldn't, or didn't want to, make any excuses for him.

"Surely you don't want me to go in without my bodyguard?"

With his jaw so tightly clamped, it was a wonder Cliff could speak at all. "Nothing's going to fucking happen to you at the Angry Parakeet. But if you don't get out of my sight and let me calm down, something might happen to you now."

"Oooh, big, strong Cliffy the cop, threatening me with police brutality. I don't know if I should be taping this for the Internet and a forthcoming lawsuit or stripping and spreading for you right here." Brett laughed and got out of the truck just as the cruiser pulled up.

Cliff sat in the passenger seat, concentrating on breathing and not succumbing to the anger boiling in his brain. It wasn't often Brett's bitchiness was directed toward him, and he'd forgotten how very much he hated it. This was more cutting than normal, but then, Cliff hadn't witnessed Brett with someone who'd dumped him before. Perhaps this was nothing more than Brett's bruised ego lashing out.

The mention of a lawsuit restrained Cliff from any further madness. No matter how irritating Brett was, it wouldn't do to antagonize him. Cliff would just have to figure out how to ignore the pointed barbs Brett aimed his way. That was the only way he'd keep his job, his sanity, and a somewhat normal blood pressure.

There was something Cliff needed to take care of now, before Brett found the most mortifying and shocking way to announce either Cliff's sexuality or their former relationship status. Or both.

A mask of indifference plastered on his face with quite a bit of effort, Cliff swung himself out of the truck's cab. He nodded at Kristi and Scott, who'd exited the car and were waiting for him with Brett.

"Scott, can I talk to you for a minute?"

Scott glanced at the two visitors, then back at Cliff. "What about..."

"Do you seriously think they'll be able to get into trouble at the Angry Parakeet in under five minutes?" Cliff's tone was a little sharp; there was no excuse for taking out his bad temper on Scott. This bodyguard gig was a publicity stunt, nothing more. It wasn't like Brett's life was in danger, just Cliff's sanity.

"Sure thing, Cliff. We'll meet you two inside."

With a smug smirk, Kristi headed for the restaurant door and disappeared through it, Brett sauntering after her.

"Scott, this is probably the worst time and place to drop this on you, but I have a feeling it's going to come up over dinner, and I want you to be prepared."

Scott tilted his head but said nothing, content to wait for Cliff to finish.

"I knew Brett back in California."

Like a puffer fish, Scott's chest expanded, and Cliff knew he only had seconds to head off some excited request for information.

"He was my boyfriend."

Everything froze as Scott paused mid-inhalation. The world seemed to hang on its axis for a moment while two possible timelines resolved themselves. Was Scott going to hate him or accept him? Cliff despised having to face this same crossroad every time someone found out he was gay, but there wasn't any getting around it aside from staying in the closet, and he wasn't willing to be that guy. Not anymore.

Seconds stretched into eons as Scott processed the information. Cliff hoped to hell Scott didn't take that long when dealing with criminals, but then, maybe it wasn't all that long when it wasn't your own fate in the balance.

There was no tightening of hands into fists nor any hand movement toward the gun on Scott's hip, so Cliff let himself relax a bit.

"Wow. *Brett Cavanagh* is your boyfriend?"

"No, *was*. He cheated on me, and it was an ugly breakup. Whether he wants to play straight, bi, or gay while he's here, I don't know. It changes depending on which demographic he's courting. Judging from some of his comments, he's going to out me while he's here."

Cliff hated to call Brett bisexual, because it wasn't so much that he was attracted to both genders but more that he was a gay man who'd sleep with anyone who could further his career. Shortly after their breakup, Cliff had come to the conclusion that their hidden relationship worked for Brett because he was an opportunistic sexual omnivore who didn't want to limit his options. Brett had an incredible—and sleazy—talent for reading an audience and acting according to whichever number on the Kinsey scale would make the most favorable impression. Too bad there wasn't an award category for that, because Brett would win by a landslide.

"Are you not out, then?"

"You're taking this rather calmly."

"Dude, you slept with a celebrity. That's so cool."

"Yeah, but it was another guy."

Scott shrugged. "It wasn't like we didn't have our suspicions back in high school. You being gay isn't a surprise. You being Brett Cavanagh's boyfriend...er, ex-boyfriend, is."

A big smile stretched muscles on Cliff's face he hadn't used in far too many weeks.

Cuffing him on the shoulder, Scott nodded. "But seriously, are you not out? Does the chief know? Because surely we can do something to shut Brett up."

Relief, as pure and refreshing as a cool breeze, trickled through Cliff, easing away most of the tension he'd been carrying around since realizing his cheating bastard of an ex was in town and possibly stalking him.

"The chief knows, and I wasn't really planning to hide it. Just wasn't going to stream a rainbow flag from the cruiser window, you know? Brett just accelerated my timeline for telling you."

"Still, he should have a little respect. Outing someone without their consent is sorta douchey."

Cliff blinked. He shouldn't get used to this easy acceptance. Despite the presence of gay-friendly Key West, Florida had still voted against marriage equality, so he was pleasantly shocked by Scott's attitude.

"Thanks, man."

"Whatever." A low buzz sounded from Scott's pocket. He pulled out a cell phone. "Hey, I gotta take this. It's my mom."

"No problem. Come join us when you're done." Instead of his sexuality, one of the things Cliff had discussed with Scott during his brief onboarding training had been parents. Scott's mom wasn't well, and Cliff hadn't exactly confided his worries about his own mother. Cliff had, however, admitted that he hadn't told her that he'd taken the job, and Scott had laughed, saying she probably already knew.

Which might or might not be true. His mother's status in town was such that she didn't necessarily get all the gossip, but between that and the handyman's death, he'd have to sac up sooner rather than later and go visit her. First, though, he needed to get through this evening with Brett and not make an ass out of himself on his first day.

He stared up at the Angry Parakeet door, teal paint faded and cracked to the point the weathered wood was visible below in several places. Anger and irritation flooded him again. That lying bastard. If Brett had just gotten into town today, how the hell had he known where the Angry Parakeet was without benefit of directions or GPS? Cliff didn't know what that meant, but he would find out eventually. Because if it wasn't that Brett had memorized directions, it was possible he was stalking Cliff. Did that ever happen? A celebrity stalking a noncelebrity rather than the other way around?

Thunder cracked, loud and ominous from the dark clouds overhead, like nature's foreshadowing. The afternoon had rapidly darkened during the short drive across town. A heavy storm was coming in. Cliff had forgotten how quickly weather could change, although he hadn't forgotten the daily "too much humidity in the air" rainfalls. This, though, was going to last longer, if his eighteen-year experience in Sandy Bottom Bay was good for anything.

One more deep, calming breath and he opened the door, cool air rushing out to greet him, reminding him just how hot and sweat-dampened he was.

CHAPTER 4

Drew let Kyle take the seat with the better view of the front door, although from the angle of the table, they could both see the Angry Parakeet entrance. Looking around, he could only assume Kyle wasn't the only one who'd heard about the possibility of Brett Cavanagh visiting their small town. Half of the occultists and paranormal practitioners were "casually" relaxing in the best restaurant and bar in the area.

The Angry Parakeet's relaxed atmosphere and outstanding food were at complete odds with the shabby, weather-beaten exterior reminiscent of old Florida shacks abused by years of burning sun, melting humidity, torrential rains, and vicious hurricane winds. More often than not, visitors were drawn to establishments that had a more well-kept Floridian feel, but this close to Haunt Fest, there were a number of tourists taking their chances on the Angry Parakeet.

Kyle wiggled in his chair whenever the door opened, his face falling each time he realized the newcomer wasn't Brett Cavanagh.

"Are you sure this is a good idea? I mean, how do we know Brett will come in here at all?"

Kyle's glare should have singed Drew's eyebrows off. "Anyone with sense wouldn't send Brett Cavanagh anywhere else, and I'm sure he's worldly enough not to be taken in by the pink plastic thrill of Flamingos or the kitsch of Specter Smorgasbord."

A laugh slipped out of Drew's mouth. "Right. Because everybody in Sandy Bottom Bay has sense." The town's economy was based on a horrific massacre almost two hundred years ago and the subsequent reputation for being the second-most haunted town in Florida. If this were any other state, they'd have been labeled crackpots and weirdoes long ago, but this was Florida, so they just blended right in.

"Fine. It's a gamble." Kyle smoothed a hand over his hair.

"Besides…what if he's trying to be incognito? He might be getting room service right this very minute. Or what if he decided to stroll along the boardwalk, absorbing the ambiance?"

Kyle bared his teeth at Drew. "So it's a *big* gamble. Do you have a better idea?"

Drew shrugged and took a gulp of his piña colada. At least he didn't have to worry about ordering a more "manly" drink. Not only was this Florida, he was out and mostly proud. Neither he nor Kyle had managed to develop a taste for beer, and it was a relief to be able to enjoy their booze. Kyle, of course, stuck to a basic vodka and diet Coke to control his caloric intake, but Drew didn't have to worry about that, and he drank a variety of sweet, fruity tropical drinks.

All of which was a way to avoid the thought that he really didn't have a better idea. Bad idea or not, this was the most exciting thing he'd done in recent memory.

"This is pathetic." Drew set his drink down and snagged a tortilla chip from the basket the waitress had left on the table.

A frigid expression froze Kyle's face, and when he spoke, his voice was low, but each syllable was clearly enunciated. "I'm pathetic?"

It had been a hard transition for Kyle, when he'd been expecting to follow his dreams of dance to a big city, and as a result, he sometimes sought the limelight in ways that left Drew squirming. Drew had a few seconds to head off the explosion, and he rushed to placate Kyle. "No, I am."

Just as quickly, Kyle switched gears, becoming offended on Drew's behalf. His much shorter friend should have been born with Drew's fiery red hair. Then he could truly look the part of the twinky virago, matching the personality that resided underneath Kyle's pale Nordic appearance. Virago. Yet another word he'd picked up from his grandma's romance novels, but this one at least he knew the meaning of.

"You're not pathetic. Why would you say that about yourself?"

"Whoa. Calm down. Just saying that this is the most exciting thing I've done in weeks. Even if Brett doesn't show up. Which, you have to admit, is kinda pathetic."

Kyle scrunched up his face. "Oh yeah, I guess you're right."

The agreement stung, just a bit. Truth hurts and all that.

With another little wiggle in his seat, Kyle sat up straighter. "We need to take a trip up to Tampa, hit a decent club, and get laid. After Haunt Fest, though. One, we're both too busy to go now, and two, we might get lucky during the festival. There are almost always a couple of cute gay college students who are nerdy or freaky enough to go buck the spring-break trend."

"There's always Eddie. If you're desperate."

Kyle's pale cheeks lit up as he blushed. He slammed a fist against his chest and lifted his nose before he spoke. "As God as my witness, I'll never be that desperate again."

Eddie might have been Drew's business rival, but he was also a hot, firm-bodied man slut.

Kyle had been ecstatic when Eddie turned his smoldering green gaze on him. At least until they'd done the deed. Kyle told Drew in gory detail the next morning about Eddie and his boring, selfish bedroom so-called skills. Which didn't even take into account that Kyle had become persona non grata among the single women. Once Eddie turned his attention back toward the female population, Kyle had been forgiven.

Drew laughed, and Kyle pursed his lips, his expression suddenly assessing.

"You could give him a try. I mean, it would be better than the nothing you've got going on now, right?"

"Oh hell no." Drew frowned at Kyle. "You just got shitty service and vicious glares. I might lose my business."

He shuddered. The thought was repellant in so many ways. First and foremost, his business truly would suffer. Eddie Price didn't do the card readings a number of the town's women seemed to like, but as a medium he could be an acceptable substitute, especially if they decided to punish Drew for taking Eddie out of circulation. Drew might not be as experienced as Kyle, but he certainly didn't need more experience with bad sex. He could get himself off just fine without risking his business and an STD by taking the village bicycle for a ride. Sleeping with Eddie was a brand of notoriety he wasn't interested in, assuming either of them were willing to set aside their professional rivalry.

"No, thank you. A trip into Tampa sounds perfect to me." A handjob or blowjob in the bathroom at a club would be a welcome respite from his own hand, although he wished Sandy Bottom Bay offered more in the way of boyfriend material. With a truly eligible man available, he might have a better chance of getting over his stupid adolescent crush on a man who was never coming back.

"Uh-huh. And are you actually going to let someone touch your dick this time? Aren't you tired of waiting for the perfect Cliff Garcia, Sandy Bottom Bay's prodigal son, to return?"

Flames licked at Drew's cheeks as Kyle's words mocked the very thought that had just flown through his mind. "Shut up." It wasn't like he chickened out of one-night stands *every* time they went to a club.

Kyle rolled his eyes. "Like anyone cares you've got a crush on some dude no one even remembers. Odds are the guy is straight. And fat. Possibly married. He might even have kids by now."

The mock horror in Kyle's tone didn't fool Drew. Just as Kyle knew Drew's deep, dark secret—his unshakable crush on Cliff—Drew knew Kyle's. If Kyle could marry a sweet guy and adopt a village of kids from Africa, he'd do it in a hot second, and he wouldn't give a damn if the guy was ripped or not. Nevertheless, Kyle's secret didn't cripple his sex life nearly as much as Drew's did.

Unfortunately, Drew was a terrible liar, and his cheeks got hotter. There was one big reason an ember of hope remained in his heart— and his cock, if he was being truthful.

Kyle's mouth dropped open as he stared, understanding slowly dawning.

"No way. No fucking way. That's why you never told me Helen Somerset was your client! She tells you stuff about him." Kyle cuffed his arm, making him slop piña colada on the table.

"Hey, watch it. No spilling the drink." It was a splurge he could barely afford as it was.

"Who cares? I'll buy you another. What does she tell you?"

Kyle's voice rose loud enough that he was drawing more attention than Drew was comfortable with, especially since he truly did feel his clients deserved whatever privacy and discretion he was able to give.

"Quiet down."

Kyle puffed up like a rooster getting ready to crow, and his whole demeanor made Drew panic.

"Please, don't do this." Drew wasn't above begging. Not only was this his livelihood, but he knew how stupid he was to hoard away whatever little tidbits Helen let slip about her son's life, letting the information fuel his fantasies and feed the crush he'd had since he was fourteen.

Somehow, his desperation got through to Kyle, and disappointed, he deflated. Leaning across the table, Kyle spoke quietly, his expression serious. "Is he gay?"

"Yes." Giddiness bubbled in Drew's blood like fizzy soda at the thought of kissing Cliff Garcia.

The answer didn't bring any approval to Kyle's eyes, as Drew had half expected.

"And where does he live?"

"Los Angeles." Those words flattened out the fizzy in his veins as effectively as Kyle's solemn nod.

"Exactly. And after leaving for college he's come home...not even once." With anyone else, Kyle likely would have retained his customary sarcastic tone, but instead his voice and expression were filled with sympathy.

Drew's stomach twisted, and his eyes burned. Confronting the reality of the situation, out loud and in the face of Kyle's simple logic, depressed the hell out of him.

"Let me buy the next round." Kyle patted his hand; there was no joy for either of them in the death of Drew's hopes.

After flagging down a waitress and placing an order, Kyle turned an intense look on Drew.

Drew raised a brow. "Should I be scared?"

"If Brett gives you even a fraction of an opening, you have to jump in there. I will selflessly leave the field open for you. Brett might not be gay, but might be gay, fucking hot, and in the same damned zip code makes your odds of getting laid shoot astronomically higher than your chances of getting naked with Cliff 'Absentee' Garcia."

Kyle's description wrung a rueful laugh from Drew, and he nodded. He wasn't about to admit he'd rather have a boyfriend than just get naked with another guy, even one as hot as Brett Cavanagh, but having to drive for miles to the nearest gay club wasn't going to put him in prime geographical proximity for anything but getting his rocks off. Might as well see if it could happen with a television star. Assuming Kyle was actually able to leave the field open for him. Not that Kyle didn't have the best intentions, but Kyle's crush on Brett was almost as intense as Drew's crush on Cliff.

"Thought we'd find you here." Drew's brother Rob slid into an empty chair, sloshing beer on the table as he did so. Rob's twin, Wyatt, sat in the fourth chair, across from Rob. Both of them were much bulkier than either Drew or Kyle, taller and all muscle. Drew wasn't a thing like his brothers, not in looks, temperament, or build. Most of his family, including his brothers, resembled Vikings: big, blond, and broad. They all had golden skin that simply turned more golden when exposed to sunlight. Drew's pale skin practically lit on fire like he was a vampire if he spent too long in the sun, with or without sunscreen. And the red hair...if it weren't for his grandma's reassurances that his grandfather—bald as an egg in every picture

Drew had seen—was a ginger, he would have suspected he was the proverbial milkman's kid.

Kyle clammed up at their sudden appearance. Not that his friend would ever admit it, but Drew knew Kyle was also crushing on one of his brothers. Which one, he wasn't sure, because Rob and Wyatt almost never did anything apart. Except commit crimes, and that was simple expedience. They'd beat more than one charge because so few people could tell them apart, and having one establish an alibi while the other was off doing...whatever...meant they almost never were charged. Arrested, sure. The local police didn't have any better opinions about the Drummonds than did the rest of the town, but when witnesses couldn't definitely identify a perpetrator, there wasn't much the cops could do. If their crimes had been worse than petty theft and fighting, the cops might have tried harder, but Drew was glad they were merciful, because he didn't want either of his brothers in jail.

"And why exactly did you think you'd find us here?" Drew figured he needed to ask, since Kyle probably wasn't going to say a word until they were alone again. At least this crush was recent and would hopefully pass as quickly as it had begun, because having Kyle act like a mannequin in his brothers' presence was getting a little irritating.

"Because that fairy ghost-hunter dude is supposed to be here."

Kyle gasped a little in outrage but still didn't say anything. Drew might have done the same thing, but getting upset over his brothers' lack of political correctness wouldn't change their behavior any. They'd actually been incredibly supportive after Drew and then Kyle had come out, and had at least stopped using the word *fag*, which Drew supposed was the best he could get. And if anyone else called him or Kyle *fag* or *fairy* or any other derogatory word...well, there weren't too many in town stupid enough to incur the wrath of the Drummond clan. Not after the first few broken noses for the less tolerant.

"You do realize we're both *fairies* too, right?"

It was meant to be a rhetorical question, but Wyatt answered anyway. "Yeah, but you're *our* fairies. Makes a difference."

As one, the twins reached out and ruffled his and Kyle's hair. A rosy blush swept up Kyle's face and disappeared into his hairline.

"You two be good and don't make fools of yourselves over this famous fairy." With that parting shot, Rob headed back to the bar, Wyatt following on his heels, leaving Drew and Kyle with scrambled bed-head hairstyles.

Kyle sat there for a second, as though deciding whether to be excited by the attention or pissed that they'd ruined the effort of however many minutes it had taken him to get his hair just right. Drew never primped as much as Kyle and never used product, so his own hair would right itself with a quick shake of his head.

"Which one?" The curiosity was killing him, and Kyle apparently wasn't going to tell him, so he'd just have to ask.

"Which one what?"

Drew snorted. Others might believe Kyle's innocent look but not Drew. "Which one of my brothers gets your motor running?" He didn't much want to think about either of his brothers' sex lives, but if he could talk Kyle out of his weird crush, maybe Kyle would move on. Not that Kyle had been able to do the same for him, no matter how hard he tried, but Drew's crush on Cliff didn't seem quite as hopeless as Kyle's on Rob or Wyatt.

Hell, his friend had a better chance with Brett Cavanagh. His brothers were relentlessly straight, and they were also kind of assholes. They'd done their best as brothers and had kept him from getting his head kicked in more than once, but he wouldn't wish either of them—romantically—on his worst enemy.

Strangely, Kyle's blush became so dark Drew wondered for a fraction of a second if Kyle was having a stroke or something.

"C'mon. You can tell me."

Kyle's blush didn't fade one bit, and he couldn't meet Drew's gaze. A sudden thought hit Drew, and he shuddered.

"Not... No. Not both of them?"

Kyle's gaze flickered upward, and in the sheepish expression, Drew read the full truth.

"Not just both of them, but both of them together? Kyle, you sick puppy! Those are my brothers."

Twincest. Maybe if he hadn't grown up with twin brothers, Drew might have seen the appeal as a fantasy, but seriously... Ick.

Kyle licked his lips and took a sip of his drink, shoulders hunched in, looking nearly as defeated as when he'd arrived home after his knee injury had destroyed his dreams of dancing professionally.

"Kyle, I insist. If Brett gives you the slightest fraction of an opening, you take it. Anything, and I mean anything, to keep you from getting hung up on my brothers." Drew did his level best not to cringe as he said those last words.

"I'm sorry," Kyle whispered, gaze still directed firmly at the table, and Drew's inability to understand why anyone would fantasize about his brothers melted in the face of Kyle's shame.

"Hey, hey." He reached over and grabbed Kyle's hand. "Don't feel bad. You've got nothing to apologize for. You can't help who you like, but I don't want you to get hurt. I know you only want the best for me when you try to take me out to get laid, try to get me over my own hopeless crush. Believe me when I say I want the same for you. You're my best friend."

The unhealthy color in Kyle's face receded, and he lifted his eyes, his expression no longer ashamed. "You're right. Why is it we're not boyfriends again?"

Drew laughed. "You need to ask?"

"Oh, right, gingers are so terribly unfashionable, and I haven't a basement to hide you out in to make sure no one knows we're sleeping together."

Drew pinched Kyle's arm before he withdrew his hand. "Shut up. The royal family and Harry Potter made gingers all the rage, I'll have you know. You just don't know what you're missing out on."

Back on familiar teasing ground, Drew relaxed. They just weren't attracted to one another, which Drew did lament on occasion. Life would be a lot simpler if he and Kyle were an item, as most of the town assumed.

The door to the Angry Parakeet opened, and like he'd done all evening, Kyle craned his head to look. This time, though, he gasped and smacked Drew's arm just as Kyle was lifting his piña colada to his lips. Coconut-pineapple froth slopped out of the glass—again—and onto Drew's shirt.

"Kyle, what the fuck?"

"It's him," Kyle whispered, staring intently at the person who came in.

Drew only got an impression of a guy in a baseball cap before he tried mopping up the wet spot on his shirt. He was wearing black—maybe it wouldn't be too obvious, although he smelled as fruity as his brothers sometimes called him.

"It's who?"

"Brett."

Drew lifted his gaze. Sure enough, under the shadow of the ball cap's bill were those famous features. Drew had expected the guy to be...not as attractive in person. He'd seen tabloids before, although they mostly focused on female celebrities without their makeup. But all actors wore makeup when they were working, and he'd expected real-life Brett to be a normal guy, maybe more fit than the average man, but not gorgeous.

He was wrong. Brett Cavanagh was every bit as delicious in person as he was on screen. If Drew were going to have a one-night stand, this might be the guy he'd want, but Kyle was kidding himself if he thought a star like Brett was browsing in Sandy Bottom Bay for a boyfriend.

Brett stood in the doorway for a moment, ostensibly looking for a table, but somehow, Drew knew he was making a deliberate entrance. No matter how incognito this visit was supposed to be, there was no doubt in Drew's mind that Brett liked being the center of attention.

A woman slipped through the door behind him and stood off to the side, as though allowing Brett his moment. Their body language didn't speak of intimacy, so she wasn't his girlfriend, but there was enough yearning in her expression to tell Drew that she wouldn't mind the role. Presumably she had arrived with Brett, because she carried a briefcase and Drew had never seen her before.

With a smile meant to be self-deprecating, Brett made his way to the bar like he was a prince or something. The more Drew watched, the more arrogance and self-absorption he saw. Still, one didn't need to like a guy to have sex with him, and sex with Brett Cavanagh would be something for the spank bank.

Conversation quieted among both the locals and some of the tourists who'd come into town early for the festival. There were a few tourists who probably wouldn't recognize Brett Cavanagh if he bit them on the nose, but Drew was surprised they could remain oblivious when everyone else's attention was centered on the man striding toward the bar, the dark-haired woman shadowing him like a lackey.

Before he reached the bar, the woman tugged at his sleeve and spoke in a low voice. Brett nodded, and they abruptly changed direction to seat themselves at a booth within spitting distance of his and Kyle's table. Brett slid into the seat that allowed him to view the entire restaurant...and allowed the entire restaurant to watch him. If Brett was truly trying to be inconspicuous, he was doing it very badly.

A flustered waitress came to get their drink orders, and for the next few minutes, Brett did nothing but peruse the menu and converse with the dark-haired woman, who appeared to be making notes. Obviously she had something to do with the TV crew. Slowly, as Brett appeared to be doing nothing but trying to order dinner, the locals' interest waned. A couple of tourists approached for autographs, which he graciously gave, but shortly thereafter, Drew and Kyle were likely the only ones paying attention.

As though he could sense their regard, Brett's gaze swept across them, and out of the corner of his eye, Drew saw Kyle give a little wave. After exchanging a few words with his companion, Brett got up and strode over to their table, sitting down.

"Well, hello there. How did I miss you two last time I was here?"

"You've been here before?" Kyle managed to stutter out the question, but Brett's large, warm hand clamped down on Drew's thigh, and all he could manage was a strangled squeak.

"Sure, sure. Scoping out the area. Research, you know." Brett smiled at Kyle and stroked a finger along his jaw like a lover would, while the hand on Drew's thigh crept ever higher.

All the saliva in Drew's mouth dried out. What the hell was going on here? Was Brett trying to pick them both up? Was he truly gay, or was he just trying to shock people? Despite the thrum of desire jerking his cock to awareness, Drew wasn't sure he was comfortable with this scenario. Threesomes weren't really his thing. Having sex with one other person seemed complicated enough without trying to add a third dick to the proceedings. Hell, he didn't even think Kyle had ever had a threesome before, and given their lack of attraction to one another, he wasn't sure having one with Kyle was the way he'd go about it...assuming either of them would even say yes.

"And who are you?"

Drew didn't miss the fact that Brett assumed introducing himself was unnecessary, which slowed the blood rushing to his groin.

"I'm Kyle, and this is Drew." Kyle's voice had taken on a breathy quality that Drew associated with flirting. Wasn't Kyle as weirded-out as Drew?

"So good to meet you. I hope I'll see more of you while I'm here. Or maybe you'd like a little work as extras?" The words dripped with innuendo, and despite the weirdness, Drew couldn't help but be mesmerized by Brett's intense gaze and the novel sensation of someone in Sandy Bottom Bay displaying such open interest in him.

"Get the fuck away from them, you pervert." Drew's eyes widened, and his gaze met Kyle's equally surprised one a mere blink before Wyatt pulled Brett up by the collar.

In a second, Brett's expression turned vicious and ugly. He faced his assailant, and Drew just wanted to die of humiliation. Brett's companion spoke rapidly into a cell phone before moving to hover at the edge of the altercation.

Wyatt continued to roar at Brett, who shouted back all kinds of stuff about freedom of speech and hate crimes. The two of them were similarly built, and under normal circumstances, it might have been a fair fight. Drew had seen the signs before; it was only a matter of minutes before the fists started flying. However, by some chance, Rob wasn't there—probably taking a leak—and Drew had to get this contained before Rob came back. He wouldn't give a flying rat fuck who started what, but if he returned to find Wyatt fighting, he'd start beating on whomever Wyatt was.

"Guys, stop it. This is stupid." Drew's voice wasn't loud enough to overcome his sheer and utter embarrassment. Was this the behavior he could look forward to if he actually brought a boyfriend home to meet his family? That thought was enough to spark Drew's own temper. He had a much longer fuse than the rest of his family, but he was still a Drummond.

"Wyatt, fucking stop this now." Drew grabbed his brother's arm while Kyle tried to get Brett to see reason. Unfortunately, Brett didn't do a damn thing to calm the situation, sneering and taunting Wyatt.

"No fucking way. I saw him, hands all over you. Pervert." Wyatt directed the last word at Brett, whose face reddened to the point of almost purple.

"Is that what I am to you? A pervert?" Drew's voice got louder, trying to outshout the potential combatants.

"No, of course not." Wyatt didn't even bother to look at him, attention still on Brett.

"So, I'm not a pervert, but if a guy is interested in having sex with me, he's a pervert? Unacceptable, Wyatt."

"Jesus, you fairies are all so sensitive." Wyatt had more to say, but Brett took exception to words Drew had heard most of his life whenever he stood up to his brothers.

"Fucking redneck homophobe!"

Wyatt clocked Brett across the jaw, but Brett managed to twist his head aside, the momentum causing Wyatt to stumble and allowing Brett to remain upright.

"If you had the guts to admit to your latent gayness, you might have had a chance to fuck these two instead of being pissed I got to them first." Brett yelled that at the top of his lungs, several onlookers gasped, and Drew lunged for his brother, no longer worried about saving Brett but just trying to keep his brother from going to jail for murder.

"What the holy hell is going on here?" A stranger in a police uniform bellowed, catching Drew's attention as everyone paused.

Drew had just registered that the stranger was a grown-up, filled-out, still-fucking-gorgeous Cliff Garcia when a blow hit him from behind. The last thing he saw was the edge of a table speeding toward his face before a shock of pain turned his vision red, followed by everything going black.

CHAPTER 5

A beefy blond about Cliff's own age, face twisted in a snarl, launched himself at Brett. And missed, taking out someone Cliff thought might have been trying to stop the fight.

However it had gone down, the miss was enough to shock everyone into stilled silence.

"Scott, get him out of here, and call for backup."

Cliff had left that asshole Brett alone for ten minutes. Ten. And somehow he'd instigated a brawl. In the Angry Parakeet, for God's sake.

Roughly shoving Brett out of the way was enough for him to see a knot of people gathered around a fallen figure on the floor. A small blond man knelt close by, holding a pale hand.

"Drew? Drew?" There was no mistaking the panic in his voice.

"Let me through," Cliff ordered. Most of the onlookers melted away, allowing Cliff to approach. Two identical faces turned toward him, skin pale and ashy, but the Drummond twins didn't move. Figured. At least he had a decent shot at not getting fired for this fiasco, considering the chief's attitude about the Drummonds mirrored his own.

"Give him room." Cliff hadn't seen who'd gone down; it had all happened too fast. But clearly someone was injured, and in all likelihood, it was a guy. Those fucking Drummonds. If some poor bystander got killed or maimed because the Drummonds were homophobic assholes, Cliff wasn't sure he'd be able to control his own temper.

"Drew? Drew?" The small blond seemed stuck on that one name, but at least Cliff could assume that was the name of the guy who'd dropped. And hadn't stirred.

"Back away, kid. Let me help him."

It was dark under the table, where the thin guy lay crumpled. Cliff pulled a flashlight from his belt and shone it.

Bright red hair reflected light back at him, crimson blood streaming from a gash on the guy's forehead providing a stomach-turning contrast. Cliff gasped; his chest constricted. His little fantasy just that morning made the redhead—Drew—seem almost like a friend. Acquaintance, at the very least. Watching him for those few minutes had told Cliff a wealth of information about his character, and all of it was good. Unlike the evil twins responsible for hurting him.

Cliff bit the inside of his lip, hoping to control his suddenly racing heart.

Focus on the job. Get the job done.

As he knelt over Drew and radioed for an ambulance, his mind repeated those two phrases, hoping to whatever deity might be listening that he'd do right by this guy and not fuck up. He'd never had to deal with anyone close to him while in a professional capacity.

With trembling fingers, he quickly checked Drew's pulse, tempted to turn him over on his back to reassure himself the damage wasn't as bad as it appeared, but that wouldn't be smart. From Drew's position and the location of the gash, he must have hit the edge of the table smack in the middle of his forehead. Depending on how fast he hit, he could have spinal issues, and moving him would be the worst thing to do for him.

"An ambulance is on the way." He gave Drew's shoulder a little squeeze, loath to leave him, but Cliff had a job to do, and it wasn't mooning over the gorgeous guy he'd wanted to get to know. Also, he wasn't sure how long he could stare at Drew, motionless and bleeding, before he lost his shit all over the place.

Turning to the blond kid, who was likely the same age as Drew, he did his best to appear confident and in control. "What's your name?"

"Kyle."

"Okay. Kyle. Make sure no one turns him over. Let the EMTs do that, in case he's got a spinal injury."

Kyle's blue eyes widened and filled with tears, but he nodded.

"Good. He'll be fine. Don't worry." Cliff was so full of shit. This could go bad in a heartbeat, especially if he didn't get some backup in here. Brawls were nasty things, and he was technically on his own against at least two Drummonds. And head wounds could be finicky and dangerous.

"Right. You two. Tell me what the fuck happened. Or wait until I get you to the station. Either way, you're spending the night locked up."

One of the twins... Cliff would like to say he'd put Sandy Bottom Bay so far in his rearview that he couldn't even remember the names of the two kids who'd done their best to make his school life miserable, but it would have been a lie. He knew the twins were Rob and Wyatt, but he'd had a hell of time telling them apart, and eight years later hadn't made that job any easier.

The only difference right now was one of the twins was staring, stricken, at Drew, and the other was bouncing on the balls of his feet like a prizefighter getting ready to take a swing. If he thought he was going to take a swing at Cliff, there might be an ugly surprise or two in store. Like the gun in his holster.

Cliff took a deep breath and pointed at the bouncing twin. If he wasn't calm, this situation would explode, and if it did, Drew might get hurt even worse. Not to mention Cliff's own health might be in jeopardy.

"Drummond... Which one are you?" The twin simply glared at him. Cliff rolled his eyes and pointed at Drummond twin one instead. "Which one are *you*?" As soon as Cliff noticed his fingers were still trembling, he put his hands on his waist.

"It was an accident. I swear." Drummond twin one was shaking more than Cliff, which seemed an odd reaction since he'd seen these guys do worse damage in the schoolyard. Why would he be afraid?

"Officer, uh..." Kyle stammered a bit.

"Garcia." Cliff didn't take his attention off the twins. As soon as some backup got here, he was arresting these two for assault.

"Officer Garcia?" Kyle sounded oddly incredulous, but Cliff had no idea why. The kid was too young for them to have been in school together, and if nothing else, Cliff looked 100 percent like a Garcia.

"Yes?"

"It was an accident. They'd never hurt Drew."

"Bastard." This from Drummond twin two, the belligerent one. That was going to get old quick. "Cliff Garcia, back as a cop. Figures."

Cliff spared a glance for Kyle, ignoring the twin's venom. At least Cliff had the police on his side. "What makes you so sure?"

"He's their brother."

Shock pushed away all other emotions, and Cliff almost stumbled. He'd known there was another Drummond kid somewhere. When he'd been at school, anyway. Presumably the various branches had spawned more Drummonds while he'd been in California. But at school, Cliff had been vaguely aware Rob and Wyatt had a younger brother, although Cliff didn't think they'd ever crossed paths. If he'd spared a moment to think about it, he might have guessed *Kyle* was their brother. He was much closer in coloring than Drew was.

Cliff closed his eyes for a moment. Did that mean giving up the prospect of getting to know Drew? He almost laughed right there in the bar. Even if Drew wasn't as intolerant as his brothers, even if he was gay, there was no way he was out of the closet. Not with violent brothers like Rob and Wyatt. And that was assuming a Drummond could keep—or want to keep—his nose clean in order to have a relationship with a cop. Not that he knew for sure, but it was probable that all the Drummonds had a record or had been in juvie. Cliff stared down at Drew, and something cracked in his chest, the death of hope. Stupid to grieve for something that could never happen, but he couldn't deny finding out Drew belonged to the Drummond clan was oddly devastating.

"Please. Tell me he'll be all right." Drummond twin one must have been the one who'd accidentally sent his brother careening into the table. Given the disparity in body type and weight—not that any of these Drummonds were fat—Drew hadn't had a chance of stopping himself. Why hadn't he woken up yet?

Sirens were audible over the steady drumming of rain on the roof, and getting louder, and Cliff barely restrained himself from running outside and yelling at them to hurry. At least he was fairly certain the worst of the tension was gone, since he could now see the belligerent twin was trying to find an outlet for the fear he felt for his brother, much like the anger curdling in Cliff's brain.

If he weren't here in an official capacity, he'd love to punch one or both of them. And Brett for good measure. Instead he drew on all his experience as a cop and became the authority figure they expected.

"The paramedics are on their way. He'll be in good hands." Also a line of bullshit. He hadn't met anyone else in emergency services yet, but he hoped they'd been hired by someone as competent as the police chief. Ruthlessly, he suppressed the desire to kneel down next to Drew and touch him, reassure himself that Drew was still breathing. Give him whatever comfort he could derive in his unconscious state.

Within seconds, paramedics and more cops swarmed into the bar, all of them borderline drenched from the downpour that had begun abruptly during the fight. The paramedics immediately assessed Drew while Cliff directed the cops to take a few witness statements, but he was going to accompany Drew to the hospital. Assuming Drew regained consciousness soon, Cliff would need to get his statement. He could send another cop, but he wanted to torture himself just a little longer, find out what Drew's voice sounded like, find out what color his eyes were. Stupid, but he was going to take whatever he could get.

He took one last look at the twins. "I want to know which one of you is which. You're going to give statements to these fine officers, understand? Got it?"

His stern, uncompromising words snapped the belligerent twin out of his temper, and the anger drained from his face. Of course, if they weren't so worried about their brother, odds were Cliff would have a mouthful of broken teeth, courtesy of a Drummond fist, but he'd take whatever advantage he could get.

"I'm going with Drew to the hospital. If he agrees this was an accident, you're in the clear. Otherwise I'm running you in. And don't think I didn't hear what you said to Brett. Hate speech can get you in big trouble, Drummond."

Kyle spoke up. "Can I ride with him?"

"You related?"

Kyle's shoulders dropped. "No. Best friend."

An odd tension relaxed in Cliff's chest, one he hadn't realized was there. For a moment, he'd expected Kyle to say he was Drew's boyfriend. Kyle was clearly gay, so maybe Drew wasn't quite as intolerant as his brothers.

Cliff reached out a hand and dropped it on Kyle's shoulder. "They won't tell you anything, but I'll make sure your statement gets taken first so you can follow along as soon as possible."

Drew was loaded onto a stretcher, backboard in place, and wheeled out of the bar. It looked like he was coming around, which was a fucking relief, although head wounds could still turn bad. Depended on how badly his brains had been rattled. Between the blood that was every bit as horrific as a slasher film and the possibility of spinal-cord injury, Cliff was terrified for the man.

One of the paramedics mentioned *fractured skull* under his breath, and Cliff's insides clenched up. Drew wasn't going to bleed out, not like some of the murder victims Cliff had seen, but at the very least Drew had suffered some sort of traumatic brain injury, which had been known to cause all sorts of complications up to and including death. Cliff's first day on the job couldn't end this way. It just couldn't. Not when Drew had breathed a tiny spark of hope into his life just by existing.

The ashen-faced twin turned to Kyle. "Call Uncle Walt. He'll be too drunk by now to drive you, but he'll send one of the cousins to pick you up. Take you to the hospital."

Cliff followed the stretcher but was still paying enough attention to realize Kyle was able to call Drew's uncle Walt without having to ask for a phone number. Kid wasn't lying about being a best friend, but if an obviously gay guy like Kyle got preferential treatment from the Drummonds, what had possessed them to start that vicious, hateful argument he'd witnessed?

DREW GROANED AND BLINKED. A stabbing, throbbing pain lanced through his brain, centering on what felt like a great, gaping crack in his forehead.

Flashing lights, wailing sirens, and people's voices were like stilettos through his eyes and ears. His thoughts scattered on shards of pain, and he had no idea where he was or why he hurt so badly.

Was he drunk? He'd never been so hungover in his life. He'd been...at the Angry Parakeet, maybe. Had he somehow drunk enough to edge into alcohol-poisoning territory? Or almost-dead territory?

"Wha..." He tried to move, sit up, something. His body was weirdly immobile, but his stomach lurched. Hands gripped his shoulder, turning him on his side as he spewed his guts out. The heaving of his stomach made the pain in his head pulse angrily in time.

Finally he was done, although the wooziness hadn't decreased in the slightest. This time he didn't try to sit up or move his arms. He tried to focus his gaze, just a bit. He had to know where he was, but the only thing visible was a swath of dark green. The monstrous effort of keeping his eyes open was too much, and he let his lids drop again.

"Hey there, careful now. We don't want a repeat of the stomach explosion."

"Sorry." He must be drunk, because even he could hear he was slurring.

"Nothing to be sorry for. You just relax. Let these guys do their work. You had an accident."

"Hurts." Work? Accident? He was so confused, but the hand holding his was warm and strong, anchoring him in some indefinable way.

CHAPTER 6

The lights were still too bright, nothing was clearly focused, and time no longer seemed to run at its normal speed. At least Drew knew now that he hadn't been stupid enough to drink until he nearly died. Then again, the endless white walls interspersed with tests and cold instruments might mean he was in purgatory. His vision swam, and he remembered a lovely nurse with a lovely IV. Drugs slightly muffled the pain in his head and kept his stomach from rebelling, and he was fairly certain morphine didn't help dead people.

"Hey there. How are you doing?"

There was that voice again. He'd heard it before, and it made him feel warm and safe. It was also the sexiest voice he'd ever heard, although sex was the last thing on his mind just now. He could barely move without pain and nausea, and his cock was about as responsive as an overcooked noodle.

Taking a slow, deep breath, Drew forced his eyes to open. Somehow he knew the owner of that voice wasn't another doctor, and he wanted to see the guy. Carefully he turned his head. While his eyes worked on making sense of the figure in front of him, he decided to answer the question.

"Shitty." His voice was crazy scratchy, and his mouth was dry enough he almost expected dust to puff out with the word.

"Would you like some water?"

Oh God. That gorgeous voice offering water. It was official. He was in love.

Drew's first instinct was to nod, to avoid using his voice, but even under the pleasant haze of intravenous painkillers, he knew that would be a bad idea. "Please."

The owner of the voice drew closer, cup in hand. The dark green clothing resolved into a police officer's uniform. Wow. Once he was feeling up to his old self, this would probably fuel a few late-night fantasies.

Strong brown fingers directed the bendy straw toward his mouth, leaving Drew grateful, because he wasn't sure he even had the energy to do that.

"Not too much, not too fast. You've already puked on me twice today."

He had? Twice? That explained why it felt like he'd swallowed a handful of fishing lures. It was also embarrassing as hell. Or it would be if his emotions weren't nicely buffered by morphine or whatever loveliness was in his veins. At least the nice cop didn't sound disgusted or irritated. Maybe cops got puked on all the time.

Drew swallowed carefully, relieved that nothing set off his tender stomach. "Sorry," he rasped out.

"Not a problem. I'm just glad your injuries weren't worse."

Injuries. Hospital. Right, he'd almost forgotten. "What happened again?" Had he been hit by a car? He thought someone might have told him what happened, but the pain or the morphine didn't let it stick in his memory. Hell, he didn't even know what day it was or how long he'd been out.

The cop pulled his chair closer to the bed and settled in. "Well, I was hoping you'd be able to tell me, but the doctor says your concussion was severe enough that you probably don't remember."

Concussion. Yes, concussion fit his symptoms. Reasonable. "So you don't know how I got it? Was it a car accident?"

Which was a little weird since he didn't own a car, and if he'd been at the Angry Parakeet with Kyle like he thought he remembered, they would have walked, not driven.

"No, it appears you were an accidental victim of a fight at the Angry Parakeet."

A fight? "Accidental, you say?"

"Yes, it seems you got in the way of your brother's fist as it was heading toward someone else's head, and you cracked your head on a table."

Huh. That wasn't going to do anything to redeem his cool factor—assuming he had any at all—from puking on the sexy-voiced cop. If only he could also forget he was such a fucking loser. His brothers were going to owe him for this for the rest of their lives. At least he didn't have to worry about the medical bills exceeding his piddly insurance plan. If one of his hot-headed brothers was responsible for this, they'd find a way to pay, even if Drew would have to be very careful not to ask exactly *how* they got the money.

"Do you remember anything about it?"

Drew shivered, that deep voice—almost familiar somehow—skimming over his skin like a caress. God almighty, those drugs were fine. If only his damn eyes would work properly. He wanted to see this guy. No way could he be as hot as he sounded.

Wait. "Sorry, what?" He wouldn't be upset if the fog in his brain cleared too. Unless that meant giving up the drugs that kept the pain at bay.

"Do you remember the fight? Going to the Angry Parakeet? Was there a reason you were there?"

Drew waved a hand in front of his face. Too many questions. Exhaustion hit him like a brick to the face. "Tired. I don't...remember." He was slurring again, but his tongue wasn't obeying any better than his eyes.

"C'mon now. Try to keep those beautiful blue eyes open a little longer."

His eyes were beautiful? They were blue, but he must have imagined the compliment. Cops didn't go around saying things like that.

Never to him. Must be wishful thinking from his fractured thoughts. If he was wishing, he wished he could make out the cop's features, but all he could distinguish, aside from the blurry green uniform, was black hair and sun-darkened skin.

"That's enough now, Officer. Mr. Drummond has another test." Those brisk tones could only belong to a nurse.

"Yes, ma'am." A warm male hand gently squeezed his arm, more comforting than Drew would have expected from a cop. "You feel better now, Drew."

Drew tried valiantly to ask if he'd see the cop again, but it was all too much effort.

DREW BLINKED, the almost blinding glow reforming quickly into the white walls of his hospital room. His head still ached like a bitch, but his mind and vision were better than the last time he'd been awake. When that had been, he had no clue. Hospitals all seemed to have a sort of timelessness about them—one in the morning, three in the afternoon, it was all the same inside. Especially when there wasn't a window visible.

As he scanned the room, a blond man caught his attention. Drew wiped the gunk from his eyes, and Kyle came into view, unfortunately still a little blurry.

"You're awake." Kyle tossed aside the magazine he'd been reading and jumped up to stand by Drew's bedside. "How are you feeling?"

Drew cleared his throat while Kyle loomed over him, staring deeply into his eyes.

"Like hammered shit." Who hammered shit anyway? Be a bit of a fucking mess, really. Apparently his mind was still a little scattered.

"You poor thing."

"Where are Rob and Wyatt?" Kyle was his best friend, and he expected him to be here, but Drew had also expected his brothers to be around. Despite their reputation, they were very protective of him.

Unless... "Shit. They're in jail, aren't they? Did they kill whoever did this to me?"

Kyle shook his head. "Oh boy, they weren't kidding about the amnesia. It's a long story, but basically they were trying to...I don't know...defend our honor or something, and Rob accidentally launched you into a table at the Angry Parakeet."

"Rob did this to me?"

"Kinda, yeah."

"So he's in jail for that?"

Kyle laughed softly. "No, they had to go to work. You've been in here all night. When they release you, I'll be taking you home and staying with you because they don't want you to be alone."

"Huh. I would have expected them to insist I go home with them. Or maybe to Aunt Pam and Uncle Walt's."

"Please. I know you better than that. I told them you'd be more comfortable in your own place with your own things. But no working. Not for a couple of days, at least. You need to rest." Kyle made a better mom than Drew's own had, and at times like this he didn't know how he'd gotten so lucky as to find a friend like Kyle.

"Thanks." Drew lifted his hand to move a couple of stray hairs that were tickling his nose and unexpectedly hit the padding of a rather large bandage. "What is this?"

Kyle clucked in his best disappointed-mother-hen style. "It's covering eight stitches. Good thing Rob wasn't *trying* to damage you."

"*How* many stitches? I'm going to look like Frankenstein's monster."

"Don't be ridiculous. You'll end up with a bitchin', uber-manly scar. I hear the ladies like that sort of thing."

The idea that he'd care surprised a laugh out of Drew, triggering a bunch of miniexplosions in his brain. Groaning, he brought his hand to his head, trying to work around the odd bulk of the bandage to rub at his temple.

"I'm so, so sorry," Kyle said, his hands fluttering as though he wanted to touch Drew but was afraid to. Nausea rolled through

Drew's belly, and he clenched his teeth, trying to fight past the urge to hurl.

"Are you going to puke?"

Drew's mind muddle had cleared enough to know shaking his head right now wouldn't be a good idea. "No. Just...laughing hurts."

So did blinking and breathing, but laughing was way worse.

"Oh good. Because if you were, Officer Hottie is on his way back, and you've already puked on him twice. Might as well make it a hat trick."

Hat trick. Funny, Kyle wouldn't even know what that term meant if it weren't for the hockey player he'd dated briefly. The only sport he and Kyle watched with any regularity was soccer. Why hide all those sexy athletic muscles under equipment?

Drew summoned up enough energy to glare at Kyle. "You just here to make me sick, or you gonna tell me what else is wrong with me?" Drew fingered the bandage on his forehead. Seemed bigger than it needed to be, considering he'd had stitches before.

Instantly Kyle's manner changed back into mother hen. "It'll be okay, really. You've got a gash they stitched up. Shouldn't scar too badly, and they said you were lucky you didn't fracture your skull. They had to do a bunch of tests, an MRI and shit to make sure you weren't bleeding into your brain."

This was going to cost a fucking bundle.

"Didn't Officer Hottie tell you about all this?"

"Oh. Yeah." Drew didn't have enough energy to explain he had no idea who Officer Hottie was, although he had a vague memory of a soothing voice telling him something, and... "Did you say I puked on him?"

Kyle rolled his eyes. "Yeah. Twice. Apparently that happens with concussions." Which they both knew, since Drew's brothers had given and received more than their own fair share.

"Hey, Kyle, hope you like decaf, because that's all they had fresh."

A police officer wearing a dark green uniform strode into the room, holding two cardboard coffee cups. He stared at Drew while handing off Kyle's cup.

"Oh, hey, you're awake. How are you feeling?"

That voice. Drew remembered that voice, and he blinked. His vision still wasn't great, but Kyle wasn't wrong. The officer was smoking hot... Blood drained from Drew's face so fast his head swam a bit.

Suddenly the cop was leaning over him. "You okay? Should we get a doctor?"

"Dude, no wonder he puked on you twice," Kyle said from what sounded like very far away. "You keep standing in the firing line."

"Do you feel sick?"

Drew breathed in and out, paying close attention to each breath, trying to calm himself. Northcliff Garcia was back. Dressed as a Sandy Bottom Bay police officer. And apparently their first introduction—and second, according to Kyle—involved Drew yakking on him. If there were benevolent spirits out there, they could prove their existence right now by opening up a hole for him to drop through. Instead, he continued to stare up into the dark, warm depths of Officer Hottie's—aka the guy he'd been crushing on for the past eight years—eyes. Kyle was in so much shit for not warning him about this.

Cliff was older now, his face and body filled out to more manly proportions. There were tiny lines at the corners of his eyes, and beyond the weariness that dulled his skin tone, there was a sadness in his eyes, a sadness Drew longed to erase but knew he'd never have the chance. Cliff Garcia was still the most gorgeous guy Drew had ever seen, but now that the man was standing in front of him, Drew realized there was far more than geographical distance getting in the way of a relationship. Their lives and upbringing were too different for them to work, and besides, what would a successful, gorgeous cop want with him anyway? Especially since he'd puked on the guy. Twice.

Fuck my life.

KYLE HAD BEEN FORTHCOMING ENOUGH to let Cliff know Drew was

twenty-two, for which Cliff was utterly thankful because in this bed, surrounded by stark white and almost as pale as the sheets he lay in, Drew looked a lot younger than that.

How had Cliff never known the evil Drummond twins had a *hot* younger brother? Granted, when he was a senior in high school, he didn't pay any attention to the freshmen, but considering how adversarial his relationship had been with the twins, he was still surprised.

Drew's bright red hair called to his fingers. He already knew how silky it was because he'd touched it more than once while Drew was asleep. Made him feel just a bit perverted, but he hadn't been able to help himself. Knowing Drew was one of the deadbeat Drummonds didn't change the fact that he looked helpless and lost in the hospital bed, puffy white bandage obscuring most of his forehead. He didn't look like a belligerent bully, but how could he not be? Once his brain recovered from its trauma, undoubtedly Drew would become as big an asshole as his brothers.

"I'm really sorry."

Sheepish and apologetic? Cliff had never seen Rob or Wyatt with that particular expression. Was this how Drew fit into the Drummond clan? Rob and Wyatt were the muscle, and Drew was the smooth talker?

Didn't matter. Drew was off-limits. For a million reasons, Cliff had to shake this little infatuation and do his job.

"Don't worry about it. But I do have a few questions about the fight."

"I'll wait outside." When Kyle spoke, Cliff startled a bit; he'd been so intent on Drew, he hadn't even realized Kyle was still in the room.

"Thank you. This won't take long."

Kyle slipped out, and Drew's look of fear returned. "Do I need a lawyer?"

Cliff took a second to examine the inflection and possible meanings hidden in that question. Was that just the most natural question for a Drummond to ask law enforcement, or had Drew remembered something that would make him culpable? Cliff didn't think anyone was going to need a lawyer out of this; he'd been up most of the night going over statements and...well...sitting right here in Drew's room. The medical staff made exceptions since he was an officer, allowing him to remain after visiting hours, and he stupidly hadn't wanted Drew to wake up alone. He'd been so confused after the accident, and Cliff had felt sorry for him. Yet more evidence of Cliff's stupidity. Ridiculous to even retain one tiny shred of interest in the younger brother of the evil twins, but that soft spot had kept Cliff at the hospital overnight.

And he'd thought he'd had some sort of victory by not falling for Brett's bullshit. Apparently he was going to have to guard himself well against falling for a sexy redhead's bullshit instead, because if ever bullshit was going to smell like flowers and sparkle like it had been dipped in glitter, Drew was going to be the source.

"You shouldn't. I just wanted to get your official statement. Despite the bruising that's coming up, you look a lot better than you have the other times we spoke."

The sheepish look returned, and Drew touched a finger to the white bandage. The guy would be lucky if he didn't end up with two prominent black eyes, but at the moment, the purplish bruising merely peeped out around the bandage.

"We spoke... It's like a dream, actually. I don't remember."

Drew wouldn't meet his gaze for longer than a second or two. Cliff wasn't sure if it was because the guy was straight and therefore unaccustomed to looking another man in the eyes, or if it was that Cliff, as the big, bad authority figure, made Drew nervous, legitimately or not.

"Regardless, I just need your statement, and then you can concentrate on getting better. Just tell me what you remember about the incident."

"Are my brothers in trouble?"

Well, that was a loaded question. Cliff wanted them to be. After all the antagonism at school, and recently armed with the knowledge that Rob and Wyatt and their whole family were troublemakers, Cliff longed to throw the book at them. The fact that one of them had hurt Drew... He didn't have to admit to anyone else how angry he still was about that, even though there was no reason for him to give Drew preferential treatment.

"Not unless you want to press charges." Even without Drew's consent, he could figure out a way to get the twins jail time, but it hardly seemed worth the effort, especially if it was going upset Drew.

"No. Please. Kyle said it was an accident, you said it was an accident, and I know they'd never hurt me intentionally."

At least one of them was confident on that score.

Cliff pulled the chair next to Drew's bedside and picked up his coffee. "Okay, then, what's the last thing you remember about last night?"

CHAPTER 7

By the end of the questioning, Drew was almost glad about his concussion. If nothing else, his addled thoughts made his first conversation with Northcliff...Cliff Garcia less terrifying. Then again, he was sort of trapped in a hospital bed, and if he moved too fast, he'd probably puke again. Later, though, he'd likely be beyond humiliated.

Cliff had been very understanding about the gaps in his memory and hadn't seemed to react at all to the revelation Drew was gay. For some reason, though, the mention of Brett Cavanagh made Cliff angry. Not that Drew remembered meeting Brett, although Cliff assured him he had and that the meeting had sparked the fight. Those words had also caused a muscle to leap in Cliff's jaw. Drew had remembered—or maybe he was remembering something he'd been told—but he was sure they'd been going to the Angry Parakeet for the express purpose of trying to "accidentally" meet Brett. Cliff hadn't been very pleased anytime Rob's or Wyatt's names came up either. Basically, he'd been scowling throughout the entire interview.

Drew pressed his lips together. How did one man get so good-looking? Drew wanted, badly, to ask why Cliff was here. At the hospital. In Sandy Bottom Bay. And apparently working for the police. But answering Cliff's questions was a lot easier than asking some of his own. It wasn't like they were friends or had ever spoken before today. The fact that his brothers and Cliff were mortal enemies during high school didn't exactly give them any common ground.

Kyle stuck his head into the room. "Are you done yet? Can I come back in?"

Cliff's cell phone rang, and he frowned at the display. "I should probably take this. Excuse me."

Drew let his eyelids drop to half-mast, partly because he was exhausted and partly because Cliff was kind enough to stay in his line of sight, and Drew wanted to mask how intently he was staring at that round, uniform-clad ass.

The painkillers and the hooked daggers still slicing through his head ensured there wasn't even a tiny wiggle at his groin, but if it weren't for those roadblocks, he'd be erecting a tent for all to see.

"Oh my God," Kyle whispered. He too was staring at that exceptional butt. "Did you know he was back in town?"

"No." There was more he'd say if he had the energy. As it was, the word came out on a defeated huff of breath.

"He's hot. I mean, you pointed him out when we were in school, but I never fixated on him like you did. Are you going to ask him out?"

"Uh, no." Terror gave those words a lot more oomph. Drew wasn't great at asking guys out—wasn't much opportunity to practice in Sandy Bottom Bay. Faced with the thought of asking out Cliff Garcia, he reverted back to that scrawny kid who would have been bullied and probably gay-bashed if it weren't for his belligerent and overprotective brothers.

"Why not? You said he was gay." Kyle's voice rose excitedly.

"Shut the fuck up, Kyle." Whispers took less effort, but it was definitely harder to convey how much he wanted Kyle to stop talking about Cliff. At least while he was still within earshot.

"He's gay; he's hot... Is he single? You need to find out. This is opportunity knocking."

Drew heaved in a breath. "I can't. Rob and Wyatt hate him, and the feeling is mutual. He probably hates me by association."

Kyle rolled his eyes. "Like you'd be the first couple whose family didn't approve. That won't matter one bit. I tell you, if that opportunity came knocking at my door? Anything and anyone else could go to hell."

"Yes, I get it. Stop beating that metaphor to death." Frowning, Drew squinted at Cliff. Whatever the phone call was, it wasn't good news. Drew waved a hand toward the door. "What's wrong, do you suppose?"

"Wrong? What's wrong is you! Did that concussion knock the gay out of you? If you don't ask him out, I will."

That got Drew's attention. "You wouldn't."

Kyle shook his head. "Of course I wouldn't. But so help me, you'd better do *something*."

Past the doorway, Cliff pocketed his phone with stiff, deliberate movements. He turned back to the room, and his tightly compressed lips and clenched jaw were immediately apparent, as was his wooden posture. Cliff might have filled out from boy to man since Drew had seen him last, but observing Cliff had practically been an Olympic sport when Drew had been fourteen, and he would have won all the medals. Cliff was furious, like Drew had only seen during clashes with his brothers.

Oh fuck. What had they done now, and was Cliff going to hate him because of it?

Cliff stomped back into the room. "You'll have to excuse me, Drew. Something has come up. I hope you feel better soon."

Kyle poked Drew's arm, and although sorely tempted to flip him the bird, Drew ignored him. From somewhere in the dregs of morphine numbing his mind and emotions, Drew found the courage to speak.

"Is everything okay?" Not the question Kyle was hoping he'd ask, but even if he and the mighty morphine cobbled together enough courage to ask Cliff on a date, he wasn't going to do it while Cliff was in this sort of mood. Not a fucking chance.

For a moment, Cliff paused, and Drew was certain he was going to get a meaningless platitude, but inexplicably, Cliff sank into the chair Kyle wasn't sitting in.

"Apparently there was a mix-up at the motel I'm staying at. I paid for a month, but they called to tell me they can't accommodate me. They need me to check out today." Cliff glanced at his watch. "In two hours."

Earlier, Drew had been too blinded by shock and Cliff's incredible looks to register how tired the guy looked. Had he been up all night because of Drew's accident?

"The big motel on the highway?" Kyle asked. "They couldn't just give you another room?"

"The manager said he was booked solid because of the Haunt Fest."

"But that's not right." Drew swallowed the rest of his words. He almost asked if Cliff thought it was some sort of discrimination, but despite his inside info about which team Cliff played on, he didn't know if Cliff was out, and it wasn't a topic he could easily broach with a near stranger.

Cliff sighed and scrubbed his face with his hands.

"Can't you just stay with your mom?" Drew put the blame squarely on the morphine for letting him say that. So far, Cliff hadn't said anything about having grown up in Sandy Bottom Bay or his childhood altercations with Drew's brothers. There was no good reason for Drew to know who the hell he was. Way to spill the beans about his stupid infatuation.

Cliff froze for a split second before he lowered his hands and peered at Drew. "Does everyone know I used to live here? The town isn't that fucking small."

A shocked look followed as he clamped his lips together. Kyle smothered a laugh, and Drew smiled. It was more than obvious that if Cliff swore much at all, he hadn't intended to do so then, but fatigue made his lips as traitorous as morphine made Drew's.

Still, Drew had to respond and not let the morphine make him admit to anything he'd regret later. "No, but everyone in town knows your mom, and I recognized you from school."

An assessing, calculating look crept into Cliff's eyes. "So we did go to school together. At the time, I wasn't even sure I knew that the evil...uh...that Rob and Wyatt had any siblings. And I feel like I would have remembered that hair, at least."

The morphine was doing a number on Drew, because he would swear up and down that Cliff's tone had been admiring when talking about Drew's hair.

"My hair was a lot more blond back then. It got really red after you left." Drew wrinkled his nose. What a stupid thing to say. Usually he was much better with words. Like Cliff would care.

"Right. Well..." Cliff looked confused more than anything else. "My return is probably common knowledge by now, but I didn't exactly tell my mother I was moving back. I had planned to stay at the motel until...until I found an apartment in town."

He didn't tell his mother? Bizarre, but that explained why Helen hadn't mentioned her son's impending return during their last reading.

"So, are you going to move back in with your mom now?" Kyle sounded far too interested in the answer, which made Drew a tiny bit nervous.

Cliff's expression said it all. He didn't want to, and Drew didn't know why. Sure, Cliff had never come back to visit Sandy Bottom Bay after he left, but Helen had never mentioned any sort of estrangement. She hadn't even hinted at anything of the sort during their sessions.

"No. There's got to be a hotel or motel around here that has a room available until I can find somewhere to live."

"I don't know." Kyle's voice was full of doubt. "It's horrible that they're kicking you out, but the Haunt Fest has grown bigger each year. You might have some difficulty finding a room until it's over."

If anything, the tension in Cliff's jaw got tighter. "Perhaps. I'll figure something out." Cliff rose to his feet, transforming from frustrated man to robotic cop in the blink of an eye. "I shouldn't take up any more of your time."

"Wait, you could stay with Drew."

Shock squeezed the breath from Drew's lungs. If Kyle's words hadn't killed Drew, he was doing a fine imitation of a fish out of water. As was Cliff, for that matter. And if Drew survived Kyle's clumsy matchmaking attempt, he was going to kill his best friend.

Cliff stared at him, and Drew could only stare back. The silence lengthened, broken only by the normal bustle and beeps of a busy hospital.

Then Kyle spoke again, his voice bright and innocent. Only Drew knew that was the sound of Kyle trying to get his own way, but the guy usually succeeded. Drew still hadn't found enough breath to cut him off, which meant whatever crazy brain child Kyle was cooking was about to be presented to Cliff, of all people.

"No, really, you'd be doing him a favor."

Cliff was still looking at Drew and found the muscle control to lift an eyebrow as though asking Drew to confirm this assertion. If Drew could have spoken at all, he'd likely have gibbered, so he remained silent.

"A favor? How so?" Cliff sounded as doubtful about it as Drew felt. What the hell was Kyle doing? Couldn't the matchmaking wait until Drew could at least hobble around on his own and without puking?

"They're going to want someone to help Drew, at least for the next few days. You don't want to leave him to his brothers' care, do you?"

"But...but..." Drew stuttered. "I thought you..." Kyle was supposed to be helping him, dammit. Not his brothers and not the guy he'd been crushing on for eight fucking years.

"Of course, normally I would do it, but I'm going to be away this weekend. And we want you better for the festival. Your business depends on those tourists."

An indefinable expression crossed Cliff's face at the mention of Drew's business, but Drew was too busy trying to unscramble his brain.

"You're going away? Why didn't you tell me?" He tore his gaze away from Cliff to stare at his friend.

"I did tell you. You must have forgotten." With a rueful smile, Kyle wiggled his fingers by his forehead.

It was true there were a number of gaps in his memory. Was Kyle telling the truth? He didn't want to confront his friend in front of Cliff, though. If Cliff hadn't realized he'd been the star of Drew's fantasies for years, there wasn't any point in *making* him realize it.

Cliff cleared his throat. "So your brothers would be taking care of you once you leave here?"

Drew lifted a shoulder in a halfhearted shrug. If Kyle really wasn't going to be around, then yeah, his brothers would have to do it. Which he was going to hate. It wasn't the first time he'd been hurt or ill. His brothers cared about him, but they were shitty nursemaids. Mostly because they were far too solicitous, hanging about and asking him a million questions; then they'd forget about him for long stretches of time, each thinking the other was taking care of him. Feast or famine, and he sure as shit didn't want to deal with that, because Kyle was right—he needed to be better in time for the festival, or he'd be in danger of losing his business and livelihood.

"What about your parents?"

Not wanting to see Cliff's reaction, Drew shifted his gaze to one of the plain white walls. There was some sort of brownish stain coming up through the paint. He really hoped it was the result of water damage and not blood or something else that had splattered that far up the wall. He reined in his fractious mind to answer the question Cliff asked.

"Mom died seven years ago, cirrhosis from too much alcohol, and Dad's in Everglades Correctional doing fifteen to twenty for manslaughter. He was sent up six years ago. Rob and Wyatt took care of me while I was still a minor, with my grandma helping out."

"Well, what about your grandma?"

Drew squeezed his eyes shut so he wouldn't start crying. Cliff had already seen him at his worst; no need to compound that with tears.

"She died a couple of years ago."

A soft gasp from Cliff dared Drew to look at the man. There was only sympathy. "I'm sorry, Drew."

Cliff bit his lip before speaking again. "This town is full of Drummonds. Aren't most of them related to you? Couldn't one of them help?"

"Oh, please, Officer." Kyle finally spoke again, breaking into the odd connection that had formed between Drew and Cliff. "You couldn't even suppress the hint of distaste when you said their name. Would you seriously want one of them to be responsible for Drew's well-being? You'd hate yourself if something happened to him."

Sensing Cliff was about to capitulate, Drew threw out a frantic attempt to stop this train wreck Kyle was determined to see through to the bitter end.

"Where would he sleep? My place is tiny."

"Oh, this head wound has done quite a number on you, hasn't it?" Oddly enough, Kyle's words were tender and every bit as mother henish as Drew had come to expect. And for some reason, Mother Kyle thought he knew best in this case and was going to make sure his vision came about. At least Drew could be sure it wouldn't be at the expense of his health; *Kyle* would never be able to forgive himself.

"If there's no room..." Cliff said after a silence that was likely only a second or two but seemed a lot longer.

"There's that minifuton in your bedroom, Drew." Kyle's sunny smile didn't have an ounce of guile. He'd clearly been hanging out with the Drummonds too long.

"Uh, yeah, there's that." Drew hadn't forgotten about the single-bed futon that folded up into a chair. With it opened, there wasn't a lot of room in the bedroom, but Kyle had slept on it more than once. But Drew hadn't ever lusted after Kyle. Having Cliff in the same room would be agony. No matter how tortuous—and how potentially embarrassing—Kyle was right about Drew needing help. The doctor had been adamant he have someone who could at least check on him regularly for the next few days, or he wasn't going to get released. Rob and Wyatt would find a way to pay his medical bills somehow, but Drew wasn't going to stay here any longer than he had to.

With the added bonus of maybe finding out if Cliff was a boxers or briefs man, perhaps this wasn't the absolute worst idea Kyle had ever had.

"I wouldn't want to intrude."

"Oh, Officer, you'd be doing both of us a favor." Kyle wisely held back on vamping it up, as he so easily could have, although he did let loose a couple of eyelash flutters.

Cliff looked up at the ceiling, the granite cut of his jaw smoothing out as he considered—*considered!*—staying with Drew. A hot, gay cop who was also one of the most honorable guys Drew had ever known was thinking about sleeping in his bedroom for a few days. Maybe all this was nothing more than a hallucination, courtesy of Drew's scrambled brains. Then again, if this was truly a product of his fantasies, Cliff would be promising a whole lot of hot and heavy sex. Surely Drew wasn't repressed enough that he was fantasizing about sharing a bedroom with Cliff like they were teens at sleepaway camp.

Cliff dropped his gaze, and Drew got sucked into deep, dark brown eyes so hypnotic he almost forgot about his pain.

"Are you okay with that? I'll find something else next week if I'm in your way too much."

No. He should say no. *No* was smart. *No* would let him hold on to his pathetic crush a little longer. But the thought of spending time with Cliff, however platonic, overrode every sensible and logical thought that swam in his murky mind.

"Uh, sure."

Kyle spoke at the same time with an enthusiastic, "Of course he's okay with it."

Cliff didn't look happy, although he did look relieved. His tiny, almost mischievous smile made Drew want to do some eyelash fluttering of his own. Swooning. This was what grandma's romance heroines must have felt right before swooning.

"Then I'd better get my stuff." A faint frown pulled at Cliff's brow. "Wait. I heard the nurse say the doctor was probably going to release you as soon as the doctor sees you one last time. I don't know how long that will be, but maybe I should wait. Surely you'll be released before my checkout time."

Kyle flapped his hands. "Don't be ridiculous. Go do what you need to do. I can get Drew home if he gets released before you get back. We can get you settled at his place after."

"What's your address?" Cliff pulled out his phone, ready to tap in the information.

"Give it here." Kyle reached out an imperious hand, and for some reason, Cliff obeyed the command. Taking Drew's phone too, Kyle fiddled with them while Cliff smiled benevolently at Drew. Drew found himself smiling back. However goofy and besotted he might appear, at least he could look his fill and blame it on the morphine later.

"There you go, Officer. Contact info exchanged. We'll text you when we're leaving here."

Cliff shook his head. "Good, but could you just call me Cliff? I'd feel a little less like I was taking advantage by bunking down with Drew."

"Certainly, Cliff."

Drew wasn't fond of the flirtatious lilt Kyle put on Cliff's name, but he appreciated Cliff's attempts to be friendly.

"Well, I'll see you later. Kyle. Drew."

If Drew squinted his eyes and imagined really hard, he was sure Cliff had said his name differently than Kyle's. Warmer, friendlier, and with a bigger smile. Wishful thinking, no doubt, but as far as Drew was concerned, it was yet another side-effect of the morphine.

They both watched Cliff's spectacular ass as he walked away.

Once he was well out of sight, Drew heaved in a breath. "What the fuck, Kyle?"

"You're welcome." Kyle's reply was unbearably smug.

All of Drew's ire left, and he deflated back into the bed. "It's not going to work out how you hope."

Kyle snickered. "How I hope? I don't have a horse in this race. But here's a chance to get to know him. I mean, not only has it been eight years since you've seen him, but it's not like you even talked to him when we were kids. Maybe you'll hate him. Maybe you'll realize your crush was justified. Maybe there won't be a spark. But this at least gives you both a chance to get to know one another."

With an irritated but gentle tap at the puffy bandage on his head, Drew said, "These are hardly ideal circumstances to get to know one another. He'll see me at my worst. How could I possibly entice him that way?"

He didn't bother to tell Kyle about the number of times he'd watched Cliff at school, although Kyle was aware of some of them. Nor did he remind Kyle that he'd been getting inside information from Cliff's mother for the past two years. It wasn't perfect, but Drew already knew a lot about what kind of man Cliff was, and none of it had served to lessen his infatuation any.

"I beg to differ. He's already seen you at your worst, when you were puking on him. That didn't scare him off."

This time, the embarrassment broke through Drew's medicated haze—must be time for another dose—and the sudden influx of blood to his face reminded him of the dull ache in his head.

The mother hen clicked back on, and Kyle rubbed his arm. "Hey. Listen to me. You at your worst is better than ninety-nine percent of guys at their best. Trust me. If he doesn't fall for you, he's either taken, straight, or lobotomized."

Kyle's comment surprised a laugh out of Drew, which immediately turned into a groan.

"Sorry, sorry." Kyle rubbed his arm a little more before he stood. "Let me see if we can either spring you or get you some more meds."

A good idea or not, Drew had to accept he was sharing a room with Cliff Garcia for at least the next few days. Instead of wasting energy wishing Kyle hadn't put him in this position, he'd better save his strength for figuring out how to hide his infatuation.

CHAPTER 8

Cliff strode out of the hospital, pretending this was normal, pretending he paid this much attention to accident victims, who were virtual strangers, every day. He was a fucking fool, but Drew's sweet face had him in complete protective mode, something he'd never really experienced with a guy he was interested in. Being a Drummond, Drew could probably take care of himself, but that didn't change the fact that he'd looked so vulnerable, bloodied and bandaged. Cliff's foolish need to protect Drew, even from his own family, had won out.

Even more foolishly, he'd been so worried about Drew that he'd stayed at the hospital overnight. When Kyle had arrived the next morning, he'd thought Cliff had only gotten an early start on the day. Which was fine by him. Letting anyone know he'd spent the night staring at Drew, afraid he was going to start seizing or slip into a coma, wasn't going to do Cliff's career any favors. If they also knew he'd spent part of that time holding Drew's hand and stroking his hair, well, his career would go up in flames. At some point, he was going to have to find a way to check Drew's record or ask Scott. Maybe both. If his criminal past wasn't terrible, and if Cliff could keep him out of hot water in the future, Sandy Bottom Bay might be forgiving of a cop getting involved with a Drummond.

Not that Cliff should even consider getting involved. But he was drawn to Drew in a way he'd never been before, and that spoke of difficulty for him. Which should come as no surprise. The Drummond twins were trouble through and through, yet Drew Drummond seemed more innocent and naive than his brothers ever had. Cliff would rather deal with Drew's brand of trouble than Brett's.

Brett.

Cliff was already out of the hospital and inside his car before he'd stopped thinking solely about Drew and let Brett's name cross his mind. Shit. Surely Brett didn't have anything to do with Cliff losing his room, did he?

No. Impossible. Cliff had never been that important to Brett while they were dating, so there was no reason for Brett to become even more douchey than he normally was. Cliff shook off his suspicions. Once he got some sleep, he'd be less paranoid. First, though, he had to rescue the meager belongings he'd brought with him. Once he got settled somewhere more permanent, he'd ship his stuff in from California, but for the time being, he only had a duffel bag filled with clothes, toiletries, and a laptop.

A quick glance at the time told him it was still early. Not quite eight. If he had one unpleasant task to take care of today, he might as well get the other one over and done with. What with all the furor at the Angry Parakeet, even if his mother hadn't yet been aware he was in town, she soon would be. Which meant a trip out to the homestead. If he got his shit done early enough, he'd see if Scott had time to meet up for a quick lunch. Not even forty-eight hours on the force and already he was going to have to ask for favors. At least he and Scott had been friends before and probably would be again. Because he'd need Scott's help to juggle his shift so that he was free to stop by Drew's periodically to check on him.

This wasn't the homecoming he'd expected.

Just as he was about to turn the key in the ignition, someone knocked on his window, and he jumped.

"What the hell?"

Scott laughed, and Cliff rolled down the window.

"Got you good. What were you thinking about so fiercely?"

Well, he certainly wasn't going to admit he was thinking about getting to know Drew Drummond better. Scott would probably understand if he admitted to wanting to fuck the man—once he was no longer injured—but getting to know him, dating, that was more dangerous.

"Nothing in particular. What are you doing here so early? I thought you'd sleep in a bit."

Scott shrugged. "I don't sleep much, and once I heard you'd been here all night, I thought I'd drop by."

Stunned, Cliff just stared. How did Scott know?

Scott just laughed again, which did nothing to ease Cliff's worries. "Hell, you have been gone a long time if you've forgotten the way a small town works. My sister Sarah is a nurse. And you, my friend, have made quite an impression on the ladies. Especially the single ones."

Cliff's face burned. He had forgotten, or perhaps just the stress of the previous day had temporarily deleted it from his mind.

Wrinkling his nose like he'd smelled something funny, Scott spoke. "But I should warn you, they're already talking about whether you're gay or not. Since Drew is, and since you stayed with him all night... Well, just thought I'd let you know they're already speculating."

"You didn't confirm one way or the other?"

"Not my place, man. Not unless you say. But if you don't speak up, one way or the other, you're going to have all the single women in this town falling all over you to give you casseroles or some such shit."

Cliff lifted a brow. "Casseroles? Is that what the kids are calling it these days?"

The joke hung there in silence for an eternal second before Scott caught on to his meaning and laughed, a great, happy belly laugh. "You know it!"

"I'm not hiding it. So if they ask you outright, you can tell them. Just don't volunteer the information, okay?" Besides, the gossip was only going to get worse once people found out he was staying at

Drew's to take care of him. He just hoped the chief wouldn't consider it a conflict of interest, because the thought of going home to Drew's place, no matter how small it turned out to be, was far more comforting than the thought of heading back to the soulless motel or the house where he'd grown up. Which only confirmed that Cliff had maybe lost his mind somewhere back around Pensacola.

"No problem, buddy. I won't ask if you were sitting with that guy because you were hoping he'd wake up enough for casseroles."

Cliff laughed, but perhaps he'd made a mistake handing that particular ammunition to Scott.

"I got his statement, if that's what you're asking."

"Uh-huh. Good. Well, where you off to now?"

Some company wouldn't be amiss, and Scott might have some insight Cliff didn't. At least with the motel thing. Scott wasn't starting his shift until two, same as Cliff.

"I have to pack up my shit from the motel. It's a long story, but want to keep me company?" He wasn't about to take Scott with him when he went to visit his mom, but he still needed to talk to Scott about their shift tonight.

"Sure thing." Scott rounded the car and jumped in the passenger side.

Cliff drove toward the highway while Scott fiddled with the radio. Once he had a station set to his liking, Scott leaned back in the seat.

"Why are you picking up your stuff? You didn't find an apartment already, did you? Or are you going to stay with your mom?"

The silence had been too good to be true. Scott was a talker and would probably never change. Still, it wasn't like Cliff had been going to keep it secret. Not from Scott, at any rate. And considering people who didn't even work at the hospital were already trying to figure out if he was gay, random people on the street were probably discussing the state of his relationship with his mother.

"No, no apartment." Really, Scott needed to think before he opened his mouth sometime. When would Cliff have had time to look at apartments? "But the manager at the motel called."

Cliff gave Scott the same explanation he'd gotten on the phone.

"Huh." Scott was quiet for a minute while he thought. "Well, it's not entirely unreasonable. I guess. I mean, you were there first, so you should get first crack, but our tourist influx is going to be a lot higher for the Haunt Fest this year, what with *Phantoms* doing a show about it. It's possible they booked accommodations for a tour bus and sacrificed your room."

Scott might speak before thinking, but he wasn't stupid. "This is true."

"Why, did you think it was because you were gay? I don't think the owner gives a shit one way or the other, as long as he gets paid."

Strangely, no, he hadn't thought of that, but since he was back in Florida, maybe he should. Not everyone would be as accepting as the chief and Scott. After all, just look at the horrible things the demon twins had said to Brett, and their own brother was gay.

"Oh yeah. You're probably right."

Cliff kept his attention on the road, trying to ignore the intent stare he sensed Scott was treating him with. As they turned onto the highway for the dull, drab drive to the motel, Cliff chanced a glance at Scott, which was apparently the opening he needed.

"You thought it was something else. What?"

"It's stupid." It had to be paranoia because he was exhausted and trying to make a good impression. "I thought it might have been Brett. Fucking around."

"Has he exhibited any other stalkerish behavior?"

"No. I mean, maybe. After we broke up, he wouldn't stop calling. And unless you count showing up here out of the blue, well, no. I'm sure it's just a weird coincidence. He does have a legitimate reason to be here."

"True enough. I know the mayor just about shit a brick when they filed for filming permits. He's been trying to convince one of those paranormal shows to come here for years, and he's over the fucking moon a show as big as *Phantoms* was the first. And of course Eddie Price has been unbearable since they asked him to do an interview for the *Phantoms* segment. Seems to think he's going to be some sort of star. Go national or some shit as a medium."

Scott's words gave Cliff some measure of relief. This was bigger than some elaborate ploy of Brett's to get him back or get back at him. Ridiculous to think he had any influence over Brett's behavior, since he'd never had any while they were dating. Brett was probably only making nice because he wanted Cliff to convince his mother to cooperate.

"How do you know all this? Didn't the TV crew get into town the same day I did?"

Laughter filled the car again. "That ex of yours...subtle he's not. He was here a couple of weeks ago, attempting a disguise, I think. He was wearing that same ball cap, grew a scruffy beard, and kept sunglasses on. But this town is filled with people who, if they're not obsessed with those shows because they believe in ghosts, are obsessed with those shows trying to figure out how they can get national fame and notoriety. And, of course, he slept with Eddie."

"He slept with Eddie? Since when is Eddie gay?" Yet another gay guy in Sandy Bottom Bay? The shock of it was the only thing that could distract him from the ridiculous notion of Brett going incognito. Cliff would have sworn incognito was against Brett's religion. Scott's casual delivery spoke of more acceptance than Cliff could have ever expected.

"Eddie's bisexual, not gay."

"I can hardly believe it."

"We do live in the modern world. Not everyone's a fan, but that's mostly because there are more single women in town than men, and Eddie tends to play them against each other. And looks more like a movie star than your ex. We get more trouble from jealousy than we do from gay-bashing."

Had Cliff stepped into an alternate universe? Or had things truly changed in Sandy Bottom Bay in the eight years since he'd been here? He wasn't exactly expecting to get bashed, not with his mother holding so many of the purse strings for the town, but this ready acceptance shocked him. One of the reasons he'd been in such a hurry to leave was because he'd thought he'd never be free to be himself if he stayed. And, of course, the ridiculous claim to fame on which this town was built.

"Jealousy? And are you sure he's bisexual?" Because Brett had charmed more than one questioning man into giving up more than the guy intended under the influence of alcohol. Generally they either ran back for the shelter of heterosexuality or came out hoping Brett would be their boyfriend.

Had Eddie slept with Drew? The thought of Drew in another man's arms sent an alarming stab of jealousy through Cliff. This wasn't good. He'd been pissed at Brett for cheating, and hurt that he'd been lied to, but this biting anger was new. And it wasn't even as though Drew had demonstrated any interest. Cliff was building sandcastles out of rainbows.

"Isn't bisexual being attracted to both sexes? Because he totally pursued Kyle. Wasn't hard to miss that. Man, the week those two did it, I'm surprised no one died."

"Kyle? Not Drew?"

Scott laughed again. "I knew you had it bad for Drew. Yeah, Kyle. He's not actually a Drummond, but most of them treat him like one of their own. Him and Drew are tight like brothers. But even that might not have saved him if the girls didn't love him and Drew to pieces. After all, it's one thing to compete with other girls, but the thought they might lose Eddie to someone with different plumbing? Yeah, things were rocky here for a bit."

Some little bit of tension Cliff hadn't realized he was carrying dispersed with Scott's words. *Tight like brothers.* Despite Kyle introducing himself as Drew's best friend, most people treated him as though he was closer. Deep in Cliff's mind, he'd thought maybe Kyle and Drew were an item and hadn't wanted to publicize the fact. But with Scott, the font of all Sandy Bottom Bay gossip, telling him different, he could relax. A bit. Besides, if Kyle really was getting it on with Drew, he wouldn't have nominated Cliff to share a room with Drew or slept with Eddie, would he?

Cliff turned in to the motel's driveway and maneuvered the cruiser to a spot near the entrance to the front desk.

"Hey, you never did tell me where you're going to stay. Because you could bunk at my place. I've got a guestroom."

Cliff flashed hot and cold. Of course Scott had a spare room. Scott hadn't even crossed his mind when he'd been wondering where he'd sleep. As soon as Kyle and Drew had offered up Drew's place, Cliff hadn't wanted to think of alternatives. He was going to torture himself with Drew's company as much as he could. Even now, with Scott presenting a perfectly reasonable, and probably more logical, alternative, Cliff didn't want to give up his time with Drew.

"Well, that's something I wanted to talk to you about. I'm actually staying with Drew."

Scott yelped and cuffed him on the shoulder. "Are you fucking kidding me? Forget your famous ex—you've got the moves. Dude was practically in a coma, and you're already moving in."

"Shut up, Scott. I'm not moving in. I don't even know Drew." But he was going to get a crash course in all things Drew, wasn't he? And while that should have scared him clear down to his toes, he couldn't find an ounce of fear inside. "But he needs someone to check in with him regularly for the next little while, help him out. He got his bell rung good."

"What about Kyle? Or Drew's brothers?"

"Please. I wouldn't trust my worst enemy's hamster to those idiots Drew calls brothers. And Kyle's got some plans this weekend. The call about the motel came while I was taking Drew's statement at the hospital, and it just seemed like..." Fate. Serendipity. Destiny. No, Cliff couldn't use any of those words. He didn't believe in shit like that, not like his mom did. "It seemed like we could both do each other a favor."

"Right. Favor." There was no missing what sort of favors Scott thought they'd be exchanging, but as much as Cliff might hope it would get to that, he wasn't betting on it. "Well, if you change your mind, the offer's there."

"Thanks, man. I appreciate it. Once Drew is back on his feet, I'll probably take you up on it."

"Sure, sure. You're helping out. I get it." Scott didn't sound like he believed Cliff, but then, Cliff wasn't sure he believed himself either. How had he gotten so intensely attached to a man he didn't know?

"Maybe you ought to call out for your shift. You've been up all night, and you've had a lot of stress for your first day."

"I can't call out. I just started yesterday. This isn't my first time working a shift on no sleep. We're cops. It happens."

"The chief will understand. I guarantee it."

"Out of the question."

"Think about it, would you? Not only are you stressed and exhausted, but you're also checking in on a guy with a head injury. How well do you think you'll be able to deal with your ex under these circumstances?"

Cliff dropped his head back against the headrest. If Brett was his normal, abrasive self, Cliff might not be able to prevent himself from punching the guy. Which would probably be much worse for his career than anything else.

"I'll think about it. I don't want to leave you shorthanded, though."

Scott shrugged. "The Haunt Fest doesn't start for a week. As long as I can convince Brett to order in, instead of trying the Angry Parakeet again, we'll be good. Two of us is overkill until the groupies and shit start showing up."

That was true. They had a few days' grace before the hordes started to descend, and from all accounts, the hordes were much bigger than he was used to—for a Haunt Fest, at any rate. Getting some decent sleep before dealing with all that wasn't a bad idea.

It only took a few minutes for Cliff to grab his stuff. He didn't have much and hadn't bothered to unpack most of what he did have. As soon as he'd tossed his duffel in the trunk, he checked out, manfully refraining from asking about the nearly empty parking lot. It sure as hell didn't look like they were booked to capacity, but this little turn of events had put him in what he hoped was a good situation, so he couldn't be too upset about it.

On the way out, he almost bumped into a woman. "Excuse me, ma'am."

"That's a new one." The snarky reply came just as he realized he knew the woman.

"Kristi. What are you doing here?"

Her expression said she could barely be bothered to speak to the shit she'd just scraped off her shoe, but she answered nonetheless. "Just paying for a reservation. If you'll excuse me."

Kristi brushed past him without another word, and his discussion with Scott in the car shed some long-needed light on Kristi's attitude. Kristi had disliked him because she'd been jealous of him—or, more specifically, jealous of his relationship with Brett. Why she still hated him, he wasn't sure, but as sure as there were birds in the sky, Kristi had wanted Brett and had been pissed beyond measure that Cliff had had him, however briefly.

Cliff frowned. What reservation could she be talking about? She, Brett, and the crew were all holed up at the hotel in town. The weird niggle that Brett was behind his eviction returned, but he carefully paid it no mind. He'd have plenty of time to talk to Brett, see if anything in his manner set off any alarms.

Time was wasting. He still had to drop Scott back at his car before seeing his mother. He wanted to leave plenty of time to get to Drew's and maybe catch a few fucking hours of sleep before he had to deal with Brett again tonight. After last night's incident, there was no way he could be left alone for a second, if only to protect the town from Hurricane Brett.

CHAPTER 9

Cliff pulled up beside a shiny black Town Car. Unless his mother's tastes had changed substantially in the intervening years, it wasn't hers. She'd never liked driving a black car in Florida, because of the heat, insisting on white or silver cars. It was the reason he'd opted for the bright blue hybrid when he'd bought his first brand-new car out in California.

He turned off the car and opened the door but didn't make a move to get out. Humid heat swirled into the car, and a faint sheen of sweat popped up on his forehead. The miasma of soggy decay, the cat-pee scent of boxwoods, and the faintest hint of the nearby orange groves assailed his nostrils. The smell of home was a comfort but also a painful reminder of his failure.

Better get it over with. At least he'd had the foresight to make sure he had someplace to be, and soon. He'd only be obligated to remain for a finite period of time.

The house he'd grown up in was old, built in plantation period and style—his family's wealth was tied up in the citrus groves. Not overwhelmingly large or ostentatious, thankfully, but the house sprawled large enough that he and his parents had rattled around a bit while he was growing up. His mother's people had been the wealthiest in the area for a long time, and previous generations had had many more family members to accommodate.

Fresh white paint coated the exterior of the house and the wrap-around porch. Although there were plenty of windows to let in the light, there was so much dark wood paneling inside that the breezy appearance of the exterior always seemed rather misleading. Inside, the staircases and doorways were narrower than modern standards, and as soon as Cliff had gotten his own place, he'd gone for every-thing modern, with clean, airy lines. The rebellion had only left him feeling oddly out of place and edgy, but it hadn't mattered. If there was anyplace like the Somerset estate in Los Angeles, only a movie star could have afforded to live there, not a cop.

That didn't mean he had any interest in moving back in with his mother.

With a huge sigh, he stepped out of the car. He needed to get this done, and sitting in the driveway wasn't going to make it happen.

At the door, he hesitated. Should he knock? He still had all his keys on his key ring, which should have told him something, despite his determination never to return to Sandy Bottom Bay. But it felt weird just walking into the house he hadn't stepped foot in for eight years.

Knocking at the door seemed a bit weird too. Was there a protocol for this type of social situation? If there was, his mother would know it, but he'd stopped listening to most of her etiquette rules a long time ago—it had all seemed so archaic. His mother's superstitions and genteel manner always made her seem to be a woman out of time.

Cliff fingered his keys for a moment before he shook his head and rang the bell. He no longer lived here, and he had no idea what his mother's schedule was like and hadn't for years. Better to be safe than sorry.

It took a few minutes before the door opened. Cliff had a moment where the world swam and realigned while he tried to make sense of Mr. Morales, his high school principal, opening the door to his moth-er's house.

This *was* still his mother's house, wasn't it?

"Cliff Garcia. 'Bout time you showed up. Your mother is in the living room."

Whoa. Mr. Morales hadn't lost that disapproving tone, at all. Cliff almost expected to be sent to detention, except he'd never gotten into trouble in school and never gotten detention. Which only made this doubly weird.

"William dear, who is it?"

Cliff gritted his teeth. William *dear*? What the hell was going on?

Neither of them bothered answering her, since it was only seconds before Cliff stepped into the living room behind *William dear* Morales.

One glimpse of his mother had Cliff wondering if she'd changed at all, but then her image resolved. She looked a little older, yes, but still as beautiful and serene as ever. And entirely unsurprised by his appearance in her living room.

He cleared his throat. "Hi, Mom."

"Northcliff." His mom smiled, and he did his best not to cringe at his full name.

"Cliff, Mom, please."

His mother let out a little sigh and wrinkled her nose. "I'm glad you were able to stop by." She stood up. "Come in. Sit down. I'll get you some sweet tea."

"Uh, thanks."

William ostentatiously checked an expensive watch. "Helen, I should get going anyway. Think about what I said." He strode over to her while Cliff sank into one of the upholstered armchairs.

His mother's jaw tightened just a bit, but Cliff knew her well enough to know that William wouldn't be getting whatever it is he wanted her to think about. *Good.*

By sheer force of will, Cliff kept from slumping down into the chair, arms crossed in front of his chest, like a sulky teenager.

"I'll see you later."

William brushed a kiss across Cliff's mother's cheek, making Cliff's lip curl for some inexplicable reason. It wasn't like his parents hadn't been divorced for years, and he never imagined them getting back together. His dad had been a fucking saint to put up with all his mother's woo-woo shit for so many years. Nevertheless, it curdled something in his gut to see another man kiss his mom, even if it was only on the cheek. Perhaps it was the possessive arm about her waist as he did so that made the gesture less than innocent.

Or it was just the shock of opening the door to his childhood home to find a man not his father there. Logically, there wasn't a good reason for his pique, but logic apparently didn't enter into it.

The door closed behind *William dear*, and Cliff's mother went into the kitchen while Cliff tried to talk himself out of his ire. Already this wasn't going well, and he'd only been here a few minutes.

A swift check of his watch had him groaning. By rights, he could easily manage an hour's visit, but not if that hour was going to feel like purgatory. Or detention. Cliff snorted at the wayward thought, and the vise around his chest eased.

His mother returned with a glass of cold sweet tea and set it down with a small plate of cookies. Cliff was a little too unsettled to try the cookies, but he gulped gratefully at the tea while his mother sat across from him.

"You look tired, Northcliff. Have you been sleeping?"

The concern grated, and it shouldn't. Cliff knew he was tired. Moving across the country would do that, with or without your best friend dying, with or without your boyfriend cheating on you. Any one of those things would be cause for sleepless nights, although he didn't really miss Brett. He'd missed having the support of a boyfriend at the funeral and could have used help packing up his apartment. He missed regular orgasms with another person, but Brett himself? Not so much. Losing Pete left a much bigger hole in his life, one he wasn't sure he'd be able to fill again.

"Been a long couple of weeks." Spending the night in the hospital watching over Drew hadn't done much to alleviate his exhaustion. "What was Mr. Morales doing here?"

Cliff congratulated himself on keeping his voice even, but his mother raised one perfectly shaped blonde eyebrow, and he knew he hadn't hidden his feelings well enough.

"Men!"

Cliff blinked. His mother rarely lost her composure like that. "Are you dating him or something?"

"William is courting me, yes."

Courting. The old-fashioned word bothered him, but his mother had always been this way.

"You never told me that." Their phone calls hadn't been frequent, but they spoke on a fairly regular basis. Sure, it had been easy to make excuses not to visit, but despite his resentment of his mother's beliefs, he still loved her.

"And you never told me you were moving back home."

Cliff squirmed in his seat. First his principal's and now his mother's disapproval had him feeling like he was a kid again. A kid in a shitload of trouble. As if he didn't have enough shit to deal with.

"No, it was...a rather sudden decision, and..." Cliff pushed out of the chair to go look out the window. "I don't know. I guess I'm still not sure if I'm here to stay."

"So why come back at all?" His mother's question was genuinely curious, with a thread of concern. For all her faults, she rarely held a grudge. Of course, he wasn't going to tell her he was home because he thought she was losing her marbles. Especially when that was only part of the equation and not the biggest part. It was, however, the easiest way he'd justified fleeing from Los Angeles. He hoped that one day his failure to make a life there wouldn't cut so deeply.

"Because I'm done with LA. And I didn't know where else to go. There was nowhere else I wanted to go, so the opening on the police force was..."

"Destiny?"

If not for a teasing hint in his mother's voice, Cliff would have lost the grip on his temper, but at least she knew just how much Cliff hated to call anything destiny or fate or kismet.

"Yeah. Maybe." He flicked at the curtain before turned back to his mother. He'd moved on from Brett and was hoping to get to know one of the Drummonds intimately and biblically. Surely he could accept his mother had moved on, years after his parents' divorce.

He sat back down. "So what has...William done to piss you off?" Cliff couldn't resist the improper word, and just as expected, his mother gave him a reproving look.

"I don't know if you're aware, but William is mayor now."

Cliff nodded. It had been a hell of shock to come back home and find out Mr. Morales had moved on from the high school, where Cliff had assumed he would be a steady feature until he was no longer able to function.

"What does that have to do with anything?"

"One of those paranormal television shows is filming at various locations over the next several days."

"*Phantoms*, yes." Cliff nearly snorted. At least his mother wasn't aware of his babysitting job and his connection with *Phantoms*' star.

"William is hoping this will be a big boost for the Sandy Bottom Bay economy."

"Mom. I can't believe you're letting them film here." It was bad enough he'd had to live with his mother's delusions of sharing their property with various dead relatives and a whole slew of massacred people who might or might not have been in his family tree, and he really hadn't believed Brett when he'd said his mother had already given permission.

"Don't be ridiculous, Northcliff. Of course I offered to let them film several places on the property, when the idea was first broached. Naturally that sort of coverage would be beneficial to the town, and you know how strong the spirits are around the estate. They've been getting stronger too, like they want to tell their story."

Stronger. She thought the ghosts were becoming more noticeable. Which was the main reason he'd been worried enough to return home. Had his mother been sliding glacially into dementia during his youth, only to have the speed of descent increase recently?

This time, Cliff did cross his arms petulantly. "Well, it sounds like you and William are totally on the same page. I don't see what the problem is." Besides believing in ghosts. Or believing in them enough for filthy lucre. He'd never pegged Mr. Morales as that type, but he knew damn well his mother believed wholeheartedly in the supernatural.

"Don't be snide, Northcliff. It's not becoming. And straighten up. No, the issue is that the...star? Producer? I don't know. Someone associated with the show wants to film me doing an interview. Answering questions about the various hauntings around the estate."

"So?" *Great.* Brett and William Morales teaming up. The thought gave Cliff the chills. The Morales estate, smaller and less acreage, bordered the Somersets', so Cliff had always had more interaction with the high school principal than he'd ever wanted.

"Ridiculous. I can understand how those California types might not understand my objection to doing something so crass, but I cannot believe William keeps trying to talk me into it. Men!"

Cliff pursed his lips. He wasn't even going to dive in, because the conflict was absurd on so many levels that he'd never be able to dignify it with the gravity his mother would expect. And if she was resorting to gender arguments, he probably wouldn't be able to pick the right side of this argument even if he agreed with every one of her statements. He took a deep breath.

"Never mind William. I'm sure he'll come around to your way of thinking." Or he'd be sent packing. "Are you doing okay? After the, uh, incident?"

A shadow crossed her face, sending a pang of guilt through Cliff. His mother was pretending to be fine, but she was upset, and Cliff was an ass for not coming out to see her as soon as he'd heard about the death.

"He was quite nice. Drank too much, perhaps, but he was a good handyman. Poor Andy."

"Did you find him?" Cliff should have asked about that sooner; it made him a horrible son that he hadn't even considered how awful that would have been for her. But she hadn't had full-time staff for years, so odds were against anyone else having found Andy.

"Oh no, dear. One of his friends was meeting him for lunch. One of the Drummond twins. He was quite shook up, poor thing."

Poor thing. Christ. Which of the evil twins had been tramping around his mother's place? Then again, it didn't matter—whichever Drummond it was, they were undoubtedly looking for a way to make a quick buck.

〜

BY THE TIME Kyle got him home, Drew was sweaty, light-headed, and in more pain. The heat in his tiny house had never seemed so oppressive before, and he slumped at the kitchen table, slick with the clammy sweat that only popped up during illness.

"I don't…" He closed his eyes and stopped talking. The heat and humidity had never affected him like they were doing right this second. Unbelievably, he was longing for the hospital bed he'd just left, with its temperature and environmental controls. He wasn't much looking forward to having Cliff see him like this either.

"Let me get you another pain pill. Then I'm going to call your brothers and have them bring over some fans. Or a window A/C unit for your bedroom. This heat can't be good for your head."

Kyle spoke God's honest truth. The heat was not doing wonders for Drew's head. Sweat formed on his scalp, and he dreaded the moment it battled past his bandage and got into his stitches.

Without another word, Kyle bustled him into the bathroom. He wasn't sure if it was because he looked pukey or if it was because the bathroom was the coolest part of the house. Drew slid gently down to the ground and turned his face to rest against the tile.

He must have fallen asleep there, because when he opened his eyes again, he was stretched out on the bathroom floor—as much as one could stretch out in a cramped five-by-seven space that already held a toilet, sink, and tub. His face was mashed up against the side of the tub, and his head rested on a pillow. The temperature had dropped a degree or two below the surface of the sun, and he pushed himself upright. He wasn't sure he had the energy to stand.

"Kyle." His voice was feeble and pathetic, but if nothing else, the house was too tiny for Kyle not to have heard him.

A few seconds later, Drew was proved right as Kyle bounded into the doorway.

"Oh good, you're awake. I can't get you into bed without some help from you."

"What the hell have I been doing, except resting? I shouldn't still be so exhausted."

"Not so. You're healing. You're supposed to rest and recuperate. But unfortunately, I can't lift you with my knee." Kyle looked away as he ran water over a cloth. "You ready to stand up?"

Drew considered it. "In a minute."

"Okay, we'll do this here." Kyle squatted, then wiped down Drew's face, the damp chill so good Drew could cry. He didn't know what he'd done to deserve a friend as good as Kyle, and he was selfishly glad that Kyle hadn't been able to move to New York as he'd planned.

"Can't you cancel your plans this weekend? Surely whoever they're with will understand." Drew tried not to sound too pathetic, but was sure he'd failed. Had to be a hookup; there wasn't anyone else Kyle spent any time with besides Drew.

"Ahem. Well. That was a bit of a white lie, really." Kyle continued to pat at his face and neck while Drew pieced together the implications.

"You lied?" Betrayal, bitter and cold, swept through him. "I thought you were my friend. How could you do this? How could you put me through this?"

"Look, everything I said at the hospital was true. This will be a good way to get to know him. Without having to worry about sex."

Drew rolled his eyes. He was pretty sure he wasn't going to have to worry about sex with Cliff—ever. Puking on a guy wasn't exactly enticing.

"And that makes it okay to lie? Jesus, Kyle."

Kyle shrugged. "I'm going to make myself scarce. If things are really terrible, I'm only a phone call away, but did you ever think that we're doing him a favor? He hasn't told his mom he's back in town. It's, like, his first day...or maybe second by now, on the job. I don't know why the motel kicked him out, but he may not have anywhere to go, not with Haunt Fest starting next week. He sure wasn't going to admit that to us, but doing this 'favor' for us and keeping an eye on you might make it easier for him to accept. Not like I got his whole life story while we were waiting for you to wake up or anything, but he seems a little private. Last thing he'd do would be to tell anyone he had to sleep in his car because he had nowhere else to go."

Once again, Drew was defeated by Kyle's arguments. Not that Kyle's arguments were necessarily watertight, but Drew didn't have the energy to try and refute them. Cliff would never buy into this fairy tale Kyle was trying to build, but maybe Kyle was right. Not about Cliff having nowhere else to go. Hell, half the nurses—male and female—in the hospital would let him bunk with them. But earlier, in the hospital, Kyle had mentioned getting to know Cliff the man instead of remaining fixated on Cliff the boyhood fantasy. Maybe sharing a place with Cliff for a few days would kill Drew's useless infatuation and let him move on.

"Fine, fine. You win."

"Of course I do. Feel like standing up now?"

The bell tinkled out front, signaling a client, and Drew groaned. "I can't do it today, Kyle. I can't be Malachi." Why couldn't this just be a hangover? At least with a hangover, he'd be just about starting to get better. The doctors couldn't give him any solid information about how long he'd have headaches or occasional blurred vision, except to say that if it lasted longer than a week, see a neurologist, and if it got worse, go back to the hospital. At least, that's what he remembered. He should probably review the paperwork they'd sent home with him. Later, though.

With a frown, Kyle stood and tossed the wet cloth in the sink. "You just wait here a minute. I'll get rid of whoever it is. I put a sign up that you were indisposed, but the door must be unlocked. Then we'll get you into bed."

Bed. His place was fucking tiny, but the bed had never felt so far away.

"Maybe it's Cliff."

"Nope. When I texted him, I told him to park in the alley at the back and come in the kitchen door. Last thing you need is someone seeing a uniformed cop going to the front of your shop to scare off the tourists. Be right back."

Drew thought Kyle might be wrong about that. Every time anyone in his family got arrested, it seemed to draw a crowd, but maybe that didn't exactly translate into sales. He'd never discussed the phenomenon with anyone.

A rapping sound, subtly different than the constant throb in his head, caught Drew's attention. Was someone knocking at his kitchen door?

"Is anyone here? Drew? Kyle?"

Ah, so Cliff *was* here. Drew waited a moment, but he didn't hear Kyle respond.

Drew pulled in a deep breath and forced himself to project his voice. "Come on in. The door's open."

Or he assumed it was. When he was home, he didn't usually lock the door. Not only did he have very little worth stealing, no one in town was that stupid. Despite last night's fiasco, his brothers were very protective of him, and from the explanations he'd been given, his concussion was a result of that. An accident of timing. Probably a good one, truth be told. Brett Cavanagh with a broken jaw would mean jail time for one or both of his brothers, whereas Drew with a concussion had been able to keep them safe. Although he still suspected there would be some harsh words exchanged next time Cliff came across either of them.

A muffled thump and a squeak told Drew Cliff had placed something heavy on the floor next to the kitchen table.

"Where are you?"

It was a good question. Where was Kyle? How long did it take to get rid of a client?

"In here." This time Drew's voice was quieter.

Cliff peered into the bathroom like he was doing a perp check— was that even what it was called? He'd only ever seen it on *Law & Order* when the cops busted into some suspect's home; he'd never seen firsthand what happened when any of his relatives had been arrested.

In seconds, the wary cop became the concerned cop as Cliff knelt beside Drew.

"Are you okay? Did you fall? How's your vision? I can call an ambulance."

The barrage of questions had Drew blinking in shock, unable to answer any questions fast enough, but he reached out a hand to stop Cliff from pulling out a cell phone.

"I'm fine." Drew let out a chuckle but stifled it quickly. "I just stopped here to rest a bit in the cool, and then I guess I dozed off."

"And Kyle left you here like that?" Anger made Cliff scowl, and like a flash of lightning, Drew had his first insight into Cliff the man. One he should have twigged to earlier, but morphine was going to be the scapegoat for a lot of things. Cliff had a temper. Drew didn't recall seeing signs of it in the teenaged Cliff, nor did he feel at all threatened, but a temper. He'd have to remember that.

"Well, he can't exactly lift me up."

Cliff's scowl eased up not at all. "Then he should have texted me instead of going off God knows where and leaving you here on the floor."

Another laugh escaped, and this one didn't feel like knives dancing in his brain, which was a big improvement. "God and I happen to know he's just in the front room, getting rid of a walk-in client. He's coming right back."

"Oh." This time Cliff's angry expression faded. "A client. Funny, I guess I never asked what you do for a living."

Drew had no trouble interpreting the odd grimace on Cliff's face. He'd seen it more than once. What did a Drummond do for a living aside from lie around drinking beer, or stealing shit and causing trouble? But he couldn't hold it against Cliff, since Drew's brothers pretty much did all that, although nowadays they fixed cars for money more often than stealing them.

"I'm—"

Kyle poked his head into the doorway. "Oh, Cliff, good. You can help me get him into bed. Then you can get settled."

"I was just getting ready to do that. I should have realized you'd have problems taking care of him, since he's so much taller than you."

Cliff's words weren't harsh or derisive, but it didn't matter. Kyle had a bit of a temper on him too.

"Excuse me. Are you calling me weak and short? I've lifted people over my head and spun around."

Cliff laughed because it sounded like Kyle was trash-talking—badly. "Of course you have."

"Truth," Drew said. "I've seen him."

"I can defend myself." Kyle snapped at him, and Drew held out his hands in supplication. "I'm a trained dancer. It was my job to hold up women over my head. I'm probably stronger than you are."

Okay, now Kyle might be stretching the truth a little, but very few people realized how much strength Kyle packed into his very compact form.

"Then why is Drew still on the floor?"

Kyle's anger shattered, leaving behind a shamed look. Drew hated to see it, because he knew it was Kyle facing the death of his dreams all over again.

"Because I blew out my knee a year ago, and it's not reliable."

Cliff gave Kyle a sympathetic smile, one that Drew wasn't pleased to see. If anyone was getting a date with Cliff out of this misguided matchmaking attempt, it had better be him, not Kyle.

"Hey, man. Injuries can happen. Don't be afraid to ask for help if you need it. Like now."

Before Drew could draw another breath, Cliff had wrapped arms around Drew's chest and hoisted him to his feet. A second later, Cliff had an arm around Drew's waist, holding him upright, while Drew's arm dangled limply across Cliff's shoulders.

As quickly as it had arrived, the tension between Cliff and Kyle disappeared. Kyle winked at him. "Let's get him into bed."

Drew wanted to groan, but most of all he wanted to lie down in his bed and go back to sleep.

They shuffled along the tiny hall into his bedroom. With a gentleness Drew wouldn't have expected from anyone, Cliff eased him under the covers before turning to Kyle.

Once Drew had relaxed back into his pillows, he remembered how long Kyle had been in his shop. "Who'd you have to kick out? Some persistent tourist? You were gone a while."

Kyle shrugged. "It wasn't anything. You concentrate on getting well."

Obviously. He needed to go back to work.

Cliff turned to Kyle. "I can stick around for a few hours now. Get set up. I'm on shift again at two, and then I won't be done until after midnight, although I can stop by during breaks."

"Sure, yeah, that will be good. I can stay with him this evening." Kyle dug around in his pocket. "Here's Drew's spare key."

Drew still had mixed feelings about handing Cliff Garcia free access to his home.

"What about your plans for the weekend?" Drew had to get some payback for this idiotic plan.

"Oh, they don't start until tomorrow." Kyle's wink made it more than clear what he intended to do for the weekend, and somehow Drew didn't think he was lying. Maybe he was going to head into Tampa by himself. No, more likely he was going to stalk Brett Cavanagh, see if he could get lucky.

Cliff, however, seemed a little uncomfortable with Kyle's blatant hint. "Right. Well, have fun."

"Oh. Yes, I'll get out of your hair. God knows this place can't easily accommodate a threesome, now can it?"

Cliff's reddened ears attested to his discomfort with the sexual innuendo, and when Cliff wasn't looking, Drew flipped Kyle the bird. He wasn't too thrilled talking about sex in Cliff's company either.

As soon as Kyle left, the kitchen door slamming behind him, Cliff sat on the bed beside Drew. "Is there a thermostat I can turn down? You and I are both used to the heat, but it's a scorcher out there today, and this can't be good for your headache."

The heat from Cliff's proximity bothered Drew more than the air temperature. Cliff was close enough to touch. One slight movement and not only could Drew touch Cliff, he could touch Cliff's cock. Feeling like total crap didn't mute the strong temptation to do exactly that. This close to Cliff's groin, Drew could clearly see Cliff was sporting a very healthy package.

"Drew?"

He flicked his eyes upward, hoping Cliff would attribute his flush to the heat of the room, not that he'd gotten caught staring at Cliff's fly.

"Uh, Kyle was going to have one of my brothers bring by some window A/C units."

Cliff's lip curled, and in other circumstances, Drew might have laughed. "They're not that bad, you know."

Maybe a cop wouldn't care that they'd done their best. They'd protected the runt of the litter—the *gay* runt of the litter—almost all his life. They'd helped their grandma put him through college for a business degree, although the funds probably weren't the cleanest, because Drew had wanted something different, better. They'd been good brothers, trying to make up for the deficit of their parents and the Drummond legacy.

"Well, you can try to convince me later." Cliff patted his arm briefly. Drew would *have* to convince the man, because even if Cliff only stayed at his place for a couple of days, he didn't want his brothers to get in trouble with the police. Not over him.

Cliff smiled down at him. "You need to rest. Will your brothers come right in when they get here, or will they knock?"

"Oh, they'll knock."

It had been embarrassing all around when they'd barged in one time while Drew had been enjoying some porn. They'd never entered without knocking again.

"Good. I'm going to bring my bag in here and set up my bed. Take a nap before my shift, if you don't mind. But I'll wake up if they knock."

The shadows beneath Cliff's eyes had deepened, and Drew

became aware of how exhausted Cliff must be. Probably rivaled Drew's head-injury- and morphine-induced lethargy.

For a moment, Cliff's hand hovered over Drew's bandage, but then he cleared his throat and stood. He headed to the only chair in the room and began fiddling with the frame to extend it out into a bed.

With drowsy eyes, Drew watched. If Cliff was going to strip down, he wanted to see it, even if Cliff didn't get entirely naked, but he couldn't keep his eyes open any longer.

CHAPTER 10

A loud thumping had Cliff sitting bolt upright. He stared around through gritty, sleep-fuzzy eyes. Where the fuck was... Right. He was at Drew's, otherwise known as the sweat lodge of death. Sweat soaked his tiny bright yellow briefs, leaving them clinging to his body. His hair was damp, and he maybe stank, just a bit. He'd long since kicked off the sheet he'd used to protect his modesty from Drew, despite Drew having fallen asleep before Cliff had even unbuttoned his shirt.

Drew still slept peacefully a few feet away, so perhaps the banging had been in Cliff's dreams, but it came again, louder this time, and recognizable as someone knocking at the door. Cliff scrambled off the futon, hoping to prevent Drew from being awakened. No sense in both of them having interrupted sleep. With a groan, he realized he'd been asleep for less than an hour. He was going to have to call in sick. He'd never be able to function. More importantly, he'd never be able to prevent himself from responding to a full eight hours or more of Brett's taunts.

The knock came again, quick and insistent. Drew frowned and stirred, leaving Cliff no choice but to answer the door in his skimpy underwear.

"What the hell— Oh, it's you." One of the evil twins stood at

Drew's kitchen door, a window A/C unit slung over a beefy shoulder. "About time. It's roasting in here."

The twin stood on the stoop and narrowed his eyes. "What are you doing here? Taking advantage of my sick brother?"

Exhaustion had blinded Cliff to what answering Drew's door in his briefs would look like, especially to a Neanderthal like one half of the Drummond twins. At least he wasn't wearing a jock. When he was planning to work, he wore briefs because they were the most comfortable under his uniform pants. But he was still gay, so they were tiny, sexy, brightly colored briefs, and he probably looked like he'd just had sex. "I can explain. Which one are you, again?"

"I'm Wyatt. And it'd better be a good explanation."

The guy was pissed as hell and holding a heavy metal object that he could easily use to crush Cliff. Antagonizing him wouldn't be smart. Unfortunately, Cliff didn't feel anything but antagonistic.

"Just looking after Drew. Kyle asked me to stay with him because he couldn't."

Wyatt's fingers gripped the A/C unit tighter, and without conscious thought, Cliff took a step back.

"In your underwear? I can't see how that is necessary. You a fag?"

It was like he was back in high school again, facing off with his adversaries, but this time Cliff had a lot more personal and professional experience with belligerent assholes under his belt.

"My sexuality isn't any of your business, Wyatt." Although the gossip meant he'd probably get an earful eventually. "None of this is your business, actually, since your brother is a grown man."

Wyatt set the A/C unit on the floor and stood, clearly poised to start a fight in Drew's kitchen, for fuck's sake. Cliff needed to choose his words carefully. He wasn't interested in taking on the more muscular man, but neither was he going to let Wyatt intimidate him.

"I was taking a nap, on the futon, while your brother rests. There is nothing going on here but me helping out an injured man." Cliff lifted an eyebrow as if daring Wyatt to contradict him. Because if truth be told, Cliff would very much like there to be another reason for him to be mostly naked in Drew's house. For the first time, he wondered how out and experienced Drew was. Even if there was someone else in this town in the closet, but willing to have a discreet relationship with Drew, the guy had to know dealing with one or both of the evil twins was a possibility.

"Fuck you!" Wyatt's voice rattled the dishes in the sink. "You think I can't see all those perverts eyeing my brother like he was some helpless girl? Rob and I, we've made sure none of them touch him. I can see it in your eyes too. I don't care who the fuck you are, but you'd better not mess with Drew. Or you'll be sorry."

Cliff slammed a fist on the table, causing more rattles. "Have you seriously been treating him like some eighteenth-century virgin heiress? What the fuck is the matter with you? And you have no say in what I do or don't do. Drew is a fucking adult." His nostrils flared as he tried to hide how much he wanted to mess with Drew, over and over. "As for threatening a police officer? I can let that slide, but if you start anything, you'll be cooling your heels in jail. Got that?"

"Please. Rob and I have been dodging arrests since that first day we met."

Good to know their first meeting, at ten years old, had been as memorable for the evil twins as it had for him. It had started with Cliff coming along the twins roughing up a younger, smaller boy and ended with a bloody fight, setting up their animosity for the rest of their school years.

Wyatt sneered. "Besides, it's kinda hard to prove shit if you don't know which of us was doing what."

Almost as an automatic response, Cliff's fist shot out, landing directly on Wyatt's nose. The satisfaction of hearing the bone break was tempered by his horror at taking the shot in the first place. Didn't stop his mouth from running off on its own, like his fist had. "Now I can tell you apart."

Wyatt's animalistic roar made Cliff wish he were wearing boots he could shake in, but he wasn't backing down. The twins had some fucking misguided notions of what it meant to be gay, and if they were trying to enforce Drew's celibacy by threatening potential suitors, he was sure he could get a restraining order against them, at least.

And he'd be there to fuck them up if they tried violating it. Assuming he didn't get kicked off the force for punching Wyatt in the first place. Not that this was the first time he'd bloodied Wyatt, but it was the first time he'd done so after becoming a cop.

"What the hell is going on here?"

Drew's voice had them both turning. Drew clung to a counter to hold himself upright. In this light, the bruising creeping down from his forehead to eyes appeared dark and menacing, especially as the rest of him looked as pale and translucent as the hypothetical ghosts this damn town was supposedly filled with. Fiery red hair resembling a bird's nest was the only thing, besides the purpling bruise and light gray boxer briefs, that wasn't ghostlike. Drew's legs trembled slightly, as though they were in danger of collapsing any minute, and Cliff struggled to focus on that, not how much he'd like to hold that lanky half-naked body against his.

Immediately the antagonism bled out of him because Drew looked on the verge of falling over, and the last thing he wanted was for Drew to be hurt any worse.

"What are you doing out of bed? You're supposed to be resting."

At the same time, Wyatt said, "Go to fucking bed, Drew."

Drew scowled at them. "And I'm supposed to sleep through you guys fighting in my kitchen?"

With a flash of clarity like a smack upside the head, Cliff realized his behavior had been just horrible. He was a guest in Drew's home and had just broken Drew's brother's nose. This was why heat waves had such a significant impact on crime rates. Tempers flared easier in the heat, and there was no denying Drew's house was just about as hot and humid as anything Cliff had experienced since he'd left Florida.

"Sorry." Cliff's voice became very quiet, and his state of undress now felt prurient and indecent like it hadn't before. Maybe it was because both he and Drew were only wearing underwear, and anyone with eyes and the knowledge that Drew had only one bedroom would leap to the same conclusion Wyatt had. Although he wasn't sure it was possible to be any more hateful than Wyatt had been in response. Cliff repressed the desire to cup his hands protectively over his package.

Wyatt snorted, then groaned, apparently having forgotten his broken nose.

"Sit down, Wyatt, and let me get some ice for that." Drew didn't make a move for the fridge, although Wyatt did obey. Gripping the counter with both hands, Drew frowned. "And don't think I missed the part that you've been warning guys away from me. Didn't we... I feel like we talked about this already. But it's fuzzy, like I dreamt it. I didn't dream that conversation, did I?"

In a flash, Wyatt turned into a chastened schoolboy. "Shit, Drew. I'm sorry. We did. Last night at the Angry Parakeet. I just... Cliff and me don't have such a great history. I shouldn't warn people away from you."

A little flash of anger directed at Cliff told him Wyatt still wouldn't be thrilled if Cliff pursued Drew. Following the pattern of years of public school, Cliff decided he was going to anyway, as long as Drew's record wasn't too bad. He wouldn't play with anyone's feelings just to spite the evil twins, but their disapproval had pushed his previous indecision about getting involved with Drew off a fucking building. If Drew'd had Rob and Wyatt protecting him the whole time, it was possible he hadn't had many brushes with the law.

"Exactly. Now let's get you cleaned up so you can install that A/C."

"You really should open up the doors to the front shop, Drew. Get some of that air back here."

"No way. I had Kyle turn those off. No sense cooling the whole place when no one's using those rooms."

"Drew, if you need—"

"I'm fine." Drew cut off whatever Wyatt was going to say with a glare, followed by a glance in Cliff's direction. Given the clean yet shabby interior of Drew's house, Cliff figured maybe Drew didn't want to spend the extra money on cooling the place down. Then again, if Wyatt was offering money, odds were he'd gotten it under less than legal circumstances, regardless of what Scott had told him about the twins working as mechanics and occasionally helping out

Andy as handymen. Cliff would let it pass, but he'd make sure he contributed where he could, since Drew was doing him the favor of giving him a place to stay.

Drew lifted one hand from where he clutched the counter, the tremors in his fingers perfectly visible.

"Let's get you back to bed. You shouldn't be up and about. I'll get Wyatt some ice for his nose." Wyatt was a big boy and could clean himself up without Cliff's help. "Then I'll help him install the A/C unit before I head in for my shift."

Drew eyed him suspiciously, and Cliff couldn't blame him. After all, they were virtually strangers, and Drew had no real reason to trust him.

"Seriously. I'm sorry about letting my temper get away from me. We can be civil, can't we?" Cliff looked at Wyatt for confirmation. The nod helped, but the blood streaking down his face probably didn't do much to ease Drew's mind.

"Please. Give it a chance."

Drew pressed his lips together before he gave a slight nod. There was no doubt in Cliff's mind that if Drew were feeling better, he'd have protested.

Cliff crossed the tiny kitchen and wet down the dishtowel before tossing it to Wyatt. "Wipe off the blood while I get Drew settled." He'd also make sure Drew got something to eat before Cliff left.

Almost defiantly, Cliff wrapped an arm around Drew's waist, savoring the feel of skin on skin and the warm, musky scent of sleepy male while he got Drew back into bed. He fussed with Drew's blankets and pain meds, trying to wait out the erection that had sprung up. No matter how contrite Wyatt might be, going back into the kitchen flaunting an erection would be like waving a red flag in front of a bull. Cliff pulled on a pair of jeans and a T-shirt, thankful he was able to hide his partial stiffy behind the denim, although he'd probably sweat through the jeans in no time.

"Cliff?"

He turned back toward Drew, hoping the resident patient hadn't noticed his totally inappropriate arousal.

"Thanks."

"For what?" Not killing his brother? Surely that didn't rate thanks. Cliff certainly hadn't shown any real restraint. His lack of control had made the decision to go in to work easier. Hopefully by the time he got back, he'd feel less like a shithead.

"For trying to get along with my brother. I appreciate it." Drew looked for a moment like he was going to say more, but his eyelids with their pale reddish-gold lashes fluttered, and he fell asleep. Cliff indulged himself for a moment by smoothing out that wild red hair, so soft under his fingertips. He wasn't ever going to be friends with Drew's brothers, but keeping the peace was part of his job description. No matter how difficult, if he wanted to get to know Drew better as a potential boyfriend, he was going to have to sac up and learn how to tolerate the evil twins.

The whole issue would be moot if Drew was a suspect in any open case files, though, so he'd better check that out as soon as possible. In fact, he should have done that before agreeing to stay here, but Drew's vulnerability had destroyed what passed for logic in his brain these days. Apparently his cock and heart were overriding his brain's decisions. Wasn't like him to make such an impulsive decision, but Pete's death had changed a lot for him. Making the decision to quit the LAPD and move back home had also been rather impulsive.

Letting himself engage in one last impulsive indulgence before he turned back to the kitchen to deal with the Neanderthal, Cliff brushed a kiss on Drew's head above the bandage. He wasn't sure when he'd become this big softy, although he'd sensed it wanting to break out while he was dating Brett. That should have been his first clue that he and Brett weren't having the same relationship. He wanted to be able express how he felt, wanted to be able to touch and kiss in tenderness without having it always be a prelude to sex. Not that he didn't want to fuck Drew into the mattress as soon as he was better, but he also wanted to be able to walk on the beach hand in hand with another man, and damned if his heart wasn't already sketching Drew into the picture.

His instinct that Drew wasn't like the rest of his family better not be wrong, or Cliff was going to be gutted.

CLIFF HAD JUST FINISHED SKIMMING through the extensive files on the Drummonds when Scott came up behind him and clapped a hand on his shoulder, scaring a year or two off his life. He fumbled for the mouse and shut down the window.

"Hey, Scott. You're here early."

"Nope. I'm actually late and was looking for you. We need to head over to the shoot."

God. He really needed some sleep if he was losing track of time that badly. Despite the lost time, he'd been able to set his mind at ease. Drew's record was squeaky clean, and even those of the evil twins weren't as bad as he'd feared. Drew's dad, yeah, he was a lot more violent, and some of Drew's cousins were clearly dabbling in drug dealing, but Drew was...not going to ruin his career.

"Checking up on the Drummonds, were you?" Scott plopped down in the seat next to him, and Cliff wanted to bang his head against the desk. For a guy who hadn't seemed to change from the big, goofy, oversize puppy he'd known in high school, Scott was far too fucking observant for his liking.

"Uh, yeah. Don't we have to get going?"

Scott nodded, accepting Cliff's diversion without any complaint. He stood and headed for the door. Cliff quickly shut down the computer and sped after him.

"Get any rest?" Scott asked.

"An hour. I think."

Scott turned and stared at him. "An hour? Are you sure you should be here?"

"I'll be fine. The worst of the tourists aren't going to arrive until midweek, so this shift should be a breeze. Watching stuff get filmed is actually pretty boring. When everyone's not waiting around for shots to get set up, they'll repeat the same segment over and over from a million different angles."

And probably in different order. The actual "haunting" parts would be filmed after dark.

"Huh. But aren't they filming ghosts or hauntings? They can't ask the ghosts to do another take."

"No, but whatever Brett or his interviewees say can be repeated again and again, then spliced together later."

With questionable footage and a bunch of idiots in the dark asking each other if they heard that noise or saw that movement or felt that chill. Complete and utter garbage, and Cliff was relieved he no longer had to pretend even the slightest belief in the supernatural. Even in Sandy Bottom Bay, no one could fault a cop for believing only in what he could see, hear, and touch.

Oddly, Scott got in the passenger seat of Cliff's cruiser and waited.

"Aren't you taking your own car?" Cliff asked as he got in and shut the door.

"Yep. In a minute. Drew's okay, you know."

Once again, Cliff had the urge to pound his head on something. He wasn't sure he was ever going to be used to everyone knowing his business.

"What do you mean?" He wanted Scott to reassure him without actually asking him to do so, which was absurd.

"C'mon. We both know why you were digging into the Drummonds' files. He's okay. Ask him out, if you want. Him and his grandma, they're the only two who seemed to have escaped being tarred by the Drummond brush. Well, maybe not quite. Some people still lump Drew in with the rest of his family, but he went to college, he owns his own house and business, and he's a good guy, as far as I can tell. If you're interested, you should go for it."

"You don't think it would look...unprofessional? Or be a conflict of interest?" Shit, shit, shit. He was way too tired. Even though Scott was an old friend, Cliff didn't like appearing vulnerable over a guy. Vulnerability was an Achilles heel that someone could exploit and use to hurt him.

"It's a small town, dude. Your options are somewhat limited, and even though some people in town lump Drew in with the rest of his deadbeat family, most don't. Most really like him. There are a number of women who keep trying to point out young gay men for him to date. Tourists, usually. Aside from the ones who think he should get together with Kyle, that is."

Cliff's insides twisted at the thought of Drew dating anyone else. Hooking up with anyone else. He was such a fucking idiot, but in light of his research and Scott's confirmation, he was going to ask Drew out. As soon as Drew was on the mend. Jealousy was a foreign emotion for Cliff, but he wanted Drew. He didn't give a damn about the so-called slim pickings in Sandy Bottom Bay. He hadn't moved out here looking for a man, and even if every man in town were gay, he'd still have zeroed in on Drew.

"Okay. Meet you at the hotel. They'll tell us where we're going when we get there." Scott exited the car and loped across the parking lot to get in his own cruiser.

THE B&B didn't look particularly menacing or haunted to Cliff, but it was apparently the feature for this part of Brett's show. A number of zealous fans had come early for Haunt Fest, filling up the rooms at the B&B and eager to catch a glimpse of Brett.

The crew was keeping the shoot locations under wraps, even from Cliff and Scott, until the very last minute. Brett had to be exaggerating how many groupies he had. This whole secretive shit was getting on Cliff's nerves. Of course, there weren't many places he wasn't familiar with in the tiny Sandy Bottom Bay, and he could make a guess at which places *Phantoms* would film.

"Right. Well, I'll take a look around, see if there's anything out of the ordinary, and you go let them know we're here."

Scott laughed. "You can't avoid him forever."

"Nope, but I sure hope my friend will cover for me when he can." A wide smile spread Cliff's lips. Avoiding Brett and asking Drew out.

Those thoughts made him a happy man, despite the exhaustion that was almost painful.

Near the end of Cliff's shift, a commotion on the other side of the B&B caught his attention. He ran toward the yelling. In the center of the incandescent white spot illuminated by the insanely bright portable lights the crew had brought with them, Brett screamed obscenities at someone while Kristi flapped her arms ineffectively and tried to talk sense into the two of them. Scott approached just then, hand poised over his gun, but relaxed his stance within seconds. This altercation shouldn't require weapons, but with Brett's harsh words, Cliff wouldn't put it past the other guy to pull out a gun and start firing.

Much as he'd like Scott to run interference with Brett, it would be better if Cliff did it.

Near as he could tell, Eddie wasn't getting what Brett had promised while they'd had sex. Cliff could relate, although Cliff had never wanted Brett to give him a bigger part in his damn TV show.

As one, he and Scott stepped between the combatants, using their bodies and bulk to move the two men away from each other.

"Mr. Cavanagh." Cliff hoped the lack of familiarity would snap Brett out of this...tantrum. Whatever it was, he'd never quite seen the like, and this was now the second day in a row he'd seen Brett lose his cool like this. "You need to calm down. Tell me what happened."

Strangely, it worked. Behind him, Eddie was still swearing, but Cliff trusted Scott to do his part. Brett took his eyes off his opponent and looked into Cliff's.

"Cliffy. I don't know if I like you calling me Mr. Cavanagh. Unless we're playing headmaster and naughty schoolboy. I'd love to discipline you while you begged Mr. Cavanagh for mercy." Brett smirked at him, but both the words and gaze only made Cliff shudder. He was 100 percent over Brett Cavanagh.

"*Mr. Cavanagh.* Tell me what happened."

Instead Brett pressed his body against Cliff's. Up close, the makeup on Brett's skin to make him attractive for the camera only looked odd and greasy under moonlight and blinding halogens.

"Don't be like that, Cliffy. You look tired, Cliffy. Why don't you come back to the hotel with me after the shoot, Cliffy? I can help you get to sleep, and I heard you might need a place to stay."

Cliff stepped back, trying to fight down the spike of anger that shot through him at Brett's words and actions. Not that Brett had admitted to anything, but Cliff had no doubt now that Brett had been responsible for him losing his room at the motel. If nothing else, the gossip vine shouldn't have extended to a newcomer that quickly. But Brett had enough celebrity status to influence someone like the manager of the motel. Fucker. Cliff just wasn't sure if it was because Brett wanted him back or wanted to piss him off. But he couldn't let it get to him.

"Thank you for your concern, but I have a place to stay. If I see any more incidents like this, I will arrest you for disturbing the peace, and you can cool your heels in jail until you can fly a fancy lawyer out here. Got it?"

Brett shivered exaggeratedly. "Ooh, Cliffy. So commanding. I like this side of you. Maybe we could go out for a drink after the shoot. I saw a very delicious redhead last night. Although..." Brett put on his pouty, thoughtful look. It was a look that had probably lost its charm a decade ago. "I think he might be indisposed. But the blond he was with was a tasty morsel as well. The three of us could have some fun."

Rage boiled up inside. Did Brett truly not realize his bizarre, skeevy, antagonistic behavior was the sole reason Drew was injured right now? And if Brett thought he was getting his slimy paws on Drew, he was mistaken. If Cliff had to, he'd sic the evil twins on Brett —again. For the first time, he found a sliver of common ground with the twins. Perhaps he couldn't continue to call them evil.

"Mr. Cavanagh. We will have no interactions besides professional ones. Are we clear?" Somehow Cliff managed to speak through a jaw clenched so tight it might spontaneously snap.

Brett rolled his eyes but stopped trying to get closer to Cliff. "No wonder you moved back here. You've become too stodgy and boring for California."

Cliff was going to leave that one alone like a week-old carcass rotting in the sun. He glanced back over his shoulder and saw the other man had mostly calmed. Old Eddie Price. He didn't seem as old as he had to their teenaged eyes and was probably younger than Brett, but he was still just as fucking crazy as all the other woo-woo believers in this town. A medium. No one could speak with the dead, and ghosts didn't exist. This town was nuts. What Cliff would give for a reason to throw the lot of them in jail.

Scott escorted Eddie to his car while the crew went on with their work, but based on what Cliff had learned from Kristi's interjections, they hadn't seen the last of him. He was still the most important of Brett's interviewees, since Cliff's mother hadn't budged on her stance.

When Scott returned, he had a sympathetic look on his face. "Dude, you look fucking beat. Why don't you take off now? These guys are only going to be a couple more hours, and I got a full night's sleep last night."

"You sure?" Cliff wanted to pull his weight, but even the minor adrenaline rush that resulted from heading off Brett's altercation was going to send him crashing, and soon.

"I'm sure. And if you don't get enough sleep, call out sick. Promise me. We've still got time before the hordes descend. You'll need to be on your toes for that."

Cliff nodded. "Thanks."

He checked Brett's status. It would be much easier if he could slip away without Brett noticing. At the moment, it appeared that Brett had gone back into the bed-and-breakfast, so Cliff took advantage and strode quickly to his car.

CHAPTER 11

Cliff stretched, the insistence of his bladder bringing him awake. He hopped out of bed and headed for the bathroom. Once his bladder was no longer screaming, he took a moment to brush his teeth. He'd taken a shower when he'd gotten back to Drew's after his shift. The tiny house was a much more reasonable temperature now, but he'd been covered in stale sweat from helping Wyatt install the A/C unit. Cliff hadn't had the time for a shower after they'd finished, so by the end of his shift he'd been quite rank. But he'd been so tired, he'd forgotten to brush his teeth and had tumbled onto the futon as soon as he'd toweled off and pulled on another pair of briefs.

He still had a few hours before his shift, so he crept back to the bedroom and onto the futon. It was surprisingly comfortable, better than some mattresses he'd slept on. Once he was comfortable, he turned on his side to look at Drew. It was how he'd fallen asleep last night, but that had happened far too soon. He wanted to look his fill.

Instead he found Drew staring back at him, hair damp and bandage missing, exposing a line of angry-looking stitches surrounded by a painful-looking bruise.

Cliff sat up in bed, prepared to leap across the small space between them. "What the hell? Are you okay?"

Drew smiled, a genuine smile, free of pain and without the sloppiness of being stoned on prescription narcotics.

"I'm fine. I feel a lot better today, actually. The shower helped."

"Shower? I was going to help you with it today."

It would have been temptation like throwing a monk into a pit of naked oil wrestlers, but he wouldn't have wanted to risk Drew getting woozy and slipping in the tub.

A faint flush colored Drew's cheeks, and he wouldn't quite meet Cliff's gaze. "I woke up a while ago, and you were sleeping so soundly. I didn't want to wake you, but I was just gross."

There wasn't any point in berating him, since it was over and Drew had survived, but Cliff felt a little cheated. He must have some previously undiscovered masochistic tendencies, since he was put out that he hadn't been able to torture himself helping Drew shower. What would that red hair look like, all slicked down and dark with water? All that smooth, wet skin. And was Drew ginger...all over?

Cliff bunched the sheet in front of him, but he couldn't stop imagining what he might have missed seeing during that shower. Hence the need for additional fabric barriers.

"Yeah. Well, that window unit is doing a good job."

"I can't believe I slept through you guys putting it in."

Cliff couldn't either because it had involved more than one whispered swear word, and the window they'd attached it to was right between the futon and Drew's bed. "You needed your rest."

Drew gave him a little smile. "Thanks for leaving me the sandwich."

"Oh, sure. No problem." The only things in Drew's place to eat were bread and peanut butter, but at least he'd been able to make a sandwich and leave it by Drew's bedside without worrying it would go off in the heat. "But that reminds me. I'm going to grab some groceries today, if you don't mind. Is there anything you want? Can't eat?"

"You don't have to do that." The hint of pink was back in Drew's cheeks, and Cliff wondered again how Drew's finances were.

"You're doing me a favor, letting me stay here. I want to feel like

I'm contributing." And he didn't want to starve to death. He liked peanut butter as much as the next guy but didn't consider a constant diet of it appealing.

"Oh, well, I guess that would be okay. I'll eat whatever."

Drew shifted, and his sheet slipped a bit, exposing an expanse of chest and a nipple, already peaked and beckoning for Cliff's mouth. He did his best to keep his gaze on Drew's bright blue eyes, but he kept flickering down to that smooth, pale chest. It was like Drew was taunting him, teasing him. His erection just got harder and more insistent.

But he was a man in control of his cock. He could ignore its demands. He could. A lengthy glance at the stitches and bruise on Drew's forehead worked as well as a cold shower. Well, maybe not quite that effective, but it helped. Drew was injured.

Self-consciously, Drew patted his forehead. "It looks hideous, doesn't it?"

Cliff had seen worse, but the sight in the mirror this morning had to have been a bit of a shock.

"It's not pretty, but it will improve quickly. Don't worry." Telling Drew it didn't change how sexy he was didn't seem particularly appropriate for a man claiming to be in control of his cock, and might even be interpreted as a heavy-handed attempt to get a "favor" in return for the favor Drew was doing for Cliff.

"I guess." Drew let his hand drop.

Right now it seemed like they were the only two people in the world, the white-noise hum of the A/C unit drowning out all but the katydids, singing in the heat and humidity outside.

Their relaxed conversation was more enjoyable than just about anything Cliff had experienced since he'd come back to Sandy Bottom Bay—hell, since he'd discovered Brett fucking around on him. And although it seemed oddly intimate to be talking while they were both in bed in their underwear, he wasn't ready to let the moment slip away. He wanted to know more about Drew.

"So, I realized I never found out what you do for a living. I assume the front half of the house is for your business." When Scott had mentioned Drew owned his own business, Cliff had almost asked what it was but realized that would make him appear just ridiculous. Hell, even *he* thought he was ridiculous for getting so hung up on a guy he knew next to nothing about.

Drew's smile disappeared, and he broke eye contact. Dread churned in Cliff's belly. Was this where all his plans fell apart?

"Oh. You never went around to the front of the house?"

"No, never really had a chance, especially since it was more convenient to park in the back alley and come in through the kitchen."

"I'm a psychic tarot reader."

Cliff froze for a moment as he tested those words in his mind. No matter how many times he ran them together, all he could hear was that Drew was admitting to being a professional con man. He stared at Drew, expecting him to take back the words, to laugh and say he was joking. But the expectant, almost hesitant expression never left his face.

"I'm sorry. Did you say psychic tarot reader?"

"Yes. I'm, uh, called Malachi the Mystic, you know, when I'm doing readings."

"So you lie to people for money." Cliff's words were full of sharp edges he couldn't contain. Yes, the profession was legitimate—barely—but that only meant Drew had managed to make the system support his scam. Cliff sat up straight, all arousal gone.

Drew tensed. "I take it you don't believe."

"Believe? Believe in what? Ghosts? Psychics? Messages from beyond the grave? You're damn right I don't, because it's all fake. This whole industry is built to take advantage of gullible, stupid, or mentally ill people. You know what else I don't believe? Is how a guy who seems pretty decent can justify taking money from people who haven't the wits or capability to protect themselves." His mother had been blowing time and money on people like Drew as long as Cliff could remember.

"Protect themselves? From what?" Two spots of color formed high on Drew's cheeks, and his voice left no doubt he was insulted. He struggled to sit up, and as much as Cliff wanted to assist, he was pretty certain Drew wouldn't want that. After all, what idiot abused a host's hospitality by belittling their profession? But he couldn't help it. He'd been blindsided by this revelation. The path had been open and clear for him to ask Drew out, but how could he do it now? Had he been wrong about Drew? What if his so-called business was tied up with the other criminal activity Cliff had seen in the Drummond family's police records?

"You aren't seriously trying to tell me you see the future, are you?" Cliff was digging himself deeper, but the bitterness over losing what he might have had with Drew leaked out into his words.

"It's not like I tell people when they're going to die or tell them what stocks to invest in, for God's sake. Most people find it fun. Entertainment, you know?"

Which didn't answer the question and solidified Drew's complicity, in Cliff's mind. If Drew truly believed, he would have said so instead of dancing around the topic. The mention of stocks raised a red flag, though. The scam could be deeper than simply pretending to be a psychic. A good con man could get all sorts of private information from an unwary client.

"Is that what you do? Use the guise of Malarky—I mean, Malachi —to get insider tips on trading? Or maybe it's an elaborate means for identity theft."

The sheet had fallen, forgotten, to Drew's waist, exposing his lithe chest, and suddenly Cliff's ire transformed into something else, something that made him breathless with want, bringing his cock back to full erection with almost painful swiftness. God help him, he wanted Drew to deny it all, because he just plain wanted Drew.

A blotchy red flush stained Drew's chest and neck before flooding up to meet his already pink cheeks. "I can't believe you...think that of me." Despite the affront in Drew's voice, his gaze slid away, and Cliff's hopes sank.

Defeated and done, Cliff let his anger drain away, and his eyes burned from the loss. If only the pervasive and driving desire for Drew would disappear as easily. The disappointment was drowning him.

"It's true, isn't it?" Cliff asked without any heat. "You're scamming people, aren't you? Just haven't gotten caught yet."

He didn't expect Drew to admit it. Cliff was a cop, after all. But the guilt was as obvious as if there were a neon billboard flashing over Drew's head.

Just as quickly, Drew's ire disappeared. He rubbed at his eyes and winced when the movement pulled at his stitches.

"I don't expect you to understand, but will you at least listen?"

Cliff pressed his lips together and nodded. If he weren't going to give Drew the benefit of the doubt, he'd have already been dressed, instead of lounging around in his briefs. Apparently his autonomic nervous system had decided in Drew's favor, overriding his brain. Or maybe it was merely his cock taking charge. That hadn't worked out so well with Brett, but he wasn't quite willing to shut down the possibility of something happening with Drew.

He sank back down onto the futon and waited. Drew dropped his gaze to Cliff's chest and licked his lips.

Fuck. Cliff just couldn't give in. Not yet. Drew needed to toss him a life preserver—anything he could use to justify this incredibly bad judgment. Or something that would throw metaphorical cold water over him and lessen the throbbing, insistent pressure in his groin.

DREW HAD NEVER REALLY UNDERSTOOD that saying about feeling your heart in your throat. Not until he was faced with the prospect of Cliff leaving, disappointed and angry, because he had the wrong idea about Drew's business. Not even the day Cliff left Sandy Bottom Bay had Drew experienced the same level of loss and desolation. He hadn't even had a chance to enjoy the fact that the worst of his pain seemed to have receded.

He wanted to leap out of bed and tackle Cliff to keep him in bed, but both the faint echo of a headache and his lingering erection emphasized that would be a bad idea. Stupid cock. Hadn't gotten the memo that just because there was only a thin bit of cotton wrapping

Cliff's hips didn't mean Drew was going to get a chance at what was underneath, or even the rest of that smooth, tanned, and incredibly exposed caramel skin.

He licked his lips. And again. He wasn't even sure his explanation would placate Cliff any, but he didn't want Cliff to look at him with that exasperated, disgusted look anymore. Besides that, he was proud of what he did.

"Most people come to me for fun. Looking for entertainment. But those that don't are often looking for a little bit of reassurance. A bit of harmless advice. A way to feel better about themselves. People leave here a little lighter, a little happier, more optimistic."

Cliff should market his skeptical look, because Drew had never seen a better one. Maybe it was something they taught at the police academy.

"Sure, a number of the tourists come in for a joke. But that's okay. I'm...uh..." Holy fuck, he probably shouldn't admit this to a man who'd pretty much accused him of all kinds of crimes. "I'm pretty good at doing cold reads."

Cliff snorted. "*I'm* pretty sure Drummonds are taught those skills in the cradle."

Ouch. He hadn't wanted such blatant, sneering confirmation that Cliff didn't have any better opinion of him than the rest of the cops in this town. It shouldn't be such a painful surprise, not with Cliff's history with Rob and Wyatt, but it was nonetheless.

"My grandmother left me this business. No matter what you think, this is perfectly legitimate. I respect my clients' privacy, and I sure as shit am not trying to get insider trading tips or information to steal identities. I decided a long time ago I wasn't like the rest of the family, and even though I'm sure you don't believe it, my brothers were very supportive of that decision."

If his family was a little more tech savvy, he might have gotten some pressure to steal credit-card information, but his grandmother's vehement insistence that the business stay clean had made it easy for Drew to maintain the status quo, especially with the backing of his brothers. Then again, having their father convicted for such a long sentence had shaken them all up, and his brothers had figured out pretty quickly it wouldn't make sense for them to protect Drew all through school, only to leave him unprotected in prison if he got caught up in their schemes.

"Sure, sure." Cliff neither looked nor sounded convinced.

"I admit, Drummonds do learn pretty early on how to exploit people's vulnerabilities. But my grandmother never agreed with all the crime. She distanced herself from the family."

God, he couldn't tell Cliff exactly what had happened. But maybe he could tell him some of it.

"I did too. I got a business degree so I could properly manage the legacy my grandmother left me." Sure, it was from a community college, but that didn't negate its value. "I am a responsible business owner. I don't ever cheat anyone, and if someone comes to me with stuff that should rightly be dealt with by the police, a psychiatrist, or a doctor, I don't fucking string anyone along with advice from the great beyond, for fuck's sake."

Cliff's eyes widened at his sudden vehemence, but Drew couldn't help it. He hated that Cliff or anyone thought he was nothing but a damn criminal. Cliff's mouth opened as though he was going to say something, but Drew was on a roll and wasn't interested in listening to Cliff denigrate him anymore.

"Most times, I'm almost a confidant. I guide them to making their own decisions, which is generally what they know is the right path; they just need a little nudge. Cold reading their nonverbal body language and cues usually tells me what they want to hear, and I give that to them. Sometimes people just need someone who'll listen to them while they talk themselves into doing what they know is right. A temporary sympathetic ear. Inexpensive comfort to people who need it. Or, as I said before, a bit of fun."

Maybe he considered himself a counselor of sorts. Not that he'd say that to Cliff, because he wasn't interested in arguing semantics. Not when this might be the most important debate of his life. Drew couldn't tell if he'd convinced Cliff, but at the very least Cliff was no longer furious.

"You've given me a lot to think about. And, well, I..." Cliff's voice trailed off as he looked almost constipated. "I like you, and I want to give you the benefit of the doubt."

A sarcastic reply welled up in Drew's throat, but that wasn't going to smooth the way any, so he swallowed it back down. "I appreciate that. I like you too." Kyle would be laughing his fucking ass off if he could hear Drew say *like* in such a laidback, nonchalant manner. Especially since his dick was feeling anything but nonchalant, even though Cliff had bad-mouthed his business.

The sentiment hung in the air for a few moments, poised to either crash and burn or maybe develop into something a little like friendship. Or more, if Drew had his way.

Then he saw it. An infinitesimal relaxation of Cliff's muscles. A smoothing of the crinkles near the corners of his eyes. Cliff deciding to let go of his animosity, at least where Drew was concerned. With some difficulty, Drew held in a whoop of victory and let his own tension bleed away. The nonsexual tension, at any rate.

CLIFF WASN'T SURE about Drew's explanation, not at all. While Drew had made some good points, Cliff couldn't help but feel the whole psychic business was on some shaky moral or ethical ground. But if Drew was telling the truth—and Cliff considered himself to be a fairly good lie detector—then Drew wasn't engaged in anything illegal, despite his family legacy.

Cliff was also quite proud of Drew for his good intentions and determination to be law-abiding, even if it wasn't always the easiest path.

Then again, his judgment might be influenced by all the naked skin and hint of ginger below the navel that was currently all he could focus on. He didn't think Drew had dropped the sheet on purpose to distract him, but his mouth watered for a chance to lick Drew's creamy skin from head to toe. The more Cliff's dick thickened, the more he wanted to believe Drew's words and the more he had to bunch the sheets over his groin to hide the fact that his briefs weren't really up to the job of containing a fierce, Drew-induced erection.

When the silence continued for several lengthy moments, Cliff dragged his gaze up to Drew's face. The man looked puzzled, and the sight of the purplish bruising and stitches softened Cliff's resolve even further. He wanted Drew, and despite his harsh words, he was willing to overlook just about anything to... He wanted to say he'd overlook anything just for a piece of Drew's sexy, sexy ass, but Cliff had never been much for one-night stands. Besides, those first few seconds Cliff had seen Drew in the grocery-store parking lot were enough for him to be thinking about getting to know Drew better in and out of bed.

The distance between them was too much to bear. Gripping the sheets in front of him, as though hiding his erection would hide his intentions, Cliff shifted from the futon to sit on Drew's bed. Those bright blue eyes widened at the sudden proximity, and unable to help himself, Cliff reached out a finger and stroked the side of Drew's face. Nearly invisible stubble rasped his finger as he trailed along Drew's jawline and down his neck. A vein beat in Drew's neck, showing Cliff the sudden increase in Drew's pulse, which matched Cliff's rise in heart rate. As much as he wanted to ravish Drew, rut against him like a mindless beast, he wanted caring, sweet sex. He wanted to kiss and suck and stroke and thrust. He wanted so much with Drew, but he had to keep some semblance of control and remember that Drew had been recently injured. Whatever he longed to do with Drew, the last thing he wanted was to hurt him.

Drew's lips parted slightly, as though he was going to say something, but Cliff took it as an invitation and gently pressed their lips together. Drew's lips firmed against his, kissing him back. A tiny knot of tension in his belly, one that had formed almost the moment he'd first seen Drew, dissolved at this very clear signal that Drew wanted this, wanted him.

Cliff cupped Drew's shoulder with his other hand and used his body mass to coax Drew back. Fortunately Drew went willingly, even going so far as to shift a little to center them on the bed. Cliff tucked his hips between Drew's splayed legs and deepened the kiss.

He had no idea how long they devoured each other's mouths, but at one point he needed to breathe. Panting, he stared down into Drew's darkened eyes. Drew's cheeks were flushed, his lips moist, and he was breathing just as heavily.

"Good morning." Drew grinned up at him.

"It's getting there." Cliff grinned back. He was hard and aching, but despite Drew's increasingly restless hip twisting, the sheets created too much of a barrier between them.

Cliff pushed himself up and yanked at the sheets. And yanked. The damn things had wound around both their legs, and most of Cliff's efforts only tightened them instead of getting him closer to Drew.

With a huff, he leaped off the bed, grabbed Drew's sheet, and tugged, flinging it to the floor.

Drew snorted, and then a laugh escaped. He snickered behind his hand, his amusement contagious. A quick glance confirmed that the sheet mishap hadn't adversely affected either of their erections.

In fact, staring down at Drew, Cliff felt his breath come fast and shallow, his amusement forgotten. Drew was slender, but his lean muscles were beautifully defined. A bright ray of sunlight illuminated flecks of gold in his fiery hair. The dark blue boxer briefs strained to hold Drew's cock, and Cliff bit his lower lip. He'd never been so indecisive in bed before, but he couldn't decide whether to strip them naked immediately or leap back on the bed and suck up a mark on Drew's neck before licking his way down to those boxer briefs and slowly revealing what lay beneath.

Regardless, Cliff's hips were still wrapped, mummy-like, in his own clinging sheet, and getting rid of it was the first step.

He wrenched the sheet off his hips and let it drop next to Drew's on the floor. Drew's gaze immediately went to Cliff's tiny briefs and the hard cock that was forcing its way past the waistband. There was no mistaking the heat in Drew's expression.

Fuck it. Cliff needed them naked now. Besides, his briefs certainly weren't doing much to contain him. Cliff hooked his thumbs in the waistband, and Drew propped himself up on his elbows, attention locked on Cliff's groin.

Slowly he pulled his briefs down, letting his cock spring free. The briefs slid down his legs to puddle on the floor. Someday he might try putting on a little strip show for Drew, but he was so fucking turned on by nothing more than kissing and a bare chest that he couldn't bear to extend this much longer.

He straddled Drew and stroked his hands over Drew's pale chest. Tiny, rosy nipples hardened under his palms, and he marveled at the contrast between his sun-darkened skin and Drew's vampiric paleness. He slid his hands lower, across Drew's belly, fingers playing with the reddish-blond treasure trail. Drew's cock jerked, brushing against Cliff's balls, the brief contact reminding Cliff that he was getting closer and closer to blowing his load. Exploring Drew's body in detail was going to have to wait until later, but he'd be damned if this all ended without him making Drew wild.

Shimmying his body down the bed, Cliff pulled Drew's boxer briefs down to his ankles.

With a groan, Cliff grabbed at the base of his cock to stave off his impending orgasm. Drew was fucking gorgeous. A ruddy pink cock rose from pubes that matched the hair on his head, and as soon as Cliff's urge to orgasm was under control, he bent over and licked the heated, salty skin of Drew's cock.

"Fuck." Drew's voice was little more than a whimper.

As Cliff had been longing to do from the first moment he'd laid eyes on this man, he opened his mouth and swallowed Drew's cock, burying his nose in Drew's red bush. There was a faint hint of soap from Drew's earlier shower, but it wasn't enough to obscure the musky scent of aroused male.

Drew shivered, and his hips twitched as though he was trying to suppress their movement. Cliff wanted Drew to fuck his mouth and come down his throat, but that wasn't all he wanted.

Again with the indecision. Fuck, suck, or rut? Fucking was out. No way was Cliff going to last long enough for either of them to glove up and slide into an ass. Drew's cock slid hot and heavy in his mouth, and Cliff could come just from blowing Drew, but he wanted to touch Drew some more. Make their first time more intimate, more special, than a blowjob like Drew could get in any gay club. He wanted to make sure Drew felt the same undeniable attraction as Cliff did.

Drew pulled gently on his hair, and Cliff lifted his head to find Drew staring down at him. A tiny smile lifted the corners of his mouth. Maybe, just maybe, Drew had been thinking along the same lines.

Willingly obedient to Drew's unspoken request, Cliff moved back up the bed and smiled down.

"You're so hot." Cliff's words weren't too romantic, but judging from Drew's blush, he didn't object.

"Not as hot as you," Drew whispered back, hands roaming freely over Cliff's back, making him shiver in delight. They'd both started to sweat, the window A/C unit not quite able to combat the scorching heat of them together.

Zeroing in on Drew's mouth, Cliff kissed him and relaxed against him, ankle to chest, although Cliff braced his arms on either side of Drew to keep from crushing him.

The press of all that naked skin together made Drew groan into Cliff's mouth, and Cliff fed the sound right back. He and Drew fit perfectly together, and another person had never felt so right.

A quick shift of Cliff's hips put their erections together, precum, saliva, and sweat providing more than adequate slick. The first thrust of his cock against Drew's had him poised on the brink again while Drew writhed in his arms. Their mouths were still locked together, and they breathed in tandem. Hips working frantically, Cliff hoped this was going to be enough to send Drew over, because his control stretched thinner and thinner every second.

Drew's fingers dug into Cliff's ass cheeks, and the sound of Drew's moans rose in pitch as they humped frantically against each other.

Fuck, fuck, fuck. Cliff wasn't going to last much longer. In a frantic bid to hold off for a few more precious seconds, he pulled out of the searing kiss, but Drew's feverish expression and kiss-swollen lips combined with the nonstop slide of Drew's hard cock against him was too much. He'd just have to get Drew off after. His balls tightened, and he dropped his face into Drew's neck, biting down where Drew's neck met shoulder.

Drew hollered his name as liquid warmth spilled between them. A mere second later, Cliff's muscles stiffened, and he exploded, cock jerking as he emptied his balls, the relief more than physical, knowing that he'd managed to bring Drew to orgasm before he succumbed.

He slid off Drew and wrapped an arm around him, tucking him close while they recovered. The earthy scent of their combined jizz hung in the air, sultry and seductive.

"Wow."

"Agreed." Because, yeah, sex with Drew was definitely *wow*. And just because he could, Cliff dropped a few kisses onto Drew's ear and neck. Although the thought was vaguely terrifying, Cliff could probably do this forever, a feeling he'd never had with another man, not even Brett, whom he'd thought he could maybe love.

"I guess I need another shower," Drew said.

"This time I'm going to help you."

Drew chuckled. "No argument here."

Drew twisted so they were facing each other on the narrow bed.

A smug smile found its way to Cliff's lips at the thoroughly sexed-out appearance of the gorgeous redhead in his arms. Cliff smoothed away the veil of hair that obscured part of Drew's face, and just as quickly, his smile disappeared as he focused again on the bruising and stitches. He'd forgotten, somehow, that Drew was injured.

"Are you in pain? Do you need some meds?" Worry for Drew and irritation at his lack of control pushed away the pleasant aftermath of orgasm.

Drew rolled his eyes and winced. "I'm just fine as long as I remember not to roll my eyes." He looked thoughtful for a moment. "And fucking. I think fucking might be out of the question for a few more days. I don't think the movement would be good."

Cliff groaned as his cock tried to make a valiant comeback,

despite the fact that they were talking about definitely *not* fucking until Drew had gotten better.

"I'm sorry." No matter what Drew said, Cliff shouldn't have taken advantage.

"You're apologizing for giving me an incredible orgasm? Are you insane? I'm hoping we'll do it again in the shower." Pink stained Drew's cheeks, and he glanced away. "Unless...I mean...maybe you don't want to. I'd understand if you didn't."

God. He'd practically humped Drew's leg while he'd been doped up on morphine and unconscious in the hospital. How was it Drew didn't know how much Cliff wanted him?

"Oh, I want you. Don't ever think I don't." Even if it maybe wasn't the wisest attraction he'd ever had, it was certainly the most consuming. He just hoped his career didn't get destroyed in the conflagration.

Drew still looked unsure, and Cliff kissed him again. "I only apologized because I'm afraid we did this too soon. You were just in the hospital yesterday, and I like to think I have some control over myself."

A shy little smile curved Drew's lips. "I like the fact that you couldn't control yourself."

Cliff needed a bit of recovery time before he could indulge again —a blowjob or handjob in the shower shouldn't be too strenuous for Drew to receive—but that didn't stop him from lightly stroking Drew's skin or enjoying Drew's tentative explorations in return. He couldn't ever remember touching someone like this just for the sheer enjoyment, without any immediate intention for it to lead to sex.

CHAPTER 12

Drew wanted to bask under Cliff's touch like a cat being stroked. This was so fucking surreal, and it was entirely possible that he was hallucinating the whole thing because, yes, he had a head injury.

Cliff Garcia was naked in his bed. Had told him he was hot. Kissed him like Drew's mouth was the only available source of oxygen. Sucked his cock, made him come, then came all over him. The jizz of his eight-year fantasy crush was currently drying on his stomach, and it was better than he'd ever imagined.

After delivering the kind of mind-melting orgasm Drew had only dreamed of, Cliff was still kissing him, touching him, and staring at him like Drew was everything he'd ever wanted. Surreptitiously, Drew passed a hand over his belly.

Yep. Jizz. If he weren't so blissed-out on endorphins, he'd consider squealing. Except that would make him look like a total dork. He'd rather keep that information under wraps as long as he could.

Tentatively, Drew reached out to do some touching of his own. Cliff was built but not bulky. Like Drew, Cliff wasn't too hairy, but what little he had was sleek and black. His pubes were carefully trimmed, and his balls were waxed. Drew had never bothered with too much manscaping; it was a lot of work when his prospects for sex were so few and far between. He'd have to find out if Cliff would prefer him to be a little less au naturel.

When Cliff had stripped off his briefs, Drew had thought he'd spontaneously combust. He wanted that cock. He wanted to make a replica of that cock so he'd have it even after Cliff got tired of him. Which he was bound to do. The stunning Cliff Garcia wasn't going to continue to hang out with a Drummond if he didn't have to.

Hell, the whole sex thing was probably in return for the favor of letting Cliff stay at his place. If that was the case, Drew was going to get as many orgasms as he could out of it and worry about the heartbreak later.

Because there wasn't much chance his heart was coming out of this intact. Not when he'd been half in love with the guy before they'd even spoken to each other. Now that Cliff was being sweet and concerned and could make Drew come until his vision blacked out...yeah, Drew was going to be a broken, devastated mess when Cliff got settled back in Sandy Bottom Bay and realized he could do so much better than slumming with a Drummond.

"Look, don't take this the wrong way, but why don't I remember you from school? Your brothers were in my face all the time, but I can't believe you never made it on my radar."

A half explanation should answer the question but without exposing just how pathetic he'd been in high school. How influential Cliff had been to his life.

"Uh. Well, I think I told you I used to be a lot blonder when I was young." Drew took a hand away from Cliff to wrap a hank of hair in his fist. "The red was one of many huge changes when I hit puberty. I also used to be a lot shorter."

"I guess the height thing happened after I left. You're taller than your brothers now, aren't you?"

Drew sighed. "Yep." His brothers had been pissed at the time, but Drew had been glad puberty had changed him enough that he'd become worse than useless at assisting Wyatt and Rob with whatever petty crimes they perpetrated. Puberty, high school, and Cliff Garcia had changed everything for Drew, who had been well on the way to following in the Drummonds' crooked footsteps.

Once upon a time, Drew had been small for his age, a strawberry-blond cutie with wide blue eyes, and perfect for his brothers to use as a decoy or distraction. Pretending to be lost or need help had more than once kept a mark from noticing either Wyatt or Rob picking their pockets, and Drew had been cute enough that no one had suspected him of complicity. He'd never quite been comfortable helping Wyatt and Rob, but he hadn't felt he had a choice. His brothers had their faults, but they'd stuck by him and protected him, and Drew felt he owed them.

"That still doesn't explain why I don't remember you." Cliff smiled and stroked his hand over Drew's shoulder before moving to trace prominent collarbones, the light touch giving Drew goose bumps.

How much to tell? They'd had sex. Once. There wasn't any indication that they'd date or have a relationship. If he admitted to his crush, would Cliff laugh it off as the folly of youth, or would he recognize the continued yearning in Drew, see him as needy and pathetic?

"Do you remember everyone in high school, especially the freshmen, when you were a senior?" Drew hedged. Drew had been a nobody, and Cliff had been one of the chosen ones.

Cliff wrinkled his nose. "No, I guess not."

The gift—or curse—puberty had brought was the suspicion he wasn't like the other boys in his class. At fourteen, other guys were starting to notice girls. At first, Drew had been able to convince himself that his indifference to girls and his desire to spend time with his friends was simply a matter of him being a late bloomer.

Until the day he'd attended his brothers' soccer practice after school, ostensibly to watch the cheerleaders practice.

Cliff Garcia had owned the soccer field that day, making the rest of the team look like bumbling idiots. Sandy Bottom Bay wasn't a bastion of sports prowess, so it wasn't exactly a challenge, but Cliff had been far beyond the other players, including Wyatt and Rob. Without even trying, Cliff had owned Drew's heart. He'd fallen head over heels into his first puppy love, and it was with a guy. Cliff at eighteen had looked like he could have played professionally for Spain, and he'd starred in every one of Drew's wet dreams and waking fantasies.

His brothers had hated Cliff with a passion and not only because he showed them up on the soccer field. Nope. Cliff was a good guy.

"You were pretty good at protecting us from bullies."

Cliff looked a little embarrassed. "I've always hated bullies. Maybe because if I'd been outed in high school, I'd have been just as big a target."

Drew suppressed a snort. Cliff could have probably come to school in a French maid outfit and still been the school's golden boy, but he appreciated that his fear made Cliff the champion of those less socially successful.

"But," Cliff continued, "I think I would have remembered protecting you, even if you were shorter and had, what, strawberry-blond hair?"

"Yeah, it wasn't me; it was Kyle." Drew hadn't needed Cliff's protection, because Wyatt and Rob had done a…well, he hesitated to say a good job of protecting him. It was rare that anyone had bullied Drew a second time, that was for sure, but his brothers' methods had tended to be a little more crude than Cliff's. Drew's fate had been sealed when Cliff protected Drew's best friend. The puppy love had strengthened and taken root in his heart. From that day on, Drew had done his best to be in a position to observe Cliff from afar the rest of the school year.

Drew had a front-row seat to the phenomenon that was Cliff and watched when he intervened on behalf of other kids. He stood up for what was right, he told the truth, he narced on kids—often Wyatt and Rob—who stole, he practically had a shiny gold halo over his head, and according to the teachers, Cliff Garcia could do no wrong. It probably didn't hurt that the entire town thought the Drummonds were troublemakers, and any nemesis of theirs was automatically going to be a golden child.

By all rights, Cliff should have been anathema to Drew, every bit as much as he was to Wyatt and Rob, but Cliff could do no wrong in Drew's eyes. Kyle had quickly picked up on Drew's preoccupation, and it wasn't long before Drew confessed to being gay. Kyle hadn't cared and had helped him hide both his orientation and infatuation.

Drew's crush had made him reevaluate his participation in his brothers' schemes. They were more forgiving of his refusal to help once his growth spurt hit and his hair color changed in sophomore year. He'd become too distinctive, too clumsy, and not nearly sweetly innocent enough to assist them.

Doing good deeds and being a nice person had begun originally as a way to ape the boy who never noticed Drew existed. It wasn't long before being a good person had made Drew feel better about himself, and even when Cliff moved away to attend college, Drew had continued being the oddball in his family. His grandmother had noticed, and they'd grown closer from that point on.

Once his brothers had figured out he was gay, he'd been not only useless for their petty theft but in dire need of more protection.

Cliff moved in closer, eyes darkening, touches becoming firmer and with more intention behind them.

"Yeah, there's no way I could have forgotten you." Cliff punctuated each word with a kiss to his throat, and a frisson of desire woke up his satiated cock.

Cliff's cock had already recovered, nudging Drew's hip and leaving tiny wet marks on his skin.

An alarm went off, but it wasn't Drew's.

"What is that?" Drew looked around, annoyed at the interruption.

"Fuck." Cliff craned his neck to see Drew's clock. "I gotta get going. Shit."

Drew fell back against the pillow. Shit indeed.

With a little eyebrow wiggle, Cliff gave him a kiss. "Maybe we can pick this up later? If I can get a long enough break?"

Like he was going to say no to another orgasm with Cliff Garcia. Not a fucking chance. "Sure thing."

"As much as I'd love to shower with you, I'd rather be able to take my time."

"Go on, shower. I'll shower after."

Cliff frowned suddenly. "I don't know if I'm comfortable with you showering while no one is here. Not for the next couple of days anyway. What if you get dizzy or something?"

Drew almost rolled his eyes again but remembered just in time not to. "I showered while you were sleeping."

"Not the same thing at all."

Stern Cliff made Drew shiver. How long was he going to have to wait until Cliff's break? Too long, that was for sure.

"Fine. I'll just wipe down." Thank God he'd taken a shower earlier, because he'd felt so grimy before, he would have been too self-conscious to have sex.

Cliff gave him an assessing look, as though trying to determine if he was telling the truth.

"I promise. No showering without you." Drew's voice lowered before he'd even realized how suggestive those words could be, and it brought back that hot look in Cliff's eyes.

"Good."

Drew listened to the shower, imagining Cliff all soapy and wet. He languidly stroked his cock, but he'd spent way too much time with his right hand over the years, fantasizing about Cliff. The next few orgasms, at least, he wanted to occur because Cliff was touching him, kissing him, fucking him.

He was going to have to open the reading room for a bit today to keep himself occupied. Otherwise the only thing he'd be able to think about would be Cliff's gorgeous naked body.

Cliff returned to the bedroom, skin still damp, and flashed him a quick smile before dressing all too quickly. The uniform, though, was fucking hot.

"You make sure you rest today, and call if you need anything, okay?"

Drew nodded. Fortunately, doing readings wasn't that stressful and didn't require any physical exertion. He wasn't lying if he said he was resting. Not really. Especially if he had a nap first. Drew fell back against the pillows, letting the unfamiliar sound of someone else puttering around his house lull him back to sleep.

⁓

ORGASMS FLOODED the system with endorphins, right? After a spectacular and unexpected orgasm with Cliff—mmm, no, *North*—he napped for a long time.

The nap and the orgasm left him feeling good enough that he could go back to work. It wouldn't quite be the intense level of Haunt Fest, and it would let him get back on his feet. He'd had lots of experience doing readings, but the past couple of days had been so unusual that it almost felt like he'd been away from his normal life for weeks.

Nevertheless, his energy levels weren't nearly as good as he'd hoped. Still, he wasn't complaining about expending maybe more energy than he should have in bed earlier. He didn't think he'd ever complain about that. The faint ache in his head reminded him he probably should be resting, but he'd never had a proper vacation, and lounging about before his busiest week was only going to stress him out.

His turban rode low over his eyes, creating a distracting shadow, but he didn't have a choice. If he put the turban where he normally did, the bandage was visible. It was bad enough that he'd had to cake on makeup to hide the bruising in his eyelids. Sadly, he had the supplies on hand. He'd met the wrong end of his brothers' elbows and fists more than once, all accidental or when he'd stupidly tried to break up fights. Rob and Wyatt were much more rough and tumble, even now, than he'd ever been.

He took a quick peek around, checking his stock of candles, incense, and herbs. He had a bunch of extras stored in his pantry. After all, who needed or could afford food? At least he was prepared for Haunt Fest.

As he unlocked the door, he pulled down the sign Kyle had posted informing his customers of his temporary closure. But when he tore it away, it wasn't clear glass left behind. There was another piece of paper stuck to the outside of his door.

Why would Kyle stick two signs on his door?

Drew pulled the door open, and his ears heated as anger gripped him. With a snarl, he ripped down a poster encouraging people to visit Eddie Price, medium extraordinaire. Bastard extraordinaire, more like. He was always trying to steal Drew's business, even though there was enough for both of them, and if his brothers ever found out, Eddie would be in trouble.

Swearing under his breath, Drew tore the poster into shreds and dumped it into the garbage can under the cash register.

The sudden rush of anger left him a bit light-headed, and he rested a hand on the edge of the counter to steady himself.

Through the window, he saw a plump woman in her sixties pause on the sidewalk, tilting her head as she stared up at the sign over Drew's door. Keeping his movements smooth and small, Drew backed out of the room, closing the velvet draperies behind him. He much preferred to make an entrance with new clients, if he could, rather than waiting to ambush them the second they walked in the door. It meant he couldn't keep as many of his new products in the front room as he'd like, but at least the fake security camera his brothers had installed kept too many things from walking away in tourists' pockets, and his brothers' reputation kept locals from stealing from him.

Drew counted to thirty after the tinkle of the bell signaling the client's arrival before he swept through the curtains with what he hoped was a mystical flourish.

"Good afternoon," he greeted the newcomer, a tourist as far as he could tell.

The woman, who'd been poking about his selection of wares, turned to face him. Although no frown was visible, Drew sensed the woman's disapproval. Her oddly uncreased forehead and substantial makeup application spoke of a never-ending battle against the ravages of time.

"You're Malachi?" There was no mistaking the disdain in her voice.

With effort, Drew kept a placid look on his face, the one he wore when he didn't dare roll his eyes. This wasn't the first time someone had asked the question and wouldn't be the last, because he did look younger than his twenty-two years. But seriously, shouldn't the outfit give it away?

"Yes, I am. Malachi the Mystic."

Her frown deepened. "You're awfully young, aren't you? My son is older than you."

Drew filed the tiny bit of personal information away. He didn't know who her son was, but anything could be of value during a reading. The Botox paralysis was going to make this reading extra difficult, since so much of his "talent" relied on expressions combined with comments or questions that unwittingly provided information. Not the best choice for his first dip back in the work pool, but with any luck, she was just a snowbird passing through and wasn't accustomed to the whole tarot-reading thing.

He smiled widely. "Well, now, there's no age of majority on psychic powers, ma'am. My granny had the second sight, and not only did I inherit the gift from her, but she trained me to use it before she passed on, God rest her soul."

His potential client weighed that information for a moment, and Drew waited for her to make up her mind. He narrowed his eyes a bit so she wouldn't notice his perusal, but he had to take this time to assess the woman because if she did decide to get a reading, he'd be hobbled by her lack of expression.

Her clothes and shoes were good quality, but not upper-crust designers. Her handbag was a Louis Vuitton, with very little wear, which Drew took to mean she'd bought it recently. Out of necessity, he'd become expert at recognizing designer handbags because he found he could discern bits about a woman's personality from her purse, but he'd not had the time, energy, or inclination to recognize specific designers of clothes or shoes.

Between the purse and the Botox, he surmised she was probably well off but not crazy rich. Maybe had a winter home in Florida to escape the cold of the north. It was probably time for her to lighten her dye job from raven black to something a little less harsh, a little less obviously unnatural. The gem on her ring finger was large, sparkly, and ostentatious, much newer and less scuffed than the simple wedding band that lay beneath. Married, for a long time to the same man, who hadn't always been well off. And more than likely just a little sentimental. Good. Sentimental he could work with.

If he could figure out if she was trying to stave off the years due to simple vanity or in an attempt to corral a wandering husband, well, that would make his job easier. But there would be time for that during the reading. Wouldn't be the first time he'd dealt with a client wondering about an unfaithful spouse.

While he made his quick assessment, she had apparently been assessing him right back. Her distrustfulness disappeared, and she smiled back, although without any discernible creasing on her forehead.

"Did you want a reading? I can sense you've got something weighing on your mind." Drew was careful to modulate his voice, lowering his tone and speaking slower than normal. He'd always found the lower tones soothed wary clients, and he almost laughed when he realized Cliff had done the same thing to him in the hospital.

Her blue eyes widened. "I do. Please, I'd like a reading. I'm Mrs. Gillespie."

"Mrs. Gillespie, it is my pleasure to make your acquaintance."

Mrs. Gillespie nodded and Drew ushered her into the reading room.

With aplomb, Drew took the deck she'd shuffled and cut, then laid out ten cards in a Celtic pattern. Generally he preferred the three lines, but the Celtic layout was usually a hit with the tourists. He asked and commented and probed in the subtle way he did every time, along with his introductory patter for brand-new clients.

The damn death card showed up, and his client couldn't quite take her eyes off it. He really needed to take it out of the deck.

Before he'd even finished discussing the first card and what it meant, he discovered that Mrs. Gillespie was wondering about her husband's fidelity and also about her son's sexuality. Drew would at least do his best to make sure Mrs. Gillespie's son didn't lose his family, if he was indeed gay, as his client suspected.

Next he tapped the death card, preparing to reassure her it didn't mean what most people thought it meant, when a flash of pain flared in his head. Mrs. Gillespie and the cards faded away while what looked like a movie clip played in front of his eyes. A large silver car, with Connecticut plates, driving on a busy highway lined with Floridian vegetation suddenly swerved into oncoming traffic, right in the path of an oncoming eighteen-wheeler. The subsequent crash, car parts flying, tractor-trailer jackknifing, cars piling up on either side as they were unable to avoid the sudden collision, was terrifying despite the silence.

"Malachi?" Mrs. Gillespie tapped his hand. "Are you okay?"

Drew blinked at her. And blinked. What the fuck was that? But his client appeared worried, and worrying clients wasn't part of Drew's business plan. He shook himself.

"Sorry, Mrs. Gillespie." If it hadn't been the death card he'd stumbled over, he wouldn't have bothered with any explanations, but he felt he owed it to her to ease her mind. He slipped his turban up. "I had an accident, and a side-effect is sudden headaches."

In a blink, Mrs. Gillespie's demeanor changed to a mother hen, just like Kyle's. "Oh, you poor boy. You shouldn't be working at all with that. Have you seen a doctor about it? My husband is picking me up soon. We could take you to a clinic or a hospital."

Drew smiled faintly even though he wasn't interested in seeing the inside of another hospital anytime soon. "I'm fine, Mrs. Gillespie. I was treated at the hospital. Just some side-effects that will go away soon. Don't worry about me."

With only a slight hitch, because he couldn't quite shake that weird vignette that had appeared so clearly, Drew continued on with his reading, giving as much comfort and guidance as he could. It sounded like Mr. Gillespie was a homophobic, cheating bastard. Mrs. Gillespie and her son were going to need to be strong.

At the end of the reading, Mrs. Gillespie was smiling, and despite his increased fatigue, Drew was able to swipe her credit card without a cringe. Accepting credit cards allowed him to bring in more business, since people carried less cash all the time, but if his brothers were more tech-savvy, he might have continued with grandma's cash-only policy. Between the credit cards and the personal information he gleaned over the course of a reading, he could easily delve into a spot of identity theft, as Cliff had suspected earlier.

If his brothers knew of the possibilities, they'd be harassing Drew on a daily basis, never mind that identity theft would put them in the same league as their cousins Jake, Nick, and Donnie, who were currently cooling their heels in a state penitentiary for the next ten to fifteen years. Or his dad, serving a sentence for manslaughter. So far, the only crimes his brothers had committed were misdemeanors, but something like identity theft? No way. Wyatt and Rob were mostly good brothers, but Drew didn't have any illusions—they weren't quite bright enough to hide their tracks for something that significant anyway.

Drew was also incredibly thankful he didn't have any misdemeanors or felonies he had to try and hide from the suspicious and observant Northcliff Garcia. Especially after the incredible morning of sex. He wasn't sure if they were heading to something relationship-like, no matter how much Drew wanted that, but if he was involved in criminal activity, Cliff would drop him like a hot potato. No doubt about it.

"You take care of yourself, dear."

"I will. Thank you, Mrs. Gillespie."

Mrs. Gillespie left, accompanied by the tinkle of the bell over his door. Drew entered the payment into his database and glanced up just as Mrs. Gillespie got into a large silver car...exactly like the one he'd seen in his weird hallucination. His breath escaped in a whoosh as a chill swept him from head to toe.

What the hell was going on?

Despite the low-level pounding in his temples, Drew ran outside, but the car turned off the main road before he could see if the plates were from Connecticut or not.

The pounding accelerated from a minor thrum to a full-fledged steel band. With a shaking hand, he grabbed a nearby light standard.

"Drew, are you all right?"

He glanced up to see Lisa Watson rushing toward him.

"Oh, hey, Lisa. Yeah, I'm fine. Are you here for a reading?"

Lisa had gone to school with him and Kyle and was assistant manager of the big bakery at the end of Main Street.

She snorted and wrapped an arm around his waist, then helped him to the front door. "I know it's my normal day, but shit, Drew, you've got a concussion and stitches. You shouldn't be working. You probably shouldn't be outside at all in this heat."

"I'm fine. Just a bit woozy." Woozy. That was all it was. His imagination and an aftereffect of getting clobbered by his brother.

"Right. You're whiter than the meringues I've got in here for the recovering victim." Lisa lifted up one of the teal boxes that were a hallmark of Mysteriously Good Confections.

"Meringues? I think I love you." Although he didn't much enjoy being called a victim.

Lisa laughed. "If you were straight, that might set my heart aflutter. C'mon, let's get you inside."

As soon as they were in, Lisa flipped his sign to CLOSED and locked up. Drew would have to remember to check his door later, in case Eddie got any more bright ideas about putting up signs.

Drew sat down in one of the front-room chairs, and Lisa set down the box. She pulled a bottle of water out of her purse.

"Here, drink this."

Grateful, Drew chugged down the water. He didn't know what had gotten into him, but if it happened again, he'd have to consider sucking it up and going to the doctor for a follow-up appointment.

Lisa chatted about business at the bakery, now that they were out of wedding-cake season and heading into Haunt Fest and Halloween territory. Drew only listened with half an ear, since they both knew it was just to fill the time until he was feeling better.

After a few minutes of him telling himself the hallucination was nothing, Drew's breathing evened out.

"You sure you don't want a reading? I feel okay now."

"I don't know, Drew. You really should be resting."

Drew rolled his eyes, suppressing the stab of pain the movement caused. "How much effort do you suppose it is, with me sitting there and dealing cards? On the house, since you saved me and brought me goodies. You might as well. I'm wearing the turban and all."

"True enough. But if you feel woozy again, you stop right away, you hear me?"

With a mock salute, Drew got to his feet and led the way into the reading room. He waved at Lisa to seat herself. She made herself comfortable in the chair while Drew got the room set up. He relit the incense, and oddly, the scent made his stomach flip. The odor hadn't bothered him with Mrs. Gillespie's reading.

"Do you mind if we don't have the incense?" Not very Malachi-like, but neither would be heaving his guts all over a client, even if it was a friend he'd known for years.

"Of course not." Lisa had an air of anxiousness or perhaps eagerness.

Drew did his best to ask what was up. Clearly Lisa had something she wanted to ask the cards, and Drew couldn't just ask outright as though they were chatting over a cup of coffee. That wasn't the way the readings worked.

After sitting heavily down in his chair, Drew prepped the cards. Lisa had done enough readings with him to do her part without any prompting, for which Drew was incredibly grateful. He was already getting tired.

Once he finally slipped into his regular patter and started focusing on the clues Lisa was broadcasting, he nearly broke out into a huge grin. Lisa thought her longtime boyfriend was finally going to pop the question at a special date that evening. Drew would never commit to an outright yes or no, because he couldn't see the future. And he didn't want to think about Cliff's objections to his job.

However, Cliff's words made Drew's reading even more circumspect. Besides, he didn't really want to get Lisa's hopes up, even though he was pretty sure Mateo knew he had a good thing with Lisa and wasn't going to let her go. Drew gave her a few oblique warnings about Mateo's family, because Drew didn't envy Lisa her prospective mother-in-law. Not one bit.

He then came to the ten of pentacles, which usually indicated financial reversal. Considering he didn't know details about Lisa's finances, it could be either good or bad, and he didn't want to freak her out. He touched the card, and unlike last time, he had no trouble recognizing the image that flashed through his mind—Mysteriously Good Confections, engulfed in flames.

Gasping, Drew shoved back from the table.

"Drew? Are you okay?"

Drew stared at Lisa, his heart racing, as he simultaneously tried to calm himself down and not alarm Lisa. The vision or hallucination or whatever it was had been far too realistic. Like the car one with Mrs. Gillespie.

What on earth had rattled loose in his brain to produce such macabre images?

"Yes. Yes, I'm fine." Or he would be once his brain stopped playing tricks on him.

Lisa crouched in front of him, her expression concerned. "Maybe you ought to close up for the day. You don't want to overdo it. Is that scrumptious police officer about?"

The unexpected question overshadowed the uneasiness his hallucination had brought on. "What do you mean?"

"You know this town. Everyone knows he's staying here. You sure work fast." Lisa winked at him.

Drew's cheeks heated. He wasn't about to admit to anything incriminating. Not until he figured out where he stood with Cliff and whether he wanted anyone to know about, well...everything. Drew wasn't even sure if Cliff was out to anyone else in Sandy Bottom Bay.

"It's not like that." Thank God his whole family were criminals. Certainly helped him lie easier, although his fair skin showed far more emotion than any Drummond wanted. "I'm giving him a place to crash, and he's looking out for me while I recuperate."

"Oh, sure, recuperate. You tell yourself that."

Lisa got ready to leave, and Drew hadn't figured out whether or not she knew who Cliff was. Presumably if the gossip had already gotten wind of Cliff staying here, then everyone must know his identity, but Drew couldn't ask. Not if he wanted to keep up the fiction that they were merely acquaintances helping each other out. His cheeks flamed hotter as he remembered how Wyatt had found them the previous day, both in their skivvies. At least he knew Wyatt wouldn't be in a hurry to share that information, which would keep them safe from confirming anyone's suspicions.

"Seriously, though, did you want me to call someone before I leave? Kyle or your new police protector?" Lisa peered at him again.

"I'll be fine. You go primp for your date tonight."

The reminder of the possibility of Mateo's proposal was all it took to distract her.

"I do have a lot to do." She kissed his cheek and pulled out her wallet.

"No charge today." Between the meringues, caring for him before the reading, and the weirdness of picturing her place of employment burning down, Drew didn't feel he deserved payment.

"Are you sure?"

"On the house, Lisa, as a thank-you. Don't you have a manicure to get to?"

Lisa's eyes widened. "Oh holy fuck, I really need to get a manicure, don't I?"

Drew barely held in his laughter as she raced out.

There were no appointments on his books for today, and he hoped that there wouldn't be too many walk-ins. He couldn't afford to turn business away, but he was too tired and too fucking weirded-out to concentrate.

CHAPTER 13

Cliff parked the car in the alley behind Drew's house and grabbed the grocery bags from the passenger seat. Scott had let him escape for an extended break before they had to pick up that asshole Brett and spend most of the evening watching him and his minions film fake ghosts and pseudoparanormal phenomena.

Of course, Scott didn't know, but Cliff had every intention of making sure Drew rested...after Cliff thoroughly tired him out.

Remembering the incredible morning was enough to send blood to his groin. He bit his lip. There was no way he should assume Drew would be up to another round. In fact, he'd been amazed Drew had been feeling well enough to have sex that morning. Hell, he'd be happy just to make Drew eat something more than peanut butter, then curl up around him and cuddle. Maybe just some lazy kisses. After all, he wasn't a ravening beast.

Drew was a cuddler, and Cliff had been pleasantly surprised by how much he enjoyed it. His previous boyfriends would primarily touch him as a prelude to sex, but there was a comfort in touching just for the sheer joy of touching, without any underlying goal. Cliff had a new goal. Cuddle with Drew as much as possible. Despite his misgivings about Drew's occupation, he had to admit he might have

overreacted. Between his mother's near obsession with the paranormal and his years-long altercations with the evil Drummond
twins, he might not have been thinking objectively. He'd mostly
steered clear of psychics and card readers and mediums and the like,
but he'd never reacted so strongly, as evidenced by his relationship
with the pseudo ghost hunter, Brett. Which only told him that he was
far more invested in Drew and who he thought Drew could become
to him, if he could make peace with Drew's profession.

Cliff let himself into Drew's place. Each time he touched the new
key on his ring, he tried not to let himself read more into it than was
intended, but this was the first time he'd had a lover give him a key. It
meant nothing, but he wanted it to mean something.

With a shake of his head, he focused on putting away the
groceries. He could cook, sort of, but with Drew's lack of supplies and
his own attempts to get settled, frozen was going to have to do.

"Drew? Are you awake?"

Obviously Drew wasn't in the kitchen, and it only took a minute
to determine he wasn't in the bedroom or bathroom. Apprehension
fluttered in Cliff's gut.

"Drew?" Stupid to call out for him when he wasn't here. Where
the hell had he gone? Despite their earlier athletics, the man was
injured and should be recovering. What if Drew had left and
collapsed or had some sort of complication?

Muffled yelling reached Cliff's ears, with the tone of an argument.
His hand went to the weapon at his hip, but after another second, he
could discern that the yelling seemed to be coming from the front of
the house and didn't have the tone that made him think there was a
real emergency.

He opened the only other door and waded through black velvet
draperies accented with embroidered symbols, presumably mystic
ones.

The scent of incense was heavy in the air, familiar in a way and
strangely pleasant. He'd want to take a better look at the room later,
but he continued through to another set of draperies and into the
store front/waiting room.

Two people were outside on the path from the street, waving arms and yelling at each other. He couldn't identify either of them, not from this angle.

"Okay, okay, what's going on here?" Cliff deepened his voice a bit and widened his stance slightly, hoping he wasn't going to have to break up yet another fight before finding Drew.

The verbal combatants turned to look at him midsentence, and Cliff lost his breath like one of them had sucker-punched him.

Eddie Price faded from his field of view as he took in Drew's appearance as Malachi.

His gorgeous hair was covered by a satiny blue-and-gold turban, which was a shame, but his bright blue eyes were ringed in dark eyeliner and, judging by the lack of evident bruising, some sort of industrial cover-up as well. Drew's eyes were possibly the sexiest things he'd ever seen, until his gaze traveled lower, to the huge expanse of pale, bare chest framed by dark blue satin. The contrast was stunning and mouthwatering, and Cliff's cock filled immediately.

He wanted to drop to his knees and worship at the cock of this mysterious, sexy man. Judging by the flick of Drew's tongue across his lips and the sudden dilation of his blue eyes, Cliff wasn't going to have any difficulty convincing Drew to go along with the plan.

First, though, he needed to get rid of Eddie without drawing attention to the tent in his uniform pants.

"Eddie Price. Becoming the town nuisance in the years I've been away?" Perhaps Cliff could have been more diplomatic, but he wanted—no, he needed—Eddie gone as soon as possible. Quicker than that, even.

Eddie glared at him, clearly not a fan of Cliff's choice of words.

"I was just trying to help, Cliffy."

Cliff lifted his lip, almost snarling. Eddie must have heard Brett's irritating pet name. "Eddie, I think you need to be moving along now."

"I haven't done anything wrong."

"Not true." Drew glared at Eddie, the sultry look vanishing. Yet another reason to get Eddie the fuck away from here. "He's been trying to steal my business. Puts up signs on my door."

No matter what Cliff might have thought about Drew's choice of profession, the surge of anger he felt on Drew's behalf wasn't exactly surprising. He wanted to punch Eddie's too-good-looking face. He didn't want Eddie sniffing around Drew for any reason, either trying to get in his bed or trying to interfere with his livelihood.

However, Cliff managed to keep those caveman instincts under control and merely lifted an eyebrow. "That'll stop, won't it, Eddie." It wasn't a question, and Eddie was smart enough to know it.

Eddie glared at him.

"Eddie?" Cliff's tone didn't allow for any argument.

"Fine, Cliffy."

"Officer Garcia," Cliff said through clenched teeth.

Eddie's lips twisted, but that didn't change the fact that he was still a good-looking man. Cliff didn't want Eddie anywhere near Drew.

"I'm leaving... Officer Garcia."

Cliff crossed his arms and waited. Eddie turned on his heel and walked away. As soon as he was out of sight, Cliff turned back to Drew.

"Are you okay?"

"Better now that you're here." Drew smiled at him.

God. Those eyes. A shiver ran down Cliff's spine, and his cock throbbed in reverence. He cleared his throat. "You are gorgeous."

"Yeah? You're extra hot in that uniform. Want to come inside with me? I can put the CLOSED sign up." The playfully cajoling tone was at odds with Drew's appearance.

"Lead the way."

Drew grinned at him and did as he said.

Cliff locked the front door behind him and followed Drew through the first set of draperies, into his reading room. There were no sounds aside from the asthmatic whir of ancient A/C units. A deep breath, and all of a sudden he realized why the scent had been familiar on his way through. It lingered in Drew's hair like an exotic spice and flavored the taste of his skin.

No wonder he'd liked the way the room smelled. It was also pleasantly cool and dim, like the interior of a movie theatre in the middle of the day. Perfect for what he intended.

He snagged Drew's shoulder before Drew was able to open the next set of draperies.

"What's wrong?"

Cliff just smiled in response and crowded Drew up against the wall. He had to look up slightly, since Drew was taller, and with a smile, swept the turban off Drew's head. At least with a bandage covering the stitches and makeup covering the bruises, Cliff found it easier to suppress the spurt of anger at the evil twins in favor of getting Drew naked.

Drew's red hair, pale skin, and smoky-lined blue eyes were such a stunning combination. After living in Los Angeles, filled with pretty men, Cliff shouldn't be so mesmerized by one man who, on paper, would be the last man he'd want to get involved with.

Wide eyes blinked at him as though confused by Cliff's sudden move, but since there wasn't a sign of pain or fear, Cliff dived right in and pressed their lips together.

Drew gasped into his mouth before returning the kiss with equal fervor, his whole body opening and welcoming Cliff in his arms.

That openness, that trust, was something Cliff had never known he'd wanted, because he'd never been with anyone who'd accepted him so thoroughly, and if he lost this, he would forever be comparing men who came after to Drew.

God, he was an idiot. They'd just met. He didn't even know if Drew topped, bottomed, both, or neither, and he was already lost. Infatuated.

At least it seemed like Drew was in the same boat. And there was no room for misgivings in the wet heat of Drew's mouth, the frantic press of cock to cock.

Cliff moved his hands from Drew's cheeks down to his shoulders, the slippery fabric under his fingers reminding him of what Drew wore. He pulled away, gratified to note Drew's blown pupils and his dismay at the end of the kiss. But the second Cliff had seen Drew, he'd had more in mind than simply checking in on him. Scott would have to understand if he got back from his break late.

"Should we go into the bedroom?"

Cliff didn't bother replying. He didn't want to wait, didn't want to leave. He wanted to have Drew right here in this cool, dim room that smelled spicy and warm, like Drew. He tucked his hands under Drew's robe and pressed them flat against Drew's smooth chest. Drew's breath hitched as his nipples hardened against Cliff's fingers.

How the fuck Drew didn't get jumped every fucking reading he did, Cliff had no idea. He slid his hands up and out, watching the dark blue satin slither from Drew's shoulders to the floor, leaving him in nothing but a pair of stretchy black pants with a substantial bulge at the groin. Drew licked his lips and shifted his arms as though he wanted to cover himself, but Cliff didn't stop touching him long enough to give him the opportunity.

Sliding to his knees, Cliff hooked fingers in the waistband and pulled them down, letting them fall to the floor as well. He leaned in, the sight of that hard, rosy cock drawing his mouth like a compass to magnetic north.

Drew's hand on his forehead stopped him in his very single-minded approach.

"What's wrong?" Cliff glanced up.

"Your uniform. You're going to do that in your uniform?"

"Why not?"

"But...but..." Drew's lips fluttered as he tried to come up with a good reason. His cock, however, didn't have any misgivings and kept bumping Cliff's face, the musky scent making his mouth water. Then again, maybe Drew had a point.

Reluctantly Cliff took his hands off Drew and fumbled with his belt, opening his pants just enough to let his cock spring out so he didn't come in his pants. Because he was definitely going to come while he sucked Drew off. He was too close right now to even think about anything else.

"But...but..." Drew repeated, this time staring at Cliff's cock. A full-body shiver raced down Drew's long form.

Cliff licked the sleek bead of precum forming at the tip of Drew's prick, making Drew shiver again. The indecision left his eyes, and he curled his hands in the fabric of Cliff's uniform, pulling him forward.

"So fucking hot," Drew muttered.

It was impossible to smile while swallowing Drew's hard cock, but it seemed as though Drew had a bit of a uniform fetish, and Cliff was more than happy to indulge his new lover.

Before long, Drew bowed to the natural instincts of his body and thrust himself into Cliff's mouth. Drew wasn't big enough to make him choke—deep throating was something he'd never really gotten the hang of—but he was able to get the entirety of Drew's cock in his mouth, burying his nose in that bright red thatch, already halfway to falling in love.

Cliff held off as long as he could, but he couldn't neglect his own erection anymore. Taking himself in hand, he stroked in time to Drew's shallow thrusts, twisting his hand at the tip. There was still so much of Drew he wanted to explore, but with a mouthful of Drew's cock, he had no regrets about a quick and dirty blowjob.

"Cliff, I'm close." Drew's voice was breathless, a sound that went straight to Cliff's cock, his balls pulling tight. They were going to hit the summit close together, and Cliff loved getting a mouthful of spunk while coming.

He used one hand to still Drew's hips, working Drew's cock with just tongue and suction while he frantically stroked his own cock.

Drew let out a few gasping moans before his cock pulsed in Cliff's mouth. Cliff swallowed, his body stiffening as the sensation and taste pushed him over the edge, and he blew his wad between his knees, vision going gray and hazy from the force of the orgasm.

Almost in reflex, Cliff gently sucked at Drew's still-hard dick until he could see clearly again.

Drew had slumped back against the wall, eyes half-closed, chest heaving in and out. Rosy patches colored his chest and neck, nearly making Cliff hard again. He'd never been with a guy who had such an obvious sex flush. There was going to be a lot of daytime fucking in their future, that was for damn sure. Cliff pulled back and licked his lips.

"That was seriously hot." Drew smiled down at him, previous unease at being naked and exposed apparently forgotten. A good orgasm would do that to a man.

"Yeah, you are." Cliff's lips twitched as Drew looked flustered.

"No, I meant..."

Cliff stood, a bit of a challenge with his dick hanging from his uniform pants and a hand covered in cum, and looked Drew directly in the eye.

"I know what you meant. And I agree, a hundred and ten percent. But I also meant what I said. Why do you think I jumped you right here? Because you are seriously fucking hot." Cliff deliberately repeated Drew's words, thrilled he could make Drew look so happy.

"Now, do you think you can give me a hand? I still have to pick up uniforms from the cleaners. This is my last clean pair of pants here."

Drew chuckled. He bent and grabbed his stretchy pants, then used them to wipe off Cliff's cock and hand before bundling them into a ball and dropping them on a nearby table.

"You're just lucky you didn't get jizz on my robes," Drew mock-scolded as he worked to tuck Cliff away in his pants, obviously realizing Cliff's hands might not be clean enough.

"Oh yeah? Why? Would you have spanked me for being a bad boy?"

Blood rushed to Drew's cheeks, and his hands trembled next to Cliff's cock. Oh, Drew had walked right into that one. Cliff kissed Drew's jaw.

"Maybe." Drew's reply was soft and hesitant, but Cliff heard the underlying desire, and he did a little trembling of his own. When Drew was better, Cliff was going to have a lot of fun with this man.

Moving back to Sandy Bottom Bay had some unexpected and very welcome perks.

CHAPTER 14

Holy shit. Drew's mind—and cock—were thoroughly blown. Northcliff Garcia, in full uniform, had stripped him down in his reading room and sucked him off. It was like a porn, but even naughtier because how the hell was he supposed to give readings from now on without blushing or throwing wood?

Not that he would have changed anything. Cliff in his uniform was almost as spectacular as Cliff completely naked. The orgasm had emptied Drew's balls and left his muscles as limp as wet noodles. In his already weakened state, and following the adrenaline-fueled argument with Eddie Price—asshole—Drew was just about ready to collapse, and the bed seemed so far away.

Which meant he was more than willing to let Cliff help him to the bedroom.

"Are you feeling okay? Maybe I shouldn't have jumped you like that." Cliff sounded so contrite as he helped Drew into bed.

Walking around his house completely naked seemed fairly decadent, since his business was attached to his home, and he sometimes had a hard time remembering it was his house and not his grandma's anymore.

"I'm feeling just fine." Wobbly, yes, but in no pain, and more relaxed than he'd been since...well, the last Cliff-induced orgasm.

There must have been something in his tone, because Cliff gave him a sharp look before grinning indulgently.

"Looks like you might get some rest after all. I'm going to finish putting the groceries away, and then I'll be back in a few hours to check on you. There's a lasagna in the freezer if you feel up to popping it in the oven."

Surreptitiously, Drew watched Cliff check out his reflection quickly in the mirror. Aside from a slight sheen of sweat, he didn't look like he'd just fulfilled one of Drew's porn fantasies in the middle of his shift. The jangle of Cliff's belt gave Drew a little thrill. The sound would forever remind him of Cliff unbuckling and pulling out his cock before giving Drew the blowjob of his life. One day he'd blow Cliff while he was in uniform, because that would fulfill yet another fantasy. He'd never imagined spanking before, but after Cliff had so teasingly mentioned it, Drew knew it would linger in his mind, whether or not Cliff had been serious. Drew wasn't sure if he wanted Cliff to have meant it or not, nor did he know if he wanted to be the spanker or the spankee or both.

"That's the best prescription ever—a blowjob every four to six hours." His dick might fall off from overuse, but it would be so, so worth it.

Cliff laughed. "I really can't make a habit of taking such long breaks. Scott will kill me."

A tiny bit of his contentment bled away. "Who is Scott?"

Leaning over the bed, Cliff kissed his nose like he was a kid, and Drew had woken up enough to wonder if he should resent the action.

"Scott Hunter. An old friend from school and my new, very straight, partner."

Oh. The tension left Drew's limbs again. Not that he had any right to be jealous. Even if he'd dreamed of being Cliff's boyfriend for a fucking long time, they hadn't even discussed if this was anything more than a convenient way to get off. There were times when Cliff looked at him and touched his face... The kisses that were tender and sweet… Those times led Drew to believe Cliff cared for him. But that didn't qualify as a relationship, and three days was hardly enough time to bring up the subject. Unless Drew wanted Cliff to run screaming the other way. He might not have had much experience with boyfriends, but getting too serious too soon was a recipe for disaster.

Smiling, Drew snuggled into his comforter as Cliff put the finishing touches on his appearance. Normally it was too hot most of the year for him to use more than a sheet, but with the new A/C unit, he was able to wrap himself in bedding, the comforter providing actual comfort in lieu of Cliff's arms around him.

His eyelids drooped, and the last thing he heard was the sound of his kitchen door closing.

~

DREW WOKE AND STRETCHED, the tepid sunlight of early evening streaming across his bed. He wiped at his eyes, his fingers coming away blackened, and he groaned. After Cliff had sucked his brains out through his dick and put him to bed like a good little boy, Drew had completely forgotten about washing the makeup off.

Listening carefully, he didn't hear anything that sounded like another person moving around in the house. He hadn't slept long enough to have missed Cliff's next break, and he didn't have the energy to get up. Without the endorphins making him sex-stupid, he remembered the readings he'd done earlier.

The readings themselves hadn't been unsettling, but the macabre visions that had accompanied them had been. Did he need to go back to the hospital? Were they true hallucinations, or were they just… nothing? Minor side-effects of getting his brain knocked about.

Even if he'd been thinking clearly when Cliff had shown up, he wasn't sure how Cliff would have reacted. Drew reached over to his bedside table and snagged his phone. Kyle had texted him a few times, wondering how he was doing.

I'm okay. Sore still. Come over for a bit?

Dunno. What about Officer Hottie? I don't want to be in the way if you're gonna put the moves on him.

Drew rolled his eyes. Kyle had a one-track mind, and Drew wasn't sure he was ready to admit that they'd already had sex. Twice. Not until he had a better grasp on what it all meant, if anything. Hell, even until he had a better sense of how Cliff would react if anyone knew they'd slept together.

Head injury, remember?

So? You can be the helpless waif. Let the big, strong cop help you into bed and shit.

Nope. He wasn't touching that. Kyle was a master at reading between the lines, and if Drew said anything in his own defense, Kyle was going to figure it out all on his own.

Never mind that. Cliff's at work. I need to talk to you.

Condom on Tab A, then into hole B. It's been so long for you, you may have forgotten how sex works.

A vein ticked in Drew's temple. He was almost grateful for the weird visions. At least he'd have solid ammunition to distract Kyle from nosy questions about his love life. Not that he could truly be angry with Kyle. They usually told each other everything, but this thing with Cliff felt different. More fragile, maybe. Or just more important. His lengthy crush didn't help, made him less objective about what was happening, and he was just going to have to figure it out for himself.

Bring pizza. Ignoring Kyle's digs was the only way to proceed, for now.

When?

Now. I'm starving. Which wasn't a lie. As soon as he typed *pizza*, his stomach started grumbling. He appreciated that Cliff had bought frozen lasagna, but he didn't have the energy or patience to deal with that.

Kyle signed off with a simple *okay.* He and Kyle had been friends long enough that he didn't have to tell Kyle what to get on the pizza. Getting pizza meant Drew had at least twenty minutes to heave himself out of bed, throw on some clothes, and wash the makeup off. All while resolutely not thinking about how much revenue he might have missed out on by being closed all this time. The exhaustion wasn't the only reason he was glad he wasn't giving any more readings tonight. He hoped Kyle could give him some peace, though, because he couldn't afford to be closed much longer, creepy hallucinations or not.

Twenty minutes, as it turned out, was enough time for Drew to sit in the kitchen and wait for Kyle, dressed, starving, and mostly feeling foolish. Perhaps he was sailing blithely along in ignorance, but he'd talked himself out of a panicked trip to the hospital. He'd convinced himself that the two creepy visions were nothing more than aberrations. If they happened again, well, then he'd reassess the issue. After all, it wasn't like he'd seen something or someone that wasn't there; it was more like a vision, or an image created by an overactive imagination. And while he certainly couldn't take TV as medical gospel, there had been an episode of *Bones* where Booth had spoken to two people and a cartoon that were complete figments of his imagination. The images that had flashed in Drew's mind weren't anything like that. Not true hallucinations, at least as he understood them.

Which meant he could chalk them up to exhaustion. And if that didn't completely assuage his fear, well, it was good enough for now.

Kyle let himself into the house and set the pizza on the table.

"Oh my God. I thought one of your brothers was bringing you an A/C unit. It's fucking sweltering in here."

Drew shrugged and glanced at the closed door to his bedroom. He had to admit, the cooler air in the bedroom didn't make his head ache, not like the muggy heat in his kitchen, but more electricity and fewer readings meant he'd be hoarding whatever groceries Cliff purchased while he was here, because Drew might not have enough money for groceries.

"I figured I'd keep the cool air in the bedroom." He wasn't about to admit he'd already sweated into his wound, and it was stinging like crazy.

Kyle glared and waved his hands around. "What? Why are you so stubborn? Your brothers are paying your electricity this month, at the very least. And your online store is going great. You should start seeing profits before the end of the year. Let some fucking cool air circulate!"

"Okay, one, I can only worry about money I've got right now, and right now I'm fucking broke. Two, since when are Rob and Wyatt paying for my electricity?"

"Since they put you in the fucking hospital, that's when."

"But they're paying the hospital bill, and they gave me the new air conditioner. Isn't that enough?"

Kyle's glare became a scowl as he marched to the bedroom door and flung it open. "No the fuck it is not. And I told them so."

It wasn't surprising that Kyle was sticking up for him, mother hen that he was, but it surprised Drew that he was taking such a hard stand against Drew's brothers. Drew opened his mouth to reply, and another scene flashed in his mind, from the Angry Parakeet. Unlike the two readings he'd done, this one he was pretty sure was a memory.

"Wait. Didn't you tell me you had the hots for my brothers? Both of them? How come you're not letting them off the hook?"

The glimmer of tears in Kyle's eyes shocked Drew. "I don't know how you can ask me that. So what if I think your brothers are good-looking? You've been my best friend for over ten years! The brother I never had."

Kyle's breath hitched, and he wrapped his arms around himself. "And for a minute or two in that bar, I thought Rob had killed you." His voice shook, and tears spilled.

Drew's eyes began to burn in sympathy, but Kyle scrubbed his hands over his eyes and got himself under control before Drew began to actually cry as well.

His voice stronger, Kyle continued. "Even now, you look like a poster child for domestic violence. No way are they getting off the hook for this. Not for a long fucking time."

Fortunately Drew had more than enough strength to stand up and wrap his best friend in a hug. Tears fell against his shirt, but he knew Kyle would be happier if Drew pretended there hadn't been any crying.

"Everything okay?"

Drew looked up at the unexpected words to see Cliff standing in the doorway, an inscrutable expression on his face.

"Hey, Cliff. Everything's fine."

Kyle coughed. "Fine. Yes. Be back in a minute." He slipped away to the bathroom without facing Cliff. Unlike Drew, Kyle could cry and still be gorgeous, but Drew knew it wasn't vanity that had Kyle hiding his tears. He didn't like to appear weak, ever, physically or emotionally.

"Come on in. Kyle was just having a little delayed reaction about my injury."

Although Drew knew Kyle wouldn't be happy he'd divulged that little tidbit, he wasn't about to give Cliff the impression that there was anything sexual or romantic going on between him and Kyle. Not when all those emotions were tied up, 100 percent, in Northcliff Garcia.

Fingers tentatively touching Drew's eyebrows and eyelids, Cliff scowled even darker than Kyle had. And Cliff looked a hell of a lot more intimidating than Kyle.

"Jeez, I think this looks even worse. I could fucking kill your brother for this." There didn't seem to be even a hint of humor in the statement. Drew didn't need both his best friend and his hoped-for boyfriend to hate his brothers. He knew why they were both upset with Rob and Wyatt, and they had reason, but Drew loved his brothers and didn't want to be running interference between everyone. Just the thought of it made him tense up.

"It's better than it looks. I swear." And it was. When Drew wasn't having sex, he had a low-grade headache, but based on how badly it had all bruised, if it hurt as bad as it looked, Drew would be back at the hospital begging for morphine.

"It didn't look nearly this bad this afternoon. Did I...did I hurt you more?"

Drew took a deep breath and reached out a hand to Cliff's chest, not to push him away but just to touch and soothe.

"I know you won't want to hear this, but I have a bunch of cover-up to go with my eye makeup. Not the first time I've got in the way of one of my brothers' brawls."

Oh, that did not make Cliff feel any better. His eyes flashed with anger, and he pulled back from Drew, fists clenched. Probably this wasn't the time to admit Drew had learned how to cover up the bruising when he was a kid, mostly because nobody wanted child services to come sniffing around. He got banged up because he stubbornly—maybe stupidly—tried to get in the middle of things, ever the peacemaker.

"That's it. I'm going to arrest him right now."

Panic seized Drew. "No. Don't."

"Don't? Are you insane?" Cliff's voice rose, and Drew darted a glance at the closed bathroom door. Last thing he needed was Kyle agreeing with Cliff.

"Listen to me. They never mean it."

"You know what that sounds like."

Drew stepped closer to Cliff and wrapped his long fingers around Cliff's fists, hoping his touch would be enough to get Cliff to unclench. "I know what it sounds like. But here's the thing—I've always hated when they fought. Hated it. I'd get in the middle, all the time. And usually get in the way of a fist not meant for me. My brothers have never hit me deliberately. Not once. I swear on everything that's holy. They don't beat me up. I just bruise easy and sometimes think I'm as big and strong as they are."

The flare of anger eased, just a bit. Drew had to press on. His brothers weren't as horrible as Cliff thought they were.

"Do you remember back in school, you used to stand up to bullies?"

"Yeah, and your brothers were the worst of them. Always seemed to go after much younger kids." Cliff's tone was hard, clipped.

"I'm not saying they were saints, because they weren't. But those younger kids? They were the ones who were bullying me and Kyle.

Rob and Wyatt didn't give a damn about giving younger kids a hard time just for sport. Only the ones who they thought were giving me and Kyle a hard time. And when they went after kids their own age? Well, they never really learned how to deal with frustrations in an appropriate way."

Drew would be forever thankful that his grandma, not his father, had been mostly responsible for his upbringing. His brothers hadn't been so lucky.

"Fuck, Drew." Cliff was completely exasperated, but the cold anger was gone. "You're not going to make me like them, you know. And dammit, I don't want to be grateful that they protected you."

"You don't have to like them." Although he'd be happier if Cliff did. "You just have to not arrest them because they pissed you off. Please, let it go."

Cliff nodded, took a deep breath and maneuvered them so he was holding Drew's hands.

"Did you get some sleep?"

"Yeah. A couple hours. I wasn't sure I'd see you again tonight."

Cliff's voice dropped. "I wanted to make sure you ate. I kinda left last time without making sure you did."

Drew's cheeks heated at the memory of just what Cliff had had in his mouth during his last break. Drew lifted the lid of the pizza box. "There's enough pizza for all three of us. You, uh, must be hungry too." Neither of them had had lunch when Cliff had been back at the house.

"Mmm. Yes. Starving." The growly sound of Cliff's voice left Drew in little doubt about what he was hungry for. "Too bad you've got company. Didn't we say something about a treatment every four to six hours?"

Drew gasped, and his cock, which he'd thought had been completely inert, plumped up at the teasing.

"Shh. Kyle will be out soon. Are you...do you want him to know?" Drew wasn't sure he did, no matter what Cliff said. Admitting to a brief fling would be devastating when he was already feeling physically fragile.

Cliff pressed his lips together and let Drew's hands go. "Perhaps you're right."

Right about what? Drew didn't know what conclusion Cliff had drawn, but he didn't think he liked it.

Kyle bounded out of the bathroom, and Drew realized he'd been in there a long time. Too long—he'd obviously been giving them time alone. Unfortunately, Kyle's well-meaning absence didn't have the result he was hoping for. And Drew couldn't even find out what Cliff was pissed off about now, not when he didn't know how much Cliff wanted the entire town to know. Hell, he couldn't even ask *that* in front of Kyle, in case the answer was "nothing." The town took too much interest in everyone's sex lives as it was; he didn't need them all to know about an extended one-night stand, if that's all Cliff saw it as.

"Are you joining us for dinner, Cliff?" Kyle's voice was syrupy sweet, and Drew was grateful he hadn't called Cliff Officer Hottie.

Cliff's nostrils flared, and he shifted his weight from one foot to another. Didn't take a psychic tarot reader to see his obvious indecision, and Drew suddenly realized that Kyle wasn't even supposed to be around this weekend. Guess they'd have to say his plans fell through, even though Kyle's plans were actually going better than anticipated, the sneaky asshole.

The radio clipped to Cliff's pocket crackled to life, calling him back to duty.

"No, thanks. I have to go. Multi-car pileup on the freeway. They're calling in all available officers."

"I'll see you later?" Drew couldn't help the plaintive tone that escaped. They needed to talk; Drew wouldn't be happy leaving things all weird and unsettled.

Cliff's expression softened, just a bit. "Don't wait up for me. I'll still have to head out to the *Phantoms* set after the crash is cleared up. I'll see you in the morning. Promise."

Drew gave him a little smile. At least Cliff wasn't running out on him. He'd have to be content with that, even though he might not be able to sleep a wink tonight.

"Be careful."

"Always." Drew managed to avoid giving Cliff a good-bye kiss, just barely.

Drew watched through the kitchen door as Cliff strode to his car in the alley, flipped on his lights, and sped away. With a little sigh, he turned back to Kyle.

"You two are totally doing it, and you didn't tell me!"

Shit.

Drew grabbed a slice of pizza and jammed half of it in his mouth to avoid confirming or denying Kyle's assumption. He wasn't sure he could believably lie to Kyle, and yet he didn't know how to respond.

Kyle copied him, chewing on a slice while he waited, staring intently.

"You can't tell anyone." Drew couldn't help looking around furtively even though there was less than zero chance of someone overhearing them in his little kitchen.

"I don't care about that, but surely you could have sent one little text that said 'we're doing it.' I thought we were friends!"

"It just...happened." Drew tried manfully to stop himself, but one more word popped out. "Twice."

"No fucking way. Are you just dying? How was it?"

Kyle's pitch was edging into painful territory.

"I can't... I don't feel right talking about it." Mostly because he didn't want to discuss how wonderful it was, only to have Cliff move out tomorrow because of...whatever had put that sour look on his face right before he had to go back to work.

"What? Why not? This is the most exciting thing to happen to you in...ever."

Sad thing was, Kyle was probably right.

"Can we just give it a break, Kyle? I just...I just want to enjoy it for now. No pressure for it to be more." Lies. But he knew admitting anything would only make it more painful, and definitely more humiliating, when it all crumbled into dust.

Kyle pouted. "Fine. But only because you've been damaged. You feel up to watching a movie tonight? Or did you just want me to head home after dinner?"

Drew considered his energy level. "Let's watch a movie. But I can't guarantee I'll be able to stay awake for the whole thing."

With his mouth full, Kyle didn't bother speaking, just lifted his shoulder in a halfhearted shrug. They'd been friends long enough that Drew knew Kyle didn't care one way or the other.

PIZZA EATEN, Drew and Kyle snuggled together on Drew's narrow bed, a bag of gummy bears between them for dessert. In Drew's tiny house, it was the only place to watch television, and without a car, it was harder for Drew to get to Kyle's place, which wasn't much bigger anyway. If there had been one more bedroom in the place, he and Kyle would have been roommates.

"I'm not lying in Officer Hottie jizz, am I?" Kyle looked around suspiciously, like he was going to whip out a UV light and get all *CSI* on Drew.

"Oh, shut up. We changed the sheets."

Kyle laughed and picked up the remote, but before he could press Start, Drew put a hand on Kyle's arm.

"You know, it's kinda weird about that accident." Drew didn't look directly at Kyle, but his peripheral vision was pretty decent. He knew damn well that Kyle was staring at him, but he'd only talked himself off the proverbial "I've got a traumatic brain injury" ledge, and he was afraid if he saw any fear on Kyle's face, he'd be right back there in a swirl of anxiety.

"Okaaaaay. Sure. Not the first time there's been a pileup there, though. Remember that time they had fog and a wildfire at the same time? That shit was bad."

"You don't think it was weird?"

"Not really. You know it could have been a localized downpour. It's Florida. Blinding rain one place and sunny and hot only a few miles away. The tourists just don't have enough experience in that kind of rain."

They sat there for a few moments, Kyle's finger resting on the

Start button, before Kyle cleared his throat. "And why do you think it's weird?"

Drew's stomach flipped. Had to be some sort of weird coincidence.

"No reason." He continued to stare fixedly at the television, despite its distinct lack of movie playing.

Kyle knew he was full of shit, so he just waited expectantly.

"It's just... I did a reading today for a tourist passing through."

Drew explained about the unusual readings he'd had, for both Mrs. Gillespie and Lisa. Saying it aloud sent chills down his spine, and his mouth dried out. Facing the possibility that something important had shaken loose in his brain terrified him. Brain surgery was expensive. Mental disorders, with medication and therapy, were expensive. How was he going to cope?

Finally he found the courage to look at Kyle, whose stunned expression didn't give Drew any hints about whether or not he should call an ambulance or have himself committed.

"Well? Have I completely lost my mind? Bleeding on the brain? Aneurysm?" Drew didn't know how he'd forced those words out, because he was almost certain there was something medically wrong. Underneath his substantial health worries was the tiny niggling fear he was going to lose Cliff over this. A boyfriend should be the least of his concerns right now, but he didn't want to face that loss on top of everything else.

Kyle's eyebrows lifted, and he shifted on the bed so he was fully facing Drew, cross-legged. "Whoa, hold on there. Are you in pain?"

"Of course I'm in pain! I'm stitched up like Frankenstein's monster and have two black eyes."

Kyle flapped his hands. "That's not what I meant. Is it worse? Different? What about blurred vision or nausea?"

"No. It's better, actually." Not that Kyle was a medical professional by any stretch of the imagination, no matter how many episodes of *House* he'd watched. But the questions were reasonable, and the fact that Drew didn't have any of those symptoms eased the band around his chest just a bit. Didn't mean he didn't have some sort of medical or psychological problem, but maybe it wasn't an emergency.

"Well, you've got a source in the police department. Use it. Find out if Mrs. Gillespie was involved."

Drew blinked at Kyle, trying to make sense of his words. No matter how many times he turned them over in his mind, he couldn't quite get them to resolve.

"I'm sorry—I'm going to talk to *Cliff* about this?" Because doing so would only prove he was out of his fucking mind.

"Sure. Rule out that possibility."

Drew scrunched up his nose. "Rule out what possibility?"

"That you're actually psychic."

Okay, now Drew did feel a little light-headed. "What the fuck are you talking about? There's no such thing as psychics."

"What about your grandmother?" Kyle looked so earnest, so calm.

Maybe Drew really was having some sort of break from reality and was going to snap out of it, only to find himself restrained to a hospital bed somewhere. Or maybe he was in a coma and the stuff with Cliff had all been a figment of his imagination.

"My grandmother wasn't psychic. She had intuition, was great at reading people's nonverbal cues, and made some insightful predictions based on a lifetime of experience. She capitalized on that and *taught* me everything she knew."

Kyle shrugged. "I don't know. She knew I wasn't going to New York if I didn't give up that part. She even knew which knee was going to get blown out. If I'd listened to her, it's possible I might still be dancing."

"What are you saying? And why haven't you told me this before?"

Looking slightly ashamed, Kyle averted his eyes. "She came right out and told me to quit the part I'd been given. Told me there was going to be a screw-up that would cost me my career. I didn't believe her. That part in *Chicago* was going to be my big break. I never told you, because I had no proof of anything. And I know you, Drew. You need proof."

The chills were back, more intense than before. There was no way his grandma could have known a careless stagehand in another city was going to leave a smear of grease on the stage floor, causing Kyle to slip, taking the brunt of the injury while protecting his dancing partner from the fall. No way.

"But...you don't believe in psychics and ghosts." Drew couldn't let it go. He did need proof, and no one had ever provided convincing evidence to the contrary. Even his interest in watching *Phantoms* had been solely for the presence of Brett Cavanagh. Certainly not for the questionable evidence Brett provided to prove the existence of super-natural events.

Kyle popped a couple of gummy bears in his mouth. "Until your grandma warned me, I didn't believe in psychics, no. But I believe in ghosts."

Drew's world wobbled. Was he the only one in this town who didn't believe in the supernatural? Underneath the shock, a hint of betrayal lurked. Kyle had been lying to him all this time.

"Oh, don't look at me like that." Kyle flicked a gummy bear at his chest. "Ghosts make perfect sense. Remnants of energy, strong emotion, remaining behind. Nothing malevolent or sentient. Just... shadows. Echoes. How else do you think I make those ghost tours so creepy? Because I believe the ghosts are there, and I've learned how to scare the shit out of tourists with them. And psychics, well, the brain is still largely untapped. Unexplored. I believe both ghosts and psychic phenomena could exist. Could have a scientific basis."

Drawing in a deep breath, Drew thought about Kyle's words. Choosing to believe as Kyle did would ease his mind a bit, but deep down he was still concerned about a medical problem.

"Shouldn't I go get checked out? Medically, I mean? Rule out...damage?"

Kyle shrugged. "So here's the way I see it. If you're damaged, I don't think it's life threatening. And yes, you could go to the hospital now or make appointments with specialists in the morning. But you can easily rule out one possibility—for free—tonight."

"I must be brain damaged, because that actually makes sense." Somehow it did, although he wasn't sure if he'd be more relieved or less if it turned out Mrs. Gillespie had been involved in the pileup. "Do you know where they're filming tonight? Probably that's the best place to talk to Cliff."

Kyle huffed and tossed another gummy bear at him. "Do I know where they're filming? Of course I know where they're filming."

Drew should have known better. Kyle was a gossip maven. Mostly because he worked with kids and teens. Their parents blabbed about shit in their kids' hearing, not realizing that the kids were going to discuss the more interesting gossip with their peers, and for some reason, the gay dance teacher was virtually invisible when those kids got talking.

"You'll take me out there?"

"I wouldn't have it any other way. Now, are you going to tell me all about Officer Hottie?"

"Not yet. Not until I can talk to him." Drew just hoped that Cliff had forgotten to be mad at him when he and Kyle crashed the film site later.

CHAPTER 15

K yle pulled to the side of the road, just before the turnoff to the Somerset estate. Drew stared in dismay at the trucks that blocked the drive, undoubtedly parked that way on purpose.

"It's obvious we aren't welcome. They're never going to let us just walk right in. After all, they must have some sort of bouncers or something besides Drew and his partner." This was a stupid idea, and he couldn't believe he'd let Kyle talk him into it.

"They might. You never know. Besides, don't tell me you don't know another way onto this property. A way to Cliff's house that isn't so obvious."

Drew went from the icy cold of panic to the heat of embarrassment so quickly he thought he might pass out.

"What are you talking about?"

"C'mon. Back in high school. Surely you 'explored' part of this property as a way to check up on Cliff."

"I wasn't a fucking stalker, Kyle." At least, not to the point of staring into the windows of North's...or rather, Cliff's house. Or at least, not often. The best way to the back of the house from where Drew had lived was to cut through the Morales property, then through the edge of the fenced-in swamp-conservation area to the Somerset estate. He hadn't done it often, because the swamp preserve was crawling with gators and the high school principal, Mr. Morales, hated all Drummonds. If Drew had been caught, Mr. Morales would have skinned him alive. The hatred hadn't exactly abated since the man became mayor, either, and if Drew ever *had* been tempted to step off the straight and narrow, the mayor would have had his business shut down within seconds.

"Uh-huh. Whatever," Kyle said after an insultingly long pause.

Drew stared out of the window even though there was very little to see in the night-darkened shadows of the trees lining the Somerset property.

"Even if I did know, we don't know where they are on the property." The front of the property was easier to get into, but the front lawn was also much more open, much more visible to people looking out windows.

Kyle snorted. "Are you fucking kidding?" He pointed through the windshield. "All we have to do is follow the bat signal."

Drew stared up into the sky in the direction Kyle was pointing, where a whitish glow lit up the treetops deep in the Somerset estate, looking for all the world like lights at the high school's football field. He wasn't sure why all the *Phantoms* episodes looked like they'd been filmed through night-vision goggles when apparently they brought in enough lighting to signal the space station.

"Okay, I guess we can find it, but seriously, Kyle, I'm not sure I'm up to tramping through the woods in the middle of the night." And that had nothing to do with his fear that he was going to make a complete ass of himself. Aside from the fact that his energy reserves were still easily exhausted, he and Kyle weren't equipped for mucking about in the woods in the dark. Kyle might have a flashlight in the trunk, but neither of them was wearing hiking boots or long pants, both of which were vital if they were going to stumble around and possibly come across a snake or two. And that was assuming no gators were taking a stroll on the property. There was no way Drew was cutting through the conservation area after dark. No fucking way.

He had no intention of deliberately wandering into gator territory if he could help it.

Kyle patted his leg. "Doesn't matter. You're on a first-name basis with one of the local cops. We're going to be able to waltz right in. Trust me."

"Shouldn't I...call him instead?" That was better. Then he wouldn't have to face Cliff looking at him like he was insane. Why hadn't he thought of this before Kyle bundled him out of the house?

"Nope. Face-to-face is better. You'll be better able to convince him of your sincere need to know, in person. Especially with..." Kyle waved a finger to indicate Drew's war wounds. "Trust me. He won't be able to deny you anything."

Drew wished he was as confident of that as Kyle, but they were here, and he was still incredibly unsettled about the whole thing.

"I suppose it can't hurt to try." As long as Cliff didn't dump him after this. Or move out. It hadn't been very long, but Drew already liked having Cliff around the house.

"That's the spirit. C'mon."

An unwelcome suspicion hit Drew as he got out of the car. It was entirely possible Kyle was pushing because this gave him a better chance at gaining Brett's attention. However, Drew wasn't interested in having an argument about it, especially since he didn't want to get stranded here if Kyle got offended and drove off in a huff. Besides, Kyle's logic had been irrefutable, although that was possibly the head wound talking.

They managed to make it all the way to the guesthouse before anyone even questioned their presence, which seemed weird to Drew. After all, he must look incredibly disreputable since he hadn't bothered with any cover-up. If he wasn't working, it was too fucking hot to bother with makeup.

Or perhaps he just looked like a zombie extra or something. Not that *Phantoms* had ever had a zombie episode, as far as he knew.

A uniformed police officer strode to where they'd been detained by a crew member. The lights might be playing tricks on Drew, but he was pretty sure Cliff hadn't suddenly turned into a blond man. His heart fluttered at the prospect of trying to explain to a complete stranger why he wanted to interrupt Cliff at work. For a completely ridiculous reason. A cop wouldn't believe in the supernatural any more than Drew did.

Fuck, fuck, fuck.

The guy smiled as he approached. "Hey there. I was going to give you the standard spiel about how the film shoot is closed to bystanders and all that, but you aren't just bystanders. Let me radio Cliff."

Drew would have raised his eyebrows in shock, but he'd learned the hard way to curb that motion. The cop turned away and spoke quietly into his radio, and somehow, Drew had no idea what he said.

"What the fuck is going on?" Drew whispered to Kyle. No way it should be this easy. No fucking way. Although…half the town must know Cliff was staying at his house. Had gossip linked them as a couple already? Drew didn't have a problem with that, but he had no idea how Cliff felt about it.

The cop turned back to them with a smile that would have been goofy if he hadn't been wearing a very official-looking uniform. "I'm Scott Hunter, Cliff's friend."

"I'm Kyle Grainger, and this is Drew Drummond." Kyle positively simpered at the good-looking blond. Ridiculous, really. After all, Drew might have the world's most useless gaydar, but there was no way Scott was gay.

Scott chuckled. "I was pretty sure I knew who Drew was. If the red hair didn't give it away…" Scott looked uncomfortable and waved a finger in the vicinity of Drew's forehead. "But it's nice to officially meet you both."

Drew smiled uncertainly. He wasn't sure how to act around Cliff's friends, mostly because he didn't know how Cliff wanted him to act around Cliff's friends. Hell, half the time he was still worried about slipping up and actually calling him North. He hoped that maybe he'd have the opportunity to get to know Scott better, but a few good orgasms and a place to crash didn't necessarily spell the foundation of a relationship, no matter what Drew hoped for or wanted.

"How's the head, by the way?"

For a single, insane moment, Drew thought Scott was asking about the quality of the last blowjob. Kyle's muffled cough-slash-laugh told Drew he wasn't alone with his mind in the gutter.

"Oh, er, well, it's not as painful as it was."

"Good, good. You had Cliff worried there."

Was that a good thing? Drew couldn't deny the sudden warmth that flooded his belly, knowing Cliff had worried about him.

Fortunately, Drew didn't have to figure out the most appropriate response, because Cliff was jogging toward them. The warmth in Drew's belly intensified, as it always did at the sight of Cliff.

SEEING DREW CALMED the initial spurt of dread Cliff had felt when Scott radioed him. There was no good reason for Drew to seek him out here, and he'd worried that something was wrong. But Kyle was standing next to him, which eased Cliff's mind a bit. While Kyle and Drew both looked slightly overwhelmed at the crazy bustle of the crew, aside from some lingering exhaustion, Drew looked... Cliff didn't know how to finish that sentence. There was no denying that Drew's good looks were temporarily marred by the bruising and stitches, but the sight of him comforted something deep in Cliff, and it was good. Cliff couldn't imagine seeing Drew would ever be bad.

Cliff skidded to a stop in front of Drew. "Hey there." He was tempted, oh so tempted, to cup Drew's face and kiss him right there in front of everyone. Stake a claim. But that wasn't the sort of thing he could just spring on Drew. Not until they'd talked about it. Not even when Drew took a tiny step forward, with a look in his eyes like he'd welcome such a gesture.

"Hey." Drew smiled, and for a moment Cliff was able to shut out everyone else and just stare into Drew's big blue eyes.

Drew licked his lips, and Cliff bit back a groan. God. He was as horny as a teenager, but it wasn't just the sex. There was something else about Drew. Something that meant he was crashing headlong into feelings he shouldn't be feeling yet. But he didn't know how to stop it, and he wasn't sure he wanted to.

Kyle cleared his throat, and Cliff finally paid attention to the other two men, both of whom were unsuccessfully hiding smirks. Maybe Cliff's dreams of a relationship—out and proud—with Drew weren't as farfetched as he feared.

"Are you okay? What's up?" Cliff peered closely at Drew, trying to assess him for medical reasons this time.

Drew shrugged. "I'm okay. I just...wanted to ask you about that crash on the highway."

Odd. "What did you want to know?" It hadn't been pretty. Lots of injuries and a couple of fatalities.

As though he could sense Drew's discomfort, Scott offered to grab a couple of coffees from craft services. Such as they were. Brett had spent the last hour bitching about the limited options available in a small town late at night, and Cliff had been only too glad to get a break from his babysitting duties.

Scott jogged off, and Kyle wandered away as though trying to give them some privacy, although Cliff had no idea why that would be necessary. He waited for an answer to his question.

"It's just that..." Drew frowned at him. "I don't want to upset you."

Fuck it. Cliff stepped forward and cupped Drew's face. "I know this has been a crazy few days, but this is more than just sex for me." God, that was fucking scary to say, especially since he felt more strongly for Drew in less than a week than he'd ever felt for Brett. If this crashed and burned like his last relationship, Cliff might never recover.

"Me too," Drew whispered and licked his lips again.

The temptation was breaking Cliff. "I want people to know we're together. Are you okay with that?"

"I am if you are. You don't mind people knowing about you? About us?"

"Not at all."

The happiness thoroughly drowned out his Brett-induced crankiness and the lingering heartsickness from dealing with injuries and fatalities at the highway pileup. He'd probably have to put up with some more shit from the evil Drummond twins, but they were just going to have to accept that Cliff was going to be in the picture as long as Drew wanted him there.

Without even glancing around to see who might be watching—and since most of the crew had been imported from California, it was unlikely they'd care—Cliff kissed Drew. Tenderly, sweetly, and with all the burgeoning feeling in his heart.

Drew pressed himself against Cliff, and Cliff fervently wished he weren't on duty. When Drew made moves to deepen the kiss, Cliff gathered the tattered remnants of his self-control and pulled back.

For a split second, Drew looked confused and hurt, until the sound of someone shouting orders reminded him where they were. "I'm sorry. I shouldn't have done that."

"Don't be sorry. If you're still awake when I'm done my shift, we'll pick up where we left off. If you're not, we'll have time in the morning." If Cliff had anything to say about it, he wouldn't be spending another minute sleeping on that futon.

"I'd like that."

"Now that we've got that settled, what brought you all the way out here?" He'd ask about Kyle's presence, but Cliff didn't give a damn if Kyle had lied about having plans this weekend. If he hadn't, it might have taken weeks or months to get where Cliff was with Drew. Or maybe even never. Without their being thrown together, Cliff might have been scared off by the thought of getting involved with a Drummond.

"The accident on the highway. I did a reading with a tourist, right before she was heading out of town, and...I was just worried she might have been involved. She was a nice older lady."

Surprisingly, Cliff only felt a tiny twinge of discomfort at the reminder of Drew's occupation. But then, it was something he'd have to accept if he was going to be in Drew's life, which meant Cliff was going to give Drew the benefit of the doubt. "I really shouldn't talk about the people involved, not until that information has been released to the public."

Tension tightened Drew's face, and he clutched at Cliff's forearms.

"Please. I need to know. Her last name was Gillespie. She was in a silver car with...with Connecticut plates."

Agitation was making Drew shake, and Cliff wasn't going to aggravate Drew's health. "I'm sorry, Drew. She was badly injured, and her husband was killed on impact. I'm not sure if she's going to make it or not, but I know they've contacted her son, who is on his way down."

Drew paled and lifted a trembling hand to his lips. "Oh my God."

"I'm sorry." Cliff didn't know what else to say. He wouldn't have expected Drew to care so much about a random tourist who'd come in for a reading.

Scott returned at that moment with coffee, and Kyle gravitated back to the group as well. Drew grabbed at the paper cup like it was a lifeline, and Cliff wished there was something else he could do to make Drew feel better.

"This is where you disappeared to." Brett shouldered his way into the circle, making Cliff's lip curl. The chief had certainly called this job right. Babysitting, through and through. None of the fans who'd appeared so far had been dangerous, and Brett had positively preened whenever one appeared and worshipped.

"Where's my coffee?"

Scott raised an eyebrow and lifted his cup before taking a big sip. "At craft services, same as mine was."

Cliff barely held in a laugh. It hadn't taken Scott long to realize what a jackass Brett could be, and the shiny celebrity adulation had tarnished far quicker than Cliff had expected.

"Aren't you going to get it for me?"

"Not hardly. We're glorified *babysitters* not glorified *waiters*."

This time, Cliff couldn't hold in the laugh, which earned him a glare from Brett. "Get your own fucking coffee, Brett. I'm sure you remember how, from back when you were one of the little people."

Brett's struggle with his temper was visibly apparent, and he pasted on his trademark smile, which Cliff knew was fake as all hell.

"You did bring me some pretties, so all is forgiven." Brett leered at Kyle, then turned his attention to Drew. Brett's expression of distaste was readily apparent even before he opened his mouth. "Well, one pretty, at least."

Between Brett's grimace and harsh words, Drew's cheeks reddened, and he moved to take a step back, away from Brett's noxious influence.

Cliff couldn't let it go, though, and wrapped an arm around Drew's shoulders. "What the fuck is wrong with you, Brett?" Drew was gorgeous, no matter how banged up he was now, and fault for the bruises could be laid squarely at Brett's feet, even if it had been one of Drew's temperamental brothers who'd actually delivered them.

Brett frowned at Cliff. "Surely you don't want him over me? Sure, he's a sweet morsel when he's not looking like a zombie, and if you want, we can play with him later. You know I never objected to bringing in a third."

Cliff flashed hot and cold, unable to believe Brett had just laid out their dirty laundry like that. Kyle and Scott had both gasped, but Drew stiffened beside him and stepped away.

"You may think you were a dream in bed, but you clearly didn't think I was, or you wouldn't have cheated on me," said Cliff. That brought another gasp from Kyle and caused Drew to step even farther away, but Cliff wasn't done. "I'm not sure when you became the biggest asshole on the planet, or maybe you always were and I just never noticed, but there is simply no cause for taking out whatever anger you have toward me on Drew. He doesn't deserve it."

Brett's eyes narrowed. "Fine. When you're back in LA, you'll be begging to get back into my bed."

What would it take to get this through Brett's thick skull? Picturing Brett as a stalker was no longer difficult. This inability to understand that someone wanted nothing more to do with him was typical of stalkers.

"I'm not coming back to LA. As I've told you numerous times." Until now, he hadn't been sure if he was planning to stay in Sandy Bottom Bay either, but if things worked out with Drew, Cliff was home for good. And surprisingly, he was more than okay with that idea. Assuming he could smooth this over with Drew.

"Please. You're not serious about wanting to stay in this little podunk town. Not when you worked so hard to leave it. As soon as you get tired of this little boy toy, you'll come crawling back to me."

Cliff clenched his fists. "Don't fucking talk about Drew like that." He was coming close to losing his cool, and he didn't think his new chief or the mayor would consider Cliff punching out a celebrity to be appropriate publicity for the Haunt Fest.

"Whoa." Scott stepped between him and Brett. "The name calling is completely out of line. Brett, I think you should take a walk, calm down a bit."

Normally Brett would have sneered at someone telling him what to do, but Scott was a big guy, and right now there was no doubt he was the authority figure a cop should be. With a curl of his lip, Brett whirled away and stomped back to where the crew was working.

Cliff didn't give a shit about Brett's temper tantrum. Sure, it might come back and bite him in the ass later, if Brett decided to complain to Chief Walker, but through the wondrous magic of breaking up, Cliff didn't have to worry about placating Brett. He was far too worried about placating Drew, who did not appear to be taking Brett's ill-timed revelation well.

"Drew. I'm sorry. There never seemed to be a good time to tell you."

Drew rubbed the back of his neck, and Kyle moved in close to wrap an arm around him. It made Cliff grit his teeth because he didn't want Kyle to be the one comforting Drew.

"I wish you had said something earlier. I feel like...I feel like Brett was laughing at me the whole time. Like this was some sort of joke on the redneck hick, and you were in on it."

The pain in Drew's words was like a kick in the stomach. "I wasn't. I swear. I really had planned to tell you. It wasn't a secret—I'd already told Scott."

Drew narrowed his eyes, some of the hurt giving way to anger. "Scott? And not me?"

Cliff held up his hands in supplication. "Not because I didn't think you deserved to know. But I suspected Brett was going to use our past relationship to try and make trouble for me at work, and I wanted Scott to be prepared. I had planned to tell you, but there really hasn't been a lot of opportunity to have a discussion with you, not since we decided we were serious about us." Cliff's stomach twisted, just a bit, at having this conversation in front of two bystanders. He'd wanted to be out and proud in a relationship, but he hadn't necessarily imagined that would include airing out a huge snafu in front of an audience.

He stared at Drew, hoping his sincerity and regret was evident in his expression. "And if I'm honest, I was hoping he'd crawl away without you ever having to deal with him. I'm sorry. I should have said something."

Frowning, Drew remained silent while Cliff wondered if the good thing they'd started was going to be over before Cliff had even had a chance to get comfortable.

After an interminable silence, Drew nodded, and a faint smile curved his lips. There was something still bothering Drew, though, and Cliff would make sure he figured out what it was, just as soon as he was off duty.

His and Scott's radios crackled, reporting a fire at the bakery on Main Street and calling in all available officers. It probably made more sense for Scott to go, since he had more experience with Sandy Bottom Bay emergency services, no matter how uncomfortable it would be for Cliff to babysit Brett.

Scott glanced at Drew before speaking. "You go. I'll stick it out with Brett until you're back."

Relief flooded Cliff, and he had to bite back a huge grin because it was hardly appropriate to be happy about a bad fire.

"Thanks, man." Cliff took a good look at Drew, who had paled considerably and was clinging to Kyle as though he was having trouble standing. "Hey. Are you okay? Do you need me to take you back to the hospital?"

"No, no. I'm okay. Just worried about the bakery. Was there anyone there at this time of night?"

Cliff might still know a number of people in Sandy Bottom Bay, but Drew and Kyle interacted with them every day and probably had a number of close friends in town. Of course this would affect them. Cliff took a step toward Drew and held out a hand.

Wan and pale, Drew gave him a tight little smile. "Be careful." He extricated himself form Kyle's embrace to touch Cliff's arm.

"I will." Cliff took a deep breath, not sure he was completely forgiven for Brett. "I'll see you tonight?"

Drew nodded. "You'd better go."

Leaving it like this felt wrong or unfinished somehow, but Cliff didn't have a choice. He had a job to do, and like it or not, sometimes it was going to trump his boyfriend...if he still had a chance to call Drew that. After one more lingering look, he jogged toward where he'd parked his patrol car.

$\sim$

DREW HELD HIMSELF together long enough for both Cliff and Scott to depart, but as soon as Scott disappeared, the shakes started.

"Holy shit, Drew. I can't fucking believe it." Kyle hugged him as he spoke.

Kyle was warm and comforting, but there was a tiny, disloyal part of Drew that wished it were Cliff wrapped around him.

"This can't be coincidence, can it?" Drew hoped Kyle would say yes, but he knew damn well they'd both been half convinced after verifying Mrs. Gillespie was from Connecticut.

"No, I don't think so. You're psychic."

"Fucking concussion."

Kyle pulled away, looking puzzled, before he started laughing.

"What's so funny?"

"Who knew? One solid knock on the head and you're a legit psychic. It's kinda weird."

Maybe it would go away. Maybe he wouldn't see any more visions. Maybe once the headaches were gone, they'd take away his new "gift." He could only hope, because he didn't know how he was going to convince Cliff he wasn't bleeding into his brain or trying to scam people.

Shakes rattled his body, and his breathing sped up. When his vision started to gray at the edges, Kyle slapped him.

"Slow breaths, Drew. In. Out."

Drew followed Kyle's breathing, letting the panic and hyperventilation subside. "This is so fucked-up."

Kyle rubbed his shoulders. "C'mon. Let's get you home and get a beer or something into you. We'll figure this out."

"I don't know if I can do this, Kyle."

Kyle hugged him again. "It might not always be bad news, honey. Try not to worry about it. We'll deal with it if it happens again. First, though, text Lisa and make sure she's all right."

"I'll do it in the car. I really need to sit down for a bit."

He was worried about Lisa, but there wasn't anything he could do at the moment, and if he collapsed out here in the dark, that would only make things worse.

THE NEXT MORNING, Drew opened his eyes, amazed that he'd managed to fall asleep at all. After receiving confirmation from Lisa that no one had been in the bakery and it was only property damage, he'd been relieved, but he'd still wanted to wait up until Cliff got home. Despite the scares and adrenaline and worry, his eyelids had drooped before midnight.

Cliff had made it home okay, though, as he was currently wrapped around Drew, warm and secure. Shifting slowly, Drew turned over so he was facing Cliff. He'd been a little thrown off by the information that Cliff and Brett had been an item at one point. How on earth could Drew possibly measure up to Brett Cavanagh? Drew wasn't famous. Millions didn't drool over him every week. But then again, neither would Drew cheat on Cliff. Drew might not be a relationship expert, but he hadn't seen anything that indicated Cliff wanted Brett back. Funny thing was, he wasn't sure Brett truly wanted Cliff back either, despite his words the previous night.

Maybe it was stupid of him, but Drew was secure in the knowledge that Cliff wanted him and only him. Whether that would still be true if Drew tried to convince him that he was psychic...well, he'd cross that bridge when he came to it. Because one of the last things he'd thought about before dropping off to sleep was that maybe there was no real reason he had to tell Cliff about his visions. As long as he didn't see anything that was life-threatening or illegal, there wasn't any point in rocking the boat.

Cliff's eyelids fluttered open. "Hi." His voice was husky and sleep-filled, rubbing along Drew's skin like a caress.

"Hi."

Cliff raised a hand to brush Drew's hair off his cheek before sliding down to the nape of his neck. With the slightest amount of pressure, Drew succumbed to both their desires and pressed his lips to Cliff's.

It hadn't taken long for them to get in the habit of sleeping together naked, and Cliff's firm erection nudged Drew's, the slide of skin on skin only ramping Drew up.

"You're so sexy," Cliff murmured into his neck before licking the skin there. One of Cliff's hands pinched at Drew's nipples, and he moaned, writhing against Cliff.

"More," Drew whispered.

Cliff grunted an affirmative before he nipped his way down Drew's chest, each touch with those straight white teeth making Drew crazy. Hovering over Drew, Cliff grinned, an evil, sensual grin, before ducking down and sucking one nipple into his mouth while pinching the other rhythmically.

Arching his back, Drew moaned, loud and long. He was going to fucking die of pleasure. Or come just from the attention to his chest.

Mere seconds before Drew blew, Cliff lifted up, still grinning, and Drew humped air, so fucking close.

"Dammit." He was desperate, but he knew instinctively that just grabbing his cock and stroking to orgasm would be cheating. "You have to do something. Please."

"What would you like?" Cliff drew a featherlight touch along the inside of his thigh, displacing the hair and tickling him while making him want to beg for a firmer touch farther north.

"Fuck me." Drew stilled for a moment. They hadn't done that yet. Hadn't even discussed it. But he wanted it now. Wanted Cliff's fat cock to fill him up.

This time Cliff groaned. "Yes. Nightstand?"

Drew nodded. Seemed a logical place to keep supplies, although it had been a damn long time since he'd needed to delve into the box of condoms.

Mere seconds later, Cliff was suited up, a cool bottle of lube rolled against Drew's leg, and slick fingers probed him.

"Now, please." Drew might not have done this often, but he'd done it often enough to know he didn't need a lot of prep.

Cliff stared at him. "You sure?"

"Yes. Do it. Fuck me."

Cliff pushed Drew's knees back and rubbed his cock over Drew's hole, teasing. Shifting his hips, Drew did his best to impale himself.

"You're so fucking hot." Cliff's gaze was riveted to their groins, and Drew could easily imagine what they looked like from that perspective. Didn't mean he wanted Cliff to stare all day.

"Please, North, please." Panic made Drew freeze, although it didn't wilt his erection any. He'd called Cliff by the name North too many times in his head, gotten too comfortable with the man, and out slipped his own special shortened name.

Cliff's reaction was gratifying and swift. He groaned and pushed his cock inside, filling Drew up perfectly. He slid home and held still, pubes crinkling against Drew's ass. He ducked his head against Drew's neck, biting with the exact pressure that made Drew fucking crazy.

Drew writhed, enjoying the stretch and burn but desperate for a hard pounding. After a few licks and nibbles, and somehow keeping his cock motionless inside Drew, Cliff lifted up and stared deep in his eyes.

With a wicked grin, Cliff answered Drew's prayers, pulling back and thrusting in with an ideal rhythm and force. Drew barely had time to breathe as they worked with each other, flexing and sweating, pleasure rising and magnifying.

A minor shift in position, and Cliff's cockhead hit Drew's prostate with every thrust, wringing tortured groans from his throat that mingled with the erotic slap of flesh against flesh.

Drew couldn't wait any longer. He needed to come so bad it was almost painful. He grabbed his cock, slick with precum, and stroked frantically. He was so turned on and absolutely desperate to come.

"That's it," Cliff gritted out. "Come for me. Come on my cock."

Drew had never been one to follow orders like that, but on command, his entire body stiffened, cock spurting and ass rippling around Cliff's dick. Cliff groaned and threw his head back, jerking helplessly in the throes of his own orgasm.

Breathing heavily, Cliff collapsed atop Drew, heedless of the jizz decorating Drew's belly. Drew sank back into sated lethargy, letting his heart rate and breathing slow. He'd come so hard he was pretty sure his legs weren't going to work, not for several minutes, at least.

Cliff pulled his softening cock gently out of Drew, disposed of the condom in the wastebasket, and grabbed a cloth to clean them up. Then, to Drew's surprise, he came back to the bed and curled around Drew, nuzzling his nose into Drew's hair. It was comforting and sweet in a way Drew had dreamed of but never experienced with any other bed partner.

"So I guess you know my full name," Cliff whispered in his ear.

Ears heating in embarrassment, Drew half shrugged. "Yeah, I guess. Um...I kinda like it."

"I don't really like it. Doesn't suit me. Sounds like it belongs to someone pampered and entitled."

Drew's lungs seized up, and his entire face flamed. The only saving grace was that he wasn't facing Cliff, but he still stiffened, wanting to get out of bed and away from his humiliation.

Cliff had other plans and flipped him over. Unable to meet Cliff's gaze, Drew stared hard at a long-healed scar on Cliff's shoulder.

Despite Drew's uneasiness, Cliff kissed him. "I like it when you call me North. In bed, at least."

The air in Drew's chest escaped in a whoosh. He hadn't completely fucked up. He glanced up and smiled at the tenderness in Cliff's eyes.

With gentle fingers, Cliff smoothed sweat-dampened red hair out of Drew's face before smiling ruefully. "I'm sorry about Brett. He can be such an asshole. Just ignore him, please."

Tiny ripples of apprehension swirled in Drew's belly. In the wake of some stellar sex, he'd forgotten Brett trying to stake a claim on the man Drew had wanted for his entire adult life.

"Is...is that why you came back? Because of the breakup?" Drew feared the answer as strongly as he needed it.

Cliff gave him a rueful smile and shook his head. "No. Brett and I broke up a few months ago. There were a number of reasons why I decided to return. Being a cop in LA is a hard, often thankless job. You see a lot of ugliness, and I was tense all the time because I wasn't out at work. Maybe it wouldn't have mattered, but I wasn't willing to risk it. Then, a few weeks after my breakup with Brett, my best friend died in an accident."

With a quiet gasp, Drew squeezed Cliff's hand, hoping to give him some comfort. "I'm so sorry."

Although his eyes reddened slightly, Cliff just smiled sadly. "Thanks. He was a great guy. But without him there, I sort of lost my way. Lost any desire to remain in Los Angeles. I know I seem like a horrible son, never coming back to visit my mother, but I spoke to her on the phone regularly. I was a little worried about her, getting older and being on her own. It all contributed to me leaping on the job opening here. I guess I'm just a small-town boy at heart."

This time, Drew was the one to brush a kiss over Cliff's lips. "I'm sorry you've had a tough time, but I'm glad you're here."

This time Cliff's smile had no sadness in it. "Me too."

CHAPTER 16

Drew couldn't believe it had only been a week—he'd never felt so connected to someone so quickly. He definitely couldn't count the years-long crush, because he'd never spoken to North until a week ago...no, he had to remember to call him Cliff. Except in bed, since Cliff was adamant that North only be used between the two of them. Which still gave Drew a warm, fluttery feeling in his belly. Just as he'd hoped, the name was something special just for Drew, and having a little secret like this was very coupley. Made Drew smile.

He'd spent the last few days distracting himself with Cliff's dick and ignoring the elephant in the room, namely his so-called psychic visions. Although he'd done a few readings while recuperating, he'd never quite been able to shake the fear that he was going to see something disturbing. He'd mostly convinced himself it was some sort of weird side-effect from his concussion, and he was glad he'd never told Cliff about it.

Haunt Fest was approaching fast, and while it made sense for Cliff to leave early to lay in enough groceries and supplies to get them through, Drew would have preferred to luxuriate in bed with him. Or have hot, sweaty sex. Or both.

Instead he pulled on Malachi's clothes because opening the

reading room would be wise; there might be pre-Fest early birds out and about. Although he still tired easily, a little extra business couldn't hurt.

The cool air, which Cliff insisted remain on, made wearing his costume almost pleasant. The memory of Cliff's first sight of him as Malachi, when Cliff's eyes darkened and he looked positively hungry, made Drew shiver and hardened his cock. Which really wasn't the most appropriate reaction when he was going to work. He gave his unruly dick a thump, hoping that the robes were sufficient to hide some unexpected tumescence.

As he passed through the reading room, he rocked to a stop and stared at the black-velvet-covered table, deck of tarot cards sitting there in readiness. He didn't want to believe he was psychic, but something weird had definitely happened, no matter how much he'd tried to pretend otherwise, and he wasn't keen for a repeat. The stomach-churning trepidation he experienced during each reading since wasn't a joy either.

Screw it. He strode over to the table, sat down, and picked up the deck. Nothing changed. No visions appeared. Any heralds of supernatural phenomena that he'd ever heard about were completely and utterly absent. But he didn't want to take any chances.

He flipped over the deck, quickly sorted through the cards to find the death card, and pulled it from the deck. He'd thought about this more than once, no matter how much it was...stacking the deck in his favor. He was a tarot reader, for fuck's sake. This he could cheat on, a little, if it eased both his mind and those of his clients. As an afterthought, he also pulled the ten of pentacles that had presaged the bakery fire. If he was going to start believing in the unbelievable, he'd rather assume those cards were cursed than that he'd somehow managed to unlock his third eye or whatever by getting knocked out in a barroom brawl. Drew slipped the two offending cards under a heavy, ornate box that held a variety of incense sticks and returned the deck to its original position on the table.

With a nod, he continued on into the front room. The first thing that caught his eye as he unlocked the door was a piece of colored paper tacked on the outside screen. He yanked open the door to find yet another sign that claimed he wasn't available for consultations, and interested clients might consider the services of Eddie Price, medium.

Fucker. Did Eddie think his brains were completely addled by the concussion and he somehow wouldn't notice the sign? Maybe he'd have to ask Cliff about getting a restraining order, because this was starting to resemble harassment. He couldn't do anything that would garner bad publicity this close to the Haunt Fest, or the mayor would string him up by his balls. Afterward, though, Eddie would find out that messing with a Drummond wasn't wise.

He crumpled the sign in his fist and threw it away, vowing not to let it ruin his day.

Between his slight alteration of the deck, the presence of Cliff in his life, and the fact that the worst of his pain had receded, Drew was happier than he could remember being in a long time. They both agreed that although their relationship was new and had had a weird start, living together had been like compressing their relationship to a much more serious place much faster than normal. They spent the mornings and early afternoons before Cliff's shifts getting to know each other, in between heating the sheets.

Humming, Drew rearranged a few of the displays, removing the coating of dust that built up so fucking fast. Never made sense to him. Florida was so humid that the dust should have been tamped down by the water-logged atmosphere, and yet he had to dust every couple of days if he didn't want his wares to look like they'd been hanging around since his grandma had been a teenager.

If the online sales got going, he'd find a way to pay someone to come in and do the cleaning and rearranging, maybe more. Maybe even man the desk during Haunt Fest, because he was pretty sure him in his costume doing all the grunt work only showed how close he was to being a complete fiscal failure. At the moment, he didn't have any other choice.

The bell over his door tinkled, and Drew quickly tucked away his duster before whirling to greet his client. It took a moment to reconcile that the man in the baseball cap wasn't a typical client but none other than Brett Cavanagh, rendering Drew speechless. Normally he'd ask a newcomer if they wanted a reading or if they just wanted to look around. Brett's money would spend just as well as anyone else's, but after everything he'd seen of Brett, Drew was incredibly reluctant to offer him a reading. What if he said yes? Considering his entitled attitude, he'd probably expect a freebie too.

"Well, well. You've got a deft hand with the makeup, don't you?"

Was Brett capable of sounding anything other than smarmy? Drew didn't bother answering. He just waited for Brett to get to the point.

"I think we might be able to use you in the interview portion of the show. You'd be famous, and you clean up really well." Brett took a couple of steps forward, and Drew had to steel himself to stand his ground.

Not wanting to stand too close to Brett didn't mean he was afraid of the man, but Drew was certain Brett would consider him duly intimidated if he retreated. If his brothers had taught him nothing else, they'd shown him how to be bullheaded, even when it wasn't in his best interest. And really, Brett might be a viper with a lecherous tongue, but he hadn't been directly responsible for Drew's injuries. Drew could take care of himself, even with a guy who was much bigger than he was—yet another valuable lesson he'd learned from Rob and Wyatt.

Brett merely smirked and ran a finger along Drew's jaw, nearly causing Drew to shudder. How could Cliff have been taken in by this oily, two-dimensional prick?

"Don't you want to be famous? It would probably only require a couple of nights filming together."

Drew resisted the urge to roll his eyes. He might be a hick redneck in a tiny Florida town, but he wasn't stupid or naive. At least, not completely. Certainly not enough to fall for Brett's over-the-top pseudoseduction.

"Why now? What's in it for you?"

Brett shrugged and took only a tiny step back. "I think you'd be good for ratings. I wish I'd had a chance to talk to you when I was doing my original scouting trip."

It wasn't possible to believe a single word Brett said. Drew didn't think he'd trust the man to give him the right time of day. But maybe he would have if Brett had approached him on that scouting trip. However it happened, Brett came across Eddie first and identified him as a conquest and patsy to be used to Brett's benefit, with no need to seek out anyone else. Close call. Drew had seen the unsavory underbelly of Brett before he'd had a chance to be hypnotized by his serpentine charm.

"Oh? But I'm sure there are a dozen people in town who would look good on camera and want to be there." Eddie Price leaped to mind. Drew would gladly give up Brett's offer—which undoubtedly had lots of strings involving nudity—to Eddie. Eddie was arrogant enough that he might even believe Brett's hogwash.

He needed to get Brett to leave peacefully. The mayor had stopped by specially to deliver Drew a warning not to fuck up whatever cachet Brett and *Phantoms* was lending to the town—like he was the only one who could fuck up—so just kicking the asshole out of his home wasn't going to fly.

The bell over his door sounded again, and he deftly stepped away from Brett to greet the newcomer. Speak of the devil. Drew didn't get a chance to ask Eddie what he was doing there, because he got right in Brett's face.

"What the fuck are you doing here, Cavanagh? You promised me that interview. You're not going to give it away to one of the fucking Drummonds."

Drew clenched his jaw. Not that he cared what Brett thought of him, but he was glad his name and all the baggage that came with it didn't mean anything to Brett.

"Eddie, Eddie. You need to calm down."

"And you need to stop putting signs on my door." Drew's words were completely ignored by both parties.

"You promised, Brett."

Brett stepped into Eddie's personal space and did the same finger-down-the-jaw maneuver he'd just finished laying on Drew. Made Eddie shudder, but in what appeared to be lust.

Oh. *Oh.* Looked like Eddie had already fallen for Brett's line of crap. Perhaps even on the infamous scouting trip.

"Promises can be broken, Eddie. Especially if it feels like you're demanding things of me."

Eddie stared into Brett's eyes. "Please. Not Drew fucking Drummond."

Okay, that kind of pissed Drew off. He and Eddie weren't best friends, but the contempt that dripped off Eddie's words was uncalled for. He pushed himself in between Eddie and Brett.

"Why not me? Brett thinks I'd be good for ratings." A part of Drew stood back and asked him what the fuck he thought he was doing, since he truly wanted no part of Brett, but Eddie had been pushing his buttons for days, and Drew was ready to blow.

Eddie sneered and poked him in the chest. "Well, you are good with makeup. Or was that whole 'I got a concussion' thing just to drum up sympathy?"

"Don't touch me, Eddie."

Brett laughed. "I just love it when people fight over me."

Drew didn't know what to do with that statement. He wasn't fighting over Brett, and he sure as shit shouldn't have been drawn into this ridiculous argument at all. Undoubtedly Brett would find the absolute worst way to spin this if Drew didn't get to tell Cliff first.

Eddie placed a palm on Drew's chest, as if daring him to do something. The bell tinkled again, bringing with it a trickle of dread. Surely the mere thought of Cliff hadn't conjured him out of thin air.

Then Wyatt roared, and the trickle became a full on *river* of dread.

"I told you to leave my brother alone, Eddie!"

Oh fuck. Eddie snatched his hand away as if Drew were on fire, before they all turned to Wyatt. Which was apparently when Wyatt realized Brett was there.

"You. You f—" Wyatt glanced at Drew, swallowing back what was undoubtedly the word *faggot*. At least his brother wasn't completely incapable of personal growth. "Fucking asshole. Haven't you done enough damage?"

"I didn't do any damage. That was you who gave your brother his war wounds." Brett taunted from his vantage point behind both Drew and Eddie. Wyatt had called it. The guy was a fucking asshole.

Wyatt clenched his fists, face turning red. Neither he nor Drew bothered correcting Brett that it was actually the other twin who'd done the damage, because there was no point. But Drew had to head off another brawl, this time in his place of business. The powers that be, namely Mayor Morales, would shut him down for sure.

His turban tilted over his eyebrows, and he swept it off his head, hoping if he looked less like a dork, Wyatt would listen to him. In a way, he wished it were Rob bellowing like a wounded bear. Not that Rob was any more reasonable than Wyatt, but Rob had been avoiding Drew since putting him in the hospital, which alternately pissed Drew off and made him sad.

"Wyatt, calm down. This is nothing." Maybe it wasn't nothing, but it was light-years away from the something it would be if fists started flying. Drew had miscalculated, though, because Wyatt's gaze was drawn to Drew's forehead, and he growled.

Even Eddie, as obtuse as he could be, must have recognized the murderous intent in Wyatt's eyes, because he also tried to talk Wyatt down while carefully edging away from Brett's ground zero. "Wyatt, seriously, don't do this."

Brett grabbed on to Drew's shoulders, using him as a shield, which only enraged Wyatt further. "Get your fucking hands off him, pervert. I'm going to drag you out of here and pound you into paste."

Another time, Drew would roll his eyes at his brother's melodramatic intimidation tactics, but for now he was grateful Wyatt was yelling and not actually carrying out his threats. Yet.

A shrill whistle blasted into the small space, acting like a bucket of cold water over the lot of them. Stunned, they stood still, wondering what was going on, until Helen Somerset appeared from behind Wyatt, a cold look on her face, like a queen ready to order executions. A police whistle dangled from a string around her wrist.

Great. He looked like a fool in front of one of his best customers and his boyfriend's mother. She'd never treated him like he was one of the dirty Drummonds, but that was bound to change after this.

Helen raised a hand and pointed an impeccably manicured index finger at Brett. "You, Mr. Cavanagh, are filming on my property by my goodwill and my goodwill alone. I would ask you not make trouble."

Brett didn't appear to be too concerned by the threat. "There are plenty of film sites around town."

"But you will have difficulty filming anywhere if I have you arrested."

"For what?" Brett gasped in surprise.

"Disturbing the peace. A minor inconvenience, to be sure, but it will give me enough time to make sure my lawyers bury you and your show in enough red tape that you'll be broke, jobless, and a joke before you slice through it all."

Drew shivered. He had no doubt Helen could and would do as she threatened. Brett was a minor celebrity on a specialty cable channel. Helen and her millions would clean him out, and it was clear that Brett had no interest in going up against the grand dame of Sandy Bottom Bay.

"And you." Helen moved her finger of doom to point at Eddie. "Quit causing trouble because you were too afraid of the Drummonds to go after the man you really wanted. It was a lost cause as soon as you slept with his best friend anyway. Deal with the consequences of that mistake."

Drew's ears heated as hot as Eddie's cheeks as he realized Helen meant Eddie had wanted him not Kyle.

"And then we come to you." Helen's gaze locked on Wyatt, who suddenly looked like he was going to lose his lunch. "You just narrowly escaped getting arrested. Again. If you truly want what's best for your brother, focus on your *legitimate* business, and control your temper. If you need more to keep you occupied, I've got a number of handyman jobs that either you or your twin would be more than capable of executing."

Wyatt nodded, chastened in a way Drew had never seen, although he certainly hadn't missed the slight emphasis Helen had made on the word *legitimate*. He'd have to talk to Rob and Wyatt later. He didn't want to lose any more family members.

"Now, then." Helen slipped the police whistle back into her purse. "Are any of you here to get your cards read?"

Like clones, all three shook their heads.

"Then I suggest you leave, as you're interfering with the running of a business. We wouldn't want to get the police involved, would we?"

Holy shit, no, they wouldn't. Drew wouldn't either—just his luck, Cliff would be the one to respond to the call. Apparently none of the other guys were too interested in facing a potentially pissed-off Cliff with a gun; they filed out of Drew's, leaving an odd vacuum in their wake. The room, always so tiny, seemed enormous in their absence.

The influx of adrenaline drained away, leaving Drew shaky and light-headed. Again.

Helen turned back, the cold, remote look on her face gone in a flash. "You need to sit down."

If Drew felt better, he'd probably be embarrassed by the déjà vu of needing so much help. Helen assisted him to a chair and sat down beside him.

"I'll be fine in a minute." Except he was confused. He didn't know why the town's leading lady was sticking up for him like a lioness. "Were you here to get a reading?"

Helen smiled sadly at him and brushed a lock of hair behind his ear, reminding him he wasn't wearing his turban. "I know this is the busy season for you, and I know you're not going to miss working Haunt Fest if you can avoid it, but can I please just...buy out the readings you'd normally do until Haunt Fest? You need to take it easy. Rest and recover so you don't make yourself sick."

Drew's mother had never acted like this around him, but Helen's concern did make him miss his grandma all the more. He just couldn't quite figure out why Helen was treating him so nicely. There didn't seem to be any ulterior motive behind it; growing up with the Drummonds, he was usually pretty good at spotting things like that.

"Thank you. I appreciate the offer, but I can't do that. If you want a reading now, though, I'd be happy to do so."

Helen peered at him for a moment before she spoke. "Okay. A quick reading, as long as you promise to take it easy."

Drew tried to shove on the turban, but Helen grabbed his hand and shook her head.

With no small amount of trepidation, Drew led her into the reading room. A glance at the incense box that hid the two problematic cards soothed him some. There was no tingle when touching the cards, no change in temperature, nothing strange. Just the normal hum of activity outside the walls of his house.

He took a deep breath and laid out three lines of cards. Almost at the end of the reading, he touched the tower, and just like last time, a picture rose clear in his mind like a movie projection on a screen, with an unreal clarity, almost like something not of his own mind.

Unfortunately he already knew what it was, and even snatching his hand away from the card didn't make it stop. Andy Wilson stood on a ladder, right before the hand of an unknown person, a shiny watch strapped around the wrist, reached out and shoved the ladder. The vision cut out before he saw who the culprit was and, thankfully, before he had to watch Andy topple to the ground.

Breathing hard, heart pounding, he blinked. Helen, wearing a concerned expression, came into focus. Drew had no idea how long his vision had taken, but it couldn't have been more than a couple of minutes. Nevertheless, if he'd checked out in the middle of a reading, it was no wonder Helen was concerned.

He sure as hell wasn't going to tell her what he'd seen. No fucking way.

Biting his lip in the hopes of controlling the fine tremors in his hand, Drew touched the card again, but whatever psychic electricity that had imbued it before had dispersed.

The damage had been done, however, and Drew could barely complete the reading. It ended up being the most stilted, amateurish reading he'd done since the first solo one his grandma had made him do. Helen had every right to complain, but instead she still looked worried. That made two of them. There was no way Drew could pass this off as coincidence or imagination. The implication of the vision was too disturbing.

"I'm sorry. I guess I'm still not quite recovered. The...uh...head injury has created some interference with the spirits." He was so full of shit. "This one's on the house, okay?"

Helen's lips thinned, but she didn't argue. "You need to take care of yourself. You've got Northcliff's phone number if you need him, right?"

Drew flashed hot and cold as he realized for the first time Helen must know exactly where her son had been staying. Whatever estrangement existed between the two hadn't done a damn thing to wither the gossip vine of Sandy Bottom Bay. Helen had probably known of the arrangement before Cliff dropped off his stuff. She couldn't know the true nature of their developing relationship, though, or she'd be warning him off like dozens of girls' fathers had done to his brothers since they hit puberty. Weren't many families who wanted their kids to get involved with a Drummond.

"Uh. Yes. Thanks."

Helen gave him another assessing look, and Drew did his best to smile as if his brain hadn't just conjured up an image of a murder, but the silence was like a black hole, trying to suck words out of his chest. How could he tell Helen—or anyone—about his visions?

"Can I ask you something?"

Helen patted his hand and waited with no hint of impatience or exasperation. If he hadn't been so rattled by the image of Andy's death, he'd have never imposed on the matron of Sandy Bottom Bay, but he liked the illusion of mothering.

"Do you believe—I mean, truly believe—in the hauntings of this town? Ghosts, supernatural activity, and all that? I know *Phantoms* is filming out at your estate, but do you believe they're going to find proof of something?"

Drew couldn't tell from Helen's expression if he'd surprised her with his question.

"The supernatural is tremendously important. It is the lifeblood of this town, and this town is my responsibility, the same as it has been for all the Somersets since they settled here. If *Phantoms* finds proof, that will only be to the good."

Helen stood and tucked another stray lock of Drew's hair behind his ear. "I'll just see myself out, but please take it easy. I don't want you to make yourself ill."

Drew nodded and waited as she made her way out of the reading room. He took several deep, calming breaths, during which the bell over his front door tinkled, heralding Helen's departure. With a rueful laugh, he realized Helen could have been a politician. She'd answered his question without him realizing right away that she hadn't come right out with a yes or no, and he had no idea which one she was leaning toward. Not that he'd ever have the guts to press her for a real answer.

With a deep breath, he gathered the cards into a stack, hoping he wasn't about to be shown any other disturbing visions.

He couldn't do another reading for anyone. Not yet. Helen was right about that. He needed to figure out what was going on, and he needed to do it before Haunt Fest started in full swing, because otherwise he'd never survive. Although he was risking Eddie's annoying business-stealing tactics, Drew needed to close up for the day.

Before anyone could drop in, Drew locked the front door and put up the closed sign. He didn't usually have too many locals come in the few days prior to Haunt Fest anyway. Most of them had too much to do to prepare for the onslaught, so he wasn't going to miss out on much income.

Turning back to the tiny desk that was his payment counter, he noticed a small bundle of paper tucked under the credit-card reader.

Two quick steps had him within reach. The bundle turned out to be a piece of notepaper wrapped around a wad of cash. There wasn't any writing on the paper, but the scent of Helen's perfume was unmistakable. The money covered the cost of ten full readings, with all the extras, and tears burned in Drew's eyes at Helen's kindness. He didn't know what he'd done to deserve her more than generous patronage, but he couldn't deny that this would ease his mind and give him the time before Haunt Fest to figure out what the fuck was wrong with his brain.

Sniffing, he held back the tears—damn eyeliner—and pocketed the cash. First thing was to get out of Malachi's robes and into something more comfortable.

~

THIRTY MINUTES AFTER HELEN LEFT, Drew found himself wandering along Main Street with no real destination in mind. He had no idea what he was going to do. Broaching a conversation with Cliff about visions of murder would be, at best, awkward and, at worst, explosive. Hell, telling Cliff about his vision might destroy their budding relationship altogether, but how could he live with himself if the vision was true and he did nothing? Andy Wilson might have drunk more than was healthy, and his reputation hadn't been improved by his frequent association with Drew's brothers, but that didn't mean he'd deserved to be murdered.

Drew sighed again and checked his phone, hoping his frantic text to Kyle would have a response. Unlike last weekend, Kyle had been desperate for a break before Haunt Fest and had headed up to Tampa to blow off some steam, planning to be back within a day or so. The screen was as blank as ever, and Drew didn't know why Kyle had chosen this particular day to abandon him, but he was pretty sure he was going to need to stop for a milkshake to console himself. Thanks to Helen's contribution, he could afford a little splurge, despite his reduced workload the past few days.

He looked up, finally paying attention to his surroundings in order to head over to the Dairy Devil, and found himself outside the police station. Had his new psychic subconscious brought him here, or was it merely another coincidence in a long line of increasingly unlikely coincidences?

Stopping on the sidewalk, he stared at the door. Cliff's shift didn't start for a couple of hours, and he was probably still shopping for groceries. Drew didn't want to face Cliff, but neither did he want to avoid Cliff until his shift started, where he'd be hanging out with Brett for hours. A sneer curled Drew's lip at the thought of Cliff's ex. What a complete asshole. That didn't stop the insidious worry that Cliff might want to return to the glamour of a celebrity boyfriend. The hustle of a big city. Cliff had been adamant about feeling at home with Drew, happy where he was, but it was hard for Drew to believe this wasn't some figment of his imagination that was going to be snatched away from him.

"Hey, Drew."

The unexpected voice made Drew jump, and he turned to see Scott smiling at him.

"Oh. Hey, Scott."

"You looking for Cliff? I haven't seen him today, but he's due out at the film site at two."

Drew hesitated for a moment, then made a split-second decision. "Can I ask you something?"

Scott shrugged. "Sure. What?"

"Is there any chance Andy Wilson's death wasn't an accident?"

A frown erased Scott's bright smile as he stared at Drew. Drew fidgeted while Scott mentally assessed his question, and they were interrupted as a couple of officers walked by and clapped Scott on the shoulder.

"Good going, Hunter. Makes it easy if the Drummonds just show up at the station to get arrested." The two cops laughed, and Drew didn't have any difficulty recognizing them as guys who would have given him a beat-down or three in school if it hadn't been for the protective nature of his brothers.

Drew's face heated, and while Scott deflected the attention of his colleagues, Drew slipped away. The Dairy Devil was a necessity more than ever. He'd never been arrested, not once, and yet there were an unfortunate number of townspeople who expected him to turn to criminal ways any second.

There were a number of park benches and tables scattered around the Dairy Devil, but Drew couldn't stand the thought of anyone else watching him, judging him.

Instead he took his milkshake and made his stealthy way to an out-of-the-way corner at Ochopee Park, conveniently located behind the Dairy Devil's parking lot. He and Kyle had devoured probably hundreds of milkshakes and sundaes in this very place over the years, hidden from staring eyes.

A headache pulsed, the focal point situated below the healing wound on his forehead. If only he had some way to hide it from view, since it felt like a neon sign proclaiming him a troublemaker. Dejected, he sucked in the sweet, thick milkshake. Mint chocolate chip had long been a favorite of his, but it wasn't doing much to elevate his mood this time. Worse than the mean-spirited mocking was the realization that Cliff had no idea what he was getting into. Not everyone hated Drew for being a Drummond and thought he was one bad day away from knocking over a liquor store, but even a few people was enough. There was no way Cliff was going to want to be with him once he realized Drew would always be a pariah in the eyes of some of the townspeople, especially the police force.

Then again, if Drew's visions were proof of psychic ability or merely the manifestation of insanity, Cliff wasn't going to be sticking around anyway.

No matter how sweet and caring Cliff had been, Drew had to face facts. The milk in his fridge would probably last longer than the relationship he'd dreamed of for years.

Sniffling, he tilted his head back, hoping to defeat gravity and keep the tears in his eyes.

CHAPTER 17

Burdened by several grocery bags, Cliff strode to the kitchen door a few hours after he'd left Drew warm and sated in bed. Almost like he'd been waiting, Drew opened the door, which meant Cliff didn't have to juggle the groceries to get in the house. Living with Drew was both comfortable and exciting in a way he'd never expected. Every time he saw the door, he knew he was coming home, and he really hoped Drew wasn't just counting the days until Cliff found his own place. Maybe it wasn't smart to feel like this so soon, but he didn't want to leave. He wanted to be with Drew, wanted to live with Drew, despite Drew's family and occupation and super-tiny home.

Cliff placed the bags on the floor and turned back to Drew. "Hey there."

"Hey, yourself."

Drew's response wasn't quite as robust as Cliff might have liked, and he hoped it wasn't another headache. Nevertheless, he leaned in and gave Drew a kiss, to which Drew responded with more than ample enthusiasm. "How are you feeling?"

Drew grinned and winked. "Better, if you're staying."

A glance at his watch confirmed that Cliff couldn't stay, not long enough to have sex and still be in uniform and out at Brett's film site. They were going to be on his mother's property again.

"Can't. Not today."

Drew's happy expression faded, and what remained appeared to be worry or anxiety, which caused a clench of panic in Cliff's gut. Had he worn out his welcome already? After all, Drew didn't really need him here any longer. They'd agreed he could stay until at least the end of Haunt Fest, when things calmed down and it would be easier for him to find an apartment, but maybe it was all too much for Drew. Especially if he'd sensed how badly Cliff wanted to stay. Perhaps Drew was feeling trapped.

Or maybe it was because circumstances had made them jump into living together without having a proper date first. They'd spent the past week ensconced in Drew's tiny house, getting to know each other and becoming so close, almost like a minihoneymoon. Drew had confided about how his boyhood crush—on Cliff, amazingly enough—had helped keep him on the straight and narrow. Cliff had admitted how rudderless and on edge he'd felt in Los Angeles, especially after Pete died. Cliff should have been terrified by how fast his feelings for Drew were growing, but he wasn't. Not a bit.

Cliff stepped close and pulled Drew into his arms, trying not to let Drew's fading bruises make him tighten in anger.

"After Haunt Fest, can I take you out to dinner? Somewhere romantic?"

"Like...a date?"

He'd come this far; he might as well jump and hope Drew would catch him. "Exactly. A date. With my boyfriend."

The whole town would see them, and Cliff wanted them to. Early on, they'd discussed being out and open, but somehow, in the intervening time, they'd really only spent time together inside Drew's house.

A sunny smile lit up Drew's face. "Oh yes. Please."

The faint terror faded away, and Cliff kissed Drew. "The Angry Parakeet, or maybe the Vineyards at the hotel?" Cliff would be happy with either.

Drew thought about it for a minute. "The Angry Parakeet. I mean...if you don't mind people knowing about us."

Joy surged in Cliff, erasing all his previous hesitation. "Drew, I *want* them to know about us. Boyfriends, remember." Just the thought of parading a boyfriend in front of coworkers would have terrified him back in Los Angeles, but here, he wanted people to know he'd staked a claim, however archaic the sentiment.

"Why don't I take you to the Angry Parakeet for lunch today?" Because he wanted to show Drew off now, not wait.

"Sure. That would be great."

"We can decide on a place for our date later. Maybe drive up the coast a bit." Farther south, the swampland merged into the Everglades, but heading north along the coast toward Tampa were a number of towns whose claim to fame was a romantic seaside. Somewhere had to be a romantic restaurant he could take a date.

Smiling, he kissed Drew, the rightness of their connection almost unbelievable. He deepened the kiss, but once his cock hardened and his hips began responding to Drew's thrusts, he pulled himself back. "Now, now, no tempting me into delinquency."

"You sure?" Drew rubbed against him, eyes dark with lust.

Cliff groaned. "Fiend."

"Sex fiend. Yep. I can make it quick, North."

North. An unexpected shiver raced down Cliff's spine at hearing Drew's special name for him. A name that promised sex and sweetness, fun and comfort. Maybe even love. The throb in Cliff's cock practically begged him to throw caution to the wind. He took another desperate glance at the time. He could flick on the lights in the squad car and speed through town, just this once. Especially if he didn't get messy enough to require another shower. The last thing he wanted to do was turn down what Drew offered.

Somehow perfectly attuned, Drew could tell when Cliff acquiesced, because the moment Cliff had decided maybe they had time for a quickie, Drew dropped to his knees and fished out Cliff's cock, right there in the kitchen, followed immediately by Drew's cock making an appearance.

"Drew, you're killing me."

His boyfriend didn't bother to respond but sucked Cliff's hard dick into the warm wetness that could convince him to sell his soul, if it didn't already belong to Drew.

Drew stroked himself while his tongue and lips worked Cliff over, and within seconds, Cliff was shuddering, almost ready to blow. Somehow Drew got better and better, and if Cliff had to die by blowjob...well, there were worse ways to go. He slid his fingers into Drew's hair and tightened, somehow managing to resist the temptation to take over the rhythm and fuck Drew's mouth to a speedy orgasm.

Holding off was utterly impossible when Drew moaned around his dick and Cliff got a whiff of the earthy musk of Drew's spunk. He shuddered, and his cock jerked, spilling down Drew's throat.

Drew pulled off, giving the tip of Cliff's dick a little lick before he sat back on his heels, debauched and angelic-looking all at once. Cliff leaned over and kissed those talented lips, savoring the taste of himself there, before he grabbed something for Drew to clean up with.

CLIFF COULDN'T KEEP the grin off his face, and his happiness was only partially due to the outstanding blowjob he'd recently received. Walking into a public place with the boyfriend he was quickly falling for, both of them out and proud, was an indescribable feeling, and he never wanted to lose it.

With a possessive hand in the small of Drew's back, Cliff ushered him into the Angry Parakeet but stopped in the entrance. The Angry Parakeet was a *find your own seat* kind of place, rather than a *please wait to be seated* place, but sudden trepidation halted his forward momentum. This was the first time he'd been back inside the Angry Parakeet while Drew was there. The table Drew had bashed his head against was clean and sitting innocuously between two tourists. Cliff didn't know what he was expecting to happen, since he didn't believe in any of the woo-woo shit, and Drew was, thankfully, standing beside him, strong and on the mend. Maybe it was the memory of Drew's close call that gave Cliff the chills, that sensation of someone walking over his grave—although they'd have to torture him before he'd utter those words aloud.

"C'mon. Let's sit over here." As far the fuck away as he could get from the place where he'd seen Drew covered in blood like he'd been the victim of a horror-film slasher. Blood was an unfortunately regular sight for a cop, but it made him squeamish when it was on people he lov—cared about.

They sat down, Cliff ensuring that not only did Drew have his back to the scene of his accident but also that Cliff had an unimpeded view of the room, with the wall at his back.

"It's okay, you know. I don't remember it at all." Drew gave him a little smile as he touched his bruised forehead.

Cliff stroked the side of Drew's face before he sat back. "But I remember, and not only does the thought of you getting hurt freak me out, but I want to beat the shit out of your brother."

"Again?" Drew teased, making Cliff laugh.

"Just because I punched the mirror image of Rob doesn't mean I don't want to give Rob a matching broken nose. Especially when I think about how easily you could have died." Cliff's eyes burned. He could have lost Drew before he'd even gotten to know him, and Cliff's life would be immeasurably darker for the loss.

"Hey." Drew grabbed his hand, and with the simple touch, public and claiming, a warm fluttering in Cliff's gut chased away the chill of fear. "We can't live in fear of what-ifs. I'm here, you're here, and we're together."

Cliff squeezed Drew's hand. Together and alive were the most important parts of the equation. "You're right. I will try to get over it."

With one last caress of Cliff's hand, Drew let go to peruse the menu. Unlike at chain places, the Angry Parakeet's chef regularly refreshed the menu, both for lunch and dinner. Still, the options weren't endless and certainly didn't require the intense concentration Drew seemed to be giving the menu.

It took no time at all for Cliff to make a decision, but when he set the menu down, Drew was still frowning at his own menu, the expression looking even more intense accompanied by the slowly healing bruises.

"Hey, are you okay?"

Drew started and lifted his gaze up. "What? Oh. Yes, I'm fine."

The waitress came by and took their orders, but that didn't entirely remove Drew's air of preoccupation. Nevertheless, he appeared to shake it off, and they managed to converse about a number of things in a comfortable manner, exactly as Cliff had believed a couple should.

He couldn't shake the idea that something was bothering Drew, and he hoped Drew would talk about it sooner rather than later. Perhaps it was too early in their relationship to push—he didn't know how Drew would react to that sort of pressure.

When their burgers had been reduced to scraps, Drew stared down at his plate and pushed around a couple of fries.

Without being obvious, Cliff glanced at his watch. He didn't want to be late for his shift—well, he sort of hated babysitting Brett and the rest of the *Phantoms* crew, but he was committed to being a good cop in Sandy Bottom Bay. On the other hand, if Drew was going to spit out whatever was worrying him, Cliff didn't want to take off and leave him hanging.

"Drew, seriously. I can tell something's bothering you. Is it something I did? Is it Brett? I can tell him to fuck off when I see him."

Drew gave him a little half smile without quite meeting his eyes. "No, it's nothing you or Brett did."

They sat there for a few more silent minutes before Drew heaved out a sigh. "Is there any chance Andy Wilson's death wasn't an accident?"

The question was so unexpected, Cliff had to blink a couple of times to parse its meaning. "Andy Wilson? The handyman who died out at my mom's place?"

"Yes. I mean, I know it was classified as an accident, but is it possible people were...wrong?"

"I doubt it." Cliff thought for a moment, wondering if he'd get in trouble for sharing what he knew. Probably not, since it wasn't an open investigation, and quite frankly, he was sort of surprised the whole town didn't know the story from front to back anyway. "His blood alcohol was high enough that there's no way he should have been up on a ladder."

Drew nodded slowly, but he didn't appear convinced, and Cliff had no idea why it would even matter. Unless... "Did your brother say something?"

"What? No. Why?"

Cliff raised an eyebrow. "If he did, you need to tell me."

Wyatt Drummond had discovered Andy's body, and if it had been up to Cliff, Wyatt would have been down at the station right after, answering a few questions. Cliff's relationship with Drew had softened him up—a bit—with regard to the evil twins, and despite the police records of others in the Drummond clan, he didn't think the twins were capable of murder. But accidental manslaughter...yeah, he didn't have any difficulty believing that could happen. The real surprise was that it hadn't happened yet, considering how free Rob and Wyatt were with their fists.

A flicker of something passed across Drew's expression, like he knew what Cliff thought and wanted to be pissed off but was also afraid that it could have gone down like that. "I promise you, he didn't say anything."

Cliff had no doubt that Drew could lie if it came down to it. After all, he'd been surrounded by champion liars from birth. But he also believed Drew was the oddball in the Drummond clan and that lying, cheating, and stealing weren't Drew's default. Cliff didn't think Drew was lying. But *something* wasn't right.

"Then what makes you think Andy's death was anything other than a tragic accident?"

Stunned, Cliff listened to Drew spin out some fucked-up tale about...cursed tarot cards? Anger built up in his chest as Drew claimed to have foreseen the pileup on the highway as well as the fire at Mysteriously Good. Followed quickly by a vision—in Cliff's mother's presence, no less—of Andy being murdered. Not that Drew could even identify the murderer. No, he only saw a hand with a watch.

The muscles in Cliff's jaw, which had just started to unlock after moving home and finding Brett prancing around, tightened up so hard a dull throb started in his temples. He clenched his fists together under the table, trying to control himself, hoping against hope that Drew was going to end this ridiculous, laughable, un-fucking-believable tale by telling him it was all a big joke. One in extremely poor taste.

Drew licked his lips, which was normally sexy as hell, but that couldn't distract Cliff. Not from this. Drew's expression was expectant and wary at the same time. And unfortunately, there was no hint that he wasn't serious. Even worse, there was every indication that he wanted Cliff to take this seriously.

"No. No fucking way. What the hell are you trying to pull? Trying to get yourself a spot in the *Phantoms* segment? You don't need to pull this elaborate bullshit to get Brett to give you an interview." Cliff's lips twisted into a sneer. "All you'd need to do is let him in your pants."

Drew gasped and pulled back as though Cliff had slapped him, but there was too much anger in Cliff for anything like remorse to take hold. Cliff stood, pulled out a couple of twenties, and threw them down on the table.

"But—"

"I have to get to work." Cliff left before he let Drew's big blue eyes, brimming with moisture, make him even think about believing this towering mountain of bullshit.

"Cliff, wait!"

Without acknowledging Drew's anguished plea, Cliff dashed for the door. He wasn't lying about needing to get to work, and if he gave any thought to what this might mean for his new relationship, the one he had such hopes for, he'd be a fucking wreck. As it was, Brett was going to sense trouble, like a shark sensing blood in the water. Cliff would have enough trouble keeping his temper with Brett, so the best thing to do was to pretend the whole discussion hadn't happened. He could worry about it after his shift. With a stabbing pain in his heart and a sick flip of his stomach, he decided he might have to crash in Scott's spare room after work.

How could he have been so happy just an hour ago?

UNABLE TO PUT Drew's story out of his mind, Cliff showed up at his mother's estate still fuming. Brett better not be a fucking ass, or Cliff was going to make a habit of breaking noses. And probably get fired in the process, so he really hoped Brett wasn't a dick. Then again, being a dick was Brett's normal state of being.

His stride ate up the ground, and before he was ready, he was already approaching the film crew. Out of the corner of his eye, he noticed a muscular blond man at the edges of the activity. Cliff couldn't think of one good reason for Rob—there was no bruising on his face—to be here. Just as Cliff decided to confront Drew's brother, Rob noticed him and slipped away behind one of the trailers.

A frowning Scott got in Cliff's way before he could chase the man down. "What is wrong with you?" Scott's voice was low, and Cliff was thankful his friend did his best to keep it down.

"What the hell is Rob Drummond doing here?"

"As far as I know, your mom hired him to pick up some of the stuff she'd hired Andy for."

Cliff gritted his teeth. He'd have to have words with his mother about that, but later. The last thing he needed today was a constant reminder of the pending implosion of his relationship with Drew. Tripping over one of the evil twins wasn't going to make it easy to put that out of his mind.

"You gotta keep Brett out of my way today. Please."

"What did he do now?"

Cliff let out a bitter laugh. "Not Brett. Drew. But Brett likes digging into open wounds and...well, let's just say the leash on my temper is frayed."

At least today's segment wasn't inside the house but in some of the outbuildings that had had various purposes over the years. Inside the house, where filming was to take place tomorrow, his mother would likely witness it if he lost his shit all over Brett. Having his mother chastise him for doing so—which she would undoubtedly do, no matter how justified—in front of the *Phantoms* crew and his new partner would likely push Cliff into homicidal territory.

"Trouble in paradise? That surprises me a little."

Swallowing around the lump in his throat, Cliff managed to get the next words out. He told himself he was only angry, but he was hurt, badly, too. Drew knew how he felt, and he'd still decided to spin out this stunt to get on Brett's show. "You said you had a spare room. Can I crash there tonight after work?"

There wasn't any hiding the surprise on Scott's face, and he glanced around before dragging Cliff away from the filming and behind a large tree. Any other time, Cliff might have found it amusing, but not today.

"Okay, what the hell is going on? I might not be in a relationship, and I realize this was sort of an intense beginning for you and Drew, but this is a pretty drastic step. Are you sure you want to do this? What happened?"

What happened between him and Drew was so personal. If anyone else had asked him the same thing, Cliff would have told them where they could shove their questions. There was also a small part of him that wanted comfort, because he didn't know if he could continue in this relationship. Drew's betrayal wasn't as bad as if he'd cheated, but it was a betrayal nonetheless.

As emotionlessly as he could, Cliff relayed the story Drew had told him.

"I just can't believe he'd go to these lengths to try and get on *Phantoms*."

Scott's eyes flared open. "He asked you to get him on *Phantoms*?"

"I left the restaurant before he could ask, because I might have broken up with him right there." Cliff's breath hitched. The thought of not having Drew in his life left him light-headed, but how could he trust Drew after this? "I don't know...I don't know if that won't still happen, but I'd rather not have to do it in front of the whole town."

The story left Scott stunned into speechlessness, and he peered around the tree as though checking for eavesdroppers. But Brett was the only one who'd care about this, and he'd been in the middle of filming a segment when Cliff arrived. At least the man had enough professionalism to harass people only when he wasn't needed for filming.

When Scott returned his attention to Cliff, he grabbed Cliff's shoulders and squeezed, presumably to comfort Cliff, although it wasn't quite doing the job.

"We should probably get to work." Now that he'd bared his soul, Cliff really didn't want to talk about it anymore. He hadn't cried since Pete died, and to do so over the actions of one of the Drummonds seemed the height of stupidity. He should have known better and listened to his brain, not his heart and cock.

Scott rolled his eyes. "We both know this is a bullshit assignment for PR purposes only. And ironically, the person Brett needs the most protection from is you. So there's no rush. We're close enough if something happens, which it won't."

Cliff dropped his gaze. He should have kept his fucking mouth shut.

Scott's fingers didn't release their grip but only got tighter. "If you don't want to talk about it, that's fine. You're certainly welcome to stay in my spare room. But I want to say one thing, and I want you to listen."

One thing. Scott wasn't capable of that sort of brevity, but Cliff was the one who'd opened the door for Scott to butt in on his relationship, so he'd just have to shut up and deal until Scott let him escape, hopefully without any tears. The important part had already been said—Cliff had a place to sleep tonight.

"I don't really think Drew is the sort to do what you're accusing him of. He didn't like Brett at all."

"Okay, I'll take that under advisement. Can we go now?"

Scott's expression hardened to stone. "I might have lied about having only one thing to say, but you're going to listen to me. You're my friend, and I don't want you unhappy. I also happen to think you're making a colossal ass of yourself, and I'm hoping to keep you from making it worse."

Cliff barely held back a snarl. He didn't need to alienate everyone in Sandy Bottom Bay in his first week. "Fine. Talk." Listening to Scott might be marginally better than dealing with Brett's taunts.

"I know you're sensitive to the whole supernatural thing here. I get why, and I know how much it pissed you off when we were in school. I know you think anyone who believes in it is a gullible fool. But let me ask you something. Is Drew Catholic? Baptist? Hell, is he a Buddhist? Muslim?"

Cliff's confusion broke through his anger, just a bit. "I don't know. It hasn't come up. We're in Florida, so I'd assume Baptist, as long as the Drummonds don't actually burst into flame the second they set foot in a church."

A tiny burst of shame had his ears heating. He didn't need Scott's disappointed expression to know he'd overstepped. Assuming he and Drew could get past this, Cliff was going to have to refrain from openly disparaging Drew's family, because that wasn't fair of him. Not at all.

"Okay, that aside," Scott continued. "I know you were an atheist in high school. I'm assuming that hasn't changed, right?"

Cliff shrugged. "No."

"If Drew had told you he was a Baptist or whatever, would you have this same reaction? Would it make you this angry? Would it be worth breaking up over?"

"No, of course not. Why would it?"

"Belief in the supernatural isn't a religion, of course, but from an atheist's standpoint, what, exactly, is the difference between the two?"

Some of the stiffness in his spine melted as shame heated his ears even further. "Oh shit. I...I fucked up, didn't I?"

"Yeah, you kinda did."

Cliff let his head drop, and he fought against the tears that had threatened ever since he'd walked out on Drew. He had all sorts of unresolved anger tied up in his mother's beliefs and the resulting breakup of his family, and he'd brought all that anger and baggage and slammed it squarely atop his burgeoning relationship.

"Oh fuck, Scott, what do I do?" Despite the fact that their current assignment was stupid and useless, he couldn't just abandon his post to chase after his boyfriend, although Drew deserved a heartfelt and groveling apology. Assuming he would even listen, and at this point, Cliff wouldn't blame him if he didn't.

Scott merely raised his eyebrows because, yeah, Cliff knew what he had to do. Apologize like he'd never apologized for anything before. After his shift, which seemed like an eon away.

"C'mon. We need to get back to work, or your ex is going to come looking for you. You sure that's not going to go anywhere?"

Cliff did his best to compose himself. He had at least eight hours of dealing with Brett's shit, if not more. "Why? You want a chance at celebrity ass?"

Scott laughed and punched him in the shoulder. "Not hardly. Just checking. Because if you gave in, he'd probably be a lot nicer to work with."

A snort escaped Cliff. "That might be the worst reason I've ever heard to have sex with someone. Just sayin'."

Scott shook his head and started walking back toward the film crew. With a sigh, Cliff fell into step behind him.

"You know, Drew asked me the same thing. About Andy."

The twitching muscle in Cliff's jaw had been getting quite the workout since he'd arrived back in Sandy Bottom Bay. Now he wasn't sure if he was upset that Drew must have gone to Scott first with this, or irritated that Drew was putting so much effort into this campfire horror story. "Really? When was that?"

"Dunno. Earlier today, outside the station. I think he was looking for you, but a couple of the guys made some comment about a Drummond making the job easier by coming to the station on his own. So he didn't tell me about his visions or whatever, assuming he was going to tell me that."

A fresh surge of anger had Cliff clenching his hands into fists. No mistake this time. However upset Drew had made him, knowing that some of his fellow officers were hassling his boyfriend was a million times more aggravating. Once word got around that Cliff and Drew were an item—assuming they still were—Cliff would knock their heads in if they continued to give Drew trouble.

There couldn't be anything to Drew's murder…theory? No, calling it a theory gave it too much credence. Notion. Cliff scrubbed a hand through his hair. He might not have had much respect for the backwater town of his birth when he'd left, but from what he'd seen of the small police department, they were every bit as professional as he could hope. But there weren't many murders in Sandy Bottom Bay. At least, not the sort of murder requiring investigation to determine the identity of the killer. Could someone have mistakenly pronounced an accidental death simply because it was so uncommon?

God. He was making himself crazy. Brett better not be an asshole tonight, or Cliff's hard-won control would snap.

CHAPTER 18

Drew stood in front of the door of the mobile home where he'd grown up. His brothers had elected to remain there until their father was released from prison, but Drew was certain as soon as the man returned, his brothers would rent an apartment or something. None of them had particularly warm feelings for the hard man who...hadn't raised them, exactly, but rather had spent time drunk in their general vicinity while their mother did the bare minimum for them as required by law.

Lunch with Cliff had been disastrous. With no exaggeration. Cliff hadn't wanted to hear one word about Drew's new skill, and he'd looked so angry when he'd left, Drew wasn't sure if he'd managed to irreparably maim the relationship of his dreams. He had no idea how to fix it either, because he couldn't ignore what he'd seen. Not when taken in conjunction with the two previous visions.

So here he was at the only other place where he might find some answers, since Kyle was still incommunicado. After a detour for another milkshake from the Dairy Devil, of course. *Thank you, Helen Somerset*. He actually felt a little less guilty for accepting her generosity, since it was her son's intractability forcing Drew to seek mint-chocolate-chip solace for the second time in one day.

He rang the doorbell, wondering if he should have gone by his brothers' auto-body shop instead. For guys who'd never been much into honest work until their father had been incarcerated, they were usually at the shop very early in the morning, though they rarely stayed past midafternoon. The town was small enough that anyone who needed to pick up their car or have emergency work done only needed to text one of the brothers, and they'd show up at the shop. Most times, they'd even be sober.

Wyatt flung the door open with a scowl, and a laugh sputtered out of Drew.

The irritated expression on Wyatt's face smoothed out, mostly. "What's so funny?"

Drew flicked a hand toward Wyatt's bruised nose and matching remnants of a pair of black eyes. "I guess we're the twins in the family now."

Wyatt rolled his eyes. "Your boyfriend is an asshole."

Despite the recent tension between them, there was still a spurt of warm-fuzziness in Drew's stomach at the acknowledgment of North-cliff Garcia as his boyfriend. It helped that Wyatt's grumbles weren't the serious "the Drummond twins are gonna pound the life out of ya" sort, not like the feral look that came into Wyatt's—and presumably Rob's—eyes whenever Brett's name came up. Kyle had caved and told Drew exactly what had gone down the night he was injured, and none of it was worth his brothers going to jail for, so he figured he'd just not mention Brett Cavanagh or *Phantoms* until filming wrapped.

"Maybe to you. But you know you rub people the wrong way. Can I come in?"

Wyatt stepped back. "Not going to be rubbing your boyfriend any way."

Drew bit his lip against another bout of laughter that wanted out, but Wyatt didn't spend a lot of time cracking jokes, so he might have been serious. Drew headed straight for the kitchen and flung open the fridge, looking for a beer. He plucked one out and hefted it in his hand.

"Middle-of-the-day beer?" Wyatt sounded puzzled, but Drew was probably the only Drummond who didn't regularly engage in pre-five-o'clock drinking on weekdays. Mostly because the majority of his family didn't hold down regular jobs.

Then he remembered the two enormous milkshakes he'd had earlier and scrunched up his face. No matter how awkward the coming conversation was, a single beer wasn't going to smooth the way. It would probably only make him puke.

"No, I guess not." Drew slid it back into the fridge.

"Hey, little man, if you want beer, you drink it."

Ugh. *Little man.* He was taller than both his brothers, but they'd coined the name before his growth spurt, and it had stuck, much to his dismay. Maybe it *was* better when his brothers called him a fairy. Regardless, the beer was still a bad idea, so he filled a glass with ice and tap water before sitting down at the kitchen table.

Wyatt grabbed the beer Drew had put back, slouched in another chair, and waited. Wyatt and Rob never, ever got nervous in silence. Probably because they'd been trained by the sheer number of times they'd been taken in for questioning. Babbling didn't happen. It was a skill Drew didn't much have, perhaps due to lack of practice, for which he was terribly glad now. He was sure Cliff, as a cop, wouldn't give him the time of day if he'd had the practice his brothers had.

The silence stretched out, but then, Drew was the one with the issue, and he should be the one to speak up. Wyatt would probably sit there, not speaking, until he got hungry.

No matter how he approached the subject, it was going to be awkward as hell. Third time was the charm, right? "Wyatt, I need to ask you something about Andy Wilson."

"What?" Wyatt's irritated growl was accompanied by a faint stiffening of his shoulders.

"I know it had to have been hard, finding the b—" Drew cut himself off. Even for his brother, calling Andy *the body* would be insensitive. Andy had been a friend to both twins. "Er...finding him dead like that. I was just wondering how come it was you that found him."

Wyatt narrowed his eyes and assessed him for a moment before speaking. "Andy'd borrowed some of my tools. I went out there to get them."

Well, that was exactly what the gossips had said, no matter how oddly coincidental it seemed. Then again, if Wyatt had been out there smoking up with Andy or doing anything borderline illegal, the borrowed-equipment excuse was at least vaguely plausible. Nevertheless, Drew suspected *tools* might be a euphemism for *weed*.

"And...there wasn't anything weird?" Oh good. *That* wasn't too vague.

"Weird how? You snooping for your boyfriend or something?"

Drew's shoulders sagged. "No. It's just..." Did he spill it out again, like he'd done with Cliff?

"Just what?" Wyatt did not sound happy.

Sweat streaked down Drew's back. Wyatt and Rob had a couple of window units, but they weren't on full blast, and the topic was stressing Drew out, so he was more sensitive than usual to the temperature. Or he was just spoiled by how much cooler his house was since Cliff took over the thermostat.

"Is there any chance Andy was murdered?"

Wyatt's nostrils flared. "And what, you think I did it? What the hell, Drew!"

"No, no." He'd never thought that. Accidental death from doing something dumb, yeah, that Drew could see, but not the deliberate murder he'd seen in his vision.

"I don't really know how to explain it. But I've started having visions. Psychic visions." Drew attempted to explain, starting with the first two visions he'd had. "And then, I saw someone topple Andy's ladder. I don't believe you'd ever be able to do that to someone."

Wyatt snorted. "Well, thanks for that."

The one significant point in the Andy vision was the expensive watch. Drew glanced at Wyatt's wrists. His brother wasn't wearing a watch, and he often didn't, working on the cars all day. The watch had looked well out of a Drummond's price range unless someone had applied the five-finger discount.

"You don't have a watch, do you?"

"No watch. It'd just get banged up in the shop. You know that."

If Drew hadn't been watching Wyatt so carefully, he would have missed it, but for a split second, Wyatt looked uncomfortable. That minuscule crack in Wyatt's armor was enough for Drew to realize his brother was lying. About something. He just didn't know what, and he couldn't bring himself to believe his brother was a cold-blooded murderer. So what was Wyatt hiding?

"So. You're letting Cliff Garcia fuck you?"

The unexpected left turn in the conversation didn't give Drew any chance at all. Embarrassment at his brother's intrusive question had his cheeks heating up. He also didn't mistake Wyatt's wording. His brother had some pretty outdated assumptions about manliness and pitching, which Drew had no interest in trying to explain. Not again.

Wyatt rolled his eyes and swallowed another mouthful of beer. "Never would have guessed him for a fairy. Of course, he's always been an asshole. Stands to reason he'd love them."

Drew sputtered. He'd thought he was inured to his brother's insensitive remarks, but somehow Wyatt had managed to shock him. And piss him off.

"What the fuck, Wyatt? You can't say shit like that. He's a cop."

Wyatt's shrug was supremely unconcerned, and Drew wanted to slap him, but that way only led to trouble. Besides, Wyatt got too much practice fighting with Rob, either against a shared opponent or with each other.

Drew sighed. He knew better than to get sucked into another pointless argument with his brother. "Rob around?" His other brother had made himself scarce since the bar brawl, guilt making it difficult for Rob to face Drew. Even Drew's text messages had gone unanswered.

"Nah. I told him about Mrs. Somerset's job offer, and he decided to pick up some of the work Andy was doing up at the estate."

Drew blinked. He remembered Helen offering his brothers work, but he couldn't get past either of them taking her up on it. Maybe the auto shop wasn't doing as well as he'd thought.

"Is everything okay for you guys?" Because even calling Helen something other than *old lady Somerset* was somewhat unusual.

Wyatt shrugged. "We're fine. Rob'll get over being an asshole eventually. You really serious about Cliff?"

Drew stared at him, trying to figure out if there was some hidden meaning in the question. Was this his brothers trying to make things easier for him and Cliff? No one in town except for he and Kyle would believe they were capable of this sort of sensitivity, but it was possible they were trying to make themselves more...acceptable to Cliff and his mother.

After a moment, he decided there was no harm in admitting the truth and nodded. Even if Cliff was no longer serious about him, after their disastrous lunch date.

Wyatt's lip curled, just a bit, but Drew knew him well enough to know it wasn't disgust at Drew having a boyfriend, but irritation at the identity of that boyfriend.

"He better treat you right, or I'll give him worse than this." Wyatt pointed at his broken nose.

Drew sighed. Just what he didn't need. More punches thrown trying to protect his honor. His eyes burned a bit at the realization that he might not have to worry about Cliff sullying that honor after today.

"What's wrong?"

Oh fuck no. Drew wasn't about to talk to Wyatt about his relationship problems. Was he? Yet Kyle had made himself scarce, the bastard, and Drew desperately wanted someone to talk to. Wyatt had been surprisingly cool about Drew's newfound abilities, but he wasn't foolish enough to believe his brother would care to hear about his "fairy" problems.

"Nothing."

"Trouble in your big, gay paradise already?"

"Just a fight." Drew rubbed his eyes with the back of his hand. He wasn't going to cry in front of his brother. He just wasn't.

"Hey." Wyatt knocked his arm with the beer bottle, which was chilly enough to make Drew flinch.

"What?" Drew glared at his brother, hoping Wyatt would mistake his upset for anger.

"Talk to him." Wyatt sounded so serious, almost knowledgeable about the topic, even though Wyatt had never had a serious girl-friend. Nor had Rob, for that matter.

"What if he doesn't want to talk to me?" Drew hated that his voice sounded so sad and defeated, but all his energy was expended in keeping the tears at bay.

"The guy's a bit of a hothead, and I might hate him even more, knowing he's corrupting my little brother, but he's...a good guy." Wyatt's words were drawn out as though it pained him to admit Cliff wasn't the devil incarnate. "Give it some time; then make him listen to you. Because we've seen fighting doesn't work."

As if the unaccustomed compassion had made him uncomfort-able, Wyatt's gaze bounced away from Drew as he stood up and stretched. "I need to take a piss. When I'm done, I'm going to order a pizza. You can stay if you want."

"Uh, sure. Okay." Drew didn't much want to go back to his own place, not when the sheets still smelled like sex and Cliff had imprinted his entire house with memories.

The weirdest thing had been Wyatt and his unexpected insight. Drew hadn't realized Wyatt had been so aware that their parents' relationship had been a piece of shit, with the constant fighting—because there was no doubt that was what Wyatt had been referring to. Oddly enough, Wyatt was probably right about how to deal with Cliff. Despite the painful knee-jerk reaction, once Cliff had had some time to consider Drew's story, he might relent. After all, they'd been through this same thing with his mother's reading.

The big question was whether Drew should wait for Cliff to come home—assuming he didn't crash at Scott's place—or show up at the film site again and insist Cliff talk to him.

~

WITH HIS BLUNDER weighing heavily on his mind, Cliff couldn't stop

fidgeting. He wanted to tell the crew to hurry the fuck up. And seriously, this had to be the most boring shift he'd ever had the misfor-
tune to endure, each hour taking forever. He checked his watch
constantly, but the seconds crawled by, taunting him. Not even
watching his mother refuse yet again to film an interview, and Brett's
subsequent pouting, was enough to give him any satisfaction.

Honestly, he was surprised that his mother's belief in the supernatural hadn't outweighed any outdated consideration of vulgarity.
Still, seeing Brett thwarted made him want to cheer his mother on.

He glanced over at Scott and made a split-second decision. "Do
you know where Andy was found?"

"Back of the main house."

Cliff stretched and made a show of looking casual. "Things look
quiet right now. I think I'll wander by the house, make sure no one is
sneaking around." Cliff wouldn't have fooled a five-year-old with that
blatant lie.

"Sounds good. I'll cover for you out here." Scott didn't say a word
about what exactly Cliff would be checking out—namely the potential crime scene—but the knowledge was there in his eyes. Knowledge and support.

Cliff owed it to himself, and the man he was falling for, to at least
look, even if giving Drew's theory any credence made him feel like an
idiot. If by some crazy twist of fate Drew was right about the murder,
Andy deserved justice. And certainly not because Andy's spirit would
otherwise be destined to roam the overgrown vegetation behind
Cliff's family home.

Full sundown wasn't for another couple of hours, but the tangled
mass of the side yard was in full shadow. His mother hadn't been
lying about her inability to find a decent groundskeeper. The area
between the house and the wilder parts of the estate was almost
indistinguishable. The side yard was positively murky. Good privacy
for the bedrooms on this side of the house, including where his
boyhood room had been, but it also meant that those rooms would
be dark even in the daytime.

Cliff pulled out his flashlight, feeling a little bit foolish for the

sudden spurt of relief when the strong beam lit up the area, the vegetation losing all sinister aspects.

Once he'd finished apologizing and Drew forgave him, Cliff was
going to spank Drew for making him freak out like this.

There wasn't much to see. It wasn't overgrown enough to provide
much protection from the torrential rains. Cliff was certain he could
tell where Andy had fallen and then been the recipient of emergency
services. The grass was slightly trampled and the soil flattened.
Nearby, there were two rectangular imprints where the ladder had
rested. Presumably those indents survived because they'd been so
deep from supporting Andy in the sandy loam. At the far end of the
house, in the most overgrown area, were two larger rectangular
imprints, still fairly clear, as this patch of lawn was the most
protected. From the dimensions, they were probably where Andy had
put his toolbox and a small cooler, likely choosing the same spots for
those items each day. There were a few more of the ladder imprints
along the back wall of the house.

At least that narrowed down the area where Andy had been working. Cliff swept the flashlight beam over the ground and into the base
of the shrubs and hibiscus plants, which were never going to bloom
again without sunlight. Granted, he wasn't a detective, but he wasn't
stupid either, and he'd been present at a number of crime scenes.
There was nothing out of place. Nothing that gave any indication of
foul play, not even the few cigarette butts scattered around that his
mother would have bitched about if she'd seen. Andy was a smoker,
and all these seemed to be the same brand, which presumably Andy
smoked.

Cliff rubbed his forehead with the back of his hand, the overgrowth making things more hot and humid, despite the shade.
Finally he shone the flashlight up the side of the house. Hell, he
hadn't spoken to his mother long enough to even find out what sort
of work she'd been having Andy do. The beam of light caught some
distinctive leaves. Apparently Andy hadn't been hired to tame the
out-of-control bougainvillea and jasmine vines, or if he had, he'd
done a piss-poor job, because vines were creeping everywhere,

creating a junglelike atmosphere. Made it doubly hard to find snakes or wandering gators in this gloom.

Huh. Andy had been drinking before he fell. Seeing a snake or gator, especially for a northerner, might have startled him enough to have fallen. Cliff would present that as an alternate theory to Drew, see if he couldn't get Drew to admit his imagination was just running away with him.

Then the aimless wandering of his flashlight beam caught the gleam of black-coated wire. He flicked off the flashlight. The wire was virtually invisible. Turning the flashlight on again, he tried to follow the wire's path. He couldn't think of anything that would require wiring out here. Not of that type anyway. It sure didn't look like the green outdoor wiring people used for patio lighting.

Heedless of potential serpents or arachnids, he pushed into what had once been flowerbeds, jasmine curling about his head. He couldn't quite reach the wire above his head, but he was mostly able to follow it. It seemed to attach to the house in the vicinity of the windows on the second floor and possibly continued up to the third floor, although the light wasn't strong enough to see for sure. It could be some sort of shoddy home security system, but if his mother had decided to install something, Cliff couldn't see her hiring the local handyman to do it. Regardless, he didn't think any home security system in the world used wiring like this. It looked like the wiring they used on bombs on TV or the kind on ceiling fans that never seemed to attach to anything at all.

This time he followed the path of the wire down. Back in a wild tangle of foliage he found a battery pack and what looked like a control board for a remote control car, wrapped in plastic.

Pulling back, he plucked leaves out of his hair and brushed dirt off his uniform as he considered what he'd found. There wasn't any doubt that Andy was responsible for whatever it was. Unfortunately, Cliff didn't know exactly what the wires were for.

First thing to do—rule out that it was actually legitimate. Which meant talking to his mother. He brushed at his uniform again before heading around to the front door.

Morales's black vehicle was parked in the drive. Cliff shuddered. The thought of his mother and the mayor doing anything, even kissing, squicked him out something fierce. Nevertheless, he needed answers now. He needed all the information he could gather before he laid himself at Drew's mercy.

This time, when he walked in, the tension was still there, but Mayor Morales didn't leave. In fact, he looked like he was going to be staying for dinner. An intimate, couple's dinner. Ick.

Cliff wasn't ready to explain anything right now, especially to his old high school principal, but he didn't know how to get the man out of the way.

"Cliff, dear, is something wrong?"

He hesitated for a moment, but he really didn't want to risk spreading a rumor that involved his own mother, despite their differences.

"No, nothing, I just want to check something out upstairs." Cliff raced up the stairs before his mother could ask any questions.

He started in the spare room first. He wasn't entirely sure he wanted to look in his own room, because he hadn't set foot in it since he'd left town. Whether his mother had left it exactly the same or entirely revamped it, both notions were equally troubling.

The spare room had updated curtains and bedspread, but the heavy furniture passed down through the Somerset family remained the same. Hot as blazes, though, and stuffy enough to indicate it hadn't seen use in a while. If the mayor was spending the night—and another little shudder ran down Cliff's spine at the idea—he definitely wasn't staying in here. A fresh coat of paint on the window frame seemed to indicate that perhaps Andy had been responsible for replacing the windows. Yet something wasn't quite right.

Cliff walked straight to the window and inspected it before flipping the latch and opening it. Nothing seemed out of place, except the vegetation was really overgrown. His mother might not have noticed how bad it was, since the master bedroom, bathroom, and sitting room were situated at the front of the house. Sliding his hands down the side of the house, he was able to feel the wires he'd seen while standing in the yard.

He paced the room, rubbing his temples. He could go check the other rooms, but there didn't seem to be much doubt about what he'd find. The windows had been wired for something. His mother might be all for creating work in town for townspeople, but even with that mantra, Cliff couldn't imagine her being foolish enough to pay for a security system that relied on a laughably amateur setup.

Cliff inspected the window frame itself, looking for some trace of the sensors he normally associated with security systems, and found nothing. Nor did he remember seeing any sort of keypad at the front door.

What the hell were those wires for? He paced some more while his mind whirled.

Every scenario he could imagine, he had to disregard as ludicrous, except for one. Even that, he might not have considered if it weren't for his mother telling him on the phone about increased spectral activity right before he'd moved back. In the very rooms where he'd seen new wiring. He suspected the attic might be similarly wired, since his mother had mentioned the spirits were more restless up there as well.

There was only one person who had anything to gain from an artificial haunting, and it sure as shit wasn't his mother.

The muscles in his jaw tightened up so fast that pain streaked through his temples. He slammed the window shut and flipped the latch to the locked position.

"Honey, what's going on?" His mother appeared in the doorway, the mayor standing just behind her.

Cliff's nostrils flared as he sucked in a breath that utterly failed at being calming. "Just need to go see a man about a haunting."

"What?"

Cliff ignored his mother's question and pushed past the mayor to get to the staircase. Brett was going to pay for involving his mother in this horseshit.

CHAPTER 19

Outside his mother's house, Cliff loped toward the outbuildings where *Phantoms* was filming. Thank fuck they hadn't done any interior shots of his childhood home nor managed to convince his mother to do an interview.

Like a predator, he prowled around the building, searching for the asshole celebrity star of the worst fucking show in the entire world. He was vaguely aware of his mother and the mayor following him, but they soon fell behind.

As soon as he spotted Brett's perfectly styled hair, Cliff made straight for him, tunnel vision muting Scott calling his name and several of Brett's underlings trying to keep him from interrupting the take. What a fucking laugh. Like *Phantoms* was some sort of earth-shattering truth or a Hollywood blockbuster.

Cliff walked right under the bright, hot lights, relishing Brett's look of shock, before he twisted Brett's collar in his fist and pushed him back against the weathered wood slats of the building. Be better to do this without all the onlookers, but Cliff was too focused on Brett to clear the crowd. Scott was there, making sure no one tried anything stupid. Cliff didn't want to have to shoot anyone today.

Behind him, Eddie let out an irritated bleat at the intrusion. Like Cliff gave a shit about interrupting Eddie's dream interview and spoiling his fifteen minutes of fame. More like Cliff was interrupting Brett's on-screen interview for a bed partner.

"I know your secret, asshole."

Brett gestured to someone behind Cliff to cut before he plastered on a smile, one of his superfake ones. "Cliffy, we're filming right now." He enunciated his words carefully, like Cliff was the village idiot.

"I don't give a fat flying fuck about your pissant little show."

The faint lines of tension around Brett's eyes were the only indication he was even remotely concerned about Cliff's anger.

"Cliff, what are you doing?" The mayor sounded thoroughly annoyed, and Cliff kept his attention on Brett, or he'd flip the bird to the man who'd hired his boss.

"My *pissant show* is the best thing to happen to your shithole of a town in, oh, forever."

Cliff needed some answers. That was the only reason he was able to hold on to the slippery reins of his temper. But if Brett didn't stop acting like a spoiled brat, Cliff was perfectly happy to let Brett cough up the answers after hanging out in jail for several hours.

"That's why you need to fake your hauntings? Because your show is so damn awesome? You're a fucking shit, Brett. And a stupid one too."

That wiped the smirk of Brett's face, giving Cliff some bleak satisfaction.

"Fuck you. I'm a hell of a lot smarter than you." Disdain dripped from Brett's words, without a hint of his previous flirtatiousness, his expression cold.

Cliff rolled his eyes. "Please. An infant could have figured out the haunting of my mother's house is a hoax. The basis of your show is as fake as your tan. Tell me, what would your adoring public think if I could prove you were a big fraud?"

The flicker in Brett's eyes was one Cliff had seen before, when Cliff had confronted him about his infidelity. It wasn't guilt, because Brett didn't care enough about other people to feel guilty for his asshole behavior. No, it was more disgruntlement at having been caught out. No matter what Brett said from here on out, Cliff knew he was responsible.

Kristi moved in and dug her crimson-painted nails into Cliff's bicep. "Stop this, Cliff. The relationship is over. Let it go. Resorting to slander will only bring lawyers into your breakup and won't get you back in his bed."

Disbelief momentarily replaced his anger, and he tossed an incredulous look at Kristi. "Are you fucking serious? I dumped him because he's a cheating asshole, remember? Oh, and good thing I'm already *out* here, Kristi."

Cliff let his gaze ice over, and Kristi paled and released her grip but held her ground.

"Just don't hurt him. Please."

That earned her a snort. He didn't know why Kristi had tied herself to Brett, but Cliff felt sorry for her, because Brett only ever looked out for himself, and Kristi would figure that out eventually.

"Let me go, Cliff. I think I could make a good case for police brutality." Brett tried to break Cliff's grip on his shirt, but Cliff merely shook him in response.

"And I think I could make a good case that you were resisting arrest."

"Arrest? For what?" Brett snarled.

"Murder."

"What?" Brett wasn't the only one who said that. The onlookers were a vague annoyance at the edges of Cliff's attention.

"You killed him, didn't you? What, he threatened to expose you?"

"I haven't killed anyone. Who are you talking about?" Brett was starting to get angry.

"Andy Wilson."

Brett paled. "Andy was *murdered*?" The last word came out as a little squeak, loud in the sudden silence that surrounded them.

"Don't play the innocent, Brett. You're not that good an actor."

All the fight left Brett. "Cliffy, you can't think—"

"Don't call me that. Brett Cavanagh, you're under arrest—"

"No, Cliff, please, don't."

Cliff glared at him but paused.

"I didn't kill Andy. I swear. I paid him to add some...enhancements to your mother's place." There were a few gasps from their audience.

Good. Brett wasn't going to deny it. "Yes. I already said that. And then you killed him to hide it."

"Jesus, Cliff. Don't you think I've seen just about every way people have tried to fake me out? They're the ones who *don't* make it on the show. If I wanted to, I could present the perfect fake haunting, and no one would know better. I *wanted* it to be discovered, just not quite yet. And not by you. I had no reason to kill Andy."

Some of Cliff's anger bled away as his resolve faltered. He'd been so sure that Brett had been up to no good. Underneath his rage that Brett had chosen Cliff's mother to screw over had been an undeniable relief that he could accept Drew's intimation that Andy had been murdered. Chalk it up to intuition or knowledge of the town or however Drew had figured out the truth. As much as Cliff wanted to be able to believe Drew, Brett made a lot of sense. The "haunting" had been amateur hour, big time.

Hell, what he'd found wasn't even evidence of murder. It barely even made a credible motive and wasn't proof of anything, especially since Andy's death had been deemed accidental. What the hell was he thinking?

"You asshole." Kristi flew in, hand raised, the slap across Brett's face as loud as a gunshot. "If this gets out, the show will be finished."

A smug smile stretched Brett's lips, and with a sinking stomach, Cliff realized Brett was no longer worried about getting arrested.

"But, Kristi," Brett simpered, "that's what I want."

Kristi's look of shock had to mirror Cliff's own. "Why? We're poised to go international. You'll be a household name worldwide."

Brett scrunched up his nose. "With you at the helm, I suppose. Thought you could drag yourself into the stratosphere with me, did you?" His tone was so unbearably condescending, Cliff wanted to slap him, and Cliff didn't even like Kristi.

"Well, yes." Kristi sounded lost and hurt. Cliff hadn't realized Kristi was going to learn the folly of trusting Brett right this very day.

"I don't want to be a household name as part of the fucking spook brigade. That's never going to A-list me."

"It won't matter." Kristi was adamant. "The network will never air this segment."

"They don't have to air it. I'll leak the fraud myself." Brett laughed. "Don't you just love social media?"

"How is sabotaging your show going to help you A-list yourself?" Cliff hadn't meant to interject, but he couldn't see how this fit into Brett's patented blend of narcissism and selfishness.

Brett's lip curled into a sneer. "I have a career-changing movie role lined up. Which I can't take because I'm contracted with *Phantoms* for-fucking-ever. After this, the network will cut me loose."

"Two years. You only had two more years on your contract," Kristi said.

The crew around them had begun to mutter, and the few words Cliff caught weren't exactly complimenting Brett. No more than he deserved.

Brett shrugged. "Two years *is* forever in this business."

Cliff had to agree. It was probably harder every day for Brett to look young enough to still be considered a rising star.

None of that was important, at least as far as Cliff was concerned. "And you chose my mother's house because…"

Brett turned that smug smile in his direction, and Cliff's hand curled into a fist. What he wouldn't give to break Brett's nose like he'd done to Wyatt.

"Well, Cliffy…"

Cliff snarled, but that didn't deter Brett any.

"Cliffy, killing your town's reputation is only a bonus."

The muscles in Cliff's jaw hardened, and a tic in his temple throbbed in time with his heartbeat. "You did this all because… because…I dumped you?"

Brett bared his teeth in a feral approximation of a grin. "No. I was going to do this anyway. I just didn't know where. Breaking up with me deserved a little payback, so in a way, you chose the location of my swan song."

Swan song. Pretentious asshole.

"Too bad I had to dick around with all these Eddie-the-medium interviews." Brett glanced over Cliff's shoulder, an overly exaggerated sympathetic look on his face. "Sorry, Eddie, honey. You're pretty, but you're shit on camera."

How could Brett manage to make Cliff feel sympathy for yet another person he didn't fucking like?

"If only your mother had consented to film an interview. Would have made this revenge ever so much sweeter."

Anger shredded Cliff's control, and he grabbed Brett by the throat, pushing him up against the side of the building.

This time, though, Scott leaped into the fray and wrenched him away. "Don't do it. It's not worth it."

Cliff struggled a bit against Scott's hold.

"What about Drew?"

The unexpected question broke through Cliff's haze. "What?"

Scott got his face into Cliff's so it was the only thing he saw. "Not that I would cry if you killed this ass, but I thought you wanted a relationship with Drew. And I like having you back in town. That will all go away if you don't calm the fuck down."

Cliff took a deep breath. Then another. Scott must have seen he'd pulled in the reins on his temper, and let him go.

Brett was glaring at him and rubbing his throat, but there wasn't a single person who appeared to have any sympathy.

"Suing the shit out of you and this town for police brutality will be icing on the cake, Cliffy." There was no hint of playfulness or flirting in Brett's tone. "Think I'll go for a walk and call my lawyer."

Scott grabbed Cliff's arm as Brett turned away.

Once, Cliff had been mesmerized by the sight of Brett sashaying away, but now he never wanted to see the man again.

The snarl on Kristi's face was truly terrifying as she glared at the crew, with a little extra laser-death stare for Cliff, and he wasn't ashamed to say he quailed, just a bit.

"If I see one word of this on social media, you'll be fired, stranded in Florida, and I'll make sure people will think the Black Death would be preferable to working with you. Got it?"

Her slender shoulders shook as she stalked toward the craft table. Probably she wouldn't be the only one who needed some sugar therapy. The crew were clearly unwilling to brave the table while Kristi was still so angry, and Cliff didn't blame them one bit. They drifted around the grounds, clumping together and whispering furiously. Eddie stalked away, angry spots of color on his cheeks, poor bastard.

The mayor had disappeared, probably to do damage control after the threat of lawsuits. Scott patted Cliff's arm. "I think I better give the chief a heads-up. In private."

Without a word, Cliff watched him head toward his patrol car, leaving Cliff mostly alone and feeling ostracized.

He had no idea what had happened, although he was almost certain he was getting fired. Hell, as soon as Kristi was done at the craft table, Cliff might as well look for a doughnut or twelve. Not like he'd have to worry about a fitness test after this debacle made it back to the ears of the chief. Unwillingly, his mind went back to his room at his mother's place.

Fuck. He might find out sooner than he'd like if his mother had redecorated or not. How could he possibly have fucked up his job and his relationship in less than a twelve-hour time span?

Like he'd conjured her up, his mother appeared in front of him, although he'd been aware that she'd observed the shitstorm as it had unfolded. What he hadn't expected was the undiluted concern in her eyes. "Are you hurt?"

Just like that, she was the mom who'd always loved him. Always. She didn't care about the opinions of however many viewers *Phantoms* had; she didn't care that Cliff had let his temper get the best of him. It was Cliff's own hang-ups and unwillingness to deal with his parents' divorce that had driven an imaginary wedge between them, and he could hardly believe it had taken a tragedy to get him to come home.

"Not physically, but yeah, I screwed up. Bad." He was so fucking fired.

She reached up and touched his face. "That's okay. You'll fix it. You're a good man, Northcliff."

Funny, his name didn't make him cringe as it usually did. Not that he was in a hurry to be known by that moniker. "I'm sorry about Brett."

"Not your fault, honey. Besides, you've traded up." There wasn't a hint of disappointment or disapproval in her tone.

Remorse made Cliff's heart ache. "I think I screwed that up too," he whispered.

"You like Drew, don't you?"

Like? Cliff had so much more than *like* for Drew. But he didn't want to admit to his mother how thoroughly he'd fallen in love with a Drummond, because it would only make it that much more painful if he lost Drew. If he couldn't fix it.

"You'll do the right thing, Northcliff." She squeezed his hand. "I'm going to head back to the house, see if I can stifle the gossip. If you need anything, let me know."

"I will, Mom."

The warmth in his tone made her blink, and she smiled at him, her eyes watery. True to her reserved nature, though, she didn't let a tear fall. That didn't bother him either. She didn't have the same exuberance as his father and his father's family, but he no longer doubted she loved him. He didn't know why he ever had.

Scott strode up, biting his lip. Dread filled Cliff. He and Scott stared at each other while Cliff waited to hear what an asshole he was. What a *fired* asshole he was.

"The chief wants to see you first thing in the morning."

Cliff's shoulders sagged. Getting fired was the only reasonable outcome, but it hurt nonetheless. "It was nice working with you, Scott."

Scott shook his head. "I hope it doesn't come to that."

Cliff didn't want that either, but he didn't hold out any hope.

~

"I CAN'T BELIEVE I'm helping you do this," Wyatt muttered, making Drew roll his eyes.

"You want me to be happy."

Wyatt said something else that Drew couldn't quite hear, but that was probably for the best, as it was undoubtedly derogatory.

Pushing through the foliage, Drew tried to make sure he didn't end up looking like he'd run his hair through a blender.

"How is it you know exactly where we're going?"

Drew shrugged as he continued to walk. They'd parked on an unpaved, overgrown access road that put them fairly close to where the *Phantoms* crew was supposed to be filming. The crew, with all their trucks and equipment, didn't have the option of using this route, and Drew preferred it. He could probably get fairly close to Cliff before he had to explain to anyone what he was doing there, although the crew had seemed to think he and Cliff were cute. Did they know about Cliff's previous relationship with the star of their show, though? And if they did, would they be rooting for Cliff and Brett to get back together?

Then again, maybe it was a moot point. Cliff might not want anything more to do with him.

"I just do."

They continued to walk, Wyatt trailing him while letting out the occasional curse under his breath before Wyatt spoke again. "Hold the fuck up." This time there was anger in his tone, and it made Drew obey. Not that he thought Wyatt would hurt him, but an angry Wyatt was one spoiling for a fight.

"What's wrong?"

His brother's cheeks were flushed red, and Drew knew it wasn't from exertion. Both twins drank a lot more than they should, but they also kept themselves in shape. A brisk walk through humid brush wouldn't make Wyatt sweat. While Drew and his brothers had vastly different complexions, Wyatt's skin flushed in the same obvious way Drew's did when he was angry.

"I knew there was something weird with this relationship of yours. I *knew* it."

Was Drew having a delayed reaction to the head injury? Between the visions and Wyatt's spectrum of emotions, he was so fucking confused.

"There's nothing weird with my relationship." Except that it was on the rocks.

"Oh, really? I knew things happened way too fast. No one moves in that quick, not when they're supposedly strangers."

"What are you talking about?"

"I'm going to string that pervert upside down by his balls and rip his pecker off." Wyatt barreled through the foliage like a wild boar on a rampage.

Drew gasped, trying to suck in breath. He had no idea what bug had crawled into Wyatt's boxers, but it had made him crazy. Even if Cliff weren't on duty with a firearm at his side, Drew wasn't about to let Wyatt's fucked-up notions about gay men make him do something stupid that they'd all regret.

"Wyatt. Wyatt!" Drew called out and gave chase. Desperation gave him the burst of speed required, and he caught up to Wyatt just as they broke through the worst of the overgrowth near the outbuildings where the film crew was working.

"Don't try to stop me, Drew. He took advantage of you."

"I *am* going to try to stop you." Drew made sure his grip on Wyatt's arm was firm even though his brother could probably get out of it if he didn't care about hurting Drew. "Cliff has never taken advantage of me, and I want to know what made you think that."

"You know your way around the Somerset estate just a little too well. How could you know that, unless that perverted asshole had been fucking you in high school? You were just a kid! And the minute he returned, you just crawled back into his bed!"

Shock widened Drew's eyes. Holy fuck, no wonder his brothers were always getting into fights, if this was the way their logic circuits hooked up information into conclusions. Drew grabbed Wyatt's other arm, putting his body between his brother and the film site, and made Wyatt look at him right in the eyes.

"Cliff had no idea who I was in high school. Not a clue. I promise you, he certainly wasn't fucking underage guys." Because Drew would have figured that out pretty quick.

Wyatt's eyes narrowed. "I would really like to kick his ass, you know. Especially if he hurts you."

"Well, you can't. No matter what. And I..." Embarrassment flashed through him. "I maybe wandered by here, back in high school."

Wyatt's face darkened, and Drew hastened to explain. "I mean...I wanted to know where he lived. I snuck in here and, uh..." Watched. Jeez. He was probably lucky he'd never been arrested for stalking, because if he hadn't been a fourteen-year-old kid in the throes of his first crush, he would have been totally creepy. Hell, maybe he was anyway, but kids could be so dumb.

Comprehension flooded Wyatt's face—neither of Drew's brothers were as stupid as most people assumed they were.

"Oh man. I remember that year now. You'd had a crush on someone—Cliff Garcia? Really? You know how much me and Robbie fought with him."

Drew shrugged. "I know. But that's actually why I noticed him."

Wyatt's mouth moved as though he wanted to growl or bare his teeth, but he settled on a muttered, "Fucking figures. Let's go patch things up with your damned boyfriend."

After giving his brother a fond smile, Drew continued on toward the TV crew. Be easier if Kyle was here, but Wyatt was turning into a surprisingly supportive companion.

CHAPTER 20

"Cliff!"

The shout caught Cliff's attention, and he turned to see Drew, red hair flying in the wind as he strode up. The sudden surge of happiness made him smile. For a brief second. Until he saw Wyatt trailing Drew.

"Oh shit." There could only be one reason Drew would be coming after him during his shift, an evil twin in tow. Drew was going to dump him and wanted backup. He wasn't going to give Cliff a chance to grovel and apologize.

His happiness fizzled, and his breath hitched. Somehow he'd get through this without breaking. Somehow.

The closer Drew got, the shallower Cliff's breathing became. At this rate, he might pass out before he had a chance to say anything to Drew.

Scott stood beside him, watching the Drummond brothers approach. "You want me to stick around for backup?"

Cliff grimaced. His love life—both ex- and current boyfriends—might be the most interesting thing to happen on this shoot. With Brett sulking in one of the trailers, there was a whole lot of nothing going on, so he could hardly blame Scott for hanging around. The offer of support was nice but unnecessary because they both knew Cliff could hold his own against a single Drummond twin.

All things considered, he'd rather grovel without an audience, but since Drew had brought a wingman, perhaps it wouldn't hurt to have one of his own.

"Yeah, thanks." Cliff's voice cracked a bit, and he cleared his throat, hoping he wouldn't sound on the edge of breaking down, although he sort of was. He couldn't even blame Drew for accusing Brett of murder, because somehow Drew had figured out something hinky was going on even if it wasn't an actual murder.

Then Drew was in front of him. "Hi."

Cliff hated that Drew sounded so hesitant and unsure. Which was his fault. But now that Drew was standing in front of him, looking sweet and delicious, Cliff had no idea where to begin.

"Hi."

Wyatt rolled his eyes and crossed his arms, looking for all the world like a bodyguard.

"I—" Drew started to speak again, but Cliff held up a hand. There was only one person in the wrong here, and he had to take responsibility for that.

"No, please, let me speak."

Pink tinted Drew's cheeks as he nodded, his gaze skipping around, landing everywhere but Cliff's face.

"Drew, I'm so sorry. I was an idiot at lunch. I know I'm having a hard time accepting your...beliefs...but getting angry about it was completely out of line."

The pleading in his voice must have registered with Drew, because those mesmerizing blue eyes finally lifted, and Drew looked him direct in the face, lips parted in what appeared to be confusion. Cliff wanted to kiss him, but he couldn't distract himself that way. Not yet.

"You said...you said some pretty awful things." Drew's voice wasn't much more than a whisper.

"I know. I was wrong." Cliff tried not to squirm at the memory of how harsh he'd been. "Please don't let my momentary stupidity change the way you feel about me."

Drew bit his lip and cracked his knuckles, and the silence stretched out too long.

"I want to be with you more than anything. I was blaming you for issues I had that were a carryover from my parents' divorce. It was stupid, and I promise I won't let it happen again." Cliff didn't know if he could admit to love yet, not this soon, but it wouldn't be long. No one had ever made him feel like this.

Wyatt pretended to gag, but Cliff couldn't let that throw him off. If he was going to have Drew in his life, he'd have to get used to the evil twins. Besides, he only cared about Drew's reaction, and the fine tension keeping Drew taut melted, just a bit. Cliff took a step closer, thankful beyond belief that Drew didn't move away or flinch.

"It wasn't my intention to upset you like that. I...I want to be with you too."

Relief made Cliff's knees wobbly. All he wanted to do was yank Drew into his arms and kiss him thoroughly enough to wipe away the fear and dread. Making up in front of witnesses while he was on duty made that utterly impossible, though.

Drew's breath caught. "If it happens again, another vision...I'll just keep it to myself, okay?"

Guilt wrenched at Cliff's heart. "No. Please don't. I know it's something I'll have to come to terms with, but I don't want to start a relationship where you feel you have to keep things from me. And... and..." God, it was killing him to say this, but recent events had planted a tiny seed of doubt in his once firmly held skepticism.

"And what?" Drew's eyes were wide and filled with hope.

"And he just accused Brett Cavanagh of murdering Andy Wilson." Scott's words were almost explosive, and embarrassment sent blood racing to Cliff's cheeks.

Cliff didn't even look at Wyatt, because he didn't give a fuck what Drew's brother thought, but Drew looked stunned to the point of speechlessness, and Cliff hastened to explain. "Uh, yes, well, I was wrong. About the murder." He was fucking this up, and he held his hands up, palms out, trying to prevent anyone from saying anything until he'd spit out his explanation.

"I don't know what you saw, Drew. I'm not convinced you saw a murder, but you definitely put me on the trail of some funny business that Andy was involved in." Which was the only reason he hadn't insisted Drew return to the doctor for another MRI.

Cliff proceeded to explain, Scott dropping in several humiliating details of his interaction with Brett. After he was done, Drew's eyes filled, but he was smiling.

"I can't believe you did that for me. I was going to tell you that I might have been wrong about my conclusions, but there were too many coincidences for me to not at least tell you about what I saw. Thank you, North."

"North? Why the fuck are you calling him North?" Wyatt asked, making Cliff groan. He didn't mind Drew calling him that, but it would weird him out if anyone else did so.

Drew turned a glare on his brother. "None of your business. Only I can call him that."

"Oh, a sex thing. Well, kiss and make up, already, so we can get the hell out of here. Cliff is still on the clock, so I'm guessing you're not staying here with him unless you want to get him fired." Wyatt grinned in a way that said more clearly than words he'd be damn happy if Cliff got fired. Sadly, soon he'd make Wyatt a happy man.

Cliff cleared his throat. "Um, about that... This might be my last day on the job. I've already got a meeting with the chief tomorrow morning, and I don't think he's too happy with how I, uh, approached Brett."

A muffled snort of laughter came from Scott. "Sorry, man, I don't want you to get canned, but you were like the lord of vengeance. It was so awesome."

Drew wasn't at all amused. "Oh my God. I'm so sorry. I never meant for that to happen. Would it help if I talked to your chief? Explained it was all my fault?"

Wyatt made choking sounds at Drew's offer to walk willingly into the police station, but Drew ignored him.

"My temper isn't your fault, and I need to control it better. That's all on me."

"But if I hadn't told you about my vision..."

Cliff shrugged. "If you hadn't said something, I wouldn't have known about Brett's hoax. I don't know if the knowledge helped at all. Brett is still determined to sabotage his show and make Sandy Bottom Bay look foolish at the same time, but at least this way the chief and the mayor can be prepared for the backlash."

Drew didn't look convinced, but Cliff wasn't interested in Drew pleading his case for him. He could own up to his own mistakes, and although he didn't want to lose his job, he was more worried about what it would mean for their fragile relationship.

"I'm sorry. If I get canned, well..."

Drew gasped, and moisture gathered in his red-rimmed eyes. "You're not...you're not leaving, are you?"

"No! But I won't have an income. I have some savings, but not a huge amount." Living in Los Angeles was expensive, and so was moving back here.

The lack of apprehension or hesitation in Drew's smile drained away the last vestiges of Cliff's fear and doubt. This was a true part-nership, the kind he'd always dreamed of. "We'll deal with that if it happens. Together we can manage."

"Yeah, we can." He was grateful Drew didn't make any noises about getting money from his mother. She'd help if he needed it, but he never wanted to rely on her, and Drew, who'd worked so hard to support himself, understood that without Cliff having to explain it.

Despite everything, this was his home. Both he and Drew belonged here, together.

Cliff reached out to draw Drew into his arms—since his job was toast, he was going to kiss his damn boyfriend—but the second they touched, Drew stiffened, his eyes blank and sightless.

"Drew? What's wrong?"

Something in his voice alerted Scott and Wyatt, and they both crowded him to stare at Drew, who gave no indication he heard or saw any of them.

~

THE VISION OF blood and swamp faded into the concerned faces of Cliff, Scott, and Wyatt. What didn't fade was Drew's sense of urgency, the sense that time was running out.

"Are you okay?" Cliff's skin tone didn't easily lend itself to paling, but he definitely looked washed out.

Physically Drew was fine, but he needed a minute to assimilate what he'd seen, and apparently the visions weren't as seamless as he'd assumed.

"Fine. I'm fine." Drew wrinkled his nose. He didn't really want to ask what happened, because that might only lend credence to the fact that he had some sort of brain injury that made him hallucinate. But he couldn't believe they were hallucinations. "Where's Rob?"

Cliff wrapped a warm hand around the back of Drew's neck. "It was like you were asleep or something for a minute. A minor seizure, maybe. Do you have a headache? Maybe we need to take you to the hospital."

Oh great. Good thing he didn't fucking own a car, or that could be real trouble.

The sense of urgency still rode him, and if what he'd seen was God's honest truth, then he was going to need help.

"Cliff... North..." Drew whispered the nickname, hoping it would put Cliff in a more receptive frame of mind. "You aren't going to like this, but please, you have to believe me. We need to find Rob and Brett."

"What?" Wyatt's voice dripped with derision. "Rob wouldn't have anything to do with that pansy."

"Except try to punch his lights out," Cliff said with a glare.

"He was perving on my brother and Kyle." Wyatt's defense of Rob's actions was loud and strident. "He was perfectly justified."

"Justified? Is that why he's been avoiding Drew? Because he felt *justified*? This is why fighting isn't the answer to every fucking disagreement in the universe, Drummond." Cliff's words were sharp and guaranteed to piss off Wyatt.

"Shut up, both of you." Drew's voice bordered on a shriek, but he couldn't handle his brother and boyfriend sniping at each other. Not now. Not when time was running out.

They both turned affronted looks on him, but Drew would worry about hurt feelings later.

"I wasn't having a goddamn seizure." He didn't think. "When I touched Cliff, I had a...vision. I'm sorry, but that's what it was. We need to find Rob and Brett right now."

Cliff's lips pressed together into a tight line, his attempt to be open-minded about Drew's visions almost painful to watch.

"Listen. I think they're in trouble. Like, they-could-die sort of trouble."

With an intensity he must reserve for interacting with criminals, Cliff stared into Drew's face as if assessing his sincerity. Maybe he was checking to see if Drew had the crazy eyes, but Drew didn't care if he sounded nuts. The vision had been pretty fucking clear, and until he saw Rob, he wasn't going to rest. Brett too, but only because Drew didn't wish death on anyone.

"What did you see, Drew?" Wyatt tensed, ready for a fight. Any guy who hurt a Drummond brother would be lucky if he managed to keep his teeth, assuming he didn't get beaten to death. Drew might not be as big as his brothers, but he'd be right there in the fray.

"Not a lot. They were tied up, bloody, and out in the swamp."

"That's not a lot to go on," Cliff said quietly.

"Listen, you bacon-flavored bastard. Either you stand behind the pansy-ass apology you just gave my brother, or get the fuck out of my way, because I'm not letting Rob end up as gator feed."

Cliff blinked, probably at the surprisingly subtle way of calling him a pig. "No one is going to end up as gator food."

"Yeah, but Cliff, they might," said Drew. "I didn't see who did that to them, but I'm sure that's what he—or she, I suppose—intended. Hide the evidence with the gators. I can't let this go, not if it means saving my brother. And no matter how much trouble Brett has been giving you, do you want him to die?"

"Are you fucking serious? What the hell is going on?" Scott didn't look nearly as goofy as he had in high school. Nope, he was a right scary cop when he wanted to be.

"Just hold on a second. No one is going to die, not if I can help it." Cliff had a scary cop voice too, and he threw a glare in Wyatt's direction. "And I'm standing behind my apology. But 'the swamp' can cover a lot of ground. And before we go off like some half-cocked search party, why don't we check if Rob and Brett are where they're supposed to be?"

"Agreed." Scott slapped Cliff on the shoulder. "But let's keep this as quiet as we can, okay?"

"Worried about your job too?" Wyatt sneered.

Scott's jaw tightened. "Actually, I'm more worried about starting a panic and/or letting a potential murderer escape before we can figure out what's going on."

Drew wouldn't be able to relax until Rob was okay, but something inside him eased at the support he was getting from all three men. At least he wasn't going to have to tromp through the swamp all by himself. He was itching to do just that, but he couldn't argue with Cliff's logic. After all, there was no guarantee his visions were in real time. They could be a future occurrence. Or, as Cliff had implied when he was telling them about the hoax, the visions could be merely representative, not literal. As much as Drew felt, deep down, they were almost snapshots of events, there was still no evidence of Andy being murdered. The fact that Cliff had gone to check at all had been amazing and heartwarming all at once.

If Drew weren't worried about his brother getting eaten by a gator, he'd want to take Cliff home and give him the blowjob of his life.

"Okay, then." Cliff grabbed Drew's hand and squeezed comfortingly before pulling out his cell phone with a flourish. "First, I'll call Brett, and you call Rob."

Wyatt pulled out his own phone, which was the wisest choice in Drew's opinion, since Rob had avoided Drew's calls as well as Drew's presence since the accident. His brother's finger trembled, ever so slightly, the only sign he was as worried as Drew.

It took just seconds to realize that when both men spoke into their phones, they were speaking to voice mail.

"Does Rob screen calls?" Scott asked. Drew wasn't surprised Scott hadn't asked if Brett did, because everyone knew that Brett was the sort of guy who did, even if Cliff hadn't just accused him of murder.

"Nope," Wyatt replied. "Not even during sex."

Drew shuddered, thankful he hadn't ever called Rob while he was having sex.

With a deep breath, Cliff put his phone away. "We'll split up into pairs so the crew doesn't get weirded out by strangers poking around unaccompanied. I think Brett went to one of the trailers. Scott, you and Wyatt check those out, since Brett might actively be hiding from me. Drew and I will check to see if their vehicles are here and take a quick run through the outbuildings. I think Rob was working up at the house, so we'll meet up there and see if we can find him there."

The plan made sense, and Drew was glad he didn't have to be parted from the comfort of Cliff's presence. But damn, the minutes were ticking by, and it was almost dark. Any minute he might start panicking and running into the brush.

CLIFF'S STOMACH TWISTED as he and Drew walked silently toward the house. Brett's shiny red truck was parked with the rest of the crew vehicles, but Rob's piece-of-shit truck was nowhere to be found. Its absence hadn't done anything to convince Drew that Rob wasn't in danger, as Cliff had half expected. The outbuildings weren't empty, but Brett and Rob were not in them, at least as far as could be told with a cursory walk-through. But absence of proof wasn't proof of absence.

The crew was scattered around, taking advantage of Brett's sulk to check their phones, eat, and smoke. A number of people were unaccounted for, including Eddie Price and Kristi. Cliff had managed to ask a couple cameramen and gaffers if they'd seen Brett around, but he hadn't wanted to rouse suspicions. Especially after the show he'd put on for them earlier.

The more they searched, the more Cliff found himself buying into Drew's unwavering belief that Brett and Rob were in some kind of trouble. Tied up in the swamp and left for gators seemed a little over the top, although it wasn't unheard of for murderers to use gators to hide bodies. Cliff was beginning to believe Drew *had* intuited something, but whatever it was didn't necessarily reflect reality.

The part Cliff was having the most difficulty with was tying Andy, Rob, and Brett together, unless all this "danger" was actually tied to the hoax Brett had hoped to...denounce? Perpetrate? Setting up a bad hoax only to reveal it himself was idiotic, but then, Brett didn't have the firmest grip on logic.

Who stood to gain by harming all three men? It hadn't escaped Cliff's attention that his interest in the matter would be purely academic tomorrow morning, when he no longer had any official capacity to uphold the law.

With that in mind, he threaded his fingers through Drew's. His sexy, forgiving, big-hearted boyfriend gave him a startled look but accepted the comfort with a sad smile. Hell, it hardly mattered if he got caught having sex in uniform in public at this point... Well, he still wouldn't, because despite his stupid actions, he was a good cop, and he was going to do his best until he no longer had a job. A little handholding was a minor infraction compared to the rest of the day.

They rounded the corner of the house and caught sight of Wyatt and Scott. Without one word exchanged, Cliff knew. There hadn't been a trace of either missing man, and neither Kristi nor Brett had returned phone calls. Unfortunately, as the situation stood now, they couldn't even call in official backup.

"What next?" Scott flicked his gaze between Cliff and Drew.

Cliff swallowed a sigh. The only information they had to work with was from Drew's visions, and they'd have to make do with that. Despite Cliff's initial unwillingness to believe, their inability to locate the two men had given him a bad feeling.

"Drew? Any way you can narrow down 'the swamp'?" There were

a couple of places around the estate, including some old orange groves that were no longer used in the Somerset citrus operation, that could be classified as swampland. Most of the town was surrounded by swampland, including a pie-shaped preservation area that separated his mom's place from the mayor's. Without some direction to go, the four of them would need weeks to comb the swamp.

Fists clenched tight, Drew shook his head. Fear whitened his face, and the beginnings of panic were clearly visible. "I don't know. I don't even know if what I see is real! I get flashed images and a...conviction about something. It's not like I got GPS coordinates or saw a signpost." Drew's voice cracked. Even if Cliff hadn't slowly been coming to believe Drew had an ability he couldn't explain, he'd be sending out a search party, if only to alleviate Drew's upset.

"Hey." Cliff wrapped an arm around Drew's shoulders and pulled him close. "We'll find them. I promise. Just breathe for a moment."

Drew shivered in his arms, and Cliff rubbed circles on Drew's back, hoping to soothe. It was a measure of Wyatt's worry that he didn't even roll his eyes at their contact. Cliff considered going into the house, but he didn't want to alarm his mother.

While the tremors abated and Drew relaxed into his embrace, Cliff's mind whirled. He wasn't entirely convinced that Rob hadn't just sloughed off work to go to a bar or something, although Wyatt had been adamant that Rob didn't screen calls from his brother *ever* —which was information Cliff could have done without.

Hell, he still wasn't sure a malevolent force was involved in Brett's disappearance. He'd been pissed and embarrassed when he'd stalked off. He'd said he was going for a walk, and if he hadn't been paying attention, he might have gotten into trouble. Maybe that's all Drew sensed. Cell service was patchy in his mom's house; it would only be worse out in the brush. Then again, did it matter if Brett got into trouble on his own or because of a malicious unknown person? Drew was still demonstrating some sort of atypical mental ability, and Cliff was going to have to accept that without qualifications or provisos.

Assuming either scenario, and assuming Drew was right about gators being an issue, there were a number of places with gators.

Retention ponds frequently had them, and they occasionally showed up in people's pools. Retention ponds and pools weren't swampland, though, and Drew had been adamant about the swamp. Gators plus swamp, and close enough to the estate that Brett could either get there on his own or with someone else coercing him... There really was only one place that fit the bill.

"I think I know where we should start looking," Drew said suddenly, the pinched look gone from his face and the stress in his voice reduced.

Cliff lifted an eyebrow. "The preservation area?"

Drew's eyes widened. "Yes, there. How did you know?"

"Well, I'm a cop, remember?" Cliff winked at Drew, willing him to remember the couple of times they'd engaged in salacious acts while he was in uniform. From the bright blush that colored Drew's face and neck, he recalled at least one just fine. "I deduced the most likely place for them to be."

"Yeah, me too. The path is close by, isn't it?" Drew asked and waved a hand toward the edge of the manicured yard. "Although it seems weird that anyone would bring Brett up here to get to the path, doesn't it?"

"There's another path by the outbuildings, but those are the two best ways to get to the preservation area from our property. In fact, I'd suggest we start with the other path. If Brett wandered away on his own, he'd have gone via that path, not the one by the house." Cliff frowned. "How do you know about the path here?"

Drew's face flamed red again. "Can I tell you later?" he whispered.

If the situation weren't so grim, Cliff would have laughed. Whatever reason Drew had for knowing about the path to the preserve was embarrassing, and he couldn't wait to find out what it was.

"Let's get going before I get my ass fired too." Scott pulled out a flashlight and gestured for Cliff to take the lead.

He'd rather not go wandering about gator-infested swamp at night, but neither did he want to leave Brett and Rob out there, possibly injured and helpless. At least it wasn't gator mating season, and the flashlights should illuminate gator eyes in plenty of time to avoid them. He hoped.

～

THE FENCE between the preservation area and the wild areas of the Somerset estate wasn't the only demarcation line. The growth in the preserve was more untamed and thicker and also had more dead brush. Although it had been some time, it wasn't difficult to see that Helen periodically had someone come in and remove dead brush and unnecessary growth. Drew couldn't help but worry, though. If a wildfire started in the preserve, it would quite easily spread to the Somerset property.

Thinking about some possible future fire relieved Drew from worrying about the present, and where his brother had ended up. He hadn't wanted to tell Cliff that Brett and Rob had been tied up in mangrove roots as though the trees in the swamp had come alive to imprison the two men. That wouldn't help his cause at all. The preserve they were entering was large; just the tip of it sneaked down between the Somerset and Morales properties. Thanks to his youthful...uh...surveillance activities, he knew there was a body of water, too small to be called a proper lake, a short distance from the fence. Last time he'd been there, he'd seen a couple of gators, so if the perpetrator of this crime was after gators, knew the area at all, and didn't want to traipse too far into the preserve, that's where Drew expected him to go.

He didn't know what he'd do if that spot wasn't the one he'd seen in his vision. Cliff and Scott were coming along because they knew he and Wyatt would go searching no matter what, but what they were doing wasn't safe, and if Drew thought about it too hard, the guilt would make him insist Cliff go home.

After climbing over the fence, which was more a perimeter indicator than a security barrier, Cliff called them to a halt and swung his flashlight beam near the ground.

"We're on the right track. Someone came through here recently."

They pushed into the brush, and Drew couldn't stop a shiver of dread. The sight of a gator wasn't cause for alarm, but heading right for them in the dark was an entirely different proposition. He crowded close behind Cliff, scanning the area for reflective eyes while Cliff concentrated on the broken brush trail he followed.

A few minutes later, a metallic gleam caught his eye on the edge of the half-assed path they were on, and he tugged on Cliff's shirt. "Look." Drew kept his voice low, the situation and oppressive vegetation making him unwilling to use a normal tone of voice.

Cliff trained his flashlight where Drew pointed, and Drew lunged forward, hand outstretched.

Cliff clamped fingers around his wrist, keeping him from the prize. "Don't touch it."

"But it's a watch. I think it's the same watch I saw in my vision." He couldn't be sure, not until he saw it full-on, but even finding a similar-looking watch out here had to make coincidence impossible. Didn't it?

"And if it is, I don't want you getting your fingerprints on it." Cliff seemed as reluctant as Drew to speak in a normal tone. He beckoned Scott to come up from his place at the back of their little procession. "What do you think?"

Drew knew what he thought—the watch belonged to whomever had killed Andy and then did God knew what with his brother—but it was clear Cliff hadn't been talking to him.

"Tough call," Scott said. "Might be nothing."

"Or it might be evidence, and we don't want to disturb it."

Scott nodded. "But neither do we want to chance it disappearing if the owner returns for it."

"Exactly."

The two cops stared at the watch for a few minutes, Drew getting more anxious by the second. Behind them, Wyatt cracked his knuckles. It would only be moments before he made some snide remark because this watch wasn't getting them any closer to Rob. Brett either, although Drew wouldn't be too upset if a gator nibbled on Brett...just a tiny bit.

"Hold this." Cliff handed off his flashlight to Scott. "I'm taking it with us."

"You sure?" Scott asked.

"I'm already getting fired tomorrow. How much worse could it get?" Cliff whipped out a zip tie and stuck it in the ground before taking a couple of pictures with his phone. Then he pulled a handkerchief out, snagged the watch, and stuck it in his pocket. "This will have to do."

"Can we get moving now?" Drew was vibrating with nervous energy.

"Rob!" Wyatt's voice bellowed. Apparently his brother had lost patience with their slow pace also.

Cliff rounded on him. "What the fuck is wrong with you?"

"What the fuck is wrong with *you?* My brother could be out there, hurt, and he might not be conveniently lying across the goddamn fucking path."

"Calm down, you two." Scott stepped between them, which was a good thing. Drew wasn't ready for another head injury just yet. "Wyatt, Cliff was just being cautious. If someone did put them out here, and that person is still here, we don't want to spook them."

"Whatever. Get going," Wyatt grumbled.

The night sounds of the swamp filled in the awkward silence that followed. But then Drew heard it. A tapping, like someone knocking on wood. It was too rhythmic to be natural.

"Did you hear that?" Drew clutched Cliff's arm.

"Yeah, I did. Let's go."

They sped along the ragged path as quickly as they could, abruptly coming to a stop with a squelch as the brush opened up around what was more bog than pond. There were a number of suspicious lumps that broke the flat expanse of the water, which could all be vegetation but probably weren't.

Cliff and Scott panned flashlight beams around the perimeter of the water, and the number of reflective eyes made Drew's heart rate increase. Off to the right, lumps of fabric lay on the water's edge, the dull silver gleam of duct tape unmistakable as the lumps morphed into men the longer Drew stared.

"Rob!" Wyatt pushed past them, but Scott grabbed his collar and yanked. Wyatt gurgled slightly at the bite of fabric across his neck. "What the fuck?"

Wyatt might be able to make that his motto after tonight, but Drew understood. He wanted to barge forward as well, but he didn't have a damn thing on him that would cut through duct tape.

Scott smiled, but for the first time, it wasn't a nice smile. "Most times, using duct tape to secure people indicates a crime scene of one sort or another. You sure you want to get your fingerprints all over it?"

"But that's our brother—"

"I know. But let us do our job, okay?" Cliff squeezed Drew's shoulder.

Both Cliff and Scott tried their cell phones and radios, but they must have been too far from civilization, which only made Drew more anxious. They were all alone out here in the dark. At least the two cops had guns with them, which might deter a murderer but probably not a big gator.

Cliff handed Drew his flashlight, donned a pair of latex gloves, and pulled out a small knife.

Wyatt's lips flattened, but he held out a hand for Scott's flashlight so he could put on his own gloves. As they got closer, Drew saw Rob's eyes flashing with anger. Without any hesitation, Cliff knelt in the muck beside Rob and peeled the duct tape off his lips as gently as possible, which Drew was both surprised by and grateful for.

"What the fuck are you doing here, Drew? Get the fuck out of here before he comes back." The first words Rob had spoken to him since his stilted apology in the hospital were furious, and most of that fury seemed directed at Drew.

"Hey. Drummond." Cliff gripped Rob's shoulder and shook. "If it wasn't for Drew, you'd be nothing more than gator droppings by the time anyone thought to look out here. The only thing I want to hear out of you is what happened, or I'm gonna leave you here for the fucking gators."

Of course, Cliff didn't wait before he started slicing through Rob's bonds as Scott did the same for Brett. He wrapped the tape inside his gloves and shoved them in his pocket with the watch. Drew had seen enough crime dramas to know Cliff was hoping to get fingerprints from the tape and was trying to preserve them the best he could out here.

CHAPTER 21

Rob and Brett sat up, rubbing their fingers to get some feeling back in them. Drew crouched by his brother, trying to inspect him for damage.

"Are you guys okay?" Cliff wanted nothing more than to find out what the hell had happened, but both men seemed a little groggy and out of it. Cliff was reeling from finding them out here. Unless this proved to be some hugely elaborate con—and Cliff had too much faith in the man he'd fallen for to believe he'd be a part of such a thing—Drew had an ability Cliff couldn't explain, and he was going to have to accept that and move on.

"Fucker had a stun gun." Rob rubbed at an angry-looking bruise on his temple.

"That's not from a stun gun," Wyatt supplied, somewhat needlessly.

"No shit, Sherlock," Rob bit out. "Stunned me first, then decided to conk me over the head. The fucker didn't realize knocking someone out doesn't work like it does on TV, so he had to stun me again. And when I see him again, I'm going to rip off his head and piss down his neck."

"No, you are not," Cliff said sternly. "You are going to let the police take care of it. Otherwise, you'll definitely be going to jail. This guy do the same thing to Brett?"

Brett was being uncharacteristically silent, which had to mean he'd either had his brains scrambled, or he was hurting more than he wanted to let on. Maybe both. And sitting here this close to gator central, hovering on the edge of shock, with possible concussions, wasn't doing either of them any good.

"Think you guys can walk out of here if we help you? Or I can head back to where I've got some reception and call some EMTs in first."

"No, don't leave us here." Brett's voice cracked, and he flicked a fearful glance out at the water. Yeah, that was exactly why Cliff didn't want to leave them here. Thankfully it had been a wet summer. During dry summers, the number of gators in areas like this concentrated just because so much of their habitat dried up, but Cliff didn't want to push their luck.

Wyatt and Drew helped Rob to his feet, leaving Brett for Scott and Cliff. Supporting the two injured men, they slowly made their way back to his mother's property.

"So," Cliff said, trying not to sound as impatient or irritated as he felt. "Anyone want to tell me who did this to you? Be nice if we could go arrest someone after we get you medical attention."

"It was the fucking mayor." Brett sneered the words, then paused their progress to puke. Yeah, Cliff would have to make sure he was checked out for concussion.

Then Brett's words registered. Cliff blinked and caught Scott's glance over Brett's heaving back.

"Oh shit," Scott breathed, mirroring Cliff's sentiments exactly.

"Guys, hold up," Cliff called to the Drummond brothers, who were farther ahead with the slightly less damaged Rob.

They turned around but didn't come closer, since Rob looked pale and greenish. He'd have to get checked for a concussion as well. Not that Cliff truly wished harm on anyone, but the universe was definitely repaying karma in kind to these two. Once Brett was ready to move on, they caught up to the Drummonds.

"Why didn't you say right away that the mayor did this to you?" Cliff asked Rob.

"The mayor?" Wyatt and Drew spoke as though they were the twins.

Rob shrugged. "Like you were going to arrest the mayor on my say-so. Please."

Huh. Rob had a point. Looking back, Cliff remembered the mayor wearing some sort of ostentatious watch, but he couldn't say for sure it was the one weighing down his pocket.

The myriad implications that would arise from arresting the mayor flooded his mind, and he looked back at Scott while the Drummond brothers whispered furiously among themselves.

"Well, that's a bit of a clusterfuck, isn't it?" Scott said with his usual insouciance. "But hey, maybe you won't lose your job."

"Or this is the most dramatic exit interview ever." Cliff rubbed at his temple, where a headache threatened. "Christ, Scott, we can't just haul these guys back to the film site. We can't let word of this get out until we talk to the chief and get the proper warrants in place. Otherwise Morales could make some serious trouble."

"You're right, but what are we going to do? How are we going to keep a lid on this for the next couple of hours? These guys need medical help, although it's maybe not a complete emergency."

"Your sister working tonight? Or do you know an off-duty EMT that you could trust?"

"My sister's got the night off, and she'll keep quiet if I ask her to. I'll call her as soon as we've got reception, but where am I going to tell her to go?"

For the first time, Cliff was grateful that they hadn't been able to call in backup. If the mayor found out his two gator-bait boys had survived and were coherent, he'd be gone before anyone figured out he was behind it all.

There was only one place Cliff could think of to go where Rob and Brett would be safe and no one would see them arrive. He only hoped his mother wasn't completely under William Morales's spell.

"We need to change direction. Hit the path that leads to my mom's estate. We can't bring them out in the middle of the crew. Not a chance."

Drew's eyes widened. His boyfriend was damn smart and understood immediately that what Cliff proposed would probably break his mother's heart. Which it was going to do as soon as she caught wind of the mayor's arrest, but Cliff was banking on his mother caring for him more than some man she was dating. A bit of a gamble, given Cliff's behavior the past few years. Regardless, this was still the best option.

"Your mom... This will be hard on her."

"I know. And I won't even be able to tell her until we've got Morales in custody; otherwise she could tip him off accidentally." Or intentionally, but Cliff didn't want to think about that. He didn't want Morales to escape or try to finish off Brett, Rob, and maybe any witnesses.

Slowly they made their way to the clearing and cell reception. Morales's car wasn't parked in the driveway, which was a small mercy. Cliff made Wyatt support Brett while he and Scott made their phone calls.

After Cliff had confirmed his mother was alone and had gotten a promise of confidentiality, he hung up and looked over at Scott.

"My sister is on her way."

"Okay, guys, let's get you in the house. Don't contact anyone, either by phone or Internet. Got it? I'll field any questions about your whereabouts should they arise." Cliff didn't think the TV crew was in any hurry to find Brett after he'd screwed them all over, and anyone looking for Rob was likely right here, so he wasn't worried about too many questions.

Brett snorted, then winced. "Bastard tossed our phones in the water."

The six of them began shuffling across the lawn, a couple of lit-up windows and the porch light shining like beacons. The yard had never seemed so large before.

"Couple of questions before we get in there. Either of you know why the mayor did this to you? And how did he get you?" Cliff could always hope Morales had succumbed to the urge to talk.

Brett cleared his throat. "After our little...uh...discussion, I went to hang out in one of the trailers. The mayor followed me and asked me to go for a walk, see if we could work things out so I didn't destroy the town. I agreed to go with him, kind of wondering what he'd offer me." Brett at least had the decency to sound ashamed.

"And then what? I'm pretty sure Morales doesn't have the kind of money that would make you reconsider. Which could also be considered blackmail, you realize."

"Yeah, I know. I wasn't about to change my mind anyway. I wanted out of the contract, and I wanted to hurt you, and this seemed like a great way to get both things. The mayor wasn't serious about offering me money anyway. He just wanted to get me out of sight. Then he stunned me, saying I wasn't going to destroy his life."

Cliff frowned. "His life? What does that mean?"

"You might have noticed how obsessed Morales is about increasing the tourist trade," Scott said. "He owns, or has invested heavily in, a number of the businesses closely tied to Haunt Fest. It's possible he could go bankrupt if we had a slump in tourist traffic."

Cliff looked sharply at Drew. "Is he involved in your business?" Because that business was also Drew's home, and he didn't want any Morales fallout to affect Drew.

"No. God, no. The mayor hates me, and I do fine without his investments." The spurt of relief at Drew's words surprised Cliff, just a little, because he wanted Drew's business to thrive, whether or not he was truly psychic. Being with Drew had opened his mind, just a bit, and the comfort of Sandy Bottom Bay and its eccentricities was slowly sucking him in.

"Rob? What about you?"

"I don't fucking know. He approached me about a job, and like this asshole, once I was out of sight of anyone, stunned me. He did think I was Wyatt, though, and figured he'd say I took off after killing Brett and also so I couldn't talk."

"Talk? About what?" Scott asked.

Cliff groaned. "We definitely have to open a full investigation into Andy's death."

"Why? Because Drew said he saw the watch in a vision?" Scott's voice, thankfully, didn't sound as though Cliff was ready for a straitjacket.

"No. If Morales found out Andy was setting up the hoax, he might have killed him to keep it from coming out, not realizing Brett was behind it all. After Brett's disappearance, having a Drummond scapegoat isn't such a bad idea, but choosing Wyatt specifically, even if he was mistaken, is significant, because Wyatt found the body. Likely Morales thought he'd be able to point the blame to a missing Drummond for both deaths, if he thought we were going to investigate Andy's death as a homicide." Cliff had exaggerated when he'd threatened to arrest Brett for murder, since he didn't have any real evidence, but the mayor, watching the whole exchange, wouldn't have known that.

Scott's sister Sarah pulled up to the house just as they approached the front door, and their arrival was noisy enough to alert Cliff's mom, who ushered them all inside.

Within seconds, Sarah had taken over, with his mom helping out, leaving Cliff and Scott free to leave and go wake up the chief. They admonished the women to tell no one what was happening here, until further notice, and then Cliff pulled Drew aside.

"I'll be back as soon as I can. Stay here, and keep an eye on things. If anything weird happens, call me immediately."

Drew smiled at him and moved into his arms. Cliff didn't care if his mom or Sarah was watching. He was just so damn glad Morales hadn't decided to take Drew prisoner. The last thing he wanted was for Drew to be hurt any more.

"I'll be fine. We'll be fine." Drew pressed his lips to Cliff's, and they kissed gently. If there hadn't been an audience, though, Cliff would have given in to the clawing need to reassure himself that Drew was safe. Somewhat barbaric, maybe, but he wanted to strip Drew naked and claim him in the most primal way. The ridge of

Drew's erection told him Drew wouldn't be averse to the notion, but for the next few hours at least, Cliff had a job to do.

An insistent buzzing nudged Cliff's hips, breaking their tender kiss. Surprisingly, it was coming from Drew's pocket. "Someone's desperate to get a hold of you. Unless you've been carrying around a vibrator this whole time."

Drew's cheeks pinkened, but he pulled out his phone. "It's a message from Kyle." Drew frowned at the display. "He's left five messages already."

"Better listen to them." For all Cliff knew, Kyle had been privy to some breaking news while their sorry group was in radio silence.

Even without it being on speaker phone, Cliff was quite able to hear Kyle's shout from the message.

"Where the hell are you? I can't find anyone. Not even the TV crew has seen you. And your brothers aren't answering their phones. I'm ready to call the cops, damn it. Or your uncle. Someone. Call me the fuck back right now, Drew."

Cliff rolled his eyes. Kyle wasn't going to be put off easily. "You think he can be trusted to keep this secret?"

"Yeah. He wouldn't do anything that would hurt me or my brothers."

Then there was only one thing to do. Cliff sighed. "Call him. Get him out here to reassure him you're safe. You can tell him what's going on, but for God's sake, make sure he doesn't tell anyone until I say he can."

"I promise. Get going. The sooner you go, the sooner you can come back."

"Listen, I was serious. I might not have a job in a couple of hours."

Drew smiled. "That's okay. We'll manage just fine"

Cliff's breathing faltered for a moment. "Really?" Cliff kissed Drew again, because this man was who he wanted to be with. More than anything.

Scott cleared his throat. "No smecking until an arrest is made, you slacker."

Pulling away from Drew was difficult, but Scott was right. "I'll text you, let you know what's going on. It might be hours, so try to get some sleep."

"Be careful."

"Call Kyle. Quick."

Drew smiled, and Cliff followed Scott out of the house.

A SHARP ELBOW in Drew's ribs roused him, making him aware of the cramped and overheated bed situation. He sat up without disturbing Kyle, who'd fallen asleep in his clothes beside him after a fitful night. Snatching his phone, he checked desperately for messages, but there was still nothing from Cliff.

Drew had been so anxious to hear the results of the mayor's arrest, he was pretty sure he'd awakened every hour during the night, although the last he remembered was the hazy gray light just before dawn, and it was now almost ten.

Having Kyle speed over last night and distract both him and Wyatt from Rob's health, despite Sarah's reassurances, had been such a comfort. Brett had recovered enough to spend his time bitching, making Drew fear that Wyatt was going to knock him out, but Helen had smothered Brett in Southern charm until he'd caved and then finally passed out.

Drew had been quick to claim Cliff's bedroom when offered, but despite the high school memorabilia that made him feel close to Cliff, he'd still asked Kyle to keep him company. Helen had managed to find sleepwear for all four of them who'd been soaked in the swamp, as well as offering hot showers and the option to launder their clothes in her washing machine. Drew suspected she had someone come in and do the laundry for her, at least the items she didn't have dry-cleaned, but that was immaterial. Kyle had been a sweetheart and done their damp, swamp-soaked laundry while they'd showered, but Sarah wanted them all to go to the doctor as soon as possible for checkups. Stagnant water could contain malicious bacteria. Goody. Another medical expense Drew didn't need.

It had been hours since he'd heard from Cliff, and Drew couldn't stop himself from sending a short text asking for an update. He might not get one, but he knew it wouldn't take too long waiting this morning before he wanted to crawl out of his skin. Drew slipped from the bed and perused some of Cliff's memorabilia. Helen had done a nice job on the room, combining reminders of Cliff with an updated decor so that it was neither a shrine to a boy who would never return nor a complete erasure of a guy who'd spent eighteen years sleeping here.

Not for the first time, Drew was aware that Helen Somerset was a sharp woman. Which made her unwavering support of him unnerving and gratifying at the same time.

"Nothing yet?" Kyle asked sleepily.

"No, dammit." Drew whirled around. "Want to help me cook breakfast? I don't want to strain our hostess's hospitality any further by expecting her to cook for us as well." Assuming Helen cooked. He wasn't really sure, and while he could tell Cliff cared about his mom, he hadn't spoken a whole lot about her, beyond the reasons for their estrangement.

"Sure thing."

Drew didn't bother changing. The pajamas were plenty modest, and he'd get dressed later. After a quick trip to the bathroom to take care of business and wash his face, he ran his fingers through his somewhat savage hair—going to sleep with it wet was never a good idea—then went downstairs while Kyle took his place in the bathroom.

Sarah sat at the kitchen table, a cup of coffee in front of her, the scent of a freshly made pot hanging lush in the air.

"You hear anything yet?" she asked.

"Nope. You neither, I guess."

She shook her head, looking hardly worse for wear. Presumably a nurse had a lot more experience with the lack of sleep that came with monitoring concussion victims. "Help yourself to coffee."

"Thanks. How are Rob and Brett?" Drew fixed himself a cup and perused the contents of the fridge.

"Doing better. Resting. I'd be a lot happier if they were properly examined at the hospital, but we'll get them in there as soon as possible."

"Kyle and I were going to make breakfast. Will eggs be okay for them?"

"Sure. Nothing too spicy, though."

"That's very sweet of you," Helen said behind him, making him jump.

"Oh. Good morning Mrs. Somerset. Would you like some eggs?"

"Thank you, no. I had some toast when I woke up, but thank you for preparing breakfast for the others. We could be stuck here for several more hours. This house hasn't been so lively in years." Cliff's mom tucked a wayward lock of Drew's hair behind his ear.

Drew knew that, but he wanted it to be over and done. And he wanted to know how Cliff's meeting with the chief had gone. Cooking might help kill some time.

"Please call me Helen, at the very least." Helen's subtle wink was so very mischievous, it was obvious she knew Cliff staying at his place wasn't at all platonic. Heat raced up Drew's face, and he ducked his head into the fridge while mumbling his thanks.

Kyle pounded into the kitchen with his customary manic energy, thankfully taking the focus off Drew, and Drew could have kissed his friend for his timely arrival.

It wasn't until breakfast was a memory and the dishes were done, leaving Drew at loose ends again, that Cliff called him. As much as he knew everyone was waiting anxiously for information, not everyone was privy to the knowledge of just who Cliff and Scott intended to arrest, so Drew ran back up to the bedroom and shut the door behind him.

"Hi. How's it going?"

"It's done. We just brought him in."

"It's over? What did he have to say for himself?"

"I can't tell you everything, although he said enough that we're going to reopen Andy's case, see if we can find some evidence that links the mayor to it. Unless he confesses, though, I doubt we're going to nail him for anything besides attempted murder."

"Oh." Drew would have liked it better if Andy got some justice, but the real world didn't tie up as neatly as cop shows implied. Cliff's now unwavering belief that Andy was murdered gave Drew a little vindication, and who knew? Forensics might find something now that they had an idea what to look for.

"I'm coming now, but I can only stay a short while. Then I have to be back." Cliff sounded so weary, which wasn't a surprise. No matter how restlessly Drew had slept, he'd still gotten a few hours that Cliff hadn't.

"As much as I'd like to see you and tuck you into bed to get some sleep, why don't you wait until you're done before you come back?"

Cliff sighed. "My mother collects gossip and town news like a dragon collects treasure. She finds out more secrets, quicker and with more detail, than the most dedicated investigative journalist, and I'm pretty sure it's because people fall over themselves to offer up information in return for one of her benevolent smiles."

Despite the seriousness of the situation, Drew bit his lip against a grin. There was definitely something about Helen Somerset that made a person want to please her, and without any expectation of financial gain.

"And your point is?" Lack of sleep was preventing Drew from putting the pieces of this particular puzzle together.

"My mom was dating the mayor. As much as I don't want to be the one to break this to her, I'd rather she hear it from me."

Drew waited a moment before he spoke again. "Did you want me to do it?"

Even Cliff's chuckle sounded exhausted. "She does like you. And I know you'd be gentle with her, but no. I need to do this. I'd like it if you were with me, though."

"Of course. Hurry home."

"Yep. Scott's going to cover for me here. See you soon."

The connection dropped, and Drew wandered back downstairs, prepared to fend off inquires until Cliff got there. Stupidly, he'd forgotten to ask what he could share with the others. He'd also forgotten to ask if Cliff still had a job.

CHAPTER 22

C liff let himself into the house, wishing he were back at Drew's and able to crash on Drew's narrow bed. Nope, first he had to break his mother's heart, and then he had untold hours of paperwork left at the station. But no one else had died, and that was a win in his book.

The unmistakable sounds of an action movie emanated from the den where his mother kept the TV tucked away. Presumably anyone not sleeping was in there, except his mother. And frankly, he had no idea where she would be. In the yard, perhaps, although her gardening skills were cursory at best.

He walked into the kitchen to grab a bottle of water. It might be October, but the heat and humidity were still close to summer values.

Hoping to get this over with as quickly as possible and without any extended explanations, Cliff pulled out his phone and sent a text to Drew asking him to come to the kitchen alone. Seconds later, his gorgeous boyfriend raced into the kitchen.

"Hey. You're wearing my old pajamas."

When Drew rolled his eyes, Cliff realized that was perhaps the least pertinent thing he could have said.

"Yeah, I figured your mom wasn't into Harry Potter. Actually, I'm a little surprised you were." Drew's ankles stuck out below the hem of the pajamas, but he was slim enough that pajamas from when Cliff was fifteen mostly fit him, even if they weren't nearly long enough.

Cliff smiled. "I never had a problem with the fictional stuff, and besides, Harry Potter wasn't quite the same as the whole Sandy Bottom Bay thing."

Drew stepped close enough that Cliff could smell the scent of his mother's shampoo in Drew's hair and the hint of lavender from her soap on his skin. Cliff certainly didn't begrudge Drew a shower—he'd showered and changed uniforms at the station—but he couldn't deny it messed with his head a bit. Didn't stop him from pulling Drew into his arms and kissing the pale lips he'd grown addicted to.

After a few minutes, he broke the kiss but kept his arms wrapped around Drew's solid, lanky form.

"North," Drew whispered.

"Drew," Cliff whispered back, his mood instantly lightened by Drew's presence and his nickname.

They stood there in silence, Cliff simply soaking up comfort in Drew's embrace. If they'd been alone, and maybe not in his mother's house, Cliff would have deepened the kiss and stripped Drew naked, but that would have to wait for later. After paperwork and several hours of sleep.

"So it went okay? The arrest."

Cliff chuckled. "We took him completely by surprise. But I need to talk to my mom and get back to the station. Do you know where she is?"

"Sitting out in the gazebo with a pitcher of iced tea, I think."

"Right. Well, I'd better get out there."

"Want me to come with you?"

Normally he would have said no, this was a family matter, but not only was he beginning to view Drew as part of his family, he'd seen with his own eyes that his mom really liked Drew. Perhaps his presence would be a comfort to her, especially since Cliff would be dropping a bomb and then running.

Then again, Cliff found it totally understandable that most people would like Drew more than him, assuming they could get over the whole him-being-a-Drummond thing. From what he'd seen, Drew had gotten all the charisma in the family.

"Yes, please. I think she likes you more than me, so I'm hoping you can make her feel better when I have to leave."

"She doesn't like me more than you. Don't be ridiculous."

"But she is very fond of you. I can tell."

Drew shrugged. "I know. She's been good to me, especially since my grandma died. I used to think it was sympathy for my grief, but I don't know what I did to deserve it."

"Probably just you being you." Cliff couldn't hold back the super-sappy sentiment, and when a pleased flushed heated Drew's cheeks, he was glad he hadn't. He grabbed Drew's hand and led him to the back door.

"What about your job?" Drew asked just as they walked through the door.

"Well, I still have one. I was surprised, but the chief said he was only planning to reprimand me, even before I handed him such a high-profile criminal." It had been a real weight off his mind.

"Oh. That's good." Oddly, Drew didn't sound like he was wholly convinced that it *was* good, but the gazebo was in sight, and Cliff could only worry about one disaster at a time.

His mom looked up as they hit the wooden steps, and she gave him a quick once-over as though checking to see if he was injured. With his eyes still dazzled from the bright sunlight, the lines on her face were erased, and Cliff was reminded of better times when he was much younger. Which made what he had to do that much more difficult.

"Well, hello there." She glanced at Drew's pajama bottoms and looked as though she was biting back laughter.

"I have to talk to you."

This time his mother looked pointedly at their entwined hands, and this time there was no suppressing her smile. "I'm so pleased for you both. Although if you were trying to keep it secret, you didn't do a very good job."

Cliff wouldn't have thought having his mother's approval of his boyfriend would matter at all, and yet her words set alight a warmth in his belly.

"Thanks, Mom. We appreciate that, but I'm afraid that's not it."

"Very well." She waved a hand, inviting them to sit down.

Drew sat in one of the oversize wicker chairs and crossed his legs, clearly knowing that Cliff wasn't going to be able to sit while he spit this out.

"Mom, I'm so sorry. We had to arrest the mayor."

His mom blinked, lips parting slightly as she processed Cliff's words. It had been a long time since Cliff had seen his mother genuinely shocked, but he was seeing it now.

"Arrested? For what?"

"Attempted murder." There was no need to mention they were opening a murder investigation as well, especially since Cliff wasn't sure they'd find enough to make a charge stick.

"Attempted murder?" she parroted. Then she glanced back at the house, and comprehension sank in quickly because his mother wasn't stupid, not by a long shot. "He tried to kill those young men? That doesn't make any sense."

Her face was as serene as ever, but the whitened skin on her knuckles as she gripped the armrests gave away her upset. Only someone who knew her well would be able to tell how thoroughly she'd been rattled.

Since he didn't know how to comfort her, he continued to pace in the small space of the gazebo.

"I'm so sorry, Mom. But it's true."

Cliff gave an abbreviated version of the discovery of the hoax and Brett's intention to sink *Phantoms* regardless of whether he took down Sandy Bottom Bay along with it.

His mom sighed. "I've known William a long time, and he never did react well to being cornered. When you factor in his investments, I have to say I'm not terribly surprised he resorted to something illegal, but attempted murder is quite shocking."

Cliff blinked. Drew appeared as taken aback as he was. "Investments?" He should have known his mother was aware of Morales's investments.

"Of course. I make it a point of trying to support all the businesses in town. William had a bit of tunnel vision and invested his late wife's money heavily in the businesses related to the Haunt Fest or the properties they rest on. A failed Haunt Fest would be disastrous for him."

"You're taking this better than I thought. You were dating, weren't you?" Had Cliff misread the situation?

She lifted one shoulder ever so slightly. "Northcliff, don't you think after all these years, I can recognize when someone is more interested in my bank balance than my personality? His attention was flattering—my status can be intimidating for a lot of men. I've known for a long time it wasn't going to be a serious relationship. But I appreciate your concern."

Those few words told him more about his mother's loneliness than he'd ever truly understood before, and he vowed in the future to be a better son.

"Nonsense, Helen. I'm certain he was interested in more than your bank balance."

His mom smiled warmly at his boyfriend, and Drew leaned over and patted her hand before pausing, a glaze veiling his eyes exactly as it had before he'd sent them into the swamp on a rescue mission. It only lasted a fraction of a second, though, not long enough to become alarmed.

"There's someone else for you anyway. Someone better."

"Dear boy. If it were anyone else but you telling me, I'd say they were full of horsefeathers." Her acceptance of Drew's prophecy made Cliff just a bit uncomfortable. After all, she'd never had tangible proof of his abilities, not like Cliff had. "I'm assuming this arrest was the reason for all the secrecy, so I guess you'd better get those men into the hospital."

Nothing about today was going as expected. Not at all. He just hoped it would all make more sense once he'd gotten a few hours of sleep.

"Thank you for putting us all up." Drew smiled, and it made Cliff happy just seeing it.

"Well, you're family, dear." His mother ruffled Drew's hair, and Cliff wondered when he'd stepped into an alternate reality. "You and your brothers."

"Uh, Mom." Was she overcompensating or something? Including the evil twins was taking things too far. "I'm glad you like Drew and all, but aren't you rushing things a bit?" Not that Cliff didn't want to rush, but it surprised him that his mother would. The last thing he wanted was to freak Drew out from overbearing parental pressure to settle down. Drew gave him a funny look that Cliff couldn't interpret.

"Thanks, er...Helen," Drew sounded hesitant. "Most people in town wouldn't want to claim a Drummond as family. Not any of us."

"True. But you're a special case, and I think with a bit of incentive, like a policeman brother-in-law, they've got it in them to do what you did—pull yourself up beyond the Drummond reputation."

"Mother!" Now she had them all but married? Drew was going to take off like he was being chased by starving gators.

As though she hadn't thrown a bunch of impossible expectations into the middle of Cliff's already unusual relationship, she ignored his outburst entirely, keeping her gaze on Drew. "I'm so proud of you, and I know your grandmother would be too."

Drew's eyes reddened for a minute. "Thank you. That means a lot."

Then she smiled ruefully. "I spoke with your grandmother a few days before she died, you know. She wasn't well enough to do any readings, but she asked to see me."

"Really? What did she say?"

"She told me you and Northcliff would end up together. And I knew you well enough by then to know that meant my son would be moving back to Sandy Bottom Bay eventually."

A shiver raced up Cliff's spine, and Drew's mouth hung open. Was this the reason she had looked out for Drew more than anyone else in town? Was this the reason she had been unsurprised by Cliff's sudden reappearance? She'd been expecting him home for two years.

"Um." Cliff didn't know what to say in response to that bomb-shell. Then again, he wasn't sure he cared why his mother accepted Drew or if Nostradamus himself had prophesied their relationship. What mattered was the end result—him and Drew together. "I have to get back to work now. Scott can only cover for me for so long."

Drew stood. "Right. Yes, well, I have to get Rob's head checked out. Thanks again, Helen."

Together they walked in silence through the yard, into the house, and then to the front door.

"That was kinda weird, wasn't it?" Drew ran his fingers through his rumpled hair. "I mean, until this week, I didn't really believe my grandmother could see the future. I just thought she was superin-tuitive."

Cliff was already a believer. Believing Drew's ability was heredi-tary made as much sense as anything else. "Well, if this is how fate works, I think I like it." Drew's lips quirked up, and Cliff gave them a brief kiss. "I'll meet you at your place later?"

Just like that, Drew's odd, distracted mood returned, but Cliff's phone was already vibrating. Probably Scott wondering when the hell he was getting back.

～

CLIFF PULLED up to the curb and parked. The sight of Drew's weath-ered door eased him, gave him a sense of comfort and belonging that he'd never thought he'd have. Home. The man on the other side of that door was home.

And after a few hours of sleep, he'd prove to Drew, in many naked ways, how grateful he was they'd found each other.

Life was, unexpectedly, good. Awesome, in fact. He was still employed, and his chief not only knew his name but had compli-mented him today on a job well done, despite the uproar arresting the mayor had caused. He had a new relationship with his mother and a rekindled friendship with Scott. He'd faced the evil twins and managed to find common ground. And his boyfriend was all he'd ever dreamed of.

There was no suppressing his smile as he walked up the footpath.

Until he got close enough to see through the screen door. Drew was in the kitchen, pacing the small room, running his hands through his hair in an agitated manner.

Cliff's mood plummeted to his toes. He'd thought his stress and exhaustion had made him imagine Drew's odd behavior, but he could no longer explain it away. Something was wrong, and he very much feared it had to do with their relationship. The drama of the past week had been intense. Now that it was over, Drew could have reconsidered getting involved with him. After all, Drew's family couldn't be too happy about it.

Cliff fingered the house key. When Kyle had given it to him on Drew's behalf, he hadn't realized how precious it would become. With trepidation weighting his shoulders, it took real effort to force the key into the lock and turn it.

The click of the lock was enough to disrupt whatever internal monologue Drew was engaged in, and he turned with a look akin to fear in his eyes. Maybe the same trepidation as Cliff's, but clearly for a different reason.

"Hi." Cliff's voice cracked, and he swallowed heavily, trying to dislodge the sudden emotional blockage.

"Hi." Drew bit his lower lip while Cliff waited for the axe to fall.

The silence stretched out, tight and painful.

"So," Drew sighed. "My head is doing better. The headaches are gone, and I'm...mostly back to normal."

"Yup. That's good." *Normal.* Cliff didn't want normal, not if it meant he and Drew weren't together.

Drew turned his gaze away from Cliff, as though the clock on the wall held all the secrets of the universe. Cliff should just grab his stuff and escape the coming blow, not linger and force Drew to do this. But Cliff couldn't leave. Not until Drew told him to go.

"I guess I don't really need a babysitter. I mean, you stayed until I was on the mend. And I appreciate it. Really."

Cliff clenched his hand so tightly around the key to Drew's house that he fully expected blood to drip onto the floor. At least the physical discomfort kept him from falling to his knees and begging Drew not to do this, which would only be embarrassing and awkward for them both.

He breathed deeply and forced himself to open his hand. With shaking fingers, he pulled the key off his ring and placed it gently on the kitchen table.

"It'll only take me a minute to grab my stuff." There were some advantages to living out of a duffel bag. He'd be able to escape before he completely lost his shit.

Drew gasped, probably because he'd expected Cliff to make a scene.

Five minutes later, there wasn't a sign in the bedroom or bathroom that Cliff had been there, living the happiest days of his life.

When he returned to the kitchen, he couldn't resist one last look at Drew, who had his arms wrapped around his stomach and hair rumpled. His...ex-boyfriend. Just thinking the word threatened Cliff's composure, and he coughed to hide the sob that nearly escaped. Drew spun around, eyes red and wet, nose shiny and swollen.

The ache in Cliff's heart was no match for the urge to comfort Drew, and he dropped his bag to take Drew in his arms one last time.

Drew bent awkwardly to bury his damp face in Cliff's neck. "I don't want you to go." The words vibrated against Cliff's skin, and for a moment, he didn't realize what he'd heard.

Then shock chased away the pain. "What?"

Drew stepped back and began to pace again. "I know this all happened so quick, but I like having you here. I don't want you to go. The place is small, but surely we could work out a way for you to have your own space if you need it."

Cliff ruthlessly quashed his rising hope. He couldn't risk hoping. Not until he'd clarified something. "I don't want to go either."

"Then why are you leaving?" Drew stared at the key on the table as though it were a viper poised to strike.

The hope wouldn't stay buried. Not when it seemed that maybe

Cliff had put the pieces together incorrectly. "I thought that's what you wanted."

"Of course I don't want that." Drew chewed on his lip again, and Cliff had to force his gaze away from the swollen, reddened flesh. "And I know it's awful of me, but I was sort of hoping you were going to be unemployed. Then maybe you'd have to stay with me. Which is stupid, because you could just move back into your old room at your mom's."

"*That's* why you were acting weird earlier? Because I *didn't* get fired?"

"I'm sorry, North. I'm an awful person."

Between Drew's confession and calling him North without any hesitation, Cliff's hope soared. He snatched up the key and jammed it back on his key ring. Then he snagged Drew's arm and pulled him to his chest, the contact of Drew's lanky body soothing the jangling pain in his heart.

"You don't know how to be an awful person. But please know, I want to stay here with you because...this is home. You make this home. I'd want this if I was destitute or a millionaire. And not because of fate or because your grandmother foresaw something. Because of you. Because you and me together work."

"Really?" Drew's eyes shone with burgeoning happiness and relief. "And what if the visions don't go away? Can you live with that?"

"I will take you any way I can get you, visions or no visions. And if you see something like you did with Andy, I will do my best to help you fix whatever's wrong. I may not believe in any other haunt or specter or spirit in this entire town, but I believe in you. I know this happened fast, but living with you only compressed our initial courtship and convinced me we were meant to be together. Whether or not your grandmother knew it years before we did."

Cliff stroked the back of his hand along Drew's cheek. The faint unshaven roughness warmed his heart and stirred his cock to immediate wakefulness. He needed Drew, naked and wanting, now.

Without much gentleness or finesse, he devoured Drew's mouth like a starving man. Cupping Drew's firm ass, he pressed their cocks together, moaning into Drew's mouth at the pressure. The fear of losing Drew had morphed into a desire so fierce Cliff felt as though he hadn't come in months. Years, even.

Panting, Drew pulled back, pupils dilated, lips open, wet, and inviting. "Wait, wait," he said breathlessly.

"I can't wait." Cliff pulled Drew's T-shirt off, then fumbled with his fly. Drew's hips jerked as though trying to coax Cliff's hands lower.

"But...don't you need to sleep? You must be tired."

The adrenaline from imagining their breakup had effectively amped him up. No doubt he'd sleep like the dead after he came, but now? He needed to have Drew again. Reassure himself like a barbarian that he hadn't lost his man.

"Not too tired to fuck you through the mattress." Cliff yanked down Drew's jeans and briefs in one quick swoop, revealing his ruddy erection, precum already slicking the tip. Only then did Cliff notice he was still wearing his uniform, and his gorgeous boyfriend's skin appeared extra pale in contrast to the dark green. "Bedroom. Now." He spun Drew around and gave him a slap on the ass, the slight sting on his palm making his cock throb in his uniform pants.

Drew sprinted, and Cliff sped after him.

"Hands and knees."

Obeying with alacrity, Drew revealed a pinkish spot on the buttock Cliff had slapped, and Cliff shuddered as lust swamped him. Drew twisted his head so he could see Cliff over his shoulder, and Cliff grinned before unzipping his fly and pulling out his eager cock.

"You..." Drew blinked. "What about your uniform?"

"I can't wait. I need you." Cliff wasn't quite that far gone, but he remembered how hot Drew had been, blowing him while he was in uniform.

Drew whimpered and couldn't take his eyes off Cliff. "Hurry, goddammit. You're making me crazy."

God. There was something so utterly decadent about Drew being completely naked while only Cliff's cock was exposed, hard and wanting.

As if he were competing in an Olympic sport, Cliff had himself gloved and slicked in record time, before prepping Drew.

He'd be forever thankful Drew was his.

"Fuck me, North." Drew's demand came out as a needy whine, and Cliff didn't have the willpower to resist. Drew naked and calling him North turned him on something fierce.

He slid inside Drew's welcoming body as they simultaneously groaned. There wasn't even a chance he could tease Drew, because he was too fucking close to blowing.

"You are the sexiest guy on the planet."

Drew's response was a frustrated growl that morphed into a moan as Cliff's fingers dug into his flanks. There was no buildup; Cliff's hips just started at a frantic pace, Drew's plaintive sounds only spurring him on.

Embarrassingly fast, his balls pulled tight against his body. He wanted to hold on long enough for Drew to come, but he didn't think he could.

"Oh God, I'm going to come," Cliff groaned out.

The words must have triggered Drew, because just as Cliff's orgasm sparked, Drew's ass clamped down on Cliff's jerking cock. Throat aching from the force of his shout, he slumped over Drew's back, lips tasting the salty, clean sweat of his man.

When he could breathe again, and they'd cleaned up a bit, Cliff lay on the bed facing Drew in what was quickly becoming his favorite position. He was truly at home, and he was looking forward to building a life with Drew.

In the whirlwind craziness of arresting the mayor, Cliff realized he'd forgotten something. "Hey, how did you know about the paths to the preservation areas?"

In a flash, the pale skin of Drew's face and chest flushed pink. It was so similar to the sex flush Drew got when he was aroused that Cliff's dick tried to rouse in response, but judging from Drew's abashed expression, the source was embarrassing.

"Um."

"C'mon. After all we've been through, you should be able to tell me anything."

Drew bit his lip, which only encouraged Cliff's unruly dick.

"I... You... It was because of you that I figured out I was gay, and I may have sneaked onto your property a time or two, hoping to get a glimpse of you."

Cliff couldn't keep a few sputters of laughter from escaping. "And did you get a glimpse of anything good?"

"No, dammit." Drew sounded so aggrieved, which was even funnier since Cliff was right in front of him, stark naked and almost ready to fuck him into a stupor.

"Good thing I locked you down early."

Drew finally met Cliff's gaze. "What do you mean? Aren't you... weirded out?"

Cliff shrugged. "Maybe if I knew you back then. But seriously, if it hadn't been for that, maybe I would have come back here and found you in a relationship."

Cheeks darkening, Drew scowled. "I wasn't exactly waiting for you."

Brushing his thumb over Drew's adorable pout, Cliff smiled. "I'm not saying you were. Did I tell you about the first time I saw you?"

Confused, Drew shook his head.

"In the Publix parking lot, before my first shift. You were buying peanut butter and bread, and I wanted nothing more than to find out if you were gay and available. If you hadn't been, my life would be...so empty."

Just like that, Drew's embarrassment faded, and his sweet smile was one Cliff wanted to see every day for the rest of his life. But it was too soon to talk about that kind of permanence, so he concentrated on bringing back Drew's sexy flush, but this time for all the right reasons.

EPILOGUE

ne year later

OCliff relaxed on the new plush couch and watched reruns of *Face Off* on the flat-screen television he'd finally gotten out of storage. He'd spent enough time in Los Angeles to have a real appreciation of the behind-the-scenes work that went into movie- and filmmaking, even if he sometimes thought that actors like Brett were entitled assholes who ruined the magic. Still, *Face Off*, with its reality style of elaborate movie-makeup monster creation, had absolutely nothing to do with police work. It hadn't taken him long on the force to start assessing every cop show he'd previously enjoyed, which destroyed a lot of the charm. He knew other cops who could turn it off enough to not care, but Cliff couldn't.

As if the mere thought of Brett conjured him up—which, after a year of living back in Sandy Bottom Bay, maybe didn't surprise or offend Cliff as much as it would have before—a commercial came on for Brett's upcoming movie.

Drew appeared beside him, and Cliff grabbed his arm, pulling him onto his lap. It was a position they'd found they both liked even though Drew was taller, and Drew fell into it with the ease of long practice.

"Is this Brett's movie?"

Again, like mere mention of his name was enough, Brett's face flashed up on the screen.

"Yeah." Cliff sighed. It looked good, dammit. After the catastrophe last year, Brett had managed to come out of it all covered in rainbows and glitter. Kristi, in a rare fit of compassion, had convinced both Brett and the studio to let the matter go without litigation and had even offered to give him and Drew a bunch of free stuff if they came out to Los Angeles for a visit.

"We going to go see it?"

"I don't know. Maybe. Not until after Haunt Fest, though. You're too busy, and if we wait, we'll find out if it's going to bomb." Cliff had his fingers crossed, but he suspected Brett had finally found what he'd been looking for.

Cliff took a good look at Drew. For now, his skin had a healthy pink tinge and no shadows under his eyes. But Haunt Fest didn't start for another day, and he hoped it wasn't as stressful and exhausting for Drew as it had been last year. At least the construction for the add-ons—this living room and a small office—had finished on time. Drew might have exploded if he'd had to deal with Haunt Fest and unfinished construction at the same time.

Oddly enough, the mayor's fears of an economic downturn had been completely unfounded. Despite the lack of lawsuit, Brett had torpedoed his show, bringing Sandy Bottom Bay a notoriety no one had wanted. But converse to expectation, paranormal tourism had exploded in the region. Hell, Cliff was no longer the newbie on the force and hadn't been for some time, after the chief had to hire another five officers.

Drew's business had also exploded. It had somehow slipped out that Drew's readings might have some truth behind them. Cliff had no proof, but he blamed Brett's loose lips. Or the twins. Who had been taken under his mother's wing, much to his dismay, although he'd been able to concede that maybe they weren't entirely evil, just misguided. Aside from a huge increase in tourist traffic to Malachi the Mystic, Drew's mail-order business had also boomed, and Cliff couldn't be more proud of his boyfriend. He'd even been able to hire

Kyle on as a part-time business manager, which allowed Kyle to teach dance classes in the evening, as he preferred.

The visions hadn't stopped after the arrest of the mayor, but Drew had only had a handful since, and no more murders. They both hoped one day the visions would cease entirely.

"Shouldn't you be getting ready?"

Drew frowned. "Malachi isn't on duty for another hour."

Cliff stroked a hand along Drew's spine, making him shiver. "You could start with eyeliner." His tone was low, coaxing. Drew didn't put on his Malachi makeup until after he was dressed, but there was something about his pale skin, fiery red hair, and that thick black eyeliner that made Cliff lose his mind.

The wicked smile that stretched Drew's lips told Cliff that he knew exactly what Cliff was asking for. Haunt Fest meant exhaustion for Drew and overtime for Cliff. This might be the last time they could play until the festival was over.

Drew hopped off Cliff and bent to take his mouth in a scorching kiss before sliding his lips to Cliff's ear. "I love you, North. Give me five minutes. Then come and get me."

"I love you too."

Just like that, instant hard-on. Their attraction had only grown as they'd fallen deeper in love. After Haunt Fest was over, Cliff had secret plans to take Drew on a trip. Sandy Bottom Bay could do without their resident psychic tarot reader for two weeks.

Neither of them had seen the leaves change color in the fall, and Boston sounded as though it would be glorious. If they happened to get married while they were there? Well, then, Cliff's life would be more than perfect.

✳ THE END ✳

AFTERWORD

I really appreciate you taking the time to read my stories and I hope you'll check out some of my other work. If you enjoyed this book, please consider leaving a review - it really helps us authors out.

I also love hearing from readers - you can contact me at kc@kcburn.com

ALSO BY KC BURN

Contemporary

Cop Out (Toronto Tales #1)

Cover Up (Toronto Tales #2)

Cast Off (Toronto Tales #3)

Tartan Candy (Fabric Hearts #1)

Plaid versus Paisley (Fabric Hearts #2)

Just Add Argyle (Fabric Hearts #3)

Banded Together

Tea or Consequences

Rainbow Blues

Pen Name - Doctor Chicken

First Time, Forever

Sci-Fi

Spice 'n' Solace (Galactic Alliance #1)

Alien 'n' Outlaw (Galactic Alliance #2)

Voodoo 'n' Vice (Galactic Alliance #3)

Union of the Snake

Paranormal

Wolfsbane (MIA Case Files #1)

Blood Relations (MIA Case Files #2)

Craving (MIA Case Files #3)

Illusion of Life

Anthologies

"The Jogger" in Grand Adventures

"The Tithe" in One Pulse

Holiday

Three Dates of Christmas

ABOUT THE AUTHOR

KC Burn has been writing for as long as she can remember and is a sucker for happy endings (of all kinds). After moving from Toronto to Florida for her husband to take a dream job, she discovered a love of gay romance and fulfilled a dream of her own -- getting published. After a few years of editing web content by day, and neglecting her supportive, understanding hubby and needy cat at night to write stories about men loving men, she was uprooted yet again and now resides in California. Writing is always fun and rewarding, but writing about her guys is the most fun she's had in a long time, and she hopes you'll enjoy them as much as she does.

For information on new releases and contests, sign up for KC's newsletter!

Find out more about KC and her books at:
www.kcburn.com
kc@kcburn.com